BEAUTY AND THE BEAST

BRIARS & BLOOD

PRAISE FOR BRIARS & BLOOD

"The stories in *Briars & Blood* delighted me with truly unique and creative retellings of my favorite classic tale. It is a beautiful book that will leave its readers enchanted and inspired."

—Lara E. Madden, Author of *Wither and Bloom*

"Beasts can take many forms. They can show their faces in the tears of grief, in the voice of anger, in the pain of despair, in the loneliness of rejection, in the paralysis of fear, or in the bitterness of unforgiveness. In *Briars & Blood*, beneath each heart-wrenching story, you'll find the story of beauty hidden behind a beast, a lesson, and a friend to carry with you long after you finish reading."

—Brooke J. Katz, Advanced Reader and Aspiring Author

BRIARS & BLOOD

ANNE J. HILL • L.A. THORNHILL
JULIA SKINNER • TASHA KAZANJIAN
ABIGAIL FALANGA • EVERLY HAYWOOD
BEKA GREMIKOVA • HANNAH CARTER

Briars & Blood

Printed in the United States of America

Paperback ISBN: 978-1-956499-17-9
Hardback ISBN: 978-1-956499-16-2

Originally published in March 2023
Published by Twenty Hills Publishing

Cover by Fantastical Ink
Interior formatting by Dragonpen Designs

Edited by Anne J. Hill, Lara E. Madden
Anna Augustine, Moriah Chavis,
Sarah Harmon, and others

Book created by Anne J. Hill, head of Twenty Hills Publishing

To ladies young and old who are told to only write happy-go-lucky fairytales—may you not fall into the trap

TABLE OF CONTENTS

THE STATUE GIRL

Julia Skinner

THE ROSE AND THE BULL

Tasha Kazanjian

BONUS MATERIAL

INTRODUCTION

Beauty and the Beast has always been my favorite fairy tale. As a child, I said that it was my favorite because it was the only fairy tale where the couple actually got to know each other before suddenly falling in love. It was more realistic to me. Now, I'm aware, there are others like that too, but I was limited to whatever Disney princess movies I was given to watch at the time, and out of that small pool, this was true.

A little bit about this project:

This is book one in a planned series of three books. We have no plan for more, but writers are known for steering off the path. Book one is Beauty and the Beast inspired stories and retellings, book two will be Snow White, and book three will be Little Red Riding Hood. Why these fairy tales? Glad you asked. I'm writing a series of three books (but again, three as of now), *The Fatebringer Trilogy,* and each book subtly has ties to these three fairy tales. They are not retellings because they veer too far from the originals (as do some of the stories in *Briars & Blood*). So these are not retellings, but *inspired by or subtle hints to* or have *Easter eggs* from these fairytales.

So for each of those tales, I've put together a collection of novellas/novelettes with several authors. I like to call these our *Crimson Books Collection*, hinging on the fact that each one has a red theme to some degree. You may wonder why the covers aren't all red if that's the name, but, just like red is often represented subtly, there is some red (or crimson) on each cover.

Some are fully fledged retellings, while others linger closer to the *inspired by* lane. The lengths, themes, and subgenres vary, but each falls under fantasy.

There are also a handful of excerpts from other Beauty and the Beast publications (either upcoming, or already out).

I'm honored to sit beside these other authors, with talents that far surpass my own. If you enjoy any of these stories, I encourage you to hunt down the author and see what else they have published. Follow them on social media, leave reviews, tell your friends, and become their number one fan. I don't just do these books to attach them to my own series, but to help other authors get their work out into the world. Each and every one of these ladies deserves a whole fleet of fans. I happen to be among these fans, and it's a bit surreal to be releasing their stories as a fan and publisher bundled up into one.

I hope you enjoy these tales!

–Anne J. Hill

BEAUTY + BEAST

HANNAH CARTER

Some days I act the Beauty
As soft and sweet as roses in bloom
When love controls me absolutely
Its fragrance enough to fill a room

Some days I free the Beast
A wall of thorns wrapped around my heart
When my worst nature gets unleashed
My words as weapons tear apart

Most days I isolate within my castle
Protect the world from me, at least
When being Beauty feels like a hassle
And I could never love this Beast

Most days, though, some scale the wall
They know the Beast, they love the Beauty
The rose, the thorns, they see them all
And somehow, still, they choose me

On low days, though, it's hard to see
Beyond the claws and snarls of Beast
To know Christ my Savior died for me
And that I'm merely incomplete

I am both Beauty and the Beast
As is everyone you meet
So thank you, those who see underneath:
It's Beautiful to love the Beast

A BEAUTY AND THE BEAST LOOSELY INSPIRED NOVELETTE

A NATHAL STORY

THE WARD AND THE WOLFMAN

ANNE J. HILL

PROLOGUE
CURSED BE THE FATHER AND SON

SODI

THE WAR HAS been raging on for far too long. Most people want to throw the Emperor and his blood-born powers off his pearly white throne. I can't say I blame 'em, either. He snatched the scepter right out of his aunt's hand, the key he needed to take over our small corner of the world in one heartbeat. Having powers is already frowned upon, but taking orders from a blood-born is unthinkable to most. That, paired with his bold assassination, split the land between Emperor Loyals and the Revolter Majority. I'd be pretty miffed if some lowly crew member of mine pushed me overboard and snagged my wheel, so I can understand the fury.

But my loyalties lie with the Emperor, a blood-born like my son. The son my wife and I chose to be ours after he was orphaned.

I'd do anything to keep my wife and children safe. Including spy on the Revolters for the Loyals. Which has led to my death.

In order to find the location of the Ageless One, who could greatly aid us in this war and bring a safe world to my son, I've had to sacrifice my life to a siren.

With the Ageless One's location and numerous other plans of our enemies in my satchel, I'm heading home to see my family one last time and deliver the letters.

I don't know how or when I will die but my doom is sealed and looming.

"Captain." A hand jerks my shoulder. "We've hit shore."

I rub my face and stand on shaky legs. "My wife. I need to see my wife."

"Of course, sir. But then you need to report to the Revolter base."

I wave him away. "I know, I know. You have the letter too. I'm going to see my wife and children. You take the letter, and I'll meet up after." I gave him parchment with a false location for the Ageless One.

He nods. "Yes, Captain."

I stumble off the ship and onto solid ground. My wife and I had chosen a house near the shore when we wed. Every winter, I'd come in from the sea and spend the freezing months with my family. That is, until the war started.

I make the distance home on foot, not stopping to find a faster transport. I have one thing on my mind—to hold my wife and children one last time.

I see the thatched roof in the distance, a welcoming cloud of smoke streaming from the chimney I built with my own hands. As I near, the glow of candlelight calls to me through the windows. When I reach the weather-worn front gate, I hear screams from inside, and the door flings open.

"Sodi!" Pela runs out and throws her arms around me. I hold her tight, her body pressed against mine.

I cup the back of her head in my hand and stoop to kiss her. It sends heat through my body. I soak her in, knowing this might be the last kiss we ever share. "I love you," I whisper against her lips. My fingers trail down her back, and I pick her up.

"I love you, too. I missed you so much." She buries her face into my neck and takes a deep breath.

I carry her inside our home. "Are the children asleep?"

She kisses my neck. "Cali is."

I squeeze her and set her down. "Go get them for me. I want to see them." She rushes off, and I lower myself onto a chair, raking my fingers through my hair.

"Papa!" Cali runs out from her bedroom and throws herself on me, soon followed by Vivace. He slinks over to me, his arms crossed. He has white stubble growing on his chin, and it makes my stomach churn with remorse.

"Vivace, my boy . . . you've grown up so much."

He nods, watching me with distant eyes. "I'm not a boy anymore."

He's right. He turned eighteen this last year. And I missed it. Just as I will miss every future birthday.

Vivace is like the Emperor—born with the generational powers passed to some. It is for him that I fight for blood-borns to live safely.

"I'm sorry, son." I hold my hand out to him.

My adopted child does not take my peace offering. "You should have been here."

I stand to my full height despite the burning protest of every muscle in my body. "Vivace . . . You know why I have to fight."

"No, I don't! You've always hated what I am!" he snaps, and I blink.

"What?" When I first found out he was *special*, I admit I reacted poorly, but I've spent years trying to make up for that. My family does not know I'm a spy for the Loyals. They *cannot* know. They believe I'm a ship captain for the Revolters. My true work and Vivace's shape-shifting powers must be kept a secret at all costs.

His eyes drop to my satchel then back to me. "Going somewhere?"

"I have to report to the Revolter base, yes." And then who knows if I will be back.

He nods and turns, heading outside. It chills me that I can't explain the truth to him before I'm gone, but it's safer for him to hate me as I fade away.

I sigh and pick Cali up, hugging her close. "I love you, honey."

She kisses my cheek. "I love you too, Papa."

"The sooner you report, the sooner you can return to us," Pela says.

My heart sinks, and I nod. "Right." I set Cali down and hug them both before heading outside. I don't bother saddling our horse, not wanting her to get lost when I don't come home.

I look around for Vivace to say goodbye, but I can't find him, and I know my time is running out. I can sense it. If I can make it to the duke's manor, from there, the letters will reach the Emperor. I trudge along as the setting sun casts blood-red rays across the sky. By the time I reach Brimwood Manor at the top of the hill, I can barely see the dark path before me.

I rap tired knuckles on the door, and the duke's ward pulls it open. "Oh. Can I help you?" She looks me over. I must be a sight to see with blood from the sea battle staining my clothes.

"Is the duke home?"

She nods and calls into the manor, "Mr. Claude?"

I smile when the duke steps into view. He looks just as exhausted as I feel.

His arms cross over his chest, and he leans against the doorframe. "I haven't seen you in a while." His eyes twinkle with his lopsided grin.

"Been busy. I have letters with the Ageless One's location and the Revolters' plans that need to get to the Emperor." I tap the satchel at my side. "The unity of the empire could depend on it."

He nods and holds his hand out. "I'll take care of that from here. You head home."

I pull the satchel from around my neck and go to hand it to him when claws dig into my back, dragging me to the ground.

"Get back inside!" I hear the duke yelling at the ward who must have stepped out.

My vision blurs. Blood pools on my back. The duke yanks the satchel from my hands and feet scurry inside the mansion.

A wolf growls in my ear. My sealed fate has come.

But fate is not my master.

I twist around, grabbing the wolf's leg and throwing him off of me. He hits the wall with a whimper. Pushing myself up, I blink several times, trying to clear my sight.

The duke steps forward and slams the front door shut behind him, protecting his ward inside. He raises a flintlock pistol and aims it at the wolf. "Back, beast!"

The white wolf picks himself up and rolls his neck, bares his teeth. The duke cocks the gun, and I catch the wolf's eye.

I know this shape-shifter.

"Claude, no, don't shoot!" I grab his wrist and try to wrestle the gun from his hand. But the wolf has his fangs in my leg, and I scream.

A gunshot rings into the night. And the duke falls to the ground. I drop the gun and see red bloom across the duke's stomach. I land beside him, the wolf tugging me down. My head smacks against something hard, and everything is muffled. Ears ringing.

The front door creaks open, and the ward stands there, trembling. The wolf lunges for her, but I grab onto his neck and pin him. The duke grips the wolf's fur and curses him for going after her, "You can't have her, you icy-hearted monster! Stay off her path." Then he tosses the satchel to his ward. With his fading breath, he mumbles something to her, and she's off running to the stables. The wolf snaps at me, but I don't let go until I hear horse hooves clipping away, until my eyes grow heavy and my arms give out. The letters will reach the Emperor. I have succeeded.

Blood seeps from my body, and I cough, ragged. I try to mutter, to tell the wolf that he's wrong—that he should let the ward and the letters go. That they're bound for the Emperor and will help bring him a future world of peace. That I'm not a Revolter like he thinks. I should have told him the truth sooner, trusted him with my secrets.

But none of those words come out.

The wolf pulls out of my limp grip and nudges my head with his nose. A quiet whimper escapes him, and he howls. I feel his fur in my fingers, and before I fade from this life, a single whisper slips from my mouth.

"I still love you, son."

But this is not *my* story. That's for another time and place. This is the story about my son, Vivace, and what happens to him after I die.

CHAPTER ONE

LIGHT DAWNS IN DARKNESS

VIVACE

MY NAME IS Vivace. My father used to say he named me after the musical term for lively and brisk because I was always in a hurry to be somewhere when I was a toddler. Never stopping to think things through before acting. Impulsive, assumption-led, angry, nervous, quiet—a silent monster.

I was two years old when my parents first met me. Apparently, I was stuck, head first, in a broken fence, clawing to get out. I'd been chasing a squirrel with the determination of an experienced hunter without taking a moment to acknowledge the fence in their yard.

I'm surprised they didn't shoot me or try to scare me off. You see, when they found me, I wasn't like other normal little boys.

I was a wolf.

And now, sixteen years later, these claws killed my father, and the red rose ward is next.

LILY

In the dark, I make my way through winding bends and rustling leaves. The lantern in my hand guides my path. Adjusting the strap on my shoulder, I glance down to ensure the letters are secure in my satchel.

I was thrown from my horse several miles back, but nothing will stop me now. It'd be worse to rest for the night in these woods. My heart beats like the ticking of a clock. Better to continue on foot than to lay in wait and become prey to the white wolf. I know the duke cursed him in his last breaths, but I'm not certain what it means.

Thump-thump

Tick Tock

The full moon peeks through tree branches losing their leaves in the autumn breeze. A distant howl makes me pick up my dress and quicken my pace.

"These letters must reach the Emperor! Do you understand? This is our final hope," the duke had said as his bloody hands pressed the satchel to my chest. "Follow the smallest road in Waning Forest. Go quickly and stop for nothing."

Those were his last spoken words to me, his ward. But his last thought—which my blood-born abilities allowed me to hear as clear as a shout—was, *Light dawns in darkness!*

Unfortunately, only my feeble lantern lights my path, and I've so long to go. I'd have gone by train, the fastest transportation there is, but trains are no longer safe since the war began a few years ago. No longer under the Emperor's control. Nothing is. The world has burst into a wild flame ever since he took over the throne.

The candle in my lantern flickers when a gust of wind brushes past, and for a moment, I think I will lose what little light I have. But it regains its strength and presses on through the night, ever my guide. I thank the Storyteller above because I've already used my last match, and this is my final candle.

Thump-thump

Tick Tock

I try not to be afraid. Afraid of the dark and the things that live in it. Afraid of what might happen if I don't reach the Emperor in time. Afraid of fires blazing across the world if our ruler can't contain them. They have stirred for centuries—coals smoldering beneath civil unrest and oppressing those of us with powers. The Emperor is the one we've been waiting for to finally stoke the flames, but things have moved too fast.

I know the letters by my side are the key to fight back those flames. Getting them to him is the trouble. Many have died to bring them this far. They contain our enemy's plans. Some spy died getting them into the duke's hands, and the duke died getting them into mine.

An owl hoots from branches above me. I shudder when it takes flight, spreading large wings overhead. I reach up and touch the red ribbon in my hair, fashioned to look like a red rose—Jazper, the duke, gave it to me the day he took me under his wing. And now he's gone. Forever.

I shake my head and focus on my path. I've been trudging on since nightfall, but this forest is no small space. It stretches from the duke's mansion, through the graveyard, and all the way to the Emperor's castle. And in the darkness, there is no end in sight.

The dirt path under my feet continues to grow smaller and smaller until I find myself pushing through thickets. My expensive new dress snags on a briar bush, ripping fabric. I try to ignore the thorns that scrape along my cheeks and arms, tearing at my skin like claws attempting to rip apart our Empire's last hope.

Thump-thump

Tick Tock

I will myself to fight through the pain and march on. Like a soldier in the dark. A soldier in a dress.

Holding my lantern low to the forest floor, I search for the faintest shadow of the path. And then, there it is, bending around a tree. So I follow it, nose nearly to the ground, until wind whips around me and . . .

the

light

goes

out.

There is no light in the dark.

Thump-thump

Tick Tock

The path was hard enough to follow before, but now, standing in the middle of this forsaken forest with nothing but the shadows from the moon to hear me, I scream. I scream because I don't know what else to do. This path was meant to lead me. To show me the way to the Emperor. To save the fate of my kind. This path was meant to end the war raging in our empire and give those like me—those with special abilities—a right to live and breathe and create their own light.

But now, there is no light in the dark.

I don't move because I'd rather stand still than head in the wrong direction. At least here I'm on the path.

The howling I'd heard in the distance returns, but this time, it's no longer distant. The monster's low growl rumbles somewhere off to my right. I imagine a wolf crouching on all fours, ready to pounce and make me his meal.

Something illogical tells me I'm safe if I stand here on this path and wait. But that's absurd.

Thump-thump

Tick Tock

The growling turns to a snarl and then another howl. Leaves rustle. Panting grows nearer. Fear throws me off of the path. Dropping the dead lantern, I run. Blind, I chase after where I think the path must be and away from the hungry wolf.

I stumble over a fallen tree and scrape both my knees through what's left of my dress. I try to ignore the blood that trickles down my legs and press on. Tears attempt to blur my vision, but there isn't much left to blur.

The wolf—I can hear him—picks up his pace and must be only feet behind me.

Thump-thump

Thump-thump

Thump-thump

I know this is the end. The end of me. The end of hope. The end of the world.

I reach for my stalker's mind with my powers and hear *Get her before the graveyard! So close! Closer!*

I've read wolf minds before and they never had such organized thoughts like this. Terror sinks in deeper, my feet pounding against twigs. This is no normal wolf.

Almost! Almost there!

The wolf snarls, and I can feel his breath as his teeth snap at me. I stumble. Search in vain for—

The path!

Up ahead, faint lights. Lanterns? And then . . . the graveyard!

The path winds toward that haunted place, lanterns growing with each step and illuminating the forest.

In a few brief strides, I'm faced with a tall rose-embroidered gate to the cemetery. I fling it open and yank it shut behind me, overly aware that even its wrought-iron bars won't do much against the wretched *werewolf.*

Thump-thump

Thump-thump

Hiding behind the gate, the beast and I lock eyes. His teeth shimmer with saliva as he crouches low, a growl rumbling from deep in his chest. Then he springs forward.

I scream and stumble away from the gate. But the wolf doesn't get in. Instead, some invisible force throws him to the ground before his claws touch the metal.

He whimpers and falls on his side.

I blink and stare at him as his form slowly shifts from white fur to flesh. A man slowly pushes up to his full height, eyes locking back to mine. He's about my age, and somehow his clothes shifted with him.

A tentative smile spreads across my lips, understanding dawning. "You can't come in here."

His fingers curl into a fist. "Yes, I can. You are mine any moment I wish."

"Then prove it." I lean forward, staring him down.

He smiles widely and walks around the edge of the graveyard, reaching his hand out and touching the gate. Whatever stopped him before doesn't now, his fingers thrumming across the bars until he finds a spot he likes. He grabs hold and leaps over, landing a few feet away from my path.

He lands on all fours, grinning up at me. "Nowhere is safe for you."

Thump-thump

My throat tightens, and I grip the satchel closer.

The wolfman saunters over to me, pausing inches from my face. For a moment we share breaths—mine ragged and his rancid. We study each other. The grin on his face intensifies. *She's mine.*

There's no point in running now. He's much faster than I am. So instead, I watch his hands reach for me. Only his fingers curl like they've slammed into a glass wall. His face twists with confusion.

My feet shift on well-traveled dirt, and as I realize the truth; it's my turn to smile. "You can't get me on the path."

I turn to take in my surroundings, ignoring the wolfman pounding at the air.

Hanging on the cemetery gate is a freshly lit lantern. I reach for it and pull it down. I again have a light in the darkness.

I start up the graveyard hill, seeing the path lead through the home of the dead. I admit to myself that I'm still afraid, and that admission frees me—renews my hope.

The wolfman stalks beside me, growling in his human throat. "You are *mine*. You can't stay on the path forever. You'll step off, and I'll be here."

I run my hand over my satchel and don't give him the pleasure of a response.

Passing through the graveyard's shifting shadows, my feet stay fast to the dirt path. I can see it better here, even in the presence of death.

"You think you're somehow safe? I killed the spy. I killed the duke. And now, I'll kill you," the wolfman growls.

I want to ask why he's siding with those who would want him dead, but I decide it doesn't matter. I'm on a mission, and indulging his taunts could prove fatal. So I press on.

Bats flit just above my head, but they're no more dangerous than the wolf while I hold to the path. But the walk upward is strenuous, and my legs tremble from the long journey. Even still, I put one foot in front of the other until I reach the top of the hill, the middle of the cemetery.

And here I lift my lantern, in the light of the full moon, with the forest around me, and see the Emperor's castle just beyond the bottom of the graveyard hill.

My heart beats steadily, and I sigh in relief.

The path widens as it nears the castle—a safe escort to my destination. The wolfman has lost. He seems to know it too. "You've beaten me this time, but I'll be back." He growls one last time before darting back into the woods, but his threats turn to ash in the light.

CHAPTER TWO

THE WRONG SORT OF MONSTER

VIVACE

EACH ATTEMPT I make to step on her path thrusts me back, and I can never reach her.

The duke's cursed words must be keeping me from her. *You icy hearted monster! Monster!* My chest feels frozen, like winter decided to come early.

But still, I hunt her down, through branches and graveyards . . .

Because curses can't stop me.

I pause when she reaches the Emperor's castle, watching her beg to be let in.

This I did not expect. The satchel was meant for the Revolters, but here she is, at the castle gate. I question myself for a moment.

But I cannot be wrong. Because if I am, that'd mean I killed my father for no reason. And that I can't bear.

So I harden my heart.

And bare my teeth.

And plan to devour the red rose woman.

When something in me freezes.

She looks over her shoulder in my direction. I feel a prick in my head.

I'll end every Revolter if I need to.

And like she can read my mind, her face falls into sorrow. She calls out from the gate, "I'm not a Revolter. I'm on your side, wolfman."

She could be lying, but dread fills me because maybe she isn't.

And I've become the wrong sort of monster in this war.

I lock eyes with her, and she holds out her hand in my direction, even though I'm hidden behind the thicket in the night.

She says, voice sweet as honey, "I've got powers too. Blood-born. You're not alone. We're on the same side. Your father was indeed a spy, but not in the way you think. He was a Loyal, just like you, spying against the Revolters."

I blink at her, knives gutting my stomach. This is all my fault. I acted too fast.

"But don't blame yourself," she continues. "You didn't know or understand. You did what you thought you had to do. You're not a wolf inside."

I dip my head, flashes of memories coming to my mind. Memories I could have misunderstood. Misplaced hatred and wrongful accusations.

All these years, he'd been fighting for me?

Fighting to create a world where blood-borns with powers like mine can live without fear of being rejected, or worse, killed?

All these years as I've hated him and reasoned he wasn't actually my father. I was adopted, so of course he had no real love for me; I'd told myself many times. He had no genuine desire to fight for a world I could live freely in.

But all these years . . .

I've been wrong.

I cry wolfish tears for the lives I ended and the lies I've believed. And there I lay, a monster forevermore, because this is guilt I'll never be rid of.

But as the moonlight peeks through the trees and shines on the woman's face, she utters words I'll never forget, "I forgive you, wolfman."

The wolf within stirs and cries for forgiveness I do not deserve.

CHAPTER THREE

ICY HEARTED

VIVACE

YOU CAN'T HAVE her, you icy hearted monster! Stay off her path.

Flashes of my father yelling, my teeth in his flesh, and the duke bleeding out fill my mind.

Blood. *So much blood.*

I squeeze my eyes shut like it'll help the visions go away, but all I see is my father's stained red face muttering, "I still love you, son."

I *am* a monster.

Even though she saw me slaughter my father and her duke, even though I chased her, threatened to kill her for the sake of the war, she tiptoes over to me and sits beside the bush. "I forgive you. I really do." Her brown hair frames her face in some fancy updo, the red ribbon holding it up and twisted to look like a rose, and she looks about my age of eighteen.

My paws cover my nose, and my white fur bristles. My heart pounds slowly, as if every beat is pushing through ice. She's been trying to convince me of this ever since she came back from delivering the satchel to the Emperor.

The blood-born Emperor who wants to protect his kind.

I can't believe my father was a Loyal just like me. *Why did my father lie to me? Why did he tell me he was a spy for the Revolters?*

The ward smiles sadly and says, "I know you must have thought I was bringing the satchel to the Revolters. Well, I wasn't. And, yes, the duke and your father are Loyals like us. I don't know why he lied to you about being a Revolter spy."

I blink at her, reminded of my sinking feeling that her blood-born powers might revolve around mind reading.

She nods. "Yes. That's it. I'm sorry. I haven't mastered my abilities."

I swallow. *So you can hear every single one of my thoughts?*

She shakes her head. "Sometimes, but not exactly. I'm still working on turning it on and off myself, but it seems to have a mind of its own."

I suddenly feel naked in front of her, even in my fur. *Oh . . .* I try to stop thinking about the overwhelming guilt plaguing me, or the duke's curse that's devouring me, or the grief over never seeing my father again, or how beautiful the ward is, or the way I feel like throwing up from the colliding emotions.

I'm sorry I killed your duke. I'm not sure if I like or hate being able to converse with someone in my wolf form. This is usually my shield against conversation.

She smiles and shakes her head. "Oh, don't worry about Jazper."

Jazper?

"Sorry. Duke Claude. He hates when I call him Jazper, as if he's not young enough to be my brother. But anyway, he's alive and well."

I freeze. *How?* Not possible. A gunshot had torn through him.

"You know the Emperor is a blood-born, right?" She pauses, only to laugh. "Of course you do. That's the whole reason the Revolters are trying to dethrone him." She brushes her brown hair behind her ear. "He's a healer. Dorian—one of our friends—found them when he returned to Brimwood. He's a teleporter, and he brought the duke and your father to the Emperor in seconds. Jaz—I mean, Duke Claude, is already prancing around the castle, planning havoc for the Revolters."

My heart races. *Does that mean my . . .* I don't dare finish.

Her face falls, and she shakes her head. "No, I'm sorry. The Emperor healed his wounds, but it wasn't enough. We're not sure why."

I wince and nod. *Right.*

The ward pulls the red rose ribbon from her hair. She brushes it between her fingers and it unrolls into one long strand. She hesitates and then holds her hand out, palm up. "May I?"

My eyes narrow, and I show my teeth briefly. But I'm ashamed of my instinctive habit and clamp my mouth shut. I lay my clawed paw in her hand. She runs her thumb over my fur and ties the ribbon around my foot.

I sniff the ribbon, perplexed, then look at her and tilt my head in question.

"To help you remember that I forgive you." She smiles.

This ward is like no one I've met before. She saw me kill my own father and attack her guardian only hours earlier, and yet, she's treating me like a friend. *Why?*

I look down at her red ribbon on my front paw. It reminds me of the one my little sister wears to church.

My stomach churns.

Now I must return home and tell Mother and Cali that Father is gone. They'll turn me out of the house for sure. Father was the one who wanted to adopt me the most. Surely they'll hate me for what I've done. I huff out a deep breath and the ribbon quivers. I cannot go home. It'll be better to run than face my mother and sister.

The ward reaches out a brave hand and runs it through the fur on my head.

I tense, suddenly ashamed to be a beast in front of her. I duck my head and feel nauseous looking at the blood that stains my claws and white fur. I hate the claws and teeth that tore flesh, so I shift my fur into skin, returning to my human body. My hands are stained red . . . so I divert my gaze.

Our eyes are now level, and she studies me. She's sitting directly across from me, and I'm beyond thankful that Father had found a way for my clothes to shift with me.

I swallow. As a wolf, I don't have to talk verbally because I can't. But now, I have no excuse.

She reaches out and adjusts the ribbon on my wrist. "I know you won't hurt me. Not now that you understand."

The duke's ward studies me, and I swallow, replaying my crimes in my head. I thought my father, the Pirate King, was a traitor in this war, a spy for our enemies, the Revolters—those who hate blood-borns like me and the magical powers that surge through my veins. So I killed him—and the duke, I thought—before they could deliver the satchel to the Revolters. I still don't know what was in the satchel, but my father had left to deliver it with such earnestness that I imagine it's highly important for the war.

"My name is Lily Roselle. What's yours?" she asks, forcing me back to the present.

I blink and run a shaky hand through my white hair. "Vivace. Just . . . Vivace." I glance at the horizon. "I need to go." *Tell my family . . .*

She smiles softly. "Would you like company? There isn't much more for me to do now that the satchel is safely delivered."

Lily's hair dances across her cheeks in the breeze, and I stifle a yawn. It's still the middle of the night, and she looks as tired as I feel. But I'm sure I look worse off than she does, her brown eyes dazzling.

"That won't be necessary. You should rest. Someone's been making your night difficult." I strain a smile because I'm the one who spent the night chasing her to the castle.

She chuckles softly, and it's the most beautiful sound I've ever heard. *Shut up, Vivace. She just saw you murder your own father, and you terrified her in the forest.* I clear my throat. "How can you forgive me?"

You can't have her, you icy hearted monster! Stay off her path.

You can't have her.

You icy hearted monster!

Monster . . .

Lily picks at the grass beside her. "Well, hearing some of your thoughts certainly helps. I can't say I wouldn't have done something similar if I thought it would protect the Emperor and this war."

I pick at the ribbon on my wrist. "I really should go." *Or run away.*

I'm beyond tired and don't want someone witnessing my thoughts right now.

"Right, yeah. Of course. Stay safe out there, Vivace. And don't forget I forgive you." She smiles again and turns back to the castle. But then she pauses and says, "I'll see you again?"

Heat rises on my cheeks, thawing me briefly. *She wants to see* me *again?* "I suppose so." I watch her go briefly before I shift back to fur and take off through the woods.

CHAPTER FOUR

BRIMWOOD MANOR

LILY

LILY!" I'M WRITING a letter to Vivace in my room at Brimwood Manner when Jazper calls for me. He has been running around like a small child. He says being on the move helps him think up ideas on how to win the war. I can't blame him. If it weren't for thoughts of Vivace consuming most of my thoughts, I would be going mad with ideas of my own.

"Coming!" I call back and quickly fold the letter. Vivace and I have been writing letters to each other for a few weeks, and when we meet in the forest, we deliver them. I've only seen him twice since that brutal night, even though he's only an hour's ride away when we meet in the middle.

The first time was rather awkward. We sat in the grass, picking at fallen leaves. But the second time was better. I brought a book, and we took turns reading until he told me about how detached he felt from his family after he told them about his father. He's been battling a chilling cold as well that concerns me. And—

"Lily!" Jazper calls again, yanking me from my daydreams.

I push my chair back, the feet shrieking on the floor, and I dart downstairs to his office. "I'm here!"

Jazper's hair is in a wild mess. His eyes are wide, and his shirt is untucked. Sometimes I forget he's twelve years *older* than me and not younger.

"What took you so long?" He peers at me and then waves his hand. "No matter. I need you to take over things for a time. I'm going away."

I nod. This is fairly normal, though sometimes I join him on the Novaturient—a privateer ship that fights for the Emperor. "To sea again?" I grip the letter behind me, rocking back and forth. Jazper better not delay my meeting with Vivace.

"No, to the circus," he teases as if that can't be true. "Yes, the sea." *Though I'd rather be at the circus right now,* his thoughts say.

I chuckle. "Once the war ends, you could open your own circus."

Jazper eyes me and then nods. "Perhaps. Here." He picks up a pile of financial books from his desk and plops them in my arms. "The books need to be done. Harper should be by to help run things if she can. If not, get Demi or Allegra or Dorian, or anyone, really, to come help."

"I can handle it, Jazper."

He pauses and squints his eyes at me. "That's *Mr. Claude* to you, tiny child ward." His lips slip up into a playful grin, and he ruffles my hair.

I slap his hand away, glare at him, and hope my hair isn't ruined for Vivace. "I haven't been a child in a year, *Jazper*."

He spins towards the door. "Oh yes, you're so old and wise now. I forgot. A full eighteen years." He grabs his tailcoat with a playful smirk. "Don't let the manor burn down while I'm away," he calls over his shoulder.

And then he is out the door, leaving me to manage an estate full of misfit blood-borns. But right now, I have one thing on my mind. *Vivace.*

CHAPTER FIVE
THE WOLFMAN'S HEART

VIVACE

LILY SHOULD BE here any moment. We said we'd meet under the old oak tree at 2 p.m. today. I pull out my pocket watch. It's half past two. If something happened to her on her way to meet me, I don't know what I'll do. I can't lose anyone else.

You can't have her. The duke's curse from that night lingers over me and tethers my heart from truly believing I could be happy with Lily.

I shiver because even though the weather is a comfortable autumn, my heart feels like winter solstice.

I'm just about to shift to my fur and sniff around for her when I hear tumbling through the trees. "I'm here!" Lily calls from horseback, and I can't help the smile that tugs at my lips.

She has been the only bright spot in an otherwise dark world.

Her hair is neatly pinned back, but a few pieces have come loose during her ride. She slows her horse and climbs off with ease. "Sorry. I had a few unexpected things to manage at the manor."

"That's all right." My hands tremble behind me, both from nerves and this cold I can't shake. We've only known each other for a few weeks, but I know she must be expecting a formal offer of courtship. Many start courting before they've even met. And now I'm hoping she didn't just hear those thoughts.

Thankfully, she chuckles and says, "No, I didn't hear."

You'd still make one hell of a spy. You know that?

She shakes her head with a giggle.

I reach for the letters in my breast pocket. Sometimes I have a hard time thinking about what to write, but it was Lily's idea, and the way her eyes light up when I hand her the small stack makes it all worth it.

Lily hands me a bundle twice the size of mine. They're tied together with a rose sticking out of the top. I take the flower off and stuff the letters in my pocket. "So . . ." I twirl the rose in my fingers.

She's standing a safe distance away from me. "How are things with your family?" Lily asks.

"Not much different."

Lily nods. She pulls a blanket off her horse and lays it on the forest floor. Lifting her dress, she sits down and looks up at me. She pats the empty space beside her. "Sit?"

I still can't fathom why Lily would be interested in someone like me, especially after *that* night. *You can't have her, you icy hearted monster!* But I sit and silently play with the flower. I've never been too great with words, but with Lily, my throat closes up. So instead, I think. *How have you been doing?*

"Mr. Claude just left, so I have to run Brimwood while he's away, which is always a bit stressful, but I'll manage." She makes busy work tucking her loose hair back into her updo.

If you need any help . . . It would get me out of the house.

She smiles, little dimples forming on her cheeks. "I would appreciate that."

I nod and swallow. My palms sweat, and I don't know what else to say. I feel like I'm supposed to be doing something, or saying something to keep the conversations flowing, but I can't think of anything. I'm no good at this. It isn't Lily. It's me. I don't deserve love, especially not after what I've done. And it's not like I can get my own heart to feel what I want it to feel anyway, coated in a barrier of ice.

Lily glances at me, then reaches over and plays with the red ribbon still on my wrist. Her fingertips graze over my skin, sending chills up my arm. "Vivace. What does this ribbon mean?"

I clear my throat as if to speak, but then, *You forgave me.*

She nods and moves her hand to my chest, nearly stealing my breath. "And now you need to forgive yourself."

A squirrel races across the branches, missteps, and slips off but grabs onto another limb at the last second and pulls himself up. He's got a big acorn in his mouth and his poofy tail twitches.

I can't look at Lily. Time has done little to soften the guilt and grief. And sometimes, when I look at her, all I see is the fear in her eyes from that night, soon followed by the blood, the screaming, the flesh tearing under my teeth and claws, curses thrown. My throat fills with bile, and I swallow it down. *I'm trying.*

Lily leans over and kisses my cheek. My heart races, and now I do glance at her, afraid my burning cheeks are turning my pale skin bright red. Whenever I'm with her, she manages to thaw the ice momentarily. I so badly want to be whatever person Lily thinks I am, but I'm only me. Impulsive, assumption-led, nervous, angry, bitter, me. A literal monster. And I won't have Lily wasting her time trying to fix me. That's not fair to her. *No one can fix a beast like me.*

So I pull away and stand up, hoping she's already read all my thoughts on the matter.

"Vivace . . ." Lily stands and grips my hand before I can leave.

I pause and study her. I can't deny how right her hand feels in mine.

"I don't want to fix you," she says. "I'm not a god. Nor am I perfect by any means."

My jaw clenches. "You've never killed anyone."

She raises her eyebrow. "What makes you so sure of that? Just because I wear a dress and live in a fancy manor, you don't think I've done things that haunt me in this war too?"

The thought had never crossed my mind. "I just assumed . . ."

"Well, I have. I've sailed on the *Novaturient* with the duke before. We all have played our part." Her grip on my hand tightens. "And what you did was no different. You fought for our blood-born kind just like I have."

My face twists. "But it was my *father*."

"You didn't know he was on our side. I'm not saying it was good. I'm just saying, please don't condemn yourself forever. Don't let it keep you from living."

I let go of her hand. "I'm not ready to marry *anyone.*"

She blinks several times. "No one was asking you to?" She looks as perplexed as I feel. "Is that what's bothering you?"

I run a hand through my white hair. "I thought that's what you'd be expecting. Courtship and then . . . that."

Lily's face breaks into a smile. "Vivace. Of course, I want that someday, but not right now. Just because some people our age are already wed doesn't mean we have to go fast. I personally happen to think these things take more time."

A wave of relief gushes through me, and I grin. "Oh."

Lily laughs and grabs my hand, pulling me back down beside her. She lays her head on my shoulder, and I wrap my arm around her waist, the weight of expectations gone.

"You need time to heal, and I'd like to get to know you better," she says softly.

I watch the squirrel race down the side of the tree and take off through the woods. "Then let's do it properly. When the duke returns, I'll ask him if I can court you." *And to remove this curse.*

Lily grins and wiggles closer to me. "And I'll make sure he doesn't push us too fast." She wraps her arms around my waist.

My chin rests on the top of her head, and I close my eyes, enjoying her company and the slowing of my anxious heart. The thought of being in love with her creeps up my spine, but I quickly replace it with, *I like you, Lily.*

She gives me a knowing look and whispers, "I like you, too, my wolfman."

At those words, something cracks inside of me. I pull her closer and bury my face into her hair. Warmth spreads through me, melting the ice that surrounds my heart. And for the first time since that awful night, an indescribable peace settles in my core.

EPILOGUE

VIVACE

SEVERAL WEEKS HAVE passed since I made plans to court Lily, and the war still rages. I doubt it will end anytime soon. The people are too furious about having a blood-born on the throne to back down.

In my wolf form, I pace my bedroom. Nothing at home has been the same since Father . . .

Mother didn't kick me out of the house, but we don't talk. Cali doesn't even pester me anymore. And all I want is to flee.

Perhaps I can find my birth family if they're still alive. Or stay at Brimwood with Lily. Or—

There's thick mumbling by my door, something about singing. But my head feels like it's underwater, and my thoughts are too heavy to pull from.

I can't get most of that dreadful night out of my head. Worst of all, Father's cries as he tells me he still loves me. The images race in my head like a train on a looping track.

Footsteps trail away from my door.

Tears fill my eyes and stick to my fur. I shake my head so they fling off. Whining, I sink down on my stomach and place my chin between my front paws.

Lily's red ribbon catches my eye. I never take it off.

Remember I forgive you. You need to forgive yourself.

Lily's words dance in my head. I can't leave without her. But staying in my father's house is choking me to death.

Heaving a sigh, I shift back to flesh.

It's time to go.

I toss several trousers and shirts into my suitcase, and then my watch, flintlock, tricorne, and topper. Father always said a smart man owns both a tricorne and a top hat for different occasions. If you want to take off to the sea, you sport the tricorne. If you want to dazzle the ladies at court, you swap it out for a topper. I happen to dislike all hats, but these both belonged to my father, and I can't bear to leave them behind.

I click the suitcase shut and sit on my bed, waiting for the sun to set. Once I hear Mother and Cali drift off to bed, I slip out of the house. I'm not sure where I'm even headed.

"Vivace?" a soft voice says behind me as I step off the porch. I turn to see Cali sitting on a step. "Where are you going?"

I frown. "You're supposed to be in bed."

She shrugs and rubs her eyes, and I realize she's been crying.

Because of me.

Wincing, I crouch down beside her. "What's wrong?" *I know the answer . . .*

Cali sniffs and pushes her straight black hair behind her ear. She looks so much like our father. "I miss you."

My head jerks, and I blink rapidly. She's meant to be crying for Father, not me. "I'm right here."

She shakes her head. "You just hide in your room all day. You never talk to me anymore. Or sing to me. Momma says to give you space, but I don't want space. I want my daddy, and I want you." She wipes at her eyes.

Have I been the one avoiding them, not the other way around?

I taste blood on my tongue and realize I've been biting my lip too hard. "I'm sorry, Cal. I know you hate me—"

"No." Her face scrunches. "My tummy is grumpy and all icky, but I don't hate you." She plays with her tiny fingers on her lap. "I kinda wanna slap you, though."

I lean my head back a little out of instinct. "Would it make you feel better?"

Cali rubs her eye with the back of her hand. "I dunno. Maybe?"

I brace myself and say, "Go ahead." *How much can a nine-year-old slap hurt anyway?*

"Really?" She glances at my face, then at her hand, and then back again.

I nod and close my eyes. "Do it."

The wait is agonizing. But if slapping me is all it takes to get my sister back, I'd rather be slapped daily than have to leave.

The air is still for several moments until I hear her start to move. I pinch my eyes shut more, forcing myself to stay still.

I feel her hand rest down on my knee to balance herself and—

She crawls onto my lap and throws her arms around my neck. The movement makes me fall back against the railing. My arms dangle, and I want to hug her back. But I can't bring myself to—until I catch sight of the red ribbon on my wrist.

Remember I forgive you.

I take a deep breath and wrap her up in my arms. She grips me tighter. "I'm sorry," I whisper in her ear. Her hair tickles my lips.

She sniffs, and her little body shakes, sobbing against me. I took this little girl's father away, and yet I'm the one comforting her. Nothing makes sense anymore. Father should be here, not me. He'd just returned home a few hours before he . . . before *I* . . .

He was the Pirate King and spent his days at sea and would only come home every few months. The times he was gone, we all would miss him so much. I used to sing Cali to sleep and promise her that her daddy would be home soon to sing to her himself. But now he never will . . .

I open my eyes and blink back tears.

The front door creaks open, and Mother steps out. Her nightgown flutters in the breeze. We look at each other. Silent.

She turns and goes back inside. I see the flicker of a candle in the kitchen. She shuffles around for a bit, pots clanking about, and after a few moments, comes back carrying three tea cups. Mother sits on the step, sets the cups beside us, and whispers, "Your father was very proud of you. Both of you."

I bury my face into Cali's hair so Mother can't see me cry. Swallowing lumps of guilt and sorrow, I let them burrow in my stomach. I haven't told anyone this, but I manage to mutter, "He . . . he told me he still loves me . . . At the end . . ."

The air is still for a moment.

Cali coughs, and I run my fingers through her hair. She's stopped crying, still cocooned against me.

"If I just leave, you two can be happy again," I whisper.

Mother squeezes my shoulder a little too hard. "We're your family, Vivace. You're not going anywhere. *You* make us happy."

I wince a little. "But how?"

She cups my chin and looks me dead in the eye. "Because you're my son, blood or not."

Tears drip down my cheeks, and Mother pulls us both against her. "Are you ready to finally talk to me?" Her eyes fall on Lily's ribbon. Mother touches it and lifts her eyebrows in question. "You haven't taken this off since that night. Where have you been sneaking off to so often?"

I feel a small smile creep onto my lips. "A new friend gave it to me. She said it's to remember . . . remember she forgave me." It feels stupid saying it out loud, and I sink back, embarrassed.

But Mother smiles for the first time in weeks. "You are forgiven." She takes a deep breath and speaks through what sounds like a thick fog. "I'm sorry, Vivace. I know this isn't your fault. I've been mad with your father and taken it out on you."

This I didn't expect. "Mad at *him*?"

She nods. "If he hadn't lied to us, if he'd just told us that he was a spy for the Loyals, none of this would have happened. You wouldn't have felt the need to chase him, to defend your kind." She shakes her head. "But I know he was protecting us. You *both* were trying to protect us, and what happened was an accident. It's not his fault, and it's not yours."

I shake my head. "No. It's my fault. I react too fast without thinking. I always have."

Mother cups the back of my head and kisses my forehead. "Maybe so. But none of us can linger there."

Cali sniffs and plays with the ribbon on my wrist. "What's her name?" she asks.

My cheeks heat. "Lily."

Mother actually chuckles. "Go see Lily more." She pats my cheek. "You're fond of her."

Cali giggles a little, and the sound warms me, or maybe it's my intense embarrassment. "Vivace is in *love* with a *girl*!"

I clear my throat. "I never said that." But the heat rising on my cheeks is sure to be giving me away. "I barely know her."

Mother smiles and sips her tea. "Well, get to know her." She stands. "Drink your tea, and it's back to bed for both of you."

I nod and squeeze Cali before letting her go. She climbs off my lap, grabs her mug, and heads inside.

Mother pauses at the front door, looks over her shoulder at me and says, "And never forget, I still love you too. No matter what, kiddo."

I give her a smile and nod. She slips inside, and I lean back on the railing, finishing my tea. The urge to flee is gone.

That night, I sing Cali to sleep.

THE READER AND THE SOULLESS

L.A. THORNHILL

CHAPTER ONE

VIOLA DALLEY SUCKED in a deep breath as she slid out of the carriage after her mistress. *Master's mercy!* The Bramwell estate was enormous. The carriage had taken nearly half an hour to reach the manor from the estate line, where two large automatons stood ominously at guard. If her mistress was correct, the estate extended well beyond the manor, down the hills, over several small parishes and farmlands. The Bramwell bloodline was ancient and reputable. And currently in danger of dying off.

"Stop gawking, Viola," Ms. Cordelia chided with a wave of her gloved hand. "You'll be bored with the manor soon enough."

Not likely.

Four years of service to the lavish Nethersoles hadn't prepared her for this. Bramwell Manor had five columns in the front, signifying the strength of the Five Fathers who founded the faiths of the Five Realms. Sunlight glinted off each of the windows. The manor itself looked to be an acre in length, but surely that was her overactive imagination playing tricks on her.

A cloud drifted over the sun, stealing the glare off the windowpanes. One window towered over the rest, and for a moment, Viola was certain she could make out the figure of a man watching them from the attic. A man with one glowing red eye.

The man vanished behind glass as the sun's rays returned and obscured her view.

"Viola!"

She jumped and nodded to her mistress. "Forgive me, Ms. Nethersole."

"Keep up." Cordelia lifted her chin and walked ahead, like a queen taking in her newly conquered land.

Viola kept in line but remained behind her mistress. "Of course, Miss."

"Don't embarrass me."

"Never, Miss."

Viola stole one more glance up at the window. The man in the window must have been her imagination.

Two manservants opened the manor doors wide as soon as Cordelia's foot touched the first step. An older man with bushy brows and deep gray hair greeted her in the entryway. His tailcoat was dark blue with a matching waistcoat underneath. His collar was tall, and his cravat a little tighter than Viola imagined necessary. Standing adjacent to him was the head butler, who eyed the eight other servants who stood in a perfectly straight line, so stiff that Viola wondered if they were permitted to breathe.

"Ms. Nethersole, a pleasure," the older man said with a gallant bow.

Cordelia curtsied and held out her hand. "Lord Bramwell?"

Lord Bramwell took her hand. "My son would be honored to greet you, but we both thought it best that you settle in first and get accustomed to the estate."

"Certainly. There is no need to expedite the matter. The union is settled between our houses, but I do not care to see his condition until then."

Viola struggled to restrain her shock. No need to expedite meeting Cordelia's future husband? The man she was supposed to be bound to, and with whom she would spend the rest of her life?

Even she had no real concept of how shallow her mistress could be.

They were led through the entryway and to the sitting room, which alone was bigger than the house Viola had once shared with her father. Her mistress sat on a plush emerald loveseat, and Lord Bramwell took the chair adjacent. Viola stood behind Ms. Nethersole, her usual position.

"I cannot express my gratitude enough," Bramwell began. "And my son—"

Cordelia silenced him with a quick wave. "Lord Bramwell, forgive me. Let's eliminate the thinly veiled speeches. You need an heir after your son, and my family needs a title. And since no one else will marry a mechanical with a title, and no one with titles will marry into a house without one, we find ourselves here today."

Viola's eyebrows rose, wondering if her mistress's sharp talk would ruin her chances for said title. Cordelia's betrothed might have been a mechanical—a human being with at least one metal limb or appendage—but he was still Lord Bramwell's son.

"You are a woman of sense. I am pleased." Lord Bramwell eyed his future daughter-in-law. "When can I expect your parents?"

"When I send for them. I must determine how to prepare them. Just how bad is your son?"

Lord Bramwell crossed his legs. "My son is a handsome man, naturally, if I may say with all humility." He held out his hand, indicating a portrait over a fireplace. "Lucius Joel Everet Bramwell. My only heir. This was commissioned shortly before the accident."

Viola turned her attention to the portrait. A young man at the beginning of adulthood stared at them with brilliant blue eyes. His auburn hair hung in loose curls. He had a small grin as if he had been unable to completely conform to the usual stoic portraits of the gentry. His features were pleasing, his jaw strong, and his nose sharp. She imagined he'd filled out more as a mature man, losing the trim build of youth, making him truly handsome.

"Quite a shame, what befell him," Cordelia said. "What is he now?"

Lord Bramwell sighed. "The trainwreck that deprived me of my wife and of my son's soul left his body quite damaged."

Viola closed her eyes and clenched her teeth behind her closed lips. She hated the belief that people who needed metal limbs somehow lost their soul. It angered her how anyone could believe that, especially a father about his own son.

"Nearly his entire left side is mechanical," Bramwell continued. "His arm, his foot, and his leg to the knee. He has a mechanical eye and lung."

"Lung?"

"He took shrapnel to the chest. He has a metal cavity with a false lung in his chest, keeping his breathing regular."

Viola returned to the portrait. *Poor lad.*

"The lung does concern me. He is still able to perform his husbandly duties?"

Lord Bramwell shuffled in his seat. "I assure you, Ms. Nethersole, there is no reason to be concerned about the prospect of an heir."

"Very well," Cordelia said. "But if there is any struggle for an heir, I will not take the blame."

"Of course not."

I cannot believe I have to stand here and listen to this.

Viola reopened her eyes and stifled a yelp. Her Gift of Reading had been awakened by her distress. The room was dark, and Lord Bramwell and Cordelia were cast in low, ebbing light, like the last flicker of a candle swirled in and out of their minds, chests, and hands. They continued talking, completely unaware of what Viola envisioned.

Her Gift from the Master permitted her to interpret people's emotions. The Gift of Reading, as some called it, although many couldn't imagine it meant reading waves of light emanating from a person. But she could see the colors of the light, the speed at which it swirled, and the direction it flowed.

It was meant as a form of empathy and healing, but Viola had to use it as a means of survival, to read those around her and stay on their good side or know when they wished her harm. It had kept her alive for five years.

"I only have one concern at this time," Lord Bramwell continued. Pale yellow light swirled through him. "The last medical automaton that attended my son had an unfortunate accident. It will be several weeks before a replacement will arrive."

"Several weeks? Why so long?" Cordelia asked.

"I only send for the best automatons to care for my son. I will not settle for some bot made from spare parts by the local tinker. He might be a mechanical, but he's still the Bramwell heir. He must survive."

Cordelia smoothed out a wrinkle in her gown. "Is he in any danger without the automaton attending to him?"

"He assures me he can manage without it, but there are mechanical needs that have arisen since his accident. I prefer for him to be closely monitored."

"I may have a temporary solution." Cordelia turned around and eyed Viola. "You have some skills with bots, do you not?"

Viola clasped her hands together, trying to mentally shut down the vision of light. "Me, Mistress?"

"Who am I looking at, Viola?" The light swirling through Cordelia quickened and deepened to a golden yellow, betraying her annoyance. "I've seen you tinkering with gears and whatnot. Can you manage an automaton?"

"I can manage an automaton, yes," Viola replied, slightly flushed. "But a mechanical person is different—"

"Is he, though?"

Viola swallowed her rebuke. To call a human an automaton was ignorant. But Viola's opinion carried little weight here.

She closed her eyes and imagined closing up her Gift inside a box. When she opened her eyes, the swirling colors had disappeared from the lord and lady. "If there is any aid I can provide Lord Bramwell's son, of course, I will."

"If I do not want an unqualified bot working on my son, why would I want some servant girl?" Lord Bramwell snapped.

Cordelia returned her gaze to her future father-in-law. "She's a good servant and not prone to silly fancy. Viola, tell him of your education."

Viola hesitated. She didn't want to lie. She had to choose her words carefully. "My mother was an engineer before she passed. She taught me well. I have no formal education, but she was the best in our town."

"And why didn't you get the proper education like your mother?" Lord Bramwell inquired, his thick brow arched.

"Because . . . circumstances changed when she died. I had to work for a living." She bowed her head. "Sir, if your son's needs are beyond my skill, I will not touch him."

Lord Bramwell let out a displeased sigh. "I suppose you will have to do. Come to my office first thing in the morning for the key."

Key . . . Why would I need a key?

Viola nodded.

"Would you like to rest from your journey, or would you prefer to tour the estate?" Lord Bramwell asked Cordelia.

"Tour. A long walk would suit me well." Cordelia stood, and Lord Bramwell followed. "Viola, unpack my things and ready my room before I return."

"Very good, Miss." Viola briskly walked out of the sitting room, relieved beyond words that she was no longer an audience to such a horrid conversation.

Worst of all, what she had seen had revealed much to her. She learned that despite all they said about his son, her mistress and future father-in-law were completely unaffected by it all. No sadness in the father. No sympathy in the bride-to-be. The most activity she perceived was Cordelia's annoyance toward Viola, which told her she needed to be more cautious.

Good Master, Viola silently prayed, *have pity on young Bramwell.*

CHAPTER TWO

THE FOLLOWING MORNING, Viola was led by the mansion's head butler, Frederick, to Lord Bramwell's office. Normally her morning consisted of carrying clean garments to her mistress, helping her dress, and then attending to an endless list of tasks. This morning, she carried just her mother's small toolkit—the only thing Viola had saved when she and her father fled—and she had no idea what her tasks would be for the unfortunate young man. To Viola's relief, the master of the house wasn't in his room.

"Lord Bramwell gave me instructions for you," Frederick said as he crossed the room and opened the top drawer in Lord Bramwell's desk. He removed a single key and held it up. "There are only two keys. Lord Bramwell has a key on his person at all times. This one is mine, and you cannot enter or leave without me. You will go to Lord Bramwell's son when he requires you, no matter how minuscule the task. Do you understand?"

I hope so.

"Yes, sir," she replied.

"I have appointed a maid to attend to Ms. Nethersole while you care for Master Lucius. You must think of yourself as his servant until you are replaced by the medical automaton in approximately a fortnight. Any questions?"

"What if I cannot help him?" Her voice trembled. "Or he will not allow me to help him?"

"Then have Master Lucius summon me, and you will return to Ms. Nethersole."

Viola nodded, half-hoping the imprisoned man would want nothing to do with her. She had never worked on someone with mechanical parts, much less organs. She didn't know if she could help the man or if she might damage him further.

"Follow me," Frederick instructed.

Viola gripped the toolkit a bit too hard, and it creaked in her hands. They walked up a flight of stairs, down the west wing, and up a winding stone stairwell to a single wooden door. It was fortified with metal strips, which ran across the body and along the edges. Where a normal knob should be was a massive lock larger than Viola's open hand. Though she couldn't see the inside of the lock, she knew what was there. One of her previous masters had been a paranoid man and had the same type of lock on his bedchamber door. Known as the Rosen Lock—named for its inventor—and for the rose-like pattern of gears and bolts that wove inside, it was expensive and virtually impenetrable without the key.

"This is the door to the attic," Frederick said as he slipped the key into the lock.

Who does this to an attic door?

Frederick said nothing as the mechanism inside clicked, spun, and ticked like a clock. Once the noise ceased, he opened the door and motioned her inside.

Locks like this weren't built to keep heirs in attics. They were made to imprison the most dangerous of criminals. The idea occurred to Viola that Lucius Bramwell may not merely be a victim of his father's cruelty but actually be cruel himself. There could be little other reason for such excessive use of restraint.

She could run. Right now. Down the stairs and vanish forever.

No, she had no place to go. It took a lot of favors to conceal her as a servant in the Nethersole household. She had to keep working for them until she heard from her father again. There was no other choice.

My Master and Keeper, protect me.

She took comfort in the idea that Lord Bramwell wouldn't endanger Cordelia Nethersole if his son was vicious. She might not have a title, but her family's wealth would ensure the Bramwells' secret wouldn't be kept if she were misused.

The floor creaked as Viola stepped inside.

Frederick locked the door behind her, and the click of the Rosen Lock pronounced her imprisonment.

The attic was exactly as she imagined it would be in an enormous estate. It was large and long, with low ceilings. Furniture covered with sheets dotted the place. Some dusty, some enveloped in cobwebs. Large paintings leaned against the opposite wall, and there were enough forgotten lamps to fill a small store. The air was humid and warm and smelled of dust and aged wood with a hint of something metallic.

She glanced down and noticed a trail of footsteps in the dust. She followed it to a little nook made by one of only three windows. There was a chair, a couch, and a kerosene lamp. A small stack of books lay on the floor next to the couch, but the dust on the jackets hinted they hadn't been used for several weeks.

"So you're the one my father found to fix me."

Viola yelped and spun around. Between two crates stood a figure bathed in shadow. A single red light shone from the darkness.

For a split second, she thought she had triggered her Gift again, casting him in a threatening red light. But she hadn't. It shone from his mechanical eye.

Viola recovered herself and curtsied, but her heart still pounded in her chest. "Good morning, sir."

"So you say," the man growled as he stepped forward, the shadow receding away.

She couldn't resist using her Gift. She had to know if she was in danger. With a few blinks, light pulsed from his body. To her utter astonishment, his light *was* as red as his eye. Red light usually depicted anger, hate, pain, and often it swirled furiously toward the source of its pain. But somehow, her imprisoned master's light ebbed off of him, like the gentle waves of the Theophilus Realm shore. The man was hurt and angry, and his emotions roiled.

"Are you done staring?" he sneered.

Viola curtsied again, buying time to close up the imaginary gift box. "I am so sorry, Master Lucius. I—"

"Joel."

"I beg your pardon?"

"If you must stick your prying hands into my chest plate, then you will call me Joel. I never go by Lucius if I can help it."

She bowed her head. "Very well, Master Joel."

"I'm a prisoner in my attic. I am no one's *master*."

"As you say, sir."

He rolled his one good eye. The blue color of his iris was a little duller than in his portrait.

The portrait in the sitting room must have been old. This wasn't a young man on the verge of maturity; he was at least ten years older than he had been depicted. His auburn hair, once curly, was now tangled and reached his shoulders. He had a patchy, unkempt beard. He was still thin, but she suspected it was more from a lack of decent nourishment than youth due to the bony appearance of his flesh side.

She had never seen a mechanical like him before. It was not uncommon for the working class to have mechanical hands or legs, despite society telling them it would strip them of their souls. They chose the loss so they could continue putting food on the family table.

Lord Bramwell's son was something else entirely. He had no family to support. He was an heir who would usually choose to be without limbs rather than without a soul. For him, it must have been a case of life or death.

He wore no shoes, so she caught a glimpse of his mechanical foot sticking out from under his dirty brown pants. His tan tunic did little to conceal his mechanical arm under the fabric or the metal across his left breast. Another plate covered the left side of his forehead down to the cheekbone, his beard just touching the end. The light of his red eye glowed as he stepped closer.

"What is your name, girl?" he asked.

"Viola . . . Pertwee, sir." It wasn't a complete lie. But she didn't dare say Viola Dalley. Not ever again.

Joel examined his new servant. If he wasn't mistaken, this was the same girl who rode in the carriage with his betrothed. He had thought her lovely with her tanned complexion and brown curls tucked gently behind her ears, though ultimately unremarkable in her gray attire next to Cordelia Nethersole. Up close, he could see she wasn't merely an intimidated servant girl who was in awe of the gentry. She was methodical, processing everything around her and judging her best action. And something in her brown eyes told him that she was clever.

Or perhaps he simply had not been in the company of a woman in so long he was allowing his imagination to run wild.

"Very well, Viola." Joel collapsed in his armchair by the window. "So examine me."

"Sir?"

He tapped his chest with his mechanical hand, both metals ringing from the contact. "You're here to make sure I'm still breathing until we get another automaton, right?"

"Yes, sir. I'm sorry." She knelt and opened up the toolkit.

"What is that?" Joel asked.

"My tools for an auto . . ."

He smirked. "Aye, for an automaton. Which is what I am."

"That is not what I said, sir."

"Isn't it?"

The servant girl looked up at him, her brown eyes sharp and calculating. So, he wasn't imagining. "Sir, I would never call anyone an automaton."

"Greaseblood?"

She winced. "No."

Joel narrowed his eyes. "What about *soulless*?"

"I'm just a humble servant, sir, with some skills in engineering. Those ideas are for theologians." She reached into her kit. "Although, for the life of me, I don't know how metal limbs could deprive someone of their soul."

"You're very opinionated for a servant," Joel said.

"You asked me a question, and I answered, sir." She removed a screwdriver as well as a small wrench. "I won't know what other tools I'll need until I look inside." She stood. "It's your lung, correct?"

Joel nodded.

"Very well. Can you remove your tunic, or should I?" She spoke calmly, but Joel didn't miss the tinge of embarrassment darkening her complexion.

"I'm capable of undressing myself." He pulled off his shirt and dropped it on the floor in front of her. This was it. This was when the pretty servant would turn and run.

Viola's eyes widened for a second and then returned to normal. "Good Master, how did you survive?"

Joel paused. That wasn't the reaction he had foreseen.

He looked at his chest. A metal box was secured in his flesh, where his shoulder and the left side of his chest should have been. The horror of it had haunted him for the first year of living in his new body, but time and despair had worn away his shock. That, and being locked up in an attic where no one but his father and the head butler saw him.

"I almost didn't," he replied, with another tap to his chest. "Unscrew here, and you can see my lung."

She hesitated. "Yes, sir."

"It's fake," Joel added, feeling a slight bit of pity for the girl. "And you can't see my other organs. They survived the crash, and my metal chest was designed to shield them."

She let out a breath. "Very good, sir."

He scoffed. "Stop calling me sir."

She carefully unscrewed his chest plate. Joel studied her expressions as she focused on her task.

"Your gaze is very distracting," she said, not meeting his eyes.

He smirked. "It's *my* chest you're invading."

"I guess we'll both have to feel awkward then." She removed the metal plate. Her eyes widened again, this time not shrinking to their normal size.

"Well?" Joel asked, his throat raw.

Viola met his eyes. "It's certainly impressive."

Joel laughed so hard that he thought he might tear his good lung. "Impressive?"

Her eyes returned to his chest. "The gears . . . mechanisms . . . it's not unlike a timepiece, only it's managing an airbag." She leaned forward, examining it closer. "How did your heart avoid injury?"

"I hardly know. Must have been the angle I was sitting at."

Viola's face scrunched as she worked on him. Joel could not resist inquiring. "Is something bothering you?"

"I'm sorry, it's just . . . now, I know I'm not a doctor—"

"You're not even an engineer."

She snorted. "Right, well, I was only wondering how this is supposed to replace your lung? I mean, it's little more than an airbag on gears. And my knowledge of organs might be lacking, but I'd imagine a lung is much more . . . complex than that."

"Of course a lung is more than an airbag." Joel shook his head. *Even a servant is smarter than my father.* "There's a good reason why hardly anyone has tried to make mechanical organs."

"So, is there more to your mechanical lung than I see?"

"I'm afraid not. When my father had me built, for lack of a better word, he was appalled at the idea of me having only one lung, even though I could live with only one. He hired a Zebulonian doctor who supposedly specialized in mechanical organs. This is what he gave me." He pointed to his chest.

Viola grimaced. "Zebulon Realm is reputed to have the best doctors."

"But clearly not every Zebulonian is meant to be a doctor."

"Then why not have it removed?"

"My father refused to believe that he paid all that money for the realm's ugliest balloon. And it's been a part of me for so long, I'm not sure it could be removed. Or what would happen to me should this thing stop working. I don't know what that charlatan did to embed it in me."

"Better keep it clean and running." She resumed tinkering with his insides.

"Aye, exactly."

She glanced up at him. "Does anything feel off, sir?"

"The airflow is a little *stiffer* than I'm comfortable with."

"Stiffer?"

"It's the best way I can describe it."

Her eyes narrowed. "I may have an idea."

"You do?"

"Yes, sir, one moment." She grabbed her toolkit and selected a smaller screwdriver and an oilcan. "May I?"

He nodded, and she immediately set to lubricating his gears and tightening up screws. Soon his lung moved in a steadier rhythm.

This was the difference between talking to a human and an automaton. A human being could understand a person's discomfort and interpret how things felt. An automaton needed to know exactly what was wrong to treat it.

He grunted. "That last thing you did stung."

"Apologies, sir. I may have turned the screws too tight." She continued working. "I've never worked on a human before."

Joel let out a breath as the pressure in his chest eased. "The last time a bot did that to me, I threw him out the window."

She paused. "I hope you won't do the same to me."

"Of course not; you listened to me when I spoke of my discomfort." He smiled. "But don't test me."

"I'm not sure if threats like that should be used against the person with a wrench in your chest."

"Ha! You have wit, Viola."

"And a will to survive, sir." She stepped back and wiped the grease off her hands. "How do you feel?"

Joel listened to the rhythm of his mechanism and moved his mechanical arm in a circular motion. "Well enough."

She replaced the chest plate and handed him his tunic. "Anything else, sir?"

Joel slipped his shirt back on. He wasn't quite ready to release her. It had been so long since he'd been in the company of a woman. But she had been through quite a bit in her first time working on him.

"That will be all for today. You may return to your mistress."

She nodded and replaced her tools.

"But," Joel said, feeling a twinge of anxiety slip through his veins, "return here first thing in the morning."

"Do your mechanisms falter so quickly?"

Unfortunately, no. "Never you mind. Just be here and bring your tools."

He instructed her to pull the chord by the door to summon Frederick to let her out. Once done, she curtsied and left the attic.

Joel remained in his armchair, massaging his chest plate as if it were still flesh.

"Done already?" Cordelia said as Viola entered her lady's bedchamber.

Viola stood by the door, awaiting her next instruction. “Yes, miss. I was able to assist Lord Bramwell’s son.”

“So you did see him.” Cordelia sat in front of her vanity, still in her sleeping gown. A servant girl with stringy blonde hair worked on Cordelia’s curls. “Is the greaseblood as frightening as this child told me?”

Viola glared at the servant girl, who blushed crimson. She didn’t need to use her Gift to figure out what she felt. “He still resembles his portrait, Ms. Nethersole. He just has mechanical limbs now.”

“Just limbs?”

“No, his face has a plate. As well as his chest.”

Cordelia looked from her reflection to Viola, her expression full of morbid humor. “So, you’ve seen the lung?”

The servant girl whimpered.

“Don’t you dare stop curling my hair, Susan.” Cordelia swatted at the timid girl. “Tell me it’s at least well hidden, Viola.”

Viola nodded. “You shouldn’t have any problem with it.”

“Did he scare you?”

Viola paused. Her mistress had never spoken to her beyond basic commands. This was strange and unnerving. “He did startle me at first. But—”

“Good thing he’s in line for a title,” Cordelia muttered.

“—It was because he caught me off guard.”

Cordelia smirked. “Sneaking around, was he?”

“I don’t presume to understand his mindset, miss.”

“Susan.” Cordelia gave a quick wave to the young servant without looking back at her. “Tell Viola all that you told me.”

The girl swallowed so loudly that Viola heard her from across the room. “I’ve never seen him, but his red eye is ever-present in the dark. The windows. The shadows in the hall.”

Viola raised an eyebrow. “Oh?”

“Yes! And you can hear him scuttle about, breaking into the chambers and stealing food. He’s everywhere at once. He must be cursed.”

Viola imagined the sardonic man in the armchair she left behind and the Rosen Lock that kept him in his attic. “I can assure you, Susan, that your master isn’t cursed. And as far as breaking into rooms and stealing food, it is his estate, is it not?”

The girl blushed again and focused on tending to Cordelia's curls. "Cursed. Soulless. Little difference," Susan muttered.

"Does he expect you to return?" Cordelia asked.

Viola nodded. "I am to return first thing in the morning."

"It seems the mechanical will have need of you." Cordelia huffed and returned to her reflection. "Be sure to educate Susan here on how things are run for me, Viola."

"Very good, miss."

The rest of her day was spent teaching the timid Susan how to properly care for her mistress, down from the time she took her tea, all the way to how she liked her bed made. The servant girl tried to share her superstitions of the man locked in the attic, but Viola shushed all of them, not caring to entertain such nonsense.

But even if Susan hadn't tried to speak of him, Viola's mind would have lingered on the mysterious heir of the Bramwell estate.

CHAPTER THREE

JOEL PACED THE floor between the attic door and his armchair, waiting for Viola to return. He was simultaneously elated at her company and ashamed that it meant so much to him. How juvenile for him to behave in such a manner. But Viola was the first person in a decade that hadn't been sickened by his appearance or called him soulless. She had stirred up his curiosity, and he wanted to talk with her again.

Again, how pathetic it was that he was thrilled at the idea of a conversation.

It's not like it's my fault. He scowled.

Footsteps echoed on the other side of the door, and Joel dove for his armchair, not wanting her to find him waiting.

The door opened, and Viola stepped inside. Frederick nodded once to Joel before closing the door. Joel's neck stiffened as he heard the lock click into place.

"So you've returned," Joel said, looking out the window.

She curtsied. "Good morning, sir."

He pointed to the couch opposite him. "Sit . . . please."

She held her toolkit up. "Why did you want me to bring this?"

"Oh, I did tell you to bring that." He waved it away. "Just drop it anywhere, and sit down."

She blinked a few times before she sat on the sofa, but she placed her equipment next to her.

Joel nodded. “Good. Now talk.”

“Talk, sir?”

“Yes, tell me about yourself.”

Viola shuffled in her seat but said nothing.

“What’s wrong?” he asked.

“I’m not used to my masters asking me to speak, sir. Especially about myself.”

He rested his head in his hand. “Perhaps it’s my boredom from being imprisoned for so long, but you intrigue me. How many servant girls have engineering skills? How many wouldn’t shrink from the sight of a mechanical as deformed as me?”

She pressed her lips together.

Joel examined her. *She’s hiding something. But what?*

He decided to take a different approach. “How long have you worked for the Nethersoles?”

“Four years.”

“Do you enjoy it?”

She frowned. “Am I permitted to speak frankly, sir?”

“Ugh.” He threw his head back. “I told you. Call me Joel.”

“It’s improper—”

“If you don’t call me Joel, I’ll call you ‘servant girl.’ Do you like that?”

She sighed. “No . . . Joel.”

“Better. And yes, be honest. I want to learn about my future bride.”

“I dislike working for the Nethersoles immensely.”

Joel covered his eyes and laughed. “I should have you speak the truth at all times.”

“I do.”

“Do you?” Joel dropped his hand. “I wonder.”

“The Almighty Master expects us to be truthful at all times.”

“Ah yes, Master of all, god of our existence.” Joel rolled his eyes. “He expects such loyalty and . . .” His voice trailed off as he saw her face contort with displeasure. Fine, his issues with the god would have to wait. Time for another question: "Do you truly think I have a soul or were you being generous yesterday?"

She sat up straighter. "I stand by what I said."

"You're a good servant of the Master, yet you say I am not soulless."

"Nothing in scriptures says having metal parts strips you of your soul."

"So you're an engineer and a theologian."

"I . . ." Her shoulders slumped slightly. "No."

"Then how can you so conclusively say that there is no text about losing one's soul?"

"Well, first of all, it is believed the Five Fathers lived over a thousand years ago, yet the first mechanical didn't exist until three hundred years ago. You know, the horrific Skin Plague."

"I remember my basic history, thank you. Since they didn't have a cure for the plague, the Five Realms were forced to create mechanical limbs to compensate for all the amputations. Fair point on the timeline, but then why is the belief so widely circulated?"

"It's a misuse of the passages 'pure of body, pure of soul' and 'the soul and flesh are both sacred in the eyes of Master, and both must be in the healthiest condition' from the Book of Zebulon. Over time it has twisted into the belief that to be mechanical is to be soulless in every realm."

"And how do you know all this?"

"I study . . . I even have a book on the subject."

Joel cocked his head. "Few servants can read, much less work as an engineer. Your mother taught you those skills; who taught you to study?"

She hesitated. "My father."

"Oh? And what did he do?"

"He was a clergyman."

"And he doesn't believe mechanicals lose their soul?"

She shook her head.

"Be careful. Ideas like that can be considered heretical."

"I'm aware." Viola looked him over. "May I ask questions?"

"Might as well."

"Why are you up here?"

Joel gripped the armrests. "Because of what I am."

“I don’t understand. Even if your father thinks you’re soulless, it doesn’t mean—”

“It is not because I’m a mechanical that I’m imprisoned. It’s because I’m a Bramwell.” He spread out his arms. “The gentry cannot be soulless. We have the money to live comfortably even if we lose our limbs. But I needed these to survive. And you can’t imagine how unseemly it is for someone with such noble blood to be a mechanical.”

She leaned forward, her posture finally relaxing. “But to be locked up here? You have an entire estate that rightfully belongs to you.”

He sneered. “But leaving my attic runs the risk of being seen by other noblemen. They know I have been ill and must be confined to my chambers. They cannot know more.”

“So you’re locked up in your attic to save face for a bloodline.”

“What a clever way of putting it, but yes, that’s exactly it.”

She held her hands out to him. “You’re the heir. Can’t you stop this?”

“It is my father’s will, and the servants help him.”

“If being a mechanical is so awful, then why even save you?”

“Because the Bramwell bloodline must continue.”

She sat back, her eyes diverted.

“What? Say what’s on your mind, Viola.”

Viola looked back at him. “Forgive me, but your father doesn’t seem that old.”

“That he couldn’t remarry himself and produce an heir? Ah, yes.” Joel shook his head. “Problem with that is he is not a Bramwell.”

“I’m sorry?”

“My mother was the Bramwell. The family name is so important that when a man marries a Bramwell woman, he must take on her name. But the name is so distinguished, they gladly do it.”

“And your mother?”

“She was on the train with me.”

Viola covered her mouth. “I’m so sorry.”

“How did you lose your mother?” he asked.

“Consumption.”

“My sympathies.”

She nodded. “What exactly happened to the train?”

Joel stiffened. That night haunted his dreams every time he closed his eyes. "The locomotive was tampered with by a heretic who wanted to punish people who disagreed with him."

Her eyes widened. "You were in the Foxborough Attack."

"Locomotive exploded. The cars crashed and tore up. Nearly lost half my body in the explosion. My mother was in the seat next to me." He moved his mechanical arm up and down, indicating on which side she sat next to him. "They never found enough of her remains for a proper burial. All thanks to Oliver Dalley the Heretic."

She paled. "I've heard of him."

"We all have. And of the innocents he killed."

She glanced away. "So they say."

Joel pushed himself out of the chair and to his feet. "Enough of this line of talk. Come with me. Bring your tools."

He walked past the covered furniture and the crates to a corner of the attic that his father and butler never traversed.

"What do you want?" Viola asked, her voice tremulous.

"Just your expertise." He stopped at a lump on the floor with a sheet over it. He grabbed the sheet and ripped it off.

"Is that . . ." Viola said, stepping past him.

"An automaton."

Viola kneeled on the floor and examined the bot. It was a simple automaton that was in several incomplete pieces. It had only one leg, two arms, and a conical stomach. Its head was round but empty.

"My father got rid of all our automaton servants when he brought home a mechanical son, except for the guards at the gate and the medical ones that tend to me. He said he hated the reminder. And I used some of the spare parts from the medical bots I got tired of to construct a hybrid bot of my own."

"Tired of them?" She chuckled. "I thought you threw them out the window."

"Never you mind." He held his hand out. "It's essentially nothing but a shell since I can't make its guts work. Can you help me?"

She picked up the automaton's hand. "Didn't imagine you to be the engineering type."

"I'm not. I'm bored."

"I can help."

"Excellent."

After an hour of tinkering with the automaton, Viola took a break and reclined against the wall. Joel remained with the bot, focused hard on the mechanism that worked the robotic leg.

She rubbed her rumbling stomach. "Joel, may I be excused for a half hour?"

He glanced at her. "From the work or the attic?"

"Both. I didn't have time for breakfast this morning, and, forgive me, but I'm famished."

"Of course, but you needn't leave for a meal." He pointed to the wall above her. "Pull the cord, and a maid will come. Give her your breakfast order."

"Truly?" She looked up at the red cord above her. "I can request my breakfast?"

"Is that so remarkable?"

"I've eaten the same oatmeal from the Nethersole's kitchen for the last four years. That's all I'm permitted."

He frowned. "Our estate can afford to give our staff a good meal. Request to your heart's content."

Viola's mouth watered. "I hardly know . . . What do you recommend?"

Joel grumbled something under his breath and resumed his work.

"Joel?"

"I don't eat breakfast," he muttered.

"You don't? Why not?"

He shrugged. "I only eat a midday meal."

"What about dinner?"

He shook his head.

"Well, no wonder you're skinnier than a wrench."

More grumbling.

Viola leaned forward. "Is that because of your father or because of you?"

He stopped working and glared. "I might be confined to this attic, but I am perfectly capable of eating when I choose. And I choose to eat only at midday."

"Very well." She clasped her hands together. "I'll wait until midday then."

Joel started. "But you're hungry."

"I'll eat when you eat. After all, I am your servant. It's improper to eat when my master does not."

He glared. "Don't be foolish. Pull that cord."

"I am perfectly capable of eating when I choose. And I choose—"

"Fine!" He threw his hands up. "Pull that cord, and order breakfast for us both."

"Wonderful." She stood and took hold of the cord. "How do you like your eggs?"

"I don't." He scowled.

"You look like a scrambled egg sort of man to me. We'll both have that."

Joel looked over his automaton as the door closed behind him, locking him alone in his dreadful attic again. Normally the sound of his father or Frederick confining him to his prison filled him with despair.

But not today.

For the first time in a decade, Joel felt something in his flesh-and-metal chest. More than just his beating heart and spinning gears.

He felt hope.

That peculiar servant girl with her set of tools had filled him with hope. It had been a long time since he'd believed that a soulless could feel anything like it.

Could Viola be right? That he still had his soul, even though he was a mechanical?

I'll leave the theology to her.

Joel laid a blanket over his automaton and left it. He slipped through a maze of crates that he'd built in case his father or Frederick got suspicious of his activity. He trusted his self-made maze would deter them from venturing far.

He reached a corner where he had two crates stacked. He moved them out of the way, revealing a map of the Five Realms he'd found in the attic four or five years ago during one of his fits of boredom. He had secured the map to the wall and studied it every night before he went to bed, memorizing every river, mountain, and city of the Realms.

More digging had permitted him a second map, one of the Abimael Realm—his realm. It wasn't much, but it allowed him a chance to study the roads leading out across the borders.

He had dreamed of escape so many times, but there was never much chance of him succeeding. He couldn't get past the door, much less out of the grounds to test the accuracy of his maps. But with Viola's help, he just might succeed in escaping the estate, something he had never been able to do. Originally, he had never intended for Viola to be anything more than a companion to pacify his imprisonment until he realized her engineering skills could be put to better use.

Joel touched the map of the Five Realms, his copper hand shimmering against it. If he could only reach one of the Neutral Realms, the patches of land not governed by the Five, he might have a chance at a real life.

Could he trust Viola? Truly?

He wanted to trust her. She was a breath of fresh air in this stagnant, dusty attic.

But the servant girl had a secret. He could see it in her eyes and the way she jumped at every sound beneath their feet. She seemed to expect something or someone to chase her. At first, he had thought she was simply on edge from being in a mechanical's company, but he had since rejected that idea.

Any woman who forced him to eat scrambled eggs wasn't intimidated by him.

But even if she was trustworthy, it didn't mean she'd risk her situation to help him escape.

If I can only get my hand on one of the keys.

He sighed and pushed the crates back to the wall. He couldn't study tonight. He had too much on his mind.

Namely, Viola.

"Until tomorrow," he said as if she could hear him.

CHAPTER FOUR

DAYS LATER, FREDERICK locked the door behind Viola, again sealing Joel in his prison cell. She bit her lip as she followed the butler down the stairs to the hallway.

"I have Lord Bramwell's business to attend to," the head butler snorted at her. "Think you can find your way to your room on your own?"

"I can. Thank you, Frederick."

"Very good." The butler turned and walked in the opposite direction.

Viola stole a glance up at the attic door, biting her lip again. She had been a servant on this massive estate for a full week, and her heart still ached whenever she left Joel behind.

If only she could help him. If only she could do something to bring him peace, or to at least bring him some joy in his captivity.

They shared more in common than she could have imagined. Both had lost their mothers. Both were imprisoned under another's will and demands. And their lives dramatically changed because of the Foxborough Incident, although it was good for her that he had no idea of that last commonality.

Viola slipped down to the kitchen, hoping the staff had a spare slice of bread or piece of fruit that they would permit her to eat. The sun had set several hours ago. Normally she wasn't hungry this late, but she and Joel had worked hard on the automaton, and it stirred up her appetite.

The kitchen cook, a surprisingly slim man for his profession, noticed the moment she stepped into his domain. He had been in a huddled conversation with a maid but turned to her and blurted, "What do you want, girl?"

Viola clasped her hands together. "I came to ask if there were any spare crumbs I could eat?"

"Aye," the cook nodded his sweat-stained forehead to the pantry. "There's a day-old bread loaf on the bottom shelf. I was about to throw it out."

And to think this staff is nicer than the ones at the Nethersoles'. "Thank you."

As Viola moved to claim the bread, the cook resumed his conversation. "It's just as I said. Our new lady is bringing her baker here! Before her own kin, she brings someone to make her sweets. As if my puddings haven't been sufficient for her distinguished tastes."

"She's a real spoiled high-born, that one," the maid replied.

Viola took hold of the bread and tore it in half. The staff might well be surprised by Cordelia requesting her favorite baker, but she wasn't. The lady had a sweet tooth that rivaled a starving child. Though she didn't indulge in large quantities of desserts, she did partake in strong decadent flavors. No simple pudding would satisfy her.

Viola bit into the bread, recalling the breathtaking scents that used to waft from the Nethersole kitchen. Her mouth watered. How she wished she had been permitted to have even a crumb of one of the desserts that she used to carry to her mistress. But no, she didn't dare. Cordelia was possessive of her delicacies.

Viola thought back to Joel, wondering when the last time was that he had eaten anything sweet. She'd known him only a week but not once had she seen him eat anything other than his dull lunch of bread, cheese, and various fruits. And, of course, the breakfast she persuaded him to order.

"When will the baker arrive?" the maid asked.

"He's already here. And I am to give him the run of my kitchen first thing in the morning. Blast him!"

First thing in the morning? Of course. The lady would not be denied her sweets any longer.

An idea struck Viola. One that would surely get her in serious trouble with her mistress if she were caught.

But she would risk it to surprise Joel. Yes, she wanted to make him happy.

The following morning, Viola kept a few extra steps behind Frederick as he led her to the attic. She gripped the mouth of her toolkit, praying that nothing but the usual scent of iron and leather would leak out. But the butler paid her no mind as she stepped through the attic door. He didn't sniff the air or ask any questions before locking the door behind her.

She sighed and eased her grip on her toolkit. *I can't believe this actually worked.*

"Joel?" She called out. She usually found him slouching in his armchair when she entered.

"Back here, Viola."

With the automaton. Should have known.

Joel's behavior around the automaton was almost obsessive. He spoke of ideas of what it could do or be and was constantly frustrated by the lack of parts to fulfill his vision. He never spoke of the bot's purpose other than being fast and strong. But, for now, she attributed it to his need for activity.

She found her master huddled over the unfinished bot, wringing his flesh and metal hands together eagerly. "So what can we do today?" he asked without taking his eyes off the automaton.

"I'm afraid we're not going to be able to tinker with him today."

Joel turned to her, his good eye darting between her face and the toolkit in her hands. "Why not?"

"Did you order breakfast?" She asked, deliberately toying with him.

He scowled. "No, you cruel girl."

She grinned. "I guess it's alright this time. This might spoil your breakfast anyway."

"Spoil?" The light in his mechanical eye flickered. "What's your game today?"

She knelt and opened up her toolkit. Instead of her tools, only a single item rested inside, securely wrapped in about a dozen napkins to protect it.

"I hope this still tastes good," she said, holding it out for him. "I did my best to keep it clean."

Joel stared at her outstretched hands. "What do you want me to do?"

"Take what I'm giving you." She chuckled.

He did and carefully unwrapped the package. Inside was a dessert the size of his palm, cut into a perfect cube. The ornamental dark and white chocolate pieces on top had broken into the napkin, but it could not be helped.

Joel stared at the delicacy for several long seconds, not saying a word. He sniffed it a couple of times before saying, "For me?"

"I didn't make it," she replied sheepishly. "I found out Cordelia's favorite baker was on the estate, and I might have nicked one of the desserts for you."

He smiled mischievously at her. "Dear Viola, you stole from the kitchen?"

"Well, it's technically your kitchen, and I brought it for you."

"Is that how you justify it?" His smile persisted.

She rolled her eyes. "Are you going to eat it or not?"

He sighed. "I haven't had chocolate since . . ."

"That's what I thought. Enjoy."

He eyed her. "Have you ever had one of these?"

"Oh no, those are for Cordelia alone. She gets upset if I stare at one too long."

"In that case," he set the dessert on the floor between them. "I'll eat one half and you the other."

"Joel, I brought this for you."

"No dessert, no breakfast."

She laughed. "Oh, you can't be serious."

"Try me."

"I know better than that."

The dessert was pulled apart and eaten slowly. Upon the first bite, Viola almost swallowed the entire thing whole, it was so delicious and creamy. From the outside the cube looked to be only a chocolate cake, but there was a special red cream inside. It tasted of strawberry and something more that she couldn't place.

Joel ate as slowly as she, savoring every bite. His eye brightened, and color flushed his face. A boyish grin crossed his lips, not like the usual sarcastic one he wielded. This smile was genuine, and, for a moment, she couldn't see the metal faceplate or the red eye. She saw Joel, whole and unbroken, smiling and full of life.

Unpermitted, a blush surged in her cheeks, and she had to avert her eyes to the automaton on the floor. A giggle hung in her throat, restrained by the last bite of dessert.

What was that?

A hand took hers, and Viola was forced to face Joel again. The blush didn't recede, but shot down her neck, through her arm, and settled in her hand as his warm fingers intertwined through hers.

"Thank you, Viola," he said.

She nodded, unable to reply.

Joel clawed his way over the boxes, feeling like a half-metal rat trying to find his way to its hole in the wall. He was looking for something. Something to ease his mind after Viola had returned downstairs.

After much clambering and metallic scraping, Joel reached the very back of the attic. It was an area he hadn't been to in about four years, when he had given up on finding a weakness in the walls or a loose plank in the floor for his escape. This time he was searching the boxes for what he needed.

Viola had given him a gift. A cake. So small, so simple, but it had come with risk. Risk of her mistress' wrath. Risk of being called a thief by the kitchen staff. Risk of punishment. All so he could have a measure of enjoyment.

But it was more than a dessert that she gave him. She gave him companionship, hope, and, most astoundingly, friendship. Genuine friendship.

He had to do something for her. There had to be something in all these crates and boxes that he could give her. An item that could compensate for his inability to do more.

With his mechanical hand, he wedged open a couple of crates and searched their contents. Blast his luck. There was little more than his mother's clothes, probably long out of style, and some small pieces of furniture. And unless his feelings could be expressed with a rusty lamp, none of these would do.

He opened up a few more boxes before giving up.

Joel wiped the sweat from his brow with his sleeve. Viola had only been with him one week, and she already had him breaking rules and climbing over boxes. What more was that girl capable of shaking up in him?

CHAPTER FIVE

THE NEW MEDICAL automaton arrived on time, but the fortnight went by far too quickly for Viola. Joel Bramwell might be moody and impatient, but steadily his distrust that had built up from a decade of imprisonment was beginning to melt away. She could see the gentleman he used to be before he was told he was a soulless aberration. He still had his sharp wit, but he also had a tender side.

Joel was the first person who had *listened* to Viola in five years. No, even longer than that. The households she'd worked in previously had been just as indifferent toward her as the future Lady Bramwell, although they weren't as demanding as Cordelia. Viola grew nauseated at the idea of Cordelia marrying Joel. He was a handful, but he didn't deserve to be married to her. She certainly wasn't good enough for him, even on his worst days.

But his father had arranged it, and the Nethersoles were more than eager for the Bramwell title and estate.

She sighed as Frederick unlocked the attic door, an event that grew more sickening with each passing day. How could a father imprison his own son? How could the butler condone it?

Viola patted her skirt pocket as she entered the attic. If this was the last day she was going to work with Joel, then she wanted to leave him something.

She found Joel tinkering with the automaton. At first, she'd believed him when he said the project was to pacify his boredom, but now she suspected there was something more. He refused to explain his full plan for the bot.

He smiled at her. "Viola, you condescend to see me another day."

She grinned. "Good morning to you too, Joel."

"Morning." He returned his gaze to the bot. "Another day in an attic."

She sat down on the floor on the opposite side of the bot. "It might be a good morning if you ate breakfast."

"Now, don't you start with that." Joel pointed at her. "I told you before; I only eat lunch and nothing more."

"Indeed. And I told you that I wouldn't eat unless you do. And I'm starving."

He huffed. "Serves you right."

"Can't you pity a poor servant girl?"

"Bah, why should I?"

She tilted her head, still grinning. They had this conversation almost every morning. And every morning, she vowed to only eat when he did.

Worked every time.

Joel was still skinnier than he should be, but in the two weeks since she'd met him, he was already beginning to fill out. She had even convinced him to clean the dust and cobwebs in the attic to alleviate his mind. It kept him active.

He stood up and pulled on a cord, signaling the staff below that he would have breakfast. He'd instructed them to bring up two meals at a time.

"You're only supposed to care for my mechanical parts," he grumbled.

"Well, I'm not an official engineer, remember?"

"Indeed I do. The infernal creaking that's now in my joints reminds me every day."

"Creaking? I've never heard any. If anything, you're less noisy."

He waved her off and busied himself with the bot.

Viola sighed again. She enjoyed her banter with him. It was unusual but diverting. Soon, it would be gone.

She studied him, her strange master in the attic. His auburn locks were still tangled over his good eye, and his overall appearance was unkempt. But there was something about him that she simply couldn't narrow down. Something that made her enjoy his companionship.

"Joel," she said, unable to disguise the sadness in her voice, "the medical automaton will be here shortly."

Joel lifted his head, his good eye narrowed. "What?"

"I'm afraid this is our last day together."

He blinked, and his red eye flickered. "Is that so?"

She nodded. "The bot should be ready by midday and stationed here for you."

Joel rested his arm on his raised knee. "Are you relieved?"

"What? No." She shook her head.

"Is Ms. Nethersole that tiresome?" He smirked.

Viola snorted. "Lucius Joel Everet Bramwell, you truly are impertinent sometimes."

He raised an eyebrow.

"Is it so hard for you to believe that I enjoy working with you?" She glared.

"I believe you enjoy tormenting me."

She crossed her arms and looked away. "I hope you regret those words someday."

"Well, I already regret telling you my full name."

She chuckled, despite herself.

"Viola, you won't even miss me."

"I won't miss your ill-timed sarcasm, that's for sure." She reached into her skirt and removed a thin book. "I brought something for you."

"You did?"

"It's the small study book I told you about. The one that taught me about the erroneous belief against mechanicals. I want you to have it."

"Ah, my little heretic is at it again."

"Joel, be serious." She held out the book. "Please read it, and keep it hidden."

He took the book and looked it over. "It's not like anyone is searching me, but you have my word. I will keep it secret."

"Thank you."

He slipped the book into his pants pocket. "Our breakfast should be here soon. Let's enjoy the rest of our morning as friends, shall we?"

She smiled. "Sounds lovely."

The breakfast was brought up by Frederick moments later, and Joel and Viola sat by the window, looking out over the grounds. They said little, enjoying their breakfast in the quiet morning.

But the peace was interrupted by the arrival of a carriage pulled by a mechanical horse.

"Who is this?" Joel asked, standing up at the window. "The Nethersoles?"

Viola shook her head. "Their carriage is much gaudier, and they find mechanical horses loathsome."

He smirked. "And yet, they intend to wed their daughter to me."

"You're not a horse."

Joel laughed. "Fair enough."

Viola joined him at the window, sipping a cup of tea. "A guest for the wedding, perhaps?"

"It's not for another month, and my father keeps my condition in the strictest confidence." He took a bite of buttered bread. "Wonder which of his friends knows my dirty secret."

"Does he have guests often?"

"Often enough to irritate me. Somehow they all believe I'm merely confined to my bed."

The coachman opened the carriage door, and a tall man with a perfect part down the middle of his gray hair and a voluminous mustache climbed out. The man wore a blue suit that barely contained his thick muscles.

"Intimidating fellow." Viola sipped again. "Who is he?"

Joel grunted. "Intimidating indeed. That is my father's old friend Sir Gast Loup, the bounty hunter."

All of the air left the attic in an instant. Viola's vision blurred. "Sir Gast Loup . . ."

"Viola!"

She blinked and turned to Joel. His hand was on her shoulder. "What?"

"You dropped your tea."

She looked down and saw the shattered teacup at her feet. Tea was soaking her shoes and pooling on the floor.

"Joel! I'm sorry! I'll clean it up." She knelt and began picking up shards.

"Just set them on the breakfast tray for Frederick." He eyed her. "Viola, what's wrong?"

Viola plastered a smile on her face. "Don't worry about it. I didn't mean to be so thoughtless."

"Do you know Sir Loup?"

She shook her head. "I've heard of him. He has quite the reputation."

"So does Dalley the Heretic, but I didn't drop anything when his name was mentioned."

"I suppose it's nerves," she muttered, setting the broken teacup on the tray.

Nerves. That was an understatement. It was true she had never met the man, by the Keeper's provision.

This was a nightmare. Sir Gast Loup had been hunting her father for nearly a decade. He promised to hang her father's skull on his mantle like a wild beast and collect the reward. And politicians and religious leaders only supported his efforts, along with the local police.

Master, my Keeper, protect me once again. Don't let him recognize me and use me to lure my father out of hiding. Not my father.

Joel touched her chin, gently drawing her to face him. "Viola, what's wrong?"

Her heart fluttered in his gaze, not from discomfort but something unexpectedly warm and tender. "I'm fine, Joel."

"You can talk to me, you know."

"I wish I could." Her voice cracked, and she stepped back from his touch. She was foolish. If the bounty hunter had ever seen her image, it would have been a picture of her as a child, and she was twenty now. Besides, no one from the gentry ever truly noticed a servant.

Except for Joel.

Joel stopped his inquiries, and neither said anything more about Sir Gast Loup.

Frederick returned for the tray and informed Joel that the medical automaton was ready.

"Send it up," Joel said. He stood at the window with his hands behind his back.

"Come along then," Frederick said to Viola with a nod of his head.

Viola swallowed and turned to Joel. "Have a good day, sir."

Joel grunted but didn't look at her.

She hesitated a moment, and, without even closing her eyes, she tried to read him. His usual red light still ebbed and flowed quietly around him. Perhaps it was a little lighter than when she first met him, not quite as angry. Viola felt like crying as she descended from the attic. Her Gift was meant for healing, but once again, she had failed.

Her mother was dead. And Joel still thought he was soulless.

"Ms. Nethersole is expecting you in the parlor," Frederick said as he set down the tray to lock the attic door.

"Thank you, Frederick."

Viola worked her way to the parlor, careful to avoid the main hallways and any chance of seeing Sir Loup. She couldn't risk it.

Viola stepped into the parlor and froze. Cordelia Nethersole stood by the fireplace laughing with the bounty hunter.

It took every ounce of Viola's strength to not flee. Survival instinct kicked in, and she opened her Gift.

"Well, look who has returned from the attic," Cordelia said, turning from Sir Loup. "About time you returned."

Viola clasped her hands together, startled by her mistress' stare. The woman looked pointedly at her with an eyebrow arched and her hands on her hips. Waves of furious red light, much darker than anything Joel wielded, swirled around Cordelia.

Did she feel threatened by Viola's interaction with Joel?

Sir Loup threw his head back and laughed. Blue light burst from his mouth. Genuine laughter. There was no light other than the usual calm yellow on his being, indicating that, at the moment, he thought nothing of Viola. "You always pay such notice to your servants, Ms. Nethersole?"

"Only when they neglect their duties to me."

Viola sucked in a breath and curtsied, keeping her head down in feigned humility to hide her face from Sir Loup. She had always favored her mother in appearance, but those who knew her father could find him in her features. She didn't doubt Sir Loup knew her father's face well. "Forgive me, Ms. Nethersole. I thought I was doing your bidding in aiding your betrothed—"

Cordelia walked across the parlor and faced her, red light darkening and drifting toward Viola like puffs from a cigar. “I told you to teach that Susan girl to take care of me as you do. That child hasn’t done a single thing right since you’ve been gone.”

That’s it? You’re mad at me for Susan’s work? “I will put everything to right, of course, miss.”

“You had better.” Cordelia huffed and turned to Sir Loup, revealing her back. Viola stifled a laugh as she saw the lady’s dress mis-buttoned and the back of her hair coming undone in drooping curls. Susan truly was bad at her work. “I was beginning to believe my betrothed somehow favored this little servant of mine,” Cordelia told Sir Loup.

Viola’s heart ached, recalling Joel’s refusal to look at her as she left. She glanced down and read her own emotions; something she rarely did. A dark gray mist drifted all around her in a way she hadn’t seen since the loss of her mother and the separation from her father. *There is no chance of Joel favoring me any long—*

Glass shattered, and metal screamed and rattled outside. Everyone turned to the window in time to see a shiny copper automaton fall past the window and crash into the bushes. It trembled and sputtered on the brush, its stomach ripped open and sparking. Glass shards fell around it like sharp raindrops.

Viola covered her mouth, and both Cordelia and Sir Loup gaped at the carnage outside the window. White light of shock burst from them all.

“Joel, you insolent child!” Lord Bramwell shouted from the floor above.

Frederick emerged at the parlor entrance. “Ms. Viola, it appears your services are still needed for the master’s son.”

Viola dropped her head, flabbergasted by the turn of events. She looked to Cordelia, whose gaze was as fierce as the black energy swirling around her.

“Yes, Frederick, thank you,” Viola said to the butler. She turned back to Cordelia. “Forgive me, Ms. Nethersole. I am needed elsewhere. But you have my word that I will stay up late tonight and school Susan once more.”

“Be sure that you do,” Cordelia snapped.

“Thank you, Ms. Nethersole.” Viola curtsied.

As she left the parlor, she felt another set of eyes on her. Sir Gast Loup followed her with his gaze, a curious green mist ebbing around him.

She couldn’t walk away quickly enough.

Frederick unlocked the attic door and ushered Viola inside. She found Joel sitting in his armchair, as usual, frowning at a servant who was already boarding up his broken window. But despite his frown, a vibrant white light flowed around him. He was happy.

"Viola, thank the Master." Joel slapped his chest. "That blasted bot nearly broke me. I need you to fix the damage he has done."

"Yes, sir," she said, repressing a smile.

"Don't start with that 'sir' business again," he said, pointing at her.

The servant finished the temporary patch job on the window and was hurried out by Frederick. Viola waited until the door closed before she replied. "Sorry, Joel."

"Better. You forgot your toolkit anyway. It's on the couch."

She removed a few tools and turned to him as he removed his tunic. She silently worked on removing his chest plate.

"I was right," he said.

"About what?"

He smiled. "You didn't miss me."

"Don't be so sure," she whispered.

CHAPTER SIX

JOEL PACED BACK and forth across the attic, just as he had the second day Viola accompanied him. He was going to take the proverbial leap of faith. He would tell Viola his escape plan.

Despite his teasing, he saw how sad she had been to leave his company and how relieved she was to return. Viola was trustworthy, and she cared for him.

There was something about Viola that told Joel that even if she chose not to help him escape, she wouldn't betray him to his father or Frederick, and most certainly not to Cordelia Nethersole.

Their automaton was the key to his escape, even more than the key to the door. If built correctly, the bot would defend Joel against anyone who came against him, or, even more vitally, against the guard bots built to keep him confined to the estate grounds.

He had every confidence in Viola's skills as an engineer. She could build that hunk of metal into a proper bodyguard.

Joel jumped as Frederick opened the door for Viola; he hadn't heard them come up the stairs. She was carrying a tray with both their breakfasts on it. She grinned as Frederick closed the door behind her.

"Well, this is a surprise," she said, lifting the tray higher. "I didn't have to negotiate with you first."

"I didn't realize they'd make you carry it," Joel grumbled.

"No matter, it's part of my job as well." She set the tray on one of the crates. "How's your chest?"

He shook his head. "Never mind about that. I want to talk to you."

"Before or after breakfast?" She pointed to the tray.

"Right, breakfast." *Blast, I didn't think this through.* "I just didn't want any of the servants interrupting."

"Can it be discussed while we eat?"

"I . . ." He shrugged. "Why not?"

He grabbed his plate and planted himself in his armchair. She, as usual, took the sofa.

Viola ate quietly, and he picked at his toast with jam.

"I'm listening," she said between bites of egg.

"Hmm? Right." He set his plate on the floor. "Can I trust you with a secret?"

"Of course."

He nodded. "Do you give me your word?"

She laid her hand on her heart. "You have my word, Joel Bramwell, that I will not tell anyone what you will tell me now in confidence."

Joel stalled. He stared at her, looking so innocent, so naïve. How could he ask her to knowingly aid in his escape? How could he ask her to endanger herself by stealing the key? His father's wrath would be great if she were caught. Perhaps he would even have the dreaded Gray Guard imprison her in their infamous Dark Ore Mines. He had the sort of power to do that, even for a small matter like stealing a key.

His father had done it before.

In the early months of his soulless existence, one servant took pity on Joel. He had stolen a key and tried to release him. When Frederick caught him, the servant was sent to the Mines for his treachery. The incident haunted Joel for years, and he swore to never ask for help again. It was said no one could live more than two years in that horrible place.

No, he couldn't risk Viola's safety like that. He would throw himself out a window and take on the automaton guards with his bare hands before he would risk her safety.

To his dismay, Joel recognized a tenderness he had toward her. One that was far more dangerous for both of them than he could have fathomed.

Not yet. I can't tell her yet.

"Joel?" she asked. Her head tilted slightly, dark hair falling gently on her shoulders.

Joel swallowed. He was in deep trouble.

"I . . ." He picked up his plate and cast her a sarcastic grin. "I've decided to name the bot 'Freddy.'"

Viola rolled her eyes. "Frederick would hate that."

"Of course he would. That's why it's perfect."

"You had me going for a moment. I thought it was something serious."

He bit into his toast. "You should know me better than that."

"I suppose I don't know you at all."

Joel took another bite. First hope, and now this. Perhaps he wasn't so soulless after all.

He would have to read that book she gave him.

Another fortnight passed. Joel and Viola spent a great number of the days building the automaton, which was steadily coming to life thanks to the parts Joel had ripped out of the medical automaton.

Viola found herself enjoying Joel's company more every day. He became more alive around her, growing less antagonistic and more cheerful. He still teased, but it was playful and affectionate, without bitterness: nothing she couldn't handle.

Except for the day before, when Joel said little to her; she couldn't handle that. She couldn't get a word out of him, no matter how hard she tried. She asked him more than once to tell her what was wrong, but Joel only grunted at her.

That night Viola couldn't sleep, wondering what had changed in Joel. And if he did decide to sever their work together, it would force her to be in more frequent company of Sir Gast Loup. But she believed she could tolerate the risk of seeing Loup more than not seeing Joel again.

No sooner had Frederick allowed her into the attic than Joel pulled her to the other end of the attic, away from the door.

"Joel, what's—"

"You said you wouldn't lie to me," he snapped.

"I haven't, I—"

Joel faced her and removed the book she gave him from his pocket. "Tell me about this."

Viola blinked, not comprehending what Joel wanted. "I told you about the book."

"Not the book." He opened the front and pointed to the inside. "What is *this*?"

Joel's finger smashed against a name written inside the book. Something her father had done when she was a child and he had given it to her. He inscribed her name so it would always belong to her.

Viola D.

"You told me your name was Viola Pertwee," Joel said, his voice strained.

"Joel . . ."

"You said you don't lie. What does the D stand for?"

Instinctively, she opened her Gift of Reading. Joel was shrouded in vibrant red that swirled around him like a tornado. She had never seen such strong feeling before, such fury. And it was all directed at her.

This can't be happening.

She shook her head. "I can't."

Joel closed the book. "I saw how you reacted to Sir Loup's arrival. You know more than his reputation. I chose to ignore it, but I can't anymore. You know him personally."

"I-I don't."

"Then you have a reason to personally fear him. That's why you want to be in the attic with me."

Viola glared, anger burning in her chest. "Aye, I have my reasons for being afraid of him, and I like avoiding him. But that is not why I want to be here."

He frowned. "You cannot convince me that you truly enjoy my company, Viola."

"I was here before Sir Loup and—"

"What is your real name, Viola?" Joel shook the book at her, red light bursting from his grip. "And why are you afraid of him?"

"I . . . I can't . . ."

"Sir Loup will be up here shortly. He has condescended to grace me with his company this afternoon."

Viola gaped. "How do you know this?"

"Frederick. Now tell me the truth, or I'll find it out from Sir Loup himself."

"No, please." She took a deep breath, bracing herself. "Pertwee is my mother's family name, and it does belong to me."

Joel watched her intently, not saying a word.

"But my full name is . . ." She swallowed. "Viola Pertwee . . . Dalley."

"Dalley." Joel shook his head rapidly, his red light bursting everywhere. "No, no. Viola, no."

"Joel, please, I couldn't tell you—"

"Not the daughter of Oliver Dalley the Heretic! Viola! How could you not tell me?" The red light slowed, but a deep blue mingled with the red. He was sorrowful.

"How could I tell you?" She choked. "I can't tell anyone. My father is in hiding. I could be used to lure him out."

"As he should be! He killed my mother and did *this* to me." He pounded his chest and the metal rang.

"No, Joel! I give you my word that my father had nothing to do with the trainwreck."

"How could you possibly know that?"

"Because we were at my mother's deathbed when it happened. News didn't reach us of the tragedy until two days later, when the police and Gray Guard tried to take him away during her funeral. No one could be more startled than he was to learn that it had been done in his name."

"So he was with you. It doesn't mean he didn't order his followers to do it for him."

"Followers? My father is a clergyman, not a cult leader. He had colleagues and students but nothing more."

"And then he abandoned you."

"No, we were hiding together for over a year, and we were almost caught. My father didn't want me running for the rest of my life. He reached out to a few friends to take me to a Neutral Realm, but I refused. I was afraid I'd never see him again. I convinced them to find work for me instead."

"With the Nethersoles."

"No, I worked through a few households before I came into their employment."

"So they do not know your true identity."

"No."

Joel massaged the flesh side of his face. "And it's just a coincidence that Sir Loup is here?"

"As far as I know."

"I don't know what to think," Joel said, turning away.

"I wanted to tell you . . . when you told me of the trainwreck . . ." She looked down. "I just didn't know how."

No words were spoken between them for a full minute. At last, Joel said, "Please, just . . . continue to work on Freddy. I can't talk to you right now."

Viola hesitated. "And Sir Gast Loup?"

"He's coming. I can't change that." He sighed. The swirling light slowed, but the colors remained vibrant. "I need to think."

Joel disappeared between the crates and covered furniture. Viola returned to the automaton at the other end of the attic and got to work. She made a few minor adjustments but nothing more. Her hands shook so badly from fear that she could hardly grip a gear, much less handle a screwdriver.

After several failed attempts at tinkering with Freddy, Viola sat in a corner and pulled her knees into her chest.

In all this time of being in hiding, she had managed to avoid so much turmoil, using her Gift to stay in people's favor, seeing what pleased them or not. Moving on when she judged they were growing too suspicious of her.

But now she was trapped, locked in the attic with Joel, whose emotions were a tsunami of hurt caused by her. She refused to manipulate him, to twist those colors to favor her. No, she felt ashamed enough for invading his privacy by seeing so much of his emotion. Her fate was in his hands now.

She quietly prayed as she waited.

Finally, the door opened, and the boisterous steps of Sir Gast Loup echoed through the attic. She held her breath as she listened to him address Joel: "Lucius, my boy. It's been too long."

"Not for those who call me Lucius," Joel snapped back.

"Now, now. I forgot. No need to be rude."

"You've visited the estate five times since I became a mechanical, and this is the first time you've spoken to me. Let's not bicker about who is rude."

"Listen, Lucius, I came up to offer my congratulations on the wedding. I will be in attendance."

"Goody. My father will undoubtedly be pleased."

Viola couldn't help smiling at Joel's sarcasm and rejection of Sir Loup's courtesy. This time she wouldn't scold him for his manner if she was given the chance.

"She's a lovely girl."

"I wouldn't know; she hasn't bothered to meet me yet. Guess she's not as generous as you."

Sir Loup tried polite conversation with Joel for another couple of minutes, but Joel would not allow it. The gentleman bounty hunter gave up and left the attic.

Viola gripped her hair as the door closed behind Sir Loup.

Joel eventually came to her corner of the attic and sat down beside the automaton. He wordlessly started working on it.

"You didn't tell him," Viola whispered.

"No," he replied.

"Why not?"

He paused. "You're the only person in my life that doesn't believe I'm soulless. I don't want you to go anywhere."

Viola blinked. "Joel . . ."

"I'm not saying I believe your father is innocent," he added quickly. "But I can't possibly believe that you were involved. Even in my cold metal chest."

"Thank you."

He grunted. "Now come back and help me build this blasted bot."

CHAPTER SEVEN

AFTER AN HOUR of work in deplorable silence, Joel threw his screwdriver down and faced her. "Is there anything else you're not telling me?"

Viola didn't flinch. She seemed to expect his sudden outburst, but she said nothing.

"Well? Viola?"

She nodded.

"More secrets. Of course." He crossed his arms. "So, Ms. Dalley, what are you keeping from me?"

"You'd never believe me if I told you."

"You can't be serious. Already I've learned that you're not only a real heretic, but you're the child of *The Heretic*—"

"My father and I are only heretics in the eyes of the Realms, not the Master's," she retorted.

"Oh, my apologies. But what will I not believe? Don't tell me you're among that sect that thinks they're Gifted, do you?"

She bit her bottom lip.

"You cannot be serious," he exclaimed, covering his eyes.

"You said that already."

"And apparently, I had to say it again." He dropped his hand. "Viola, of all the absurd—"

She crossed her arms. "I understand you're upset at me, but I can assure you that my Gift is quite real. I don't think I could have survived on my own without it."

He drummed his mechanical fingers on his metal knee. He was upset and betrayed, but he so badly wanted to trust her. And a mad curiosity about his servant girl seized him now, much like when he first met her.

Just shows you what being locked up in the attic for a decade will do to you.

"Go on then," he said sarcastically, "enlighten me."

She sighed. "I'm a Reader."

"A what?"

"Reader. The Gifts of the Master come in many forms. Healing. Teaching. Understanding. And so forth. My Gift falls under healing. I can, in a way, read people's emotions."

"How could that possibly be a manner of healing?"

"Like acute empathy. I can see the turmoil or hurt and try to help heal the emotion, but . . ." Her head dropped. "The last few years, I've only used that knowledge to try to survive. I've read people to manipulate them rather than to heal. I never knew if it was wrong, but since the Master never took the ability from me, I kept going."

"Oh, perfect." Joel looked at the ceiling. "I've got a healer in my attic, but she only 'reads' emotions."

"You think it's easy?" Viola snapped. "I watched my mother die of consumption, and I couldn't heal her. I watched my father grieve, and he wouldn't let me console him. And then we learned of the . . ."

"Of the Foxborough train wreck?"

She nodded.

"Did you ask your father about it?"

"I-I did. The reports were so horrific, and everything pointed to him being the mastermind. I asked to read him to see if he had. Oh, Joel . . . the pain I read in him. For the deed done in his name, and the pain from my doubt of him. You can't comprehend it. I'm sorry for what happened, but I give you my word that my father had nothing to do with it. He suffered for it as well."

"But why would someone frame him?"

"I don't know! For ten years, I've wondered. The only thing I can think of is that someone powerful—a politician maybe—feared his voice, his teachings. And so they set him up to take the blame."

"Are you suggesting the government killed hundreds on a train, mutilated me, just to blame one heretic?"

"It's incomprehensible. But my father didn't do it."

Joel stared down at their bot. "I vaguely remember my father mentioning something about the investigation into the Foxborough tragedy when I was recovering. Originally, they didn't suspect foul play. Just a defect in the engine."

"What changed?"

"I don't know. I only know that my father told me Dalley the Heretic was the true cause of the wreck."

Viola shook her head. "With all my heart, I'm certain that my father didn't do it."

"Because you read him."

"Yes."

He cocked his head. "Have you ever read me?"

She paled.

He scoffed. "I'll take your silence as a yes."

"Joel, I—"

"How many times did you read me?"

Her eyes narrowed. "Oh, so my Gift isn't so absurd anymore?"

He matched her gaze. "It seems real enough to you. How many times?"

"Three . . . maybe four times."

"Viola!"

"I wasn't trying to influence you." She threw her hands out. "The first time was because I was locked in an attic with a stranger. I wanted to know if you were a threat. The other times . . ."

"What?"

She sighed. "I wanted to know if you cared when the medical bot was replacing me. And a few hours ago when you were so angry."

"So all of it was to protect you."

"You've been in an attic!" Her face burned bright red. "I'm sorry that you've been imprisoned. I truly am. But I've been living in fear for as long as you've been here. I should be better than this, but I've had to survive. Alone."

Joel closed his eyes and rubbed his forehead. He was still hurt, still frustrated, but she was right. For all his pain and loneliness, he was safe in his prison. It wasn't a life, it wasn't fair, but neither was her fate. Heretic or not, she deserved better.

He crawled past Freddy and sat down next to her. She watched him with a mix of confusion and fear.

"I'm sorry too," he said.

"You believe me?" she asked.

"I don't know what to believe." Joel took her hand. "But as I said, you're the only person in my life who doesn't think I'm soulless." His voice cracked. "And that means more to me than you will ever know."

"And your friendship means everything to me. You listen to me." Viola gave him a sad smile. "Most of the time."

Joel wanted to come back with one of the snarky witticisms that he loved to tease her with, but he had none. Somehow it felt inappropriate at the moment.

She rested her head on his shoulder and curled her free hand around his arm. Joel's heart beat so fiercely he was sure it would echo against the metal box in his chest. He wondered if she could hear it. Or if she could read what he was feeling.

The warmth of their clasped hands slipped up his arm.

Joel glanced up at the ceiling again, not daring to look at her.

He couldn't marry Cordelia Nethersole, not even for a day.

He was in love with his little heretic.

What am I going to do?

CHAPTER EIGHT

A FEW DAYS later, Joel had an unexpected visitor while Viola was making some minor adjustments to his lung mechanism.

"Father," Joel said, gripping his armchair.

Viola stopped her work and turned to curtsy before Lord Jasper Bramwell.

His father gagged and shielded his eyes. "Please, girl, cover him up!"

"Forgive me, Lord Bramwell." She hurriedly replaced Joel's chest plate.

Joel met her eyes, and she mouthed "sorry" as she tightened the last screw.

"Don't be," he whispered.

He and Viola had managed to patch up their differences and resumed their teasing behavior, but there was something different now. They both understood the burden of each other's situations, and the threat of Sir Gast Loup. They were no longer just friendly master and servant: they were survivors.

"You can look now, Father," Joel said, slipping his tunic back on.

"And your glove?" his father asked.

Joel sighed. "Viola, please."

She nodded and retrieved his glove from the windowsill. He begrudgingly put it on. It occurred to him then that Viola had never once asked him to cover up his hand.

"Should we invest in a mask as well?" Joel snapped.

"Don't think I haven't considered it," Lord Bramwell retorted. He waved to Viola. "Send her away. I want to talk to you alone."

"Please remain at the stairs, Viola," Joel said, rubbing his chest. "This one area still feels stiff, I'll need you to tinker with it a bit more."

"Very good, sir." She curtsied to the men and disappeared down the staircase.

Joel dropped back into his armchair. "So, Father, to what do I owe the pleasure of your company this time?"

His father crossed his arms. "You have me concerned, Joel."

"Good Master, what astounding news."

"Don't be smart with me, boy. Remember, I am your *father*."

"I can never forget," Joel muttered.

"What was that?"

Joel rested his head on his hand. "Go on, Father. In what way have I disappointed you this time?"

"You have not met Ms. Nethersole yet. I have presented you with multiple opportunities, and every time, you refuse."

Joel frowned. "I wasn't aware that she was done indulging in our estate."

"Luckily for you, she is pleased with our estate."

"You mean lucky for you."

Lord Jasper Bramwell rolled his shoulders. "The Bramwell line must carry on, Joel. An ancient and revered line—"

"Means nothing to me anymore." Joel's voice raised as he stood from his armchair.

"That's only because you have no soul."

"What if I'm not soulless?" Joel asked without thinking. "What if this is truly how I feel?"

His father's eyes narrowed. "What did you say?"

Joel pressed his lips together. His changing views on mechanicals and the Master needed to be kept to himself. He was in no danger for him in this attic, but there was always danger for Viola, the only real change in life in the last few months. It wouldn't take an engineer to figure out who was influencing him.

He shrugged. "It's just my smart mouth, Father. I know what I am. And I know what needs to be done."

"Then why threaten your engagement for an affair with a servant?"

"Affair . . ." Joel's vision blurred red, and it had nothing to do with his mechanical eye. "What do you think happens up here?"

"We both know why a man would keep a servant girl in his chambers."

"I would never!" Joel shouted. "Yes, she does more than tend to my lung, but not what you think." He pointed to the door. "She's not afraid of mechanicals, so I saw an opportunity for someone to talk to, to discuss the outside world with."

"You have me and Frederick."

"For ten years, it has only been the two of you. By the Fathers, can't you see what a difference even a servant girl means after a decade in an attic talking to two old men?"

There was more to Viola and him, so much more, but that was none of his father's business. "Not only that," Joel continued, trying to turn the conversation away from Viola. "I hadn't spoken to a woman in a decade, and I'm about to be married. This might be just an arrangement between our families, but I'd still like to be able to hold a conversation with my wife if she permits."

Lord Bramwell nodded. "Well, it is to my relief that you haven't willfully ignored Ms. Nethersole. But I expect you to meet her soon."

Joel's anger eased slightly, seeing his lie had worked. "You will let me out before the wedding?"

"Only once, to formally meet her. Her family is still awaiting her impression of you before they arrive."

Aye, they must brace their nervous dispositions before seeing my wretchedness. "Pick the day, Father."

"Tomorrow. Dinner and dancing ought to do away with any misconceptions."

Joel swallowed. "As you wish."

"You need to take responsibility for your actions," his father added. "I hope you intend to make up the lost time to Ms. Nethersole. And I can help with that." He reached into his waistcoat pocket and removed a diamond ring. "This was your mother's. A Bramwell heirloom. I was going to give it to you on your wedding day, but perhaps presenting it to Ms. Nethersole sooner will ease the insult of your behavior."

Joel took the ring with his flesh hand and palmed it. Five diamonds sparkled on the gold band. The ring was simple but ancient. Crafted by the first

Bramwell for his beloved wife, if memory served Joel correctly. Despite what the Bramwells had been reduced to, this heirloom was still a symbol of love and devotion.

He gripped the ring in his hand. His father was right about one thing. It was time to take responsibility for his actions. He knew what he had to do. After all these weeks, he finally had the perfect gift to bestow on Viola. He wasn't certain that she reciprocated his feelings; it would be a miracle if she did, but he could give her the ring and his promise to protect her. If he couldn't escape to keep that promise, Viola could take the ring and use the money to start a new life, free from the Nethersoles and Sir Loups of this world.

"I will offer this to the worthy woman, Father."

"Excellent." Bramwell glanced at the door. "I suppose you want your servant returned to you."

"Yes, you didn't give her a chance to finish her work."

His father removed the key to the attic from his coat pocket. "Tomorrow, Joel."

Joel nodded, sweat gathering under his collar at the sight of the key. He hadn't felt so eager for it in six years.

As his father left, Joel slipped the ring into his pocket and sank back into the armchair. Viola returned moments later.

"What was that about?" she asked.

"Quite a lot." He put his head in his hands.

"Joel, what's wrong?" Viola hurried to his side and placed her hand on his shoulder.

He looked up at her. "Has your mistress behaved differently to you since you started working with me?"

She sat down on the sofa. "She has."

"How so?"

"Well, it's hard to say. She hasn't ever been kind to me, but she's always just seemed bored with me. Lately, she's been rather rude and angry."

"And you don't know why?"

"She said something once about the servant Susan being insufficient. But . . ."

"But what?"

She glanced away. "I know you don't believe me, but the anger I read in her was unlike anything I've seen in her before."

Joel sighed. "Right, I believe you."

"You do?"

"Because I know why she's angry." He recounted the conversation between him and his father without mentioning the ring. Viola listened in mute shock, covering her mouth.

"I'm so sorry, Viola. I never meant for them to speak so shamefully of you."

She dropped her hand. "It's not your fault. I should have seen it. I've just gone so long without drawing attention to myself, thanks to my Gift."

"Now I have brought more attention to you." He slammed his mechanical fist on the armrest. "And when that blasted bounty hunter is a guest."

She swallowed.

He tapped his chest. "Forgive me, but these gears still feel off."

"Of course." She picked up her tools from the floor.

"Promise me you'll be especially careful when you leave the attic," Joel said as he removed his tunic.

"I always am."

"I mean it. It pains me that I cannot protect you."

She waved her screwdriver in front of his face. "I've been doing this a long time, Joel."

He took her hand in both of his. "But Sir Loup was never in the other households."

"You're truly worried about me?" she asked.

"I am."

She smiled wearily. "Don't worry, Joel. I'm Gifted."

"Yes, yes you are." He released her hands and allowed her to resume working on his chest. "How much longer do you think we have until we get Freddy working?"

"Odd question under the circumstances," she said, grabbing her oil can.

"I have my reasons," he muttered, the ring in his pocket suddenly heavy.

"We haven't tried to turn him on for a week now. We can try again, but I'm afraid we're short on some parts."

"If I had Frederick give you the money needed, could you acquire the last parts in town?"

She eyed him. "You've never told me why you're so determined to build Freddy, but I know it's not just because you've been bored."

"For your sake," he whispered, "that's all you need to know for the time being."

She paused. "How does your chest feel?"

"Good. Thank you."

She replaced his chest plate. "Are you silent because you still don't trust me?"

"I was more offended that *you* didn't trust *me*." He grunted. "But I've never known what it was like to care for someone other than myself."

They moved to the back of the attic where Freddy, their automaton, lay under a blanket. They had worked diligently on him for weeks, but building a bot from the carnage of other bots wasn't easy. Many parts didn't fit smoothly together, and Freddy looked more like an amalgamation of metal pieces than an automaton. Freddy had changed a great deal since Joel first started his plan. The bot's hands were large, his legs long. His body was now cylindrical, and his head was square and much too small for his proportions.

Viola opened the bot's chest and connected a few wires. "I still don't understand why you just didn't reprogram a medical automaton that your father bought."

"Because it wasn't what I needed."

Medical automatons were skinny, thin-plated, and slow. No, they were not at all what he needed.

Freddy's eyes lit up as soon as Viola closed the automaton's chest. The bot sat up, and his eyes flickered.

"Looks like that's the best he can do," Viola said. "But he's close to being functional."

"Cover him back up." Joel dashed across the room and pulled the cord, summoning Frederick. "I'll send you to town with the money you need."

"Won't your father take issue with me buying spare parts for you?" she asked.

"I'll send you to town under the guise of picking up a gift for your mistress. Purchase both and conceal the parts."

"A gift for Ms. Nethersole?" Viola looked perplexed.

"Yes. I, unfortunately, must meet her tomorrow."

"Oh."

Joel studied her. "Something wrong?"

"No, just . . . why can't I go tomorrow morning?"

"Well, I need to dance with you."

"You what?"

He laughed. "Trust me, my heretic."

CHAPTER NINE

VIOLA BREATHED DEEP in the open air of the midafternoon as she stepped out of the carriage. A swift breeze whipped through her hair, and she had to brush the loose strands out of her eyes. She had been in the attic for nearly two months with Joel, and the fresh air had never felt so brilliant.

They couldn't even open a window in the attic to enjoy the breeze. Lord Bramwell had ordered the windows sealed after Joel fell out of one in his first escape attempt. Her heart sank as she recalled Joel telling her how he had tried to climb down some hanging vines but instead plummeted into the brush, breaking his mechanical leg and his flesh arm.

He had had other escape attempts with even less success than the first.

Poor Joel. He doesn't deserve this.

"How long, girl?" the coachman asked as he stepped down from his carriage.

"One hour, if you please," Viola replied.

The coachman frowned. "An hour?"

"You want to shop for a gift for my mistress?"

"No, no, I don't." He whipped out a pipe from his vest pocket. "Take your time."

Viola entered a few shops before she found an appropriate gift for Cordelia Nethersole. The woman was so expensive in her taste and vain in her appearance, it was difficult to find a gift that would sufficiently please her. But eventually, Viola selected a parasol made of fine silk. Her mistress was very concerned about her fair complexion and never turned down a chance for another parasol.

Now that the trivial matters were out of the way, she could focus on the real reason she had been sent to town.

Keeping well out of sight of the coachman, Viola slipped into the local repair shop. There she was filled with warmth at the familiarity of the gears, wires, tools, and bulbs that decorated the shop like flowers in a greenhouse.

Her mother's workroom had been a lot like this. Metal, grease, and hard work.

But there was no time to reminisce. Joel was expecting her to return, and he needed her help with completing Freddy.

And dancing? What is that madman talking about now?

Her purchases were wrapped in a couple of small parcels, which she easily concealed in the pockets of her dress.

As she made her way back to the carriage, a cabby in a hansom pulled up alongside her. "Need a ride, miss?"

She shook her head. "No, thank you, sir. I have a ride."

"Not even a ride back to the Bramwell estate?"

Viola stopped. "Have you been following me, cabby?"

"Why no, miss. I happened to be driving by, and I saw you leave."

Viola opened her Gift of Reading while she replied, "Then you also saw me leave in the carriage that's now waiting for me."

The cabby smiled, and the yellow light swirling around him brightened. He was an older gentleman, roughly Lord Bramwell's age, with a trim white beard, dark skin, and quiet brown eyes. He wore a simple cap and a grey suit. He seemed harmless enough, even by her Gift's standard, so why was he following her?

"Do you enjoy books?" the cabby asked. "I bet you're quite adept at *reading.*"

Viola's eyes widened.

"You will read no threat in me, Viola." The cabby patted the seat next to him. "I'll drive you to your carriage free of charge."

"How do you—"

"We all have our gifts."

There was still nothing alarming to be read in him. His color hadn't shifted, and the waves around him were steady and peaceful.

"Very well," she said, closing her Gift and stepping onto the hansom.

"Name's Anthony Hammond." He offered his hand, and she shook it. "Noble Poet and cabby."

"Poet?" Viola gasped. "Truly?"

"Indeed."

Noble Poets were men and women who had memorized the original sacred texts from the Master, long before the Five Realms changed them to fit their purposes. Like ancient poets who quoted whole plays and legends to audiences straight from memory, so did these poets have the entirety of the texts memorized.

They often traveled the Realms incognito and discreetly spread the true texts to anyone who would listen. She had heard tales of engineers, fishermen, and teachers being poets. Why not a cabby? Who else could better travel across the realms without raising suspicion?

"I've never met a poet before," Viola said.

"Well, that's between you and me for now." He nodded. "I have traveled a long way. I went to the Nethersole manor and learned of the eldest Ms. Nethersole's journey and how she had taken you with her. I can't tell you how happy I was to find you just now."

"You were looking for me? Whatever for?"

"To give you a message from your father."

"Papa." Viola gripped the parasol. At last! After all these years! "Is he well? Where is he?"

"He is in good health but is on the move again. He believes he has finally found a place of safety for him to settle for a while, and he wants you to join him."

"Safe? Has he finally resolved to move to a Neutral Realm?"

"Not him. It is an island that has come to embrace his teaching, far from the Realms' wicked lies about him."

Viola clasped her hands. "Is there no hope the lies will stop?"

He shook his head. "I can't reveal how I know, but I can tell you with certainty that the Foxborough Incident was a tragic accident caused by a few greedy men in the engine industry who sold worn and aged parts as new. They have been quietly imprisoned. And yet the hunt for your father continues."

Her heart ached, but she wasn't surprised either. "He's settling on an island."

"Yes, outside the Realms altogether but still where there is great need. But we must leave now if we wish to catch the train to the port."

"Port?"

Anthony laughed. "Have you not been listening? It's an island. We have to go by ship."

Viola turned away. It was all happening so fast. The very thing she had dreamed of for years had finally happened. Her father was reaching out to her. She had deliberately remained in the Abimael Realm so her father could find her easily, risking her life for the chance of finding him again.

Her hand slid into her pocket, touching the parcel. *Joel.*

"I can't," she whispered.

"You can't?" Anthony exclaimed. "Why not?"

"If you had found me two months ago, I would have begged you to speed me away to the train station. But I cannot leave him. Not like this."

The cabby studied her. "Him?"

"I befriended Joel Bramwell. He is betrothed to my mistress." Her voice cracked. "He's been a prisoner in his own home because he's a mechanical. His father keeps him under lock and key."

Anthony scowled at the manor on the horizon. "Wicked man!"

"Yes, Lord Bramwell is. And I can't say for sure, but I do believe Joel wants to escape his imprisonment. I want to help him in any way I can. I can't leave."

"You can't leave without seeing him free, or you can't leave him?"

Viola glanced away. Only too late did she recognize her own growing feelings for Joel. There could be no other reason she had hated to tell Joel the truth of her parentage. She didn't want him to turn against her, didn't want him to hate her.

She had spent the entirety of her adult years in servitude, in hiding. And somehow, she felt more seen and free in the attic with him than ever before.

And more than anything, she wanted him to see himself not as soulless but as the man she saw. A man who could be loved.

Was loved.

Viola was in love with him.

And she couldn't leave him in the attic, believing he was soulless and married to someone heartless.

"Both," she replied.

Anthony brought his carriage to a stop. "Is there any hope of getting him free tonight?"

She shook her head.

"Even if there were," Anthony mused, "not every island is friendly to mechanicals. Your father has hope for the one he's settling on, but it would take time. A Neutral Realm would be best for him."

"I agree."

"If you and he can get away in the next few days, I'll arrange passage for two to the nearest Neutral Realm. I have a few friends who can make it so that no policemen or Gray Guard will think twice of your tickets. Now, you'd be on your own from there."

Viola grabbed his arm. "I'd be forever indebted to you if it were possible."

"And I'd send word to your father about your situation."

"No, not yet." Viola lowered her voice. "Sir Loup is a guest for the wedding."

Anthony's eyes widened. "Right, that explains the nervous chatter going about the town. If you two can escape, I'll personally race you to the station myself and away from that man."

Viola nodded. "How long can you give us to escape?"

"I can likely drive by the manor for the next three nights without drawing attention. Can't promise anything after that. But I will be driving those nights in search of you."

"Thank you. It's all we can ask for."

Anthony dropped Viola off behind the first shop she had entered earlier. She walked through the shop and back to the Bramwell carriage.

She had so much to tell Joel that she could hardly wait to get back to the attic.

Thank you, thank you, Provider.

There was still a great risk, and she wasn't sure what Joel was planning or if Anthony's offer would appeal to Joel. But she was so confident in this turn of events that she was sure he would approve.

Once she reached the manor, she was immediately accosted by Frederick who took the parasol from her. "I will discreetly take Ms. Nethersole's present to the attic."

"I thought I was still expected back in the attic," Viola said, confused.

"Ms. Nethersole is demanding your service tonight. I will explain things to Master Joel."

Viola bit back her frustration. If she fought now, she might not see Joel tomorrow. "As you say, Frederick."

"We all have our jobs, miss," Frederick frowned at her. "And know our places."

She recalled Joel's words earlier about what his father believed they were doing in the attic. "I never forget my place."

"I certainly hope not."

Viola wasn't sure what was worse. People thinking that she was capable of having an affair, or people believing she was less worthy than someone they thought was soulless. But she had long ago learned to stifle her feelings for the sake of being ignored.

"Where is my mistress now?" Viola asked, determined to change the subject.

"Dining with Lord Bramwell and Sir Loup."

This can't get any worse. She gave a quick curtsy and made her way to the dining area.

She had just reached the dining hall entrance when Cordelia and the two gentlemen exited. The lady laughed and engaged merrily with the men, enjoying their full attention. But Cordelia's face turned to ice as soon as she beheld her. Viola didn't need to use her Gift to figure out what her mistress was feeling toward her.

Viola curtsied to them. "You sent for me, miss."

"I did, witless girl," Cordelia said, spite bleeding from her lips. "I need both you and that child Susan to help me prepare for the dance tomorrow. And I know you will be quite busy with my betrothed in the morning."

Viola bit her tongue. *You don't deserve him.*

"Oh pity the servant, Ms. Nethersole," Sir Loup said as he drew near to Viola. "She can't help it if Bramwell requires a pet."

"I blame myself," Lord Bramwell said, shaking his head. "My son has had too little companionship. I should have visited him more often."

Ms. Nethersole shook her head. "Do not be dismayed, my lord. You've said yourself how difficult your son has been since he lost his soul."

If Viola bit down any harder, she'd cut through her tongue. How badly she wanted to defend Joel.

"Very true, Ms. Nethersole," Sir Loup agreed, his eyes on Viola. "After all, this servant has been with your family for quite some time now. She could be a valuable asset to the young Bramwell."

Cordelia scoffed. "She has only served my family for four years."

"Oh? I was led to believe she had been with you longer."

"No, she came from another household. Highly recommended thanks to her skill with automatons."

"A servant engineer," Sir Loup said. "How unusual."

Viola's heart raced faster than a steam engine.

Sir Loup was starting his hunt.

"I serve my masters as best I can," Viola said, silently praying her fear wasn't noticeable in her voice.

"Let's see you put that into practice now. Come along, girl." Cordelia Nethersole waved her to follow.

Viola had never been so happy to follow her mistress.

She shuddered and felt Sir Loup's eye on her as she walked away.

CHAPTER TEN

THE DAY ARRIVED that Joel was to meet Cordelia Nethersole. Viola educated Susan once more on how to do Ms. Nethersole's hair properly and had all her mistress's evening garments laid out to prepare for the dance. Once Cordelia was satisfied with the preparations, Viola was sent back upstairs to help prepare Joel.

"Make him tolerable," Cordelia said as Viola left.

"Yes, miss."

"And Viola," her mistress added. "You will be returning to my family's service once this is over."

Viola nodded. "I understand, miss."

If she did nothing else that day, Viola had to tell Joel about Anthony and his passage to the Neutral Realm. If she couldn't get away, perhaps he still had a chance for a new life.

She found her companion in his usual snarky manner.

"Here to make me tolerable, Viola?" Joel asked, slumped in his armchair.

Viola shook her head. "Be nice, Joel."

"Always."

She ushered him to his feet. "I will make you more than tolerable. I will make sure even Cordelia will regret her words about you."

"So she has been talking ill about me." Joel chuckled. "You're a clever engineer, my dear Viola, but not a miracle worker."

"You don't need a miracle. If you would only smile the way you did in that portrait downstairs, you would be dashing."

He eyed her. "And if I don't want to smile for her?"

Viola frowned as she sat down on the sofa. She didn't care if he smiled for Cordelia. She only wanted him to smile for her. But her feelings didn't matter.

"Joel, we need to talk."

Joel had been awake nearly all night worrying about her. She hadn't returned after her trip to town, and Frederick had ignored all his questions about why Viola hadn't come back to the attic. The parasol was enough to let him know that the trip to town had been partially successful. But where had she been?

"Joel, we need to talk."

"Yes, we do." He leaned forward in his armchair. "Where were you last night?"

"Cordelia demanded my service. Didn't Frederick tell you?"

"No, he brought that atrocious parasol and my suit for the dance and left."

"Of course he did." She reached into her pockets and removed a couple of parcels. "I managed to purchase what we needed."

"You are a miracle worker." Joel clasped his hands together and winced. His flesh hand was no match for his mechanical.

"What are your plans for Freddy?" Viola asked, holding up the parcels.

Joel frowned, his relief diminished. "Viola, for your sake, don't ask—"

"You want to use him to escape, don't you?"

He pressed his lips together.

"How?" she asked firmly.

"If my father were to find out my plans—"

"You think I'd tell him?"

"No, but if he thought you knew, he'd ship you off to the Dark Ore Mines for the rest of your life."

She set the parcels down on the sofa. "It doesn't matter. I understand enough at this point, and I've been making my own plans for your escape."

He blinked. "You have?"

Viola recounted the extraordinary tale of meeting the cabby in town, the man's connection to her father, and his offer to provide a means of escape for the two of them.

The part about her father reaching out to her struck Joel to his core.

"But I may have run out of time," Viola said sadly. "Cordelia is sending me back to her house tomorrow. But I know Anthony will still help."

Joel hardly heard what she last said. "Do you mean to tell me that you had the chance to leave yesterday and be reunited with your father, and you didn't take it?"

"Well, yes."

"Why not?"

She blushed. "Because I want to help you."

Joel's mind raced, and his heart could barely keep up. "Viola! Are you mad? You had a chance at freedom!"

"I can't just leave you. I can't—"

He dove out of his armchair and fell to his knees in front of her. He scooped up her hands in his. "My beautiful, mad heretic. You should have left without me."

She started at his sudden movement but quickly recovered. "No, never. Not without you."

"And neither could I leave this attic if you go back to the Nethersoles." He kissed her hands. "Ever since you came into my prison, I stopped merely being a survivor of that blasted trainwreck. I became a human being. I no longer believe I'm soulless, and it's not because of something from your book, it's because I felt my heart and soul come alive with you."

Tears streamed from her eyes. "You mean it?"

"I do." He dropped his head. "I love you, Viola."

She removed her hands from his, and Joel thought for sure she was rejecting him. But then her hands slid to his chin and drew his head up to face her.

Without a word, she pressed her lips to his.

She kissed him!

Joel could hardly process what happened as she pulled away.

"I love you, too." She smiled.

She loved him.

In a breath, Joel wrapped his arms around her, flesh and mechanical, and kissed her again. Her arms slid around his neck, returning his kiss and embrace.

Joel took it all in. Her lips, her warmth, the scent of her hair and skin.

She was a beautiful soul, and she loved him.

They slowly broke apart.

"Looks like my father did have reason to worry," Joel chuckled.

Viola rolled her eyes. "Oh, stop."

He sat on the sofa next to her. "No, never again."

She laughed.

Her laugh meant the Realms to Joel. And he understood in that moment that if he wanted to continue to cherish her laugh and company then he needed to open up completely to her about his plans. She became involved the instant she arranged for Anthony to meet them. There was no going back.

Joel took up the parcels. "Do you recall the automaton guards at the gate?"

She nodded. "They're awfully big."

"Indeed, and their sole purpose is to keep me in."

"What?"

"After a few escape attempts, my father was convinced I would never stop. So he purchased automatons who constantly monitor the estate grounds and search for me. Two are always at the gate, but there are at least two others constantly on the prowl."

"Your estate is enormous. Surely you can get past them?"

"I can't even get out of the attic. And believe me, those automatons are fast. Once I'm spotted, I can't outrun them."

"So, Freddy is your bodyguard."

"In a way. I need him fast and strong. Just strong enough to hold off the bots until I can get past the estate line."

"Could the guards overtake a hansom?"

"I don't believe so."

"Then we only need to get to Anthony; forget the estate line."

Joel took her hand. "Do you trust him? Will he take us to a train station?"

"I read him. He was sincere."

"Right. I'll take your word for it." He glanced toward his concealed automaton. "The only other thing is we have to get me and Freddy out of the attic."

"Can't we leave tonight during the dance?"

"Perhaps, but Freddy would still be in the attic. And Sir Loup will be at the party."

Viola shuddered. "Sir Loup . . . he spoke to me last night. I know he's suspicious."

"Do you think he knows who you are?"

"If he did, he'd be dragging me away this instant."

"True. We better leave before he's convinced."

"We need the key to the attic."

Joel nodded. "I'll try to get Frederick's key tonight."

"No, Joel." She squeezed his hand. "I will get the key and let Freddy out of the attic while you distract the others during the dance."

He sucked in a deep breath. "This is everything I didn't want. I didn't want you directly involved in this escape."

She cocked her head. "Then how did you intend for me to leave with you?"

"Well . . ." he coughed. "I might have imagined I'd ask you as I was escaping?"

"You mean sneak down, you and Freddy, to my room and ask?"

"I admit it wasn't the most well-thought-out plan . . ."

"Not at all." She tugged at his hand. "Come on, Joel. We have much to do before the evening."

"Right. Dinner and dancing." He scoffed. "My father wishes to humiliate me."

"Can't you dance?"

"I haven't danced in a decade." He pointed to their automaton. "That bot can dance better than me in its current state."

"I'm sure you can dance better than a broken automaton, but only just."

"Cruel girl."

"Save the insults for the haircut."

"No! Do not touch my hair! I forbid it!"

CHAPTER ELEVEN

"WHAT IS MY purpose, Master Joel and Mistress Viola?" Freddy asked, his lightbulb eyes shining.

Viola took in their hard work. Freddy the automaton was six feet tall at full height, and though still the most awkward looking bot to memory, he seemed capable of meeting their needs. He had learned their names well enough, so the next round of programming should work.

"He works," Joel said, breathless.

"How does it feel?" she asked.

"What?"

"To have hope."

Joel chuckled. "It's brilliant."

"My purpose, if you please," Freddy reiterated.

"Your purpose," Viola instructed, "is to protect me and Joel from harm. Harm from both man and automaton should the need arise."

"Protect." The bot squeezed his massive hands as if testing his wired muscles. "Protect."

"Is it good that he's repeating?" Joel asked.

"Yes, it's his way of computing my words. I'll elaborate more on what it means to protect, but it's a start."

"I've never known a bot to do that."

Viola smirked. "Perhaps because you destroyed them first."

"Right . . ." Joel scratched his head.

Viola worked on Freddy's programming for another half hour. When she was certain he would follow their orders, she put him back to sleep and covered him up.

"Now what?" Joel asked.

"Now we tame that horrid mane of yours."

Joel grabbed his hair. "I told you, no."

After an hour of bickering, Viola convinced Joel to allow her to trim his hair down a few inches and comb out the tangles. Next she polished the metal plate on his face, giving him a nice shine. She then coaxed him to shave his beard to a more respectable state.

"Feel better?" she asked.

"I would if this was for you and not that horrid woman downstairs."

"It is for me." She smiled. "And it will make your father less suspicious."

"Fair enough." He tugged at his tunic. "I suppose I must change as well."

"Right, well. I'll be over there." She slipped away to the other side of the attic, giving him some privacy.

Viola stared out the window as she waited, looking in the direction of the gate. Did they truly have a chance? Or were they fighting a losing battle?

It didn't matter if it was hopeless. They had to try.

"Well, am I hideous?" Joel asked.

Viola turned around, and her eyes widened. Joel stood nervously a few feet from her, tugging at his cravat tie. He wore a deep blue tailcoat, a white waistcoat, and grey pants. He also wore white gloves, ensuring that only the metal on his face was visible.

"You're not hideous," Viola replied, heat filling her face. "You look handsome."

He grumbled. "This is a waste of time."

"I completely disagree." She giggled.

"If I must do this." He held out his hand to her. "I'm not going to have my first dance in a decade be with Ms. Nethersole."

She slid her hand into his. "I can't say I've danced recently either."

"Good thing no one's here to see us embarrass ourselves."

"We don't have any music." She stepped closer.

"Can you sing?"

"No."

"Neither can I. We'll have to manage."

He swept her up in his arms, and together they stepped into the clumsiest waltz in dancing history. They laughed as they misstepped and teased as they forgot to turn. But after several blunders, they fell into step, dancing and holding each other close.

Viola rested her head on his chest, relishing his warmth.

"Joel?"

"Yes?"

"This may sound strange, but may I read you?" She had promised him to never read him again without his permission first.

He paused. "You may."

She closed her eyes and imagined the Gift box. When she opened them again, she found herself surrounded by the most brilliant orange light—like the first embers of dawn. It wove around them, engulfing them in warmth.

"Wow."

"What?"

"I've never seen color like this before." Tears welled up in her eyes.

He drew her closer. "I love you."

The light vibrated with his words, and she didn't think she had ever seen anything so beautiful.

"We're going to escape, Joel," she said. "I know it."

He stopped their dance. "I know we're going together, but I want to make one thing clear, and since I'm dressed up, I might as well do it now." He knelt on one knee and removed a ring from his coat pocket. "Will you marry me, Viola?"

Viola covered her mouth. "Y-you mean it?"

"I know this is sudden and in the middle of our escape plan, but I can't wait any longer. This ring, as well as my heart, belongs to you. No one else. You don't have to say yes. Nothing about our escape will change—"

She threw her arms around his neck, cutting off his explanation. "Yes, Joel!"

Joel tugged at his cravat for the thousandth time, and he held the parasol gift in his other hand. Viola was gone. Back to her chamber, waiting for the opportune time to find the key to the attic. If they were lucky, they could escape during the dance, only needing to let Freddy out of the attic. But if no opportunity arose, she would try to let them both out that night.

Joel closed his eyes. *Master, if you are as Viola said, then give us this. Please.*

It was already a miracle that she'd agreed to marry him, but now they needed a chance to finally live. No longer hiding in servitude or trapped in an attic.

"Do you need me, Master Joel?" Freddy asked, still concealed behind his crates.

Joel shushed him. "Not now, Freddy. Stay quiet until we command you."

The lock on the door clinked and groaned, and Joel readied himself. Frederick stood in the open doorway. "Lord Bramwell and Ms. Nethersole await you, Master Lucius."

"Thank you, Frederick."

Joel reminded himself to be on his best behavior. His anger at his father and sardonic comments would have to wait. Nothing would endanger his life with Viola.

He stepped out of the attic for the first time in a decade—at least through the door and not falling out an open window. It was strange and exhilarating. And he resolved to not return to the attic ever again. He would find the means to escape during the dance.

Frederick led him through the halls as if Joel couldn't recall the layout of his own home. Most likely his father had ordered the butler to guard him.

You are wise to suspect me, Father.

He reached the parlor where his father, Ms. Nethersole, and Sir Loup chatted by the hearth.

"Ah, my son, you're on time." His father held his hand out in Joel's direction. "Ms. Cordelia Nethersole, allow me the privilege of introducing you to my son, Lucius Bramwell."

"Joel," he corrected as he bowed. *Watch your tongue.*

She curtsied. "Pleasure to meet you."

"Pleasure is all mine."

Her nose curled, and her lips contorted with disgust upon her second look at him. "You couldn't have worn a mask?

Joel glared. "My apologies. Perhaps I should have come down with a burlap sack on my face."

"Joel," his father warned.

"Right, forgive my impertinence, Ms. Nethersole. Attics are ill-equipped to improve manners."

"I should say so," she said, nose still out of joint.

He might have cared about her reaction if he had planned on submitting to the arrangement. For now, they both had to tolerate the formalities of the evening.

He held out the parasol. "For you."

She eyed the gift. "Quite lovely, but I do wish you had wrapped it."

"How do you suggest I wrap a—"

"Joel," Lord Bramwell grumbled. His father eyed him, waiting for the ring to follow the parasol.

The ring was back in his coat pocket until Viola could wear it without drawing suspicion, and he would not take it out until then. For now, he mouthed a "not yet" to his father to pacify him.

A servant stepped into the parlor, much to Joel's relief. "A gram for you, Sir Loup."

The bounty hunter nodded and took the telegram. He tore it open and read it.

"Favorable news, my friend?" Lord Bramwell asked.

The man smiled. "Indeed it is, Jasper."

Joel looked hard at the man. He wished he had Viola's Gift of Reading at that moment or any gift to learn what news pleased the bounty hunter so much. He resolved to keep an eye on the man.

Viola held her breath as she slid through the halls to Lord Bramwell's office. She had seen Frederick let Joel out and escort him away. That meant that Lord Bramwell's key should still be in his desk. She prayed that he would not need the key that night.

She stepped into his office and rushed to the desk. She pulled the top drawer open and gasped.

Both keys were gone.

She grabbed her hair. *Now what?*

She rushed out of the office. She had to tell Joel. They had no choice but to wait until everyone was asleep and—

From out of the shadows stepped Sir Gast Loup, grinning and holding a gram in his hand.

"Viola Dalley," he said, a wicked gleam in his eyes.

Viola froze. *Oh no.*

CHAPTER TWELVE

JOEL COULD NOT focus on his dance steps. As if it wasn't awkward for two people who didn't like each other to dance together, it was made even more worse by his father watching them with a nervous intensity.

This was pathetic. When Joel was a boy, the dance hall had been filled with people, laughing and dancing joyously to the music of no less than a five-piece band. Now every step he took echoed loudly against the white-washed walls, every grunt from his father bounced off the wooden floors, and the song from the single automaton with a barrel organ in his chest could not muffle Cordelia's snorting at his movements. And Sir Gast Loup . . .

"Where's Sir Loup?" Joel said, running up to his father and leaving his flabbergasted partner. He had been so focused on not stepping on Ms. Nethersole's feet that he didn't notice when Sir Loup left.

His father pushed his shoulder and pointed to the waiting Ms. Nethersole. "Get back out there and dance."

"I will, but where is he? I need . . . to ask him a question."

"It can wait."

Joel glanced behind him. Ms. Nethersole stood alone in the center of the room, tapping her foot.

"Father, I need—"

"Let me go!" Viola screamed.

Sir Loup returned to the dance hall, dragging Viola by the wrist. Fear wracked Joel's insides as Viola winced in pain under the bounty hunter's massive grip.

"What are you doing?" Joel shouted.

"What's the meaning of this?" Ms. Nethersole demanded, stomping toward Sir Loup. "Unhand my servant."

"Forgive this display, Ms. Nethersole." He pulled Viola in front of him, holding her up by her wrist. "But this is a dangerous woman. The only child of Oliver Dalley the Heretic."

Joel's heart sank into his stomach.

"How do you know this?" Joel's father asked.

"My gram. It confirmed my suspicions. The Heretic had only one child. A daughter. Though her first name is unknown, her mother's maiden name was found."

"Pertwee," Ms. Nethersole said, glaring.

"Indeed."

She waved him off. "Do what you want with her, Sir Loup."

"I intend to." He bowed before Lord Bramwell. "I must beg your leave to miss the wedding, Lord Bramwell. This is the first real progress I've made in hunting her father in years."

"I don't know where he is." Viola glared.

"Doesn't matter. I'm sure he'll surrender for you."

Joel's mind spun. He wanted to attack Sir Loup then and there. But Loup was twice Joel's size and far more fit than a young man who'd been trapped in an attic for a decade. He had to be decisive, or Viola and her father would be destined to die in the Dark Ore Mines.

The dread of the attic was no longer an issue. Only Viola mattered.

Think! Freddy is in the attic. Sir Loup has Viola. What can I do?

Truth was, there was only one thing he could do.

Joel walked toward Sir Loup and Viola, glaring at her. She looked confused as he approached.

"Listen well, Dalley," Joel snapped, "and *read* my lips."

Understanding lit her eyes, and she blinked rapidly. He hoped she could see that he was not angry at her and somehow would understand what he was doing now.

"I trusted you. You were my companion. What were you doing? Did you find what you were looking for in my company?"

She shook her head. "I did not find what I was looking for."

So the keys are still with Father and Frederick.

"After all that has happened, I want to make one thing clear." Joel made a show of removing his gloves and dropping them on the floor. "Trust me and our mutual friend."

Her eyes widened, and she shook her head again.

"What's going on?" Sir Loup asked.

"What are you saying, Joel?" his father asked.

"Just one last command to this heretic." Joel took a deep breath. "Run!"

With every ounce of strength in him, Joel drove his mechanical fist straight into the unguarded jaw of Sir Loup. The bounty hunter's head jerked back, and blood gushed from between his teeth as he bit his tongue. The man recoiled and grabbed his face, releasing Viola in his stupor.

Viola made a frantic dash for the door. She looked behind her. "Joel?"

"Go! Run, Viola!"

She kept running.

In an instant, his father and Frederick grabbed Joel by the arms.

"What do you think you're doing?" Lord Bramwell demanded.

Joel struggled in their grasp. "She didn't do anything!"

Suddenly Sir Loup grabbed Joel by the cravat. "You knew who she was."

"I did, and I didn't care." He cast a glance at Cordelia Nethersole who looked offended by the display. "I love Viola Dalley."

"Back to the attic with you," his father shouted, "while I clean up your mess with Ms. Nethersole. Sir Loup, please assist Frederick with removing my soulless offspring."

"With pleasure," the bounty hunter glared, blood trickling along his lips. "And don't think you've succeeded. Your servant girl won't get far."

Sir Loup and Frederick dragged Joel back to the attic. He struggled the entire way, begging them to let him go, never letting on that this was exactly what he wanted.

They reached his loathsome attic door, and Frederick slipped the key into the lock. The gears turned and clinked.

"Freddy!" Joel screamed at the top of his lungs. "Freddy!"

Frederick looked at him. "You have never called me that. What are you—"

The door opened.

"Freddy! Protect!"

The door swung wide open, and Freddy the automaton's massive frame filled the doorway. "Yes, Master Joel."

In a flash of metal, Frederick was grabbed by the throat and flung into the attic, crashing into the crates. Freddy turned and punched Sir Loup square in the chest. The bounty hunter fell down the steps, pulling Joel down with him. Together they stumbled and crashed onto the floor.

"Master Joel! Forgive me!" Freddy hollered as he hurried down the stairs.

"I'm fine," Joel said, scrambling from the bounty hunter, who was reeling from the blow. "Keep this man on the ground."

Joel ran up the steps and picked up the key off the floor. The key that had long sealed him away.

"Oh, Frederick," Joel said.

The butler groaned, sprawled on the floor by a crate.

"Enjoy my old room. I'm sure Father will find you here in a day or two." Joel slammed the door shut and locked it. The clicking of the Rosen Lock had never sounded so sweet.

He dashed down the stairs, pleased to find Sir Loup still writhing in pain. "Freddy, lock him in the attic, too."

"Yes, Master Joel." The automaton grabbed the bounty hunter's arms and lifted. Immediately, the bot's entire body creaked loudly.

"Stop! Stop!" Joel gasped, waving his hands. "He's too heavy for you, Freddy. Drop him and follow me. We have to catch up to Viola."

"Very good, Master Joel." He released Sir Loup, and the man dropped hard, hitting his head on the wooden floor.

Joel winced. "Well that knock ought to keep him here."

They ran back to the dance hall, where Joel found his father imploring Ms. Nethersole to stay. She screeched when Joel returned with Freddy at his heels.

"Joel!" His father exclaimed. "What in the Realms!"

Joel pointed at him. "Freddy, grab his arm but do not break it."

Freddy was on his father in an instant, snatching up his arm at the elbow. His father squirmed frantically. Ms. Nethersole fled, screaming the whole way.

"What do you want?" Lord Bramwell asked, gasping.

"First, a small portion of what belongs to me." He searched his coat pockets until he found his father's coin purse. The man never went anywhere without a substantial amount to spend and flaunt his importance. Joel held up the purse. "This should sustain me and Viola for a month or so."

"You dare! And with a Dalley?"

Joel looked at his father's waistcoat. "Oh, look. My grandfather's pocket watch. That'll help as well." He snatched it up. "There. I've claimed my inheritance, Father. You can have the rest, including my title for all I care."

"That girl's father—"

"Was probably framed. But that's irrelevant right now. I only want Viola."

"You'll never get away. The automaton guards will bring you back, Joel. The Bramwell line cannot die!"

Joel smiled. "That's for me and Viola to decide. Not you."

"How dare you—"

"Father, I've learned a lot from Viola, and I choose to follow the Master she serves, the one who sees me as someone worth loving and rescuing."

"Soulless and a heretic." His father clamped his teeth. "You shame me and your mother!"

There was so much more Joel wanted to tell his father. To pour out his hurt and anger on the man here and now. For keeping him a prisoner in his own home for ten years, feeding him lies of being soulless and only having value to sire another generation. To say how wrong his father was. But there was no time, forcing him to settle for: "Maybe someday I'll learn to forgive you."

Joel turned to Freddy. "Release him."

"As you command, Master Joel." The bot freed him.

"Don't try anything," Joel said quickly as his father massaged his arm. "Freddy won't like it."

His father's eyes bulged at Freddy.

Joel and his automaton ran for the front door, desperate to catch up to Viola. To his astonishment, she stood on the road several yards away, waving to him. "Joel! Joel!"

He rushed to her, and she dove into his arms. "Viola, are you well?"

"Bruised but fine. Oh, Joel, I'm so sorry about—"

"Not your fault. And I'm sorry about giving you a scare back there."

She stepped out of his embrace. "Enough apologies. Let's find Anthony."

He took her hand. "Stables are this way. We'll grab a horse."

They had reached the entrance to the stable when the horses started neighing and snorting.

"What's wrong with them?" Viola asked.

Joel stopped outside the door. "I don't—"

"Master Joel!" Freddy called out.

A guard automaton came hurtling out of the stalls, red lights flashing, metal hands outstretched for him. It ran on one enormous ball instead of feet, fast and agile. Joel pushed Viola out of its reach just as it grabbed him by the shoulders. But the moment Joel was caught, Freddy grabbed the guard bot.

"Protect Joel!" Viola shouted. "Break the automaton!"

"Breaking." Freddy pulled the bot's arm out of its body, sparks flying. He punched the bot in its round head.

Joel fell to the grass, metal parts crumbling around him.

"Did I break it, Mistress Viola?" Freddy asked.

"Yes, well done," she replied.

Joel patted the ground, overcome by the feeling of grass against his skin, despite the madness around him. "I had forgotten what grass feels like."

Viola came up from behind him and helped him to his feet. "That too can wait, my love."

"Right. Right."

They quickly mounted the nearest horse that was without a saddle and only wearing its reins. Though it had been a decade, Joel quickly felt comfortable riding again.

Freddy ran as fast as he could behind them, keeping up with the horse's pace.

"Where is Anthony supposed to be?" Joel asked over the hoofbeats.

"Driving around. I'm sure he'll be within view of the front gate."

"Let's hope so."

After a few difficult minutes of saddleless horse riding that rubbed Joel's out-of-practice thighs raw, the gate loomed on the horizon, along with the two guard automatons. Still no sign of any other. Joel counted on the ornate, wrought iron gate to be unlocked as his father had taken to relying on the guard bots for protection.

Joel brought the horse to a halt. "Freddy, run on ahead and damage those automatons."

"Like the last one?" Freddy asked.

"Yes, Freddy."

"Very good, Master Joel." Freddy sprinted ahead, his massive fists clenched and ready.

They watched in silence as Freddy reached the gate. He ran his fist through the round head of the first bot. It shuddered and then fell forward, sliding off Freddy's fist. Their automaton then went to work on the second bot.

"They're not attacking him," Joel observed.

"No, they're programmed only to find you or anything human. They may not be able to read other automatons."

"I think we built him too well." Joel laughed as the second bot was rendered a pile of torn metal and sparks.

The air erupted with an enormous explosion. Their horse neighed and kicked up its front legs. Joel and Viola tumbled off, crashing to the dirt as the horse fled.

"What was that?" Viola asked, groaning.

Joel looked up and saw a horseman with a blunderbuss racing toward them.

"Sir Loup," Joel said through clenched teeth.

"Oh, Keeper, no!"

Joel jumped to his feet, pulling Viola up behind him. Sir Loup overtook them and brought his horse between them and the gate.

"Did you really think you could escape me?" Sir Loup sneered, pointing the weapon's muzzle at them.

"We thought we'd try," Joel said. "After all, you have gotten rusty in your years."

"You always thought you had wit, Lucius," Sir Loup spat. "But you're just a gullible mechanical child looking for attention. I'm going to drag you back to that attic and get paid by your father and then take great pleasure watching you cry from your window as I—"

"Protect! Protect!"

Freddy threw himself at Sir Loup, his metal fists throwing rapid punches. He struck the man in the arm. The bounty hunter cried out and fired wildly in the dirt. His horse screeched and reared back. Sir Loup fell off the saddle, but his foot was caught in the stirrup.

"Protect! Protect!" Freddy continued to yell.

The horse, frightened by the metal guardian, kicked and reared again. In his panic, the horse kicked its owner square in the face.

Sir Loup stopped struggling.

Viola cried out and buried her face in Joel's back. Joel watched in shock as the horse took off running, Sir Loup's corpse dragging along with it.

Joel shuddered and pulled Viola along. "Keep running, Viola! Freddy, follow!"

As they reached the gate, a whirring sound came from behind them. The final automaton was charging after them, arms outstretched.

Their loyal automaton ran straight at the last guard, and the two collided with a terrific crash. Both bots blew apart at the impact.

"Freddy!" Viola screamed.

"Protect . . ." Freddy said as his lights went out.

Joel tugged at her hand. His heart ached at the loss of his creation, but he had to get Viola to safety first. "He fulfilled his purpose. Come on!"

They ran past the gate and up the road, not looking back.

CHAPTER THIRTEEN

VIOLA WRAPPED HER hands around Joel's arm and rested her head against his shoulder. People at the train station were staring at the flesh woman and mechanical man, but she didn't care. They were mere moments from freedom, and she was deliriously happy.

Anthony stood by his hansom carriage, handing the tickets to Joel and giving instructions, "Now, this will get you straight to southern Neutral Realm by tomorrow morning. I sent a gram ahead, and my brother Samuel will be there waiting for you. He will find you passage to whichever Neutral Realm you decide to stay in unless you choose to stay there."

"Too close to this Realm," Joel said, taking the tickets. "I want to get to the farthest Neutral Realm we can."

Viola touched Anthony's hand. "Thank you, my friend. We're indebted to you."

Anthony patted her hand. "There is no debt. Your father is my friend, and I am more than happy to help."

Joel looked down at the tickets. "I can hardly believe this is happening."

"Believe it, lad." Anthony grinned at them. "And just a reminder, my brother is a minister, and there is no law against flesh and mechanicals marrying in the Neutral Realm."

Joel coughed, and Viola chuckled.

"Just so you know."

Joel reached into his pocket and pulled out a pocket watch. "Here, I want you to have this."

Anthony waved him off. "Thank you, but no. That'll benefit you far more than me, and it's a clue that I helped you should I be questioned."

"True." Joel replaced the watch and pulled out the coin purse. "Sincerely, sir, let me give you some coin. Knowing my father, you should take your cabby out of this Realm as well."

"Fair enough, lad."

They said their final goodbyes, and Joel and Viola walked hand in hand to the train.

After a few minutes of ticket and baggage checks, they were seated.

They said nothing until the train whistled, and the wheels started turning.

Once they were on their way, Joel turned in his seat and removed the Bramwell wedding ring from his pocket. She giggled as he slipped it on her finger. He kissed her hand before kissing Viola's lips deeply. "We made it."

Viola smiled and traced his jawline with her finger. "Are you happy?"

"Read me and find out."

She did, and she was elated to see his being a shining gold color mixed with the orange of his dawning love.

"I love you, Joel," she said, tears in her eyes.

"My soul loves you."

THE STATUE GIRL

JULIA SKINNER

PROLOGUE

AATOON WAS GOING to die. He could tell from the bitter scent of magic in the air, and the ashen rubble he stood upon. Though, no one else could see the ash clinging to the soles of his boots. Or smell the magic. Only him.

Other Sceptori could, of course. But the others were gone, dwindled away into extinction. There were far too few when Aatoon was a child, and he'd known it even then: their time was coming to an end. The air was changing. The magic was no longer what it once was.

And yet, Aatoon still clung.

No longer.

Today, the truth would, at long last, be told.

Another herald of his upcoming death was the yellow lamplight spilling from the grand entrance of the Lyhedrune castle. Two guards leaned on either side of the castle's arched doorway. Tipping his chin upward, he stalked up the flight of stairs leading to the door. The guards moved forward to meet him as he reached the top step.

"The castle is closed, old man," the first said. He was a large brute of a person with barely any magic glittering around him. Aatoon disliked him immediately. "Prince Sorik is not seeing anyone until tomorrow."

Liar. He was seeing someone right now.

Aatoon looked up at the dark, star-speckled sky. Inventors claimed the stars were merely other planetary things, set ablaze—like the sun. But he knew better. They could only dream of the things he saw.

The stars were pulsing pockets of pure, golden magic.

And he could feel them. Draw upon them. *Use* them.

"Open the door," he said softly.

The first guard laughed—a harsh, mocking sound that reminded Aatoon of his childhood and his mother. He always hated her laugh. With a sigh, he reached his hand to the side and touched the swirling particles of magic that dusted the air around him. Warmth met his skin. *This* magic everyone could see. It was always there, hanging in the air. The more powerful you were, the more golden light gathered around you.

The magic poured into his skin, transforming his features into the image he pictured in his mind: a feral, bearish beast.

Sceptori usually had only one or two forms they could shift into. But Aatoon had mastered five. If people looked like what they were on the inside, he was convinced this would be his natural face—the face of a monster.

That reminded him of his father.

He bared his fangs at the two men.

They stumbled back.

"Sceptori!" the first yelped.

The second hurriedly swept into a bow. "Please, forgive us. We did not know."

Aatoon narrowed his eyes. *That's the problem, isn't it?* No one treated people with respect simply because they were human beings. No, you had to have some sort of authority or esteemed title—*or the ability to destroy entire kingdoms*—to receive such treatment.

But they had a right to be afraid. He *could* destroy entire kingdoms. In a way it was his job to do so.

"Indeed." he casually shifted back to his normal form. "The door?"

Avoiding his eyes, the guards stepped to the side, and swung the door open. Aatoon straightened his hole-ridden tunic, and stepped past them, into the brightly lit foyer.

"Sir?" the second guard said.

Aatoon paused, and looked back. The guard was younger than the other man. There was something in his quiet, dark eyes that Aatoon liked. Maybe it was the way the magic gleamed within them, like stars in the night sky.

"Have you come to judge us?" His voice trembled.

"I do not judge," Aatoon answered. "I teach."

He continued through the foyer. Light pooled from giant lamps fastened along the walls and ceiling, their rays glinting off a wide staircase directly ahead. At the top was a balcony, set against a wall with nine doors.

The castle pulsed with light, a by-product of the late king's obsession. Many of the Drune citizens thought it was because King Riik Lyhedrune had an irrational fear of the dark. Others thought it was some strange display of wealth.

They were all wrong, of course.

Riik hadn't been afraid of the dark. He'd been afraid of the things that lived inside the darkness. Jagged, skittering little creatures brought to life by an extremely powerful curse. Aatoon had crafted it to teach the man to let go of the fears controlling his every decree.

But the king hadn't learned his lesson.

At the top of the stairs, Aatoon chose a hallway on the far right. It was a long corridor; the lights in it were nearly blinding. He sighed and lifted a hand to shield his eyes as he strode down. He headed for the door at the very end As he neared, he could hear the faint lilt of agitated voices, drawing him like the song of a siren.

I am going to die.

The thought itself was not what made his stomach feel like it was going to be retched from his body.

It was the knowledge of how he planned to die.

The feeling. This . . . emotion. It was not something he was accustomed to. It made him feel uncomfortably *normal*—and that wasn't something he was supposed to be capable of.

Carefully easing the door open, Aatoon peeked inside. It was the king's office. Three guards loomed behind a woman in a green ball gown, their backs to him. A young man faced them, eyes fixed on the woman.

"Let me explain," the young man was saying. As he spoke, golden specks of magic danced around him. As a boy, he'd been trained in the art of negotiation. That, combined with his father's wealth, had gotten him pretty much anything in life.

But riches and pretty words cannot save your life, now. Can it, dear prince?

"I understand perfectly," the woman said. "I just don't care."

It was hard to think of her as that—a woman. To Aatoon's eyes, she was perpetually eight years old. The girl he'd found at the edge of a pond, crying. That child had been very different from the girl he'd spent every waking moment mentoring the last year and a half.

Prince Sorik stared at her for a long, long time, panic slowly creeping into his eyes. Aatoon shook his head. Today, the boy was going to learn a lesson: you cannot hurt someone and then expect them to come running to save you.

"Lorlie," the prince said, voice rasping, "I'm going to die if you don't help me! Please. You're the only non-Sceptori who can wield the magic so well." There was an unusual vulnerability in him, which contrasted sharply with the proud capable heir he always presented.

Lorlie tipped her chin upward in one jerking, defiant gesture. "And I needed you when I was in that tower."

"It wasn't that simple! There were complications, and talk of war, and—"

"I honestly don't care, Sorik," Lorlie said, voice clipped. "I got myself free on my own. Heal yourself."

There was a shocked pause. The prince was so focused on her that he didn't appear to notice as Aatoon slipped into the room. "That's your final decision?" he said.

"Yes."

His eyes went cold, hard. The look of someone who was willing to do anything to stop their nightmare from coming true. *Just like his father.* "Very well," the prince said. "If you won't willingly help me, I will have to convince you in other, less pleasant ways." He nodded toward the guards. "Take her to a cell."

Aatoon smiled—though he didn't feel anything inside. Her back still to him, Lorlie shifted, ever so slightly widening her stance as if she was bracing herself for impact.

The moment the guards reached for her, she flung her right hand out, fingers arched. The magic screamed through the air, a sudden eruption of power, reacting to her emotions. The golden dust became a golden claw that ripped through the air. The three guards crumbled almost simultaneously, crimson spraying across the spotless, pale floor.

Then Lorlie turned on the prince.

Aatoon glanced sideways at the guards, now a bloody mess on the floor. Their dark red garbs were shredded, as if a monster had torn into them.

In a way, a monster *had.*

But they were still alive. *They don't deserve to be, though. She should have killed them.* He shook the thought away. That wasn't her job. She wasn't a Sceptori.

Sometimes he forgot that.

Across the room, Lorlie shoved Sorik against the wall. Golden light dripped from her fingertips, staining his beautiful, pale suit.

"You deserve to die," she spat. "Do you hear me, Sorik? You *deserve* it. When they stick your useless body in the dirt, it will be the happiest day of my life!"

Lies.

She could fool others. Yet Aatoon knew the truth. He opened his mouth to announce his arrival, but hesitated as Lorlie raised her magic-drenched hand.

When she spoke, her voice came out as cold and hard as stone. "I could finish the job early."

"Lorlie, wait," Sorik pleaded.

Aatoon folded his arms, watching with interest. Honestly, it would probably be a mercy to put the boy out of his misery. He wasn't going to learn his lesson in time to save his life. His father hadn't.

Time seemed to stretch an eternity as they stood there. A beast and a prince charming too selfish to save her.

Finally Aatoon, sighed. "Aren't you going to save him, princess?"

She jerked at his voice, hurling the magic she'd been gathering at the far wall. Deep gashes slashed through the polished wood, splintering it into ugly shreds. She fixed her blazing gaze on Aatoon. "What are you doing here?"

"You were captured," Aatoon said.

Lorlie, in response, just rolled her eyes. She knew him. She knew he hadn't come to save her.

No one will ever come to save her.

That's why she had to learn to do it herself.

Striding past her to the young prince, Aatoon leaned close to him. The bitter twang of death was faint, but present on Sorik's skin. Even the magic around him had dwindled to a dull pulse. If Aatoon looked close enough, he could see the faint shadow of the curse, invisible to most eyes, eating away at the boy's face, revealing the ugly monster inside.

"King Cyphrani's Sceptori is still alive," the prince stammered. "We thought you . . . might have died during the attack."

"Is that so?"

Sorik gave a slight nod. "How did you escape the dragon?"

Aatoon smiled. "I do hope you learn before it is too late, my dear boy." He turned to Lorlie, who was watching with narrowed eyes. *So untrusting.* She hadn't been, once upon a time. "As for you, child, I have a confession."

"Make it fast," she snapped. "I want to leave."

Shaking his head, he walked to the window and peered out at the darkness beyond. When he first met Lorlie, she'd been just a little broken thing, unwanted and unloved. An accident. Her parents had only desired one child, not a second. And certainly, not one so naturally unrefined. In her, he had seen . . .

Himself.

For the first time in his life, he hadn't been alone. He hadn't been the only monster no one cared about.

"Aatoon?" Lorlie said. He ignored her, focusing, instead, on the nauseating way his stomach was twisting upon itself. Sceptori were not supposed to be capable of experiencing emotions.

And yet, he *did* feel.

For his upcoming death.

But more deeply than that, for Lorlie.

It was a strange, protective nudge deep inside that made him want to give her a life better than his. To ensure she did not remain hated and alone.

So he'd concocted a final lesson. One that would heal all the ways he—and the world—had shattered her. It simply required him to speak one truth. The truth that would condemn him to death.

He slipped his hand into his pocket, touching the small watch he carried everywhere. It had been his mother's, passed down for generations. He twirled it on his finger every time he cursed someone, the action helped him to focus more. To remember why he did the things he did.

Judge the monsters of the world. Teach them the lessons everyone else is too scared or uncaring to.

That was how he got his curses so precise.

Aatoon turned, at last, to face her. She hadn't moved. An irritated expression crept across her face. She likely thought he was simply testing her patience. "Do you remember," he asked softly, "the night your kingdom was destroyed?"

Her scowl deepened. "That's not important."

"*Do* you?"

"Yes."

He nodded. "It was me."

"What?"

Meeting her confused gaze, Aatoon spread his arms in a sweeping gesture. "It wasn't a random dragon attack that wiped your kingdom from the face of this earth. Your parents failed to learn their lesson."

The magic began to swell around him as he smiled a lifeless smile at Lorlie—the girl who had become like a daughter to him.

"*I* killed them."

CHAPTER ONE

MARKUS

"Once upon a time, there was a girl who turned to stone. No one remembers her name, only that she was a princess, in an age of kings and Sceptori."

–From *The Book of Legends, Volume Forty-Nine*

1,000 Years Later

STONE STATUES TOWERED behind the Cursed Garden's black metal fence. Markus bounced his leg as he waited in the ridiculously long line winding from the front of the Garden's looming gates. He scanned the statues peeking above the fence. The blue midday sky was a fitting backdrop behind the creatures encased in gray. Some of them had long, jagged horns. Others reached upward with claws as long as he was tall.

The Cursed Gardens held thousands of statues that had been carved during the Age before the magic had vanished from the world. Tourists came from all over to behold the mythical creatures and figures found in the old lore records.

Leaning forward, Markus tapped the shoulder of the man in front of him, who was wearing a lime shirt two sizes too small for his bulky arms. "You see that wyvern over there?" Markus asked, pointing to one of the statues beyond the fence. The massive, reptilian figure was impressive even from such a distance. It stood reared up on its hind legs, wings spread like a pair of gray, rage-filled canvases. "That's Cringefold the Burnt. Lore says he's named for the terrible jokes he'd tell his victims before burning them to a crisp."

The man twisted to glare back at Markus.

Shut up! Markus told himself. But then he spotted the statue beside Cringefold and couldn't help but point it out. "And that bulbous creature there? It helped Cringefold in the Battle of—"

"Go bother someone else," the man snapped.

Right.

Markus bit the tip of his tongue, trying to ignore the invisible weight poking at the edges of his mind. He started to count the number of people ahead of him, then gave up after around fifteen and pulled a notebook from his pocket. If he closed his eyes, he could still smell his grandfather's scent between the pages, a mix of leather and ink.

"Wish you were here," Markus whispered. The man in front of him glanced back again with a scowl. Biting his tongue harder, Markus looked down at the yellowed pages. Gently, he flipped through them, one by one. They were all blank. Sometimes, growing up, he'd sneak to the doorway of the bedroom he shared with his grandfather, and he would watch him sit there and stare down at the endless whiteness. Grandfather never wrote anything.

But one day, Markus would. Once he found something worthy of writing.

He flipped through it a second time, then slipped it back into his pocket. As the line shuffled forward, he glanced over his shoulder. A mother with bags under her eyes stared at the ground as her daughter excitedly jumped up and down. Four teens laughed behind them, golden glitter drenching their t-shirts in honor of the magic that used to drift in the air. Beyond that, a young couple wearing matching cloth fairy wings stood on their toes to catch a peek at the statues. The line continued on, seemingly endless.

He and his grandfather had spent years talking about coming but had never been able to afford the entrance fee. Markus fingered the coin pouch on his belt. He had delivered pizzas at the Saucy Hut for four years to save up for this. And still, he wouldn't have had enough if Zek Lyhe, the Garden's owner, hadn't lowered the prices last week.

But Grandpa's not here.

Images of the white-walled hospital room where his grandfather had died drifted through his mind. It didn't seem fair that Markus was here, fulfilling one of his dreams when his grandfather could not.

A small, aching emptiness surfaced in his chest. *I just wish . . .* He cut off the thought and straightened his shoulders. *Stop it, Markus*! This was not the place for dwelling on such things. He sucked in a deep breath, turning his focus back to Cringefold's magnificent form once more. *I'm actually here.*

The line moved forward, and the man in the lime shirt stepped up to the ticket counter. A woman in a formal suit stood behind it. She handed a charcoal-black ticket to the man, then waved him through the gates.

Markus took the man's place at the counter. "Hi! I'd like to purchase a ticket for the day."

"Certainly." The woman flashed a polished smile. "That will be seventy-five bron."

Markus dug in his coin pouch and handed her seventy-five small bronze coins. The woman checked the amount, then placed the coins into a safe box and pulled out a ticket. Grabbing a hand-held hole puncher, she clicked a hole through the center of it. The action reminded Markus of a rat with enchanted teeth from the *Book of Legends, Volume Fifty*. It could bite holes through sheets of metal. As a kid, Markus had pretended that the rats he saw rooting around in the alleys at dusk were superpowered descendants of that rat. He'd even tried to tame one, once. He still had the scars to prove it.

The ticketbooth lady held the slip of paper out.

Markus snatched the ticket and continued forward, into the world of his grandfather's stories.

Woah.

Markus paused just inside the gates and took in the one hundred acres stretched out in a maze-like, glorious mess. Food carts and souvenir booths packed the crowded center. Paved paths of smooth, white concrete spiraled outward, running between endless rows of statues. Everyone seemed so small in the shadow of all the stone figures.

Markus jogged over to a crab with the girth of a medium-sized dog. Crouching, he inspected the wooden plaque in front of it. *Clute Charter*, it read, *originates from the Age of Kings. Discovered by Waine Lyhe.* Markus reached to touch it but paused as he glanced at the 'Do Not Touch' sign a few inches away.

"Oh, fine," he muttered, making a face at it.

Straightening, he glanced farther down the row. The familiar, lithe form of a cockatrice snagged his attention.

No way! Markus jogged over. The creature looked mostly like a chicken but had a serpent's tail and a lizard-like face that ended in a beak. Even carved from rock, its feathers somehow looked soft. He knelt so he was eye-level with the cockatrice. Its head was tilted upward, cocked in a curious sort of way. *Captain Brain*, the plaque read, *originates from the Dwindling. Discovered by Nella Lyhe.*

"Hey buddy," he said.

"Are ya talkin' to a statue?"

Markus looked up. An old man and woman stood a few steps away in front of a dainty, fairy-like figure.

"No," Markus said, a smile sliding over his face. "I'm talking to Captain Brain."

The old man blinked. "Young man, you do know that isn't a person, right? It's a hunk of prettified rock."

Actually, it was more than that. It was history. *Their* history. Statues like these could be found in rubble all across the world, and they could be linked to many of the characters in the old stories. Some variation of these creatures had actually existed back before the world's magic vanished.

"Did you know that Captain Brain here could control the minds of anyone she locked eyes with?" Markus said. "The Lorists claim she was the terror of the Dwindling before a clever peasant girl outwitted her one day, cursing her into stone." He tapped the statue on its beak, and smiled wistfully. What would it have been like to live in an Age like that? When creatures, man, and magic all lived together? He glanced back at the man and his wife. There was no flash of excitement in their eyes, no awed grin. He met their blank stares, cheeks burning. It was like he was speaking a completely different language.

He turned back to Captain Brain. *Maybe one day they'll see you.*

Maybe one day, they'll see me.

That was a wish he kept carefully tucked beside the tiny ember deep inside of him. The one that was angry at his grandfather and the world for treating him like he was nothing. The one he pretended didn't exist.

Giving the cockatrice a quick wave, he continued past the couple. Statue after statue towered against the sky, and each summoned a memory of his grandfather's voice, reciting their names and tales.

Halfway down the aisle, a sudden trail of warmth flashed across his palms and settled in the pit of his gut. It was like a breath of hot air, except inside of him. Markus jolted to a stop. *What in the . . .* He could have sworn that the warmth was pulling him forward, toward the end of the aisle, like tiny strings tied around his body, *tugging tugging tugging*. It was the strangest sensation. Mouth going dry, he slowly walked toward the end. A path running lengthwise divided the end of the row and a mess of others twisting outward, all leading deeper into the Garden. Tourists hadn't yet traveled this far, from what he could see. The thrumming cacophony of human voices was nothing more than a distant hum. Overall, though, this section of the Garden looked like everywhere else. Gray statues atop decorated pedestals. White concrete sidewalk . . .

Still—

As the foreign sensation increased to a jagged jolting in his gut, the hair on the back of his neck rose.

"Hello?" His voice echoed around him.

This is silly. I'm imagining things. Or I'm dying. All valid options, all valid options.

Rubbing his palms together, he turned to go back but stopped short. At the foot of one of the rows, a few aisles down was a familiar small figure atop a white pedestal.

A stone princess.

CHAPTER TWO

MARKUS

"The day she was born, the kingdom rejoiced. They loved her, even more than her elder sister, even more than the magic."

– From *The Book of Legends, Volume Forty-Nine*

THE STATUE WAS dwarfed by the other massive creatures lined beside her. Markus cocked his head, studying the finely-carved stone hair that flared away from her face like flames. A painted green ball gown billowed around her as if the carvers had captured her mid-twirl. One small hand reached outward, her glassy gaze passing over his shoulder, searching for something—or someone—he couldn't see.

"Woah." The word fell from his lips softer than a prayer.

Familiarity tugged at his core. He walked over and glanced at the plaque. *The Forgotten Princess.*

"*Once upon a time . . .*" His grandfather's voice came back to him. Markus squinted as he tried to recall her story. "*There was a girl who turned to stone.*"

Snippets slipped through his memory.

"*None were as fair, as beautiful, as kind, as she.*"

He approached the statue, reaching a hand out to touch its outstretched palm. The stone was far warmer than he'd expected.

"*. . . her name was lost to memory.*"

"And yet, here you are," Markus whispered. Who she was may have been wiped from history, but this statue was here, proving she had once existed.

What would it be like to have everyone forget you? His stomach twisted uneasily. As a child, he'd had nightmares about everything vanishing and him being left alone in a silent world, abandoned by everyone who could have seen or heard him. The memory sent shivers down his spine, even as his face flushed at the childish fear. He gave himself a small shake. "Oh well." He smiled up at the statue. "Anyway, it's been a pleasure to meet you, Princess."

In the back of his mind, he could hear his grandfather lecturing him about talking to inanimate objects. But in his experience, they were the best listeners.

Besides, maybe the magic is out there, listening.

He passed the Forgotten Princess and strode toward a set of gnome statues huddled around a fake stone fire.

"Hiya, gnomes!" he said. Something thudded behind him, and a person gasped. Markus turned. *What—*

The white pedestal glared back at him, empty.

Empty?

He rubbed his eyes. Where the Forgotten Princess once stood was nothing more than open air. A pedestal as blank as the pages of his grandfather's notebook. Retracing his steps, he rounded the podium and froze mid-step. "Are you okay?" Markus stammered.

A young woman knelt on the ground, palms planted against the concrete. Her dark hair hung in tangled strings around her face, obscuring most of her features. A torn green gown bunched around her legs, the pieces of fabric ripped and fraying.

He gaped.

It can't be . . . There's no way . . .

The girl coughed, a rasping, violent sound that tore through her entire body.

"Hey." He dropped to a knee and reached out to steady her. "You okay? What happened?" The moment his hand touched her shoulder, she jerked away. Twisting, she slammed a fist into his face. Markus fell backward, bright flashes blurring his vision, blending with the sudden pain. Blinking, he carefully brushed his fingers against his now burning nose, then quickly pulled them away again. Bright drops of blood trickled down his fingertip. His stomach curled, and he barely kept from vomiting.

Weak boy, his grandfather's voice snipped harshly through his mind. Markus swallowed, sucked in a slow, deep breath and looked up. The girl had pushed herself to her feet and was slowly scanning the Gardens.

"What did you do that for?" Markus said. He gingerly wiped his nose again and—pointedly not looking—rubbed his hand on his shirt. "Hello?"

The girl turned. Pale gray eyes met his, and he found himself leaning away.

"Don't touch me." The words rolled off her tongue with a clipped, elegant accent. The kind of sound you'd expect from royalty.

Markus glanced at the empty pedestal.

"Tell me," she demanded, "the location of this place, the Age, and the name of your current king."

"Current king?"

The corners of her mouth twitched downward. "Oh great, you aren't deaf. Wonderful."

"I don't . . ." Markus paused and rubbed his forehead. "We don't have a king. *Who* are you, again?"

"None of your business."

"You just punched me for no reason," Markus said. "I think that makes it my business."

"Just tell me what Age it is!" she snapped.

Markus instinctively flinched away. "Fragments," he said. "It's the Age of Fragments." The Age of trying to piece together everything they'd lost during the Dwindling when the magic and world descended into chaos.

"I don't know what that means," she said flatly.

Where did you come from? Markus looked back at the empty pedestal, then at her again. An impossible suspicion lurked at the edges of his thoughts. *But there's no way she could be . . .*

"Are you," he hesitated, "the statue?"

The girl looked at the pedestal. A startled expression twitched briefly across her face as if she hadn't noticed it there. He studied her. There was a dark, ash-like substance smeared on her cheeks and dress.

"How long ago was the Age of Kings?" she asked, still staring at the pedestal.

Markus blinked. "Uh, that would have been before the Dwindling. So, around a thousand years ago."

She muttered something.

"What?"

The girl turned back to him and lifted her chin. Something hard and fierce glinted in her eyes. She reached an arm to the side as if grasping for something to steady herself with. Her hands were speckled with dark red stains.

Red like blood.

She paused, then frowned, and looked down at her hands. Markus shifted nervously. Should he say something? Go get one of the Garden workers? She looked like she'd been through something horrible.

Reaching her arm out again, the girl twitched her fingers. "Where . . ." She glanced at her crimson-stained fingers again, and her face suddenly went pale. "Wait. Where is it?"

"Where is what?"

"The magic." The girl turned and locked her gaze with his. "Where is the magic?"

Um. Markus licked his dry lips. "There isn't any."

"Liar." Panic pinched her features.

"No," he said. "Really. Magic doesn't exist anymore. As far as we can tell, it began acting erratically during the Dwindling, then just vanished altogether." Markus shrugged.

As she stared at him, the shadows puddling beneath the statues seemed to pour into her eyes. "That's impossible," she whispered.

"I don't understand what's going on," Markus said.

"No. You don't." The girl started walking down one of the rows. "Follow."

Immediately, the tugging in his chest intensified, a warm rope wrapping around his very bones. He pressed his hand against his chest, staring after the girl.

I'm going crazy, aren't I? Goosebumps prickled down his arms.

"Are you coming?" she snapped over her shoulder. Sucking in a deep breath, he followed.

What in the seven tales is going on?

CHAPTER THREE

LORLIE

"That day, amidst the celebrations, the magic gathered above the newborn princess's cradle. She did not have a golden-carved hole inside of her, as the Sceptori did. But the princess *was* special, the magic could sense it. Special, indeed."

–From *The Book of Legends, Volume Forty-Nine*

AFTER ONE THOUSAND years, Lorlie Cyphrani woke to light. Golden, warm light pierced pinpricks through the dark cloak smothering her. A tingling ran up her hand into her arm, spread to her chest, and zapped through the rest of her body, breaking apart the shell she'd been trapped in.

Then the warmth, the light, vanished.

And she'd found herself kneeling in a graveyard of cursed souls.

She strode down a row of statues, memories pounding against her skull. Her past had been broken up, disgruntled by the curse that had turned her to stone. Now her thoughts swirled together in a chaotic mess. Faces without names merged with the shadowed walls of a tower. In the back of her mind, screams echoed, sharp and desperate. Memory after memory overshadowed by a stark, red film. She pressed a palm to her forehead and tried to focus through the haze. Up ahead, she could hear people—a lot of them. Their voices sounded strange, more . . . blunt, lacking the musical lilt they should have held. As guttural and different as the barking of a seal and the singing of a bird.

And the air. Lorlie frowned. There was something wrong with the air.

"Can you please tell me what is going on?" The boy's footsteps thudded lightly against the concrete behind her, but she didn't need to hear him to know he was following. She could feel it in her chest—his nearness. It was a chain wrapped around her lungs, tugging and slackening depending on his proximity. She'd encountered this specific sensation before. It was due to a tether spell. A curse that could bind two people or objects together.

She *hated* it above all the other curses.

Which was exactly why she'd been punished with it.

"How are you alive?" the boy pressed.

"I've always been alive," she said, her teeth grinding against the words. Or, at least, she thought so. Her memories were still sorting themselves out. She paused at the end of the row. It let out into a wide space with endless waves of people and large, ugly booths.

"But." The boy stopped beside her, leaving a wide gap between them. "You—the statue— Were you the statue?"

Lorlie thought of the empty white pedestal and the words on the plaque beside it.

The Forgotten Princess.

Forgotten.

A ballroom flashed through her mind, huge and overwhelming, filled with people in glittering dresses. Magic danced in the air around them. But she stood in the corner, alone, tiny. Invisible to the swirling partiers.

That's it. The realization jolted her. *The air. The air is empty.*

There was no golden dust in the air.

She'd never seen the world without those glittering specks constantly drifting around. Now, there was just a void. The loss of magic curled her toes, physically ailing her. It was so *wrong.*

The boy cleared his throat, and Lorlie forced herself to look him in the face. He had dirt brown eyes with matching hair that brushed the edges of his shoulders. His forehead was scrunched in confusion as he studied her. He couldn't be much younger than her, somewhere around twenty, even though he looked much younger.

He called this time the Age of Fragments. She frowned. There was no magic, and he didn't seem to know her.

Forgotten.

It echoed in her mind, and she shook the thought away.

The magic hasn't been gone for long. Otherwise, their language wouldn't have been preserved so well.

But he knows nothing about what these statues actually are.

She jutted her chin toward the statues. "They're all alive." One of them was old Cringefold, his ugly face turned upward toward the sky. She could hear his voice, arrogant, grating against the inside of her skull as he laughed at his own stupid jokes. Honestly, she wasn't surprised to see him here. The idiot got what he deserved.

"They're all alive?" the boy slowly repeated.

"Yes."

"Wait. How? How is that possible? They don't look alive."

"They're cursed," she said with a dismissive flick of her hand. It was a common punishment. If you caused enough trouble, made enough enemies of powerful individuals, you got cursed. If you were lucky, you were simply turned to stone for eternity. If you weren't . . .

Well, her tether curse was enough explanation of what happened *then.*

To be tied to another person, dependent on them. A shudder ran through her. It was worse than dying. It took away the very base of a person's freedom, cinched chains around your ability to choose.

"Cursed?" the boy said. "The lore mentions that a lot, but they're still alive? I thought a stone curse kills you."

"No." She scanned the crowd. The skin along her arms crawled at the prospect of walking among all those people. "They're—*we're*—still alive. Asleep." Her thoughts were beginning to quiet, memories clicking into place.

A thousand years . . . Lorlie shook her head. What was she supposed to do after all this time?

First of all, I need to get out of this place.

She could almost hear her mentor's—and consequently, the man who'd cursed her—voice instructing her on how to survive in a strange place.

Telling her how to blend in. As if he'd been training her for this very moment.

He hadn't been.

He hadn't cared if she lived or not.

And why would he? a small voice deep inside of her asked. A dash of crimson, dark and condemning, dripped through her mind.

He's dead because of me.

"Let me get this straight," the boy said. "Every single one of these creatures is alive and just sitting in their little stone prisons waiting to be released? So they could wake up at any moment? How does no one know—"

"Shut up." Hugging her arms around herself, Lorlie marched into the center and shoved her way through the obnoxious crowd. Stares burned against her skin as people paused and turned, and the boy's presence blistered at her heels. She pointedly ignored all of them. Finally breaking free of the clamor, Lorlie headed toward the huge gated entrance. There was a booth on the other side of it, and a line of even more people waiting to get in.

"Where are we going?" the boy asked, and she rolled her eyes.

So many questions.

She strode for the exit. A line of buildings stood on the opposite of the street outside the gates. They were huge, towering far into the sky. But they were also crudely made, void of the graceful curves and designs she remembered them having.

"What's your name?" the boy pressed as they walked across a curious set of metal tracks running down the center of the road.

"None of your concern."

"Fine, fine. I'll just call you 'Princess'."

She risked a glance over her shoulder. He was a few steps behind her. A contagious grin twitched at the edges of his mouth.

"I'm Markus," he said, catching her gaze. "Markus Clint."

"Saying it twice doesn't make it sound better."

"Sure it does! Good for the ole memory, too."

Lorlie rolled her eyes. Following the sidewalk down the row of buildings, she turned right at the first intersection they came to, out of view of that cursed place she'd been imprisoned. Her next order of business was to find new clothes. A ball gown from the Age of Kings obviously didn't blend in very well here.

Above each doorway was a wooden sign with the building's purpose or name engraved on it in bold letters. Some of the buildings were painted in golden dots or with etchings of tiny pixies, griffins, and other creatures. The images somehow looked out of place behind the metal tracks, and strangely dressed people. *It's like they took my world and smashed it into this one.* Just a few buildings down, she spotted a shop named the Fairy Boutique. *Perfect.* Jogging over, she threw open the glass door and stepped in. She was met with a circular, wide room with a high ceiling. Blue glitter sparkled from the walls, reflecting off a huge chandelier hanging at the center. Rows of clothes fanned outward from the front desk.

"Hi!" the young woman at the desk said. She smiled so widely it looked like she was a wolf baring its fangs. "Welcome to the Fairy Boutique! How can I help you?"

"You can't," Lorlie said.

"Uh, what Princess here means," Markus said from where he stood in the open doorway, "is that she has to do some browsing first. But thank you so much!"

The woman's gaze flicked between Lorlie and Markus for a few heartbeats. She finally flashed another fake smile and began scribbling something down on a piece of paper. Lorlie chose an aisle at random, sensing Markus on her heels. She wrinkled her nose as she walked. This was the type of clothing people liked now? The stitches were all wrong. Even she could see that—and she was nowhere close to being a seamstress.

"Why is the magic gone?" Lorlie paused to study a blue skirt.

"You're asking me?"

She shot him a glare. "Yes." *Idiot.*

"I have no clue."

Lorlie jerked the skirt from its hanger, and the hook snapped with a startling ferocity. She squeezed the fabric, staring down at her blood-speckled knuckles as they turned white. "You don't know," she repeated.

"No," he said. "But, there are theories. For example, one of the more popular explanations is that the magic was linked with the Sceptori. When they disappeared, so did the magic."

Lorlie froze. *Sceptori.*

She could see her curser's face. His eyes—deep and ancient, somehow reflecting her own soul.

"*You are a beast,*" the voice she wanted to forget rasped through her mind. It opened the hole inside of her. One she'd created with her own blade a thousand years ago.

"*Just like me.*"

The evidence stained her hands. She could feel it sinking into her veins, curling around her heart. Guilt, anger, and something else—all mixed and mashed together.

"So," Markus continued, oblivious, "I think they must have been, like, a magic source or something? Or perhaps the thing that made them vanish affected the magic as well? Either way, I would bet the Sceptori are the key. I've often wondered . . ." His sentence drifted off. "Anyway, do you know anything about it?"

Lorlie turned away. "I don't know." Her voice came out flat and distant. Markus opened his mouth to say something else, and she held up her hand. "No more questions."

Continuing down the row, she picked up a shirt and jacket before retreating to a changing room. Dumping the wretched gown on the floor of the changing room, she gave it a firm kick. It had been 'given' to her when Sorik, her ex-fiance, abducted her and tried to convince her to save his life.

She hadn't, of course.

She wasn't in the business of saving people.

After changing, she ducked back out of the room and found Markus standing where she'd left him. He stared at the far wall of the boutique, a few strands of hair had fallen over his eyes.

Why him?

Why had her curse chosen him, of all the people who'd probably passed through that graveyard, to wake her?

"If you're alive," Markus began softly, "and the other statues can be brought to life as well . . ." He turned and met her gaze. His eyes didn't hold the hard glint she was used to when people looked at her. *He's not even afraid.* She shifted, feeling thoroughly unsettled. "Does that mean the magic is back?"

"No," Lorlie said. There was no warmth in the air. No magic dancing at the edge of her fingers, waiting to be used. It was gone. Everything she'd ever cared for was gone.

"Then how are you here?" Markus asked.

He sounded so sincere. So oblivious. Lorlie drew a deep breath. "Unfortunately, I've been unconscious for a thousand years, so I don't know. But the magic isn't here." She gestured toward him. "It can leave traces, a residue, so to speak. Curses and blessings, they all remain active, even without it." She hesitated. "Or, at least, that was what we figured would happen if something happened to the magic."

Lorlie brushed past Markus and headed to the front desk. The woman was still there, scribbling away on a notepad. There was a ring on each of her fingers, and they clinked with every motion she made. Lorlie stopped in front of the desk. The woman was drawing diamonds over and over. Dozens of penciled jewels.

What a waste.

After a moment, Lorlie let out a long sigh. "Do you want to be paid, or do I just walk out of here?"

The woman startled and looked up. "Oh! I'm so sorry." Her face reddened.

"I'll be taking all of this." Lorlie motioned to her clothes. Markus paused beside her, and Lorlie barely suppressed a flinch. He was far, far too close.

The woman smiled. "Perfect! That will be"—she paused for a moment—"twenty-five copper."

Instinctively, Lorlie reached upward, curling her hand around the air. She remembered, too late, that the magic was gone. Back in her day, all you had to do was reach into your personal store of magic and hand it to whoever you owed. They could then keep and use that magic as needed.

But . . .

She suddenly felt sick. How did these people live without magic?

The woman stared at her. "Are you okay, dear?"

Markus placed a handful of small, round metal pieces on the counter. "Uh, I'm sure she's just fine. Perfectly normal, in fact. Here."

Trembling, Lorlie spun and stomped out of the boutique. People paid with pieces of metal now? *How is metal worth anything?*

A crudely made, long metallic box with windows rattled past on the tracks. Through the windows, she could make out the shapes of people inside it. *What is that? Some kind of automatic carriage?* She followed down the sidewalk, watching as it drew farther away.

A few buildings down from the shop, the chain around her chest tightened painfully; one by one, her steps became sluggish and heavy. When the street around her began to blur, Lorlie stopped and glanced down at her hands. They stung as gray stone crept over her fingertips. A sweeping cold rose from deep inside of her, chasing away any trace of warmth.

If she kept walking away from where Markus was, she'd become a statue again.

The voices would stop.

The memories would be gone.

The pain—the pain would . . .

She squeezed her eyes closed. The chain *pulled* at her to turn around and go back. To preserve what little life she had left.

"*Monsters don't deserve to live.*" Her words. Her voice. Spoken to the only person she'd thought cared about her.

A small flame rose in the pit of her stomach as she thought of him. Lorlie curled her hands into fists. She would not let this curse defeat her. She *would* bring the magic back, she would break her curse, and she would make everyone who had ever hurt her pay.

Just as she'd done before.

CHAPTER FOUR

MARKUS

"The magic blessed her. It filled her veins with thrumming life and dusted her pale cheeks with gold."

–From *The Book of Legends, Volume Forty-Nine*

MARKUS SAT IN an ocean of lore. As he leaned forward, flipping a page here, a page there, he didn't see black ink on yellowed, crisp paper. He saw people—legends dancing fiery rings around his apartment. Each one of the battered books held what Lorists guessed to be history. There were a lot of unknowns, a lot of abrupt endings and assumptions. Most people nowadays didn't even bother to read any of it.

Still, there were others who believed the magic of old would return one day.

Markus gently eased a folded map out from between the pages of one of the books near his foot. He gently smoothed it out, the paper crinkling under his hands. Ancient kingdoms and landmarks from the Age of Kings stared up at him in faded ink. *The Drune Kingdom. Siiph Kingdom. Farrow Kingdom. Winge Kingdom.* At the top left, another sector was marked, but its name had been scribbled over, making it unreadable.

Where are you from, Princess?

He glanced over his shoulder at his bedroom's doorway. He could just catch a glimpse of her sitting on the bed with an open book in her lap. After buying new clothes, she insisted on finding someplace 'safe.' So, here they were, at his dusty, cluttered apartment. She'd turned her nose up at the sight of it but hadn't said anything. Probably because right now, he was the only help she had. She had quickly—without asking—commandeered his bedroom, along with Volume Forty-Five of *The Book of Legends*, which contained the only account of her existence, as far as he knew.

Markus shook his head. She certainly wasn't very princess-like. Or legend-like.

In fact, she wasn't *anything* like he'd imagined.

Legends were supposed to be kind, eloquent, and graceful. But she was—

Markus chewed on his lip, staring blankly at the map. Since the very first story his grandfather had ever told him from the lore, he'd dreamed of how amazing it would be to meet one of the legends. And here he was, in the presence of one of them. But so far, all she had done was scowl a lot, ignore his questions, and make demands. Disappointment settled in his gut.

Maybe she just needs to rest. Get her bearings. He could imagine how disorienting it must be to wake up in a completely different world, a thousand years away from everything you knew and loved. *She could, however, at least wash the suspicious-looking red stains off her hands*, he thought, idly bouncing his knee.

"Do I even want to know what you're doing?"

Markus jumped and looked up. Standing in the open doorway of his bedroom was the princess. Her hair was still a tangled mess, and her new clothes were wrinkled. Looking just as ill-tempered as before, she cocked an incredulous eyebrow at him

Smiling, he nodded toward the book in her hands. "Did you find anything?"

"Oh, of course," she said with a roll of her eyes. "I found that you people know absolutely nothing about anything useful." She held up *The Book of Legends*. "Why in the myths would anyone waste resources making this stupid thing?"

The ember sparked inside of him. How could she say that? It was history! The stories within those pages were amazing. Magical. They were . . . they were . . . Markus bit back the retort burning on his tongue, forcing his smile to stay put. "Is the story about you not accurate?"

She leveled a flat stare at him. "No. This is absolute trash. Who would ever think that it was even remotely true?"

Me.

My grandpa.

Markus fingered the edges of the map.

Basically everyone else in the world.

"Do you have anything else left from the Age of Kings?" she asked.

"No," Markus said. "There's nothing left except fragmented records and random artifacts. Even all of the castles were destroyed during the Dwindling." The specifics of that dark Age were still largely unclear. But something had happened at the end of the Age of Kings that made society fall apart. Kingdoms burned. All form of civilization descended into chaos. People were left without magic or leadership, left to flounder in the ashes of everything they'd once known.

Just thinking of how terrified they must have been, how confused, how *lost*, made Markus want to find some way to go back in time, look them in their eyes, and tell them that the world didn't stay dark. That the story didn't end there like he was sure they must have thought it would. Society had slowly rebuilt. Slowly healed.

And now here they were, generations of people who knew nothing about living in a world with magic.

He drew a slow breath. "Here, look at this." Hopping to his feet, he gingerly picked his way across the cluttered floor to where she was standing. He held out the map.

With a scowl, she took it. "And I'm looking at this because—?"

He waved toward the books on the floor. "We can change the world! Obviously."

She stared at him for a moment, then slowly lowered her gaze to the map. She brushed a finger over the kingdom's name that had been marked out, and a shadow flickered across her face.

"See," Markus said, "you could set the record straight. You could tell us what it was like back then and fill the missing holes in our lore."

Her fingers whitened as she tightened her grip on the paper. It crunched beneath her grip, and a little section of the edge tore. Markus winced, a surprising flash of anger flaring through him. He'd taken great care to keep his lore collection in the best possible shape. "So?" he said, the word clipped.

"I," she said slowly, "am not interested in being your stupid history book. I am not here to save a bunch of people from their worthless lives. I'm here to break my curse." She dropped the map on the ground and folded her arms.

Markus shifted his eyes from the girl to the map. It lay at her feet like some discarded, unwanted piece of trash. Carefully, he took the anger threatening to break free and pressed it down, down, down. "Okay." He forced another smile. "That's all right. We can worry about it later. Anyway, isn't your curse broken?"

Her face darkened. "No. The turning-to-stone thing is only part of the curse. It's really a tether spell." She paused, as if expecting him to understand what that meant.

"Is that—" He picked up the map. "—supposed to mean anything to me?"

"Apparently not," she muttered.

Markus gently placed the map on his small dining table, then turned back to Lorlie. "Okay, so, what's a tether spell, exactly?"

"It means you and I are stuck with each other until I can break my curse. If we get too far, I turn back to stone and can only wake up if you touch me again."

Oh. Markus self-consciously tucked his hands behind his back. "Cool, cool. So how do we break your curse?"

"We could try having you shut up for five seconds."

Markus shrugged, still smiling. But inside, But inside, the words were a punch to the gut. His heartbeat squeezed painfully against his chest. His grandfather had said things like that. Flippantly. As if it had never crossed his mind that words could hurt worse than any blade or bullet or punch.

It doesn't matter.

But it did.

She turned away, considering the front door. "Who owns the place we were at?"

"The Cursed Gardens?"

"Yes."

Markus almost asked why she needed to know that but quickly bit off the question. "The Lyhe Foundation. They're probably the most important corporation in the world right now. They handle the research of everything related to the lore and magic."

"Lyhe . . ." she murmured. "Who is in charge of this . . . foundation?"

He folded his arms, then raised an eyebrow. "How about this: you answer my question, and I answer yours."

She didn't look up. "Fine."

"How do you plan on breaking your curse? Is there a way to bring the magic back?"

"That's two questions," Lorlie said, scowling. "And if you must know, I need to find a pocket watch that would have been near wherever your Lyhe-people found me; that should break my curse. Meanwhile, yes, I intend to figure out what happened to the magic. I can't believe you live like *this.* Without it." She shook her head, looking flustered.

Markus wasn't certain what living 'like this' meant, but if she could bring the magic back . . . if that was even a possibility . . . He nodded. "Zek Lyhe, he owns it."

She pursed her lips. "It's a family business, I assume?"

"Yes. Actually, he just recently inherited it a few years ago, after his parents died in a transport accident."

"Good," she said.

Good?

"I'm going to pay him a visit." Stalking to the front door, she threw it open and stepped out.

CHAPTER FIVE

LORLIE

"None were as fair, as beautiful, as kind, as the second-born princess of this vast kingdom."

–From *The Book of Legends, Volume Forty-Nine*

LORLIE WAS TRAPPED again. A beast in a cage. Only this time, the bars were invisible, and she didn't have magic to fight her way out. The hallway outside of Markus's apartment was dark and dingy. With bottles and crumbled wrappers littering the sides of the floor and yellow ceiling lamps that flickered in and out of death. Voices clamored from behind the closed doors, some happy, some arguing. Somewhere, she thought she heard someone crying. She dragged her steps until she felt Markus enter the hallway behind her. His door clicked shut.

"You want to meet with Zek Lyhe?" he said, sounding incredulous.

'Lyhedrune,' you mean.

She pressed her lips together. That name belonged to a person who was unforgivable. A person she hated. *And yet . . .* Emotion swelled in her chest, overwhelming and searing.

Her ex-fiance, Sorik Lyhedrune, was supposed to have died a thousand years ago from a curse. But if this Zek Lyhe was a descendent of his, as she suspected, then . . .

Did he break his curse?

A little flutter of relief passed through her. She scowled, shoving it away. *I couldn't care less what happened to him.*

"Lorlie, why do you want to meet with Mr. Lyhe?"

She glanced up. They reached the stairs at the end of the hallway, and she started down them. "If he's in control of all the artifacts and cursed, then there's a good chance he knows where the watch is."

"The one that will break your curse?" Markus said, puffing slightly from the descent.

"Yes."

"And why is this pocket watch important?"

Lorlie reached the bottom of the steps and headed for the exit. Outside, the sun was just beginning to rise, and the light settling across the city was soft and pale. But not golden. She flexed her fingers, pausing on the sidewalk. "How do I find him?"

"Why is the watch important?" Markus repeated.

She huffed. "It belonged to the person who cursed me." The words came out slow and cold. "He was always dangling it around, asking if I could see it like I was some blind idiot. It was the last thing he showed me before I became stone."

"And you think it'll break your curse because?"

"Because it's a test." She squinted at the silver tracks crisscrossing over the middle of the road. "He was obsessed with teaching lessons, and he'd always give me obscure tasks to complete, like finding a single piece of horse hair in a bale of hay to teach me to be thorough. This is just another one of those." A long metal box like she'd seen the previous day rattled down the tracks toward them. Lorlie watched it suspiciously. "Trust me. He tied my curse to the watch. And if the magic disappeared shortly after, he probably had something to do with it as well."

Markus grunted. The metal box thing screeched to a stop beside a canopied bench on the sidewalk. "It's called a tram" Markus said. Lorlie glanced sideways at him. He shot her a knowing smile, then started toward the machine-tram-thing.

She narrowed her eyes, following as the tether between them tugged.

"This will make a stop on the street where he lives," Markus explained as they reached the tram. He checked some numbers posted on the side of it, then nodded. A narrow doorway slid open, revealing an interior with sets of hard chairs attached to each side. At the front, right across from the entrance, a man with a twirled mustache sat in front of a panel of controls.

Lorlie followed Markus through the ridiculously narrow path dividing the seats. There were a few passengers scattered through the rows, but all of them appeared to be fully consumed with their own thoughts and didn't bother looking up. He slid in a chair on the left and moved to the part closest to the chair. Pausing beside the row, Lorlie frowned. Should she just sit on the second chair next to him? Or in one of the other rows?

"What's wrong?" he asked, glancing at her curiously.

"Nothing." After another moment of hesitation, she sat down in the space next to him and folded her arms self-consciously. She didn't like being this close in proximity to people. It made it far too easy for them to stab her, or knock her out, or capture her.

Stop it! She scowled at the back of the seat in front of her. *You're being ridiculous. No one even remembers who I am anymore.*

And Markus certainly didn't pose any threat, of that, she was certain.

Darkness blinked at the edges of her vision, bringing with it a creeping, engulfing chill. *His* voice lurked there. The one who cursed her. The one who took everything from her.

He gave you everything, too, a small part of her whispered.

Lorlie gritted her teeth. An image rose to the forefront of her mind: a man with a lean, scrawny frame, like a withering tree, standing beside her father.

And then that same man kneeling on the ballroom tile in front of her, studying her with calculating, knowing eyes.

That man, shadowed, as he stood outside her tower prison's door, holding freedom in his words.

His crumpled remains lay in the rubble of her home, clothes drenched crimson, hand stretched toward her.

"*A lesson,*" he'd whispered. "*The last. See, Lorlie. See them.*"

"Can I ask you a question?" Markus asked. Lorlie flinched, and the memory began to fade. The tram rattled as it eased along the tracks. She looked down at her hands and realized with a sickening jolt that she hadn't washed the blood off of them yet.

"Princess?"

A bitter taste crept across her tongue. "Don't call me that."

"What happened to you? Why were you cursed?" He asked as if he hadn't even heard her. She shifted in the seat, and she could feel his eyes on her, but she refused to look up. "What kingdom are you from, anyway?"

"That's a lot of questions."

"They're important questions."

No, they aren't.

They were questions about the past. Things she didn't want to remember, let alone talk about to a stranger. She pressed her palms against her knees. "Someone cursed me." *Someone I cared about very much.*

Someone I killed.

"And the same person destroyed my kingdom, killed my entire family, and got me locked up in a tower for a long time. That's all you need to know."

"Huh," he said. "That is nothing like the story in the lore."

"You shouldn't believe everything you read."

Sighing softly, he leaned back in the chair, fingers twitching. Markus had a kind of energy about him like he could never quite be still. Something was always in motion, his mouth, his fingers, his bouncing leg. "I was raised by my grandpa," he said. For a moment, he just let the sentence hang there in the air as if it held some sort of significance.

"And?"

"He was a hard man. He worked in the factories and was, y'know, always tired and stuff. But he'd always tell me a story right before bed. From the lore. That's where I first heard about Cringefold the Burnt, Viv of the Isle, and you."

Lorlie looked up, meeting his gaze. His eyes were a mud brown, but they had a strange sparkle in them. Almost as if they were smiling at her. She frowned and tipped her head back against the plastic seat.

"Anyway," he said, "my grandpa would have loved to meet a real legend."

A strange, wiggly sensation twisted through her chest. To hear herself spoken of as if she were something other than human—it almost made everyone's views of her more concrete. More real.

She wasn't a princess.

Or a daughter.

Or a prince charming's one true love.

She was the thing no one wanted. A beastly villain marring the pages of some child's fairytale. Fingering the edge of her wrinkled shirt, she tried to imagine Markus as a little boy, sitting on a bed, listening to an old man tell stories of fantastical creatures, and a girl who was nothing more than a lie on paper.

The tram turned onto another street, and Markus started bouncing his leg. He glanced out the window, then back again. "So, what's your name? If we're going to be working together to bring the magic back, I might as well know it."

Lorlie clenched her jaw. It was a simple question. Easy. But her answers were complicated.

"*Beast*," her Curser's voice whispered.

"*Princess*," her dead people claimed.

"*Accident*," her parents hissed.

"*Nothing*," her sister cheered. "*You are nothing, nothing, nothing.*"

"Lorlie," she finally said. "My name is Lorlie Cyphrani."

"Nice to officially meet you, Lorlie." He actually sounded like he meant it. She curled her lip in disgust.

He held out his hand, which was a little awkward with the small space. "I'm Markus Clint."

"You mentioned that."

He laughed. "I know. But it's worth saying again, right?"

Lorlie studied him for a moment before shaking his hand. "I guess."

A few minutes later, the tram shuddered to a stop. "Cranbary Street!" the driver announced. He pulled a lever, and the doors swung open.

"Here we are!" Markus nodded toward the open doors. "The Lyhe Mansion will be just down a short way from this stop, so we can get off here."

Lorlie stood and led the way to the exit.

"Usually," Markus said from behind her, "this tram is packed with tourists coming to see the mansion, but it's too early for that."

Nodding absently, she stepped off the tram, glanced down the street, and froze. A few feet down the sidewalk was a tall black fence, the same as the one around the Cursed Gardens.

And inside of it was a castle.

CHAPTER SIX

MARKUS

"Through the years, she grew, as did her blessing. She learned to heal wounds that were thought beyond repair, and many came seeking her aid."

–From *The Book of Legends, Volume Forty-Nine*

EVERY TIME MARKUS saw the Lyhe Mansion, it took his breath away. He stepped off the tram behind Lorlie and gawked at the majestic structure. Dark red bricks formed a curved, two-story structure with five impressive cylinder towers rising from the black-tiled roof. As Markus walked towards it, he got the distinct impression that the mansion had simply grown there. It just felt *right*. In its shadow, the other mansions on the street were blocky and dull, out of place, as if they were intruders on this beautiful creation's land. He came to a stop in front of the fence and rested his hands on the bars.

Here he was again, looking in on a dream. Just as he had done so many other times throughout his life.

First with his grandfather.

Now, alone.

A wistful longing filled him, like a soft ache of loss. The people inside those walls—the Lyhe family—knew the lore in an intimate way no one else in the world did. It was their job and had been for generations. In fact, Markus didn't even know when they'd first become the caretakers of the lore. It just seemed to be a natural part of the world, similar to how the mansion felt here on this street.

"I thought you said there was nothing left."

Markus blinked, remembering that he was not actually alone. He turned and found Lorlie a few steps behind him. She stared, pale, at the mansion.

"What?" he said.

"Nothing left," Lorlie repeated. "That's what you said." She slowly walked forward, gaze hooked on the structure. "You said all of the kingdoms, and their buildings, had been lost. That there was nothing left except for fragmented records and random artifacts."

"Well yeah," Markus said, "that's true."

"Then what is *that*?"

What is what? He glanced at the mansion again, confused. A short-cropped green lawn filled the space between the inside of the fence and the mansion. Manicured bushes in the shape of roses ran down both sides of the road leading up to the flight of black stairs at the entryway. Just like always. There was nothing out of the ordinary as far as he could see. "Lorlie? What are you talking about?"

"That!" She jabbed a hand in the mansion's direction.

"What?"

"That's Sorik Lyhedrune's castle!"

Markus frowned. "Castles don't exist anymore. They were all destroyed in the Dwindling. Also, I have no clue who that is." *Though . . . 'Lyhedrune' is suspiciously close to Lyhe.*

"Oh really?" she said, turning on him. "Then what am I looking at?"

"Um, a mansion inspired by the old castles?" All the blueprints and the castles had been destroyed, but they still had descriptions of what they had looked like. The Lyhe's specifically designed their home to show their appreciation for the old times. It took ten years to fully build, according to a bibliography Markus read on Nella Lyhe, Zek's great-great-great grandmother. He was about to tell Lorlie such when he noticed the look on her face.

Red rose in her cheeks, harsh and angry. She looked ready to punch someone. Unconsciously, Markus reached up to rub his still-sore nose, where she'd hit him the day before. *Which had been accidental. She'd been confused.* "I don't see," he began carefully, "how that could be a castle from a thousand years ago."

"Seriously?" she spat. "You're going to argue with me about this?"

Glancing at the mansion, he opened his mouth, then clapped it shut again. *She would know. But . . .*

He'd spent forever combing the records for any type of drawing of the old castles. He'd found none. *None.* Everyone—including the Lyhe family and Lorists—said that the only remains of the royal homes were piles of overgrown rubble.

"It was supposed to have been constructed only a few generations ago," Markus said, frowning at the red bricks.

"Lies," she said dismissively as if she wasn't destroying everything he knew.

He ran a hand through his hair. "Who is Sorik Lyhedrune?"

"Just shut up." She pivoted toward the mansion. "I'm done answering questions."

The words stung. Markus stared at her, slowly shaking his head. This was someone who had actually touched *magic*. Someone who had held it, probably wielded it.

She could have been anyone she wanted to be.

And yet, this was who she had decided to become.

This abrupt, angry human being with bloody fists.

The tight, shadowed sense of disappointment enveloped him. Which was silly . . . He was the presence of someone he'd only heard of in stories! He had no right to be disappointed. After all, who was to say legends were supposed to act one way, right?

But this isn't a legend, he thought. This was someone who treated him like everyone else in the world did.

Can I really blame her, though?

He wasn't exactly someone anyone should want to pay attention to.

Swallowing past the lump in his throat, Markus motioned toward the closed gates. "So, what do you want to do, then?"

"Where does your precious Zek Lyhe keep all of the artifacts he finds?" Her voice was tight with barely controlled rage.

He paused, thinking of Zek, the magic, and everything about the lore he apparently didn't know. *So much for being a Lorist one day.*

"Markus." Lorlie shot him a sharp glare.

"Warehouses," he said, forcing a smile. "They take all the artifacts and statues not on display to the warehouses on the other side of the city."

She nodded. "Good."

"How come?"

She scowled, and Markus thought she would tell him again that she wasn't interested in answering any questions, but instead, she said, "You know that answer."

He paused. "The watch?"

She nodded, and his heart started to beat faster. "And this watch will possibly bring the magic back?"

"That's my guess."

Markus bit the edge of his tongue to keep himself from peppering her with more questions. *If I had magic,* he couldn't help but think, *if it would just come back, I could be someone people actually liked.*

Someone worth seeing.

Lorlie glanced at him. There was an intensity there in the depths of her eyes, and it burned—as if they were flames searing straight into his soul. "So," she said, "ready to go break into some warehouses?"

CHAPTER SEVEN

LORLIE

"But where there is beauty and light, darkness always lurks at the edges."

–From *The Book of Legends, Volume Forty-Nine*

THREE WEEKS LATER, they were still searching. Lorlie glared at the looming metal structure of the last warehouse. Each storage building had been filled with remnants of the old world. But none of them contained the key to Lorlie's freedom. Numbly, she walked to the door set into the side of the structure. Secondary entrances like this one were consistently neglected by the guards patrolling the front of the warehouse, which provided them with the opportunity to get in and out without anyone ever knowing. She quickly picked the lock and eased the door open just wide enough to slip in. Markus followed. The door clicked shut, and they were plunged into the darkness.

Pausing, she tilted her head back, staring at the black surrounding her. It was so thick; she could feel it pressing against her skin like an icy palm. It took her back to the tower where she'd once been imprisoned.

The watch isn't going to be here. She knew it. Still, she inched forward until she was met with the hard frame of one of the shelves that ran down the length of the warehouse. Running her hand along the rack, she carefully felt each of the objects on it. A small rectangle box. A ring. Some sort of folded cloth. A cup.

A small rustle indicated Markus sorting through the items on the shelf directly across from her. They'd manage to develop a sort of system for working together over the weeks, though it still felt strange to have someone always around. Especially someone so energetically *happy* as Markus was.

But it was nice to not be alone.

That was a dangerous, dangerous thought.

People like her always ended up alone.

Time slunk by as they searched aisle after aisle. But there wasn't anything even close to resembling a pocket watch. The longer it went, the less Lorlie could force herself to actually pay attention to what she was doing.

It had been a thousand years; what if the watch had been destroyed?

He would never allow that. Would he?

The watch had been precious to the man who cursed her, as it had belonged to his father. Surely he would have found a way to preserve it, wouldn't he?

"Hey, Lor," Markus whispered from the shelf opposite to her. "This fork is glowing."

Lorlie turned. Markus was a faint outline in the darkness. In his hand, he held up a fork that was pulsing with sky-blue light.

"Put that away," she hissed.

"What does it do?"

Lorlie glared at him, although he probably couldn't see.

"Well?" he insisted, holding the fork towards her.

"How am I supposed to know?"

"You're the magical artifact expert!"

"Yes, well, I only know about the ones created or used during my lifetime." She turned back to the rack and continued feeling around. "I'm sure there are plenty of artifacts that were made after I was trapped in my stupid curse."

He sighed softly. A moment later, she heard the slight thud of his retreating footsteps.

She tried to focus on the objects in front of her.

A wooden rod. The skeletal rim of an eyeglass. What felt like a telescope with cracked lenses. She picked them up, fingered every angle, and gently set them back down.

Where is it?

Many of the artifacts had been created by powerful magic holders who knew how to combine the correct curse or blessing to create a magic-infused object. Many of them still worked, a discovery that had been exciting at first. But despite hours of trying to feel the magic in them, all she'd been able to sense was the cold running in her own veins. Like the cursed statues, the objects contained mere residues left over from the magic.

Lorlie reached the end of the aisle and pressed her palms flat against the rack, closing her eyes. But her eyelids couldn't keep out the darkness in the warehouse. It didn't stop the chill creeping down her spine. It couldn't mend the hole in her chest or the memories that bled in her mind.

Standing there, heart squeezing in her chest, she watched the tower's stone walls rise to life around her. It was small, claustrophobic, with a window barely the size of her head. The smell of rotten air tickled her nose. Lorlie could have sworn she felt chains cinched around her wrists once more.

She leaned her forehead against the metal rack.

"*Lesson one,*" her curser's voice said. For a moment, he was there, standing in the darkness in front of her, just as he had that day in the tower. Messy brown hair. Hazel eyes. He leaned forward, locking her gaze with his. "*No one is coming to save you.*"

Not him.

Not her fiance.

No one.

So she'd picked herself up from that tower floor and saved herself. "I don't know if I can do that this time," she whispered. The words wisped in the air, barely making a sound.

Maybe it wasn't worth it.

Maybe it would be better to just turn back to stone.

CHAPTER EIGHT

MARKUS

"That darkness found the princess."

–From *The Book of Legends, Volume Forty-Nine*

PAIN SHOT THROUGH Markus's brow as his forehead connected with a hard edge.

Ugh . . . Not again.

The shelf creaked as it wobbled, and he grabbed the metallic object to steady it.

"Markus?" Lorlie hissed from across the aisle.

"Ran into a shelf," he mumbled.

It was the third time that day he'd almost brought the entire warehouse crashing down on them. "How am I supposed to navigate this place without any light?"

Lorlie, as usual, didn't respond.

Besides, even if she did, she'd probably say the same thing she'd said during each of their break-ins.

"*Use your hands, idiot.*"

Rubbing his forehead, he slowly inched along the shelf. Hundreds of artifacts were stored in the Lyhe warehouses. Objects he'd only ever read about. Many he'd never heard of. And now, there he was, *touching* them.

It was almost as good as finding an actual dragon's hoard.

A needle of guilt pricked at him. He didn't like the idea of breaking into anywhere, especially not a place owned by one of the most powerful families of the Age. *But this is important.* They had the chance to bring the magic back! Surely that made it worth it, *right?*

His hand brushed something smooth and cool and circular. It felt like glass. He picked it up. "Hey," he whispered. "Come here."

"What?" Lorlie suddenly appeared beside him, and his heart threatened to leap from his chest. "Did you find it?"

"Uh, no." Markus held out the artifact. "But what's this?"

"I don't have time for this," she muttered. But she took it anyway, bringing it close to her face so she could inspect it.

A heartbeat later, a pure white light sprang to life from the object in her palms. Markus let out a soft gasp. It was a crystal ball. Inside, white light swirled. It looked like the Milky Way. Lorlie held it up, and the light fell across her face, making it look as if her skin was glowing from an inner source of light.

"It's called a star," she said.

"A star?"

"Yes." She gave him a look. "But not the kind in the sky."

Markus grinned. "*Obviously.*"

She turned and surveyed the row they were standing in. Swords, compasses, hand-held mirrors, and so much more were all placed meticulously on the shelves. There were tiny tags attached to each item with what Markus guessed were the items' names. The star's light bounced off of them, bathing the entire aisle in a luminous glow.

"My grandpa would have loved to see this," Markus said. It was a quiet remark that didn't need an answer. But for some reason, it still stung when Lorlie didn't say anything. He reached out to brush his fingers on an elegant little mirror with blue glass. *'Fairest,'* the tag attached to the handle read.

Beside it was a folded bundle of gray cloth.

Markus picked it up. The tag was nestled inside its first fold.

'*Ghostmaker.*'

He shook it out, discovering that it was a wrinkled cloak. "Huh." He turned to show Lorlie, but she'd already walked over to the end of the aisle. Although she was still holding the artifact, the light remained all around him, sticking to the shelves and floor, stretching out like a carpet between him and her.

Um.

"Lorlie?"

She paused and glanced back. Markus motioned at the light.

"That's what it does," she said. "The light will retract once you get closer to it."

Sure enough, as he walked over, the light lapped at his heels, vanishing from the space behind him. It was as if the star was purposely supplying him with light. He took the orb from Lorlie and studied it. The light trickled around his hands, up his arms. "Hi," he wanted to whisper to it. He bit the tip of his tongue to keep the word in. "How is this working without magic? It doesn't make sense."

"I don't know, Markus."

He frowned. Now that he was holding the star, she no longer looked ethereal. She looked exhausted. The cold light cast a ghostly shadow across her face.

He'd often seen the same expression on his grandfather. It was a look of someone who was exhausted from years of carrying a weight they should never have had to pick up—years of fighting back an endless ocean.

In his grandfather's case, Markus had been that burden. Guilt, sharp and smothering, stabbed through him.

He glanced down at the star, then back at Lorlie. "Are you okay?" he asked.

Her scowl deepened. "Of course."

It wasn't true, though.

It never had been, no matter how much his grandfather had insisted that he was fine. No matter how many fake smiles Markus himself plastered on. No matter how much anger Lorlie threw at those around her.

Why do we always lie?

He handed the star back. "I guess we should keep looking."

"It doesn't matter," she said. "It's not here."

"Technically, we still have the rest of the warehouse to check. It could still—"

"It *isn't.*" With that, Lorlie slammed the star on the shelf and stomped back the way they had come. A heartbeat later, the light from the artifact blinked out, and Markus was drenched in darkness once again.

It was then, standing in the black, waiting for his eyes to adjust, that he heard the scraping sound of the warehouse's gigantic door opening.

CHAPTER NINE

LORLIE

"Watching her grow—as the magic did—year after year, the Darkness came to hate her. She was everything it was not. And so it desired to destroy her. If only to remove one more thing that reminded it of the monster it was."

–From *The Book of Legends, Volume Forty-Nine*

LORLIE DOVE BEHIND a rack. Bright sunlight flooded into the warehouse, turning the rows closest to the open door grayish and engulfing the ones farther back, where she was, with shadows. The distinct sound of footsteps clicked against the concrete floor.

"Mr. Lyhe said to search them all?" a man said. It echoed in the wide space.

"Yeah," a second, slightly deeper voice replied. "He's been uptight lately."

"Cause of the stolen statue?"

"Yep."

Lorlie shifted into a practiced crouch and peeked through the slit between the shelves. She could make out two guards in maroon suits picking their way down the path that ran through the center of the rows.

They each carried sticks with light that beamed at the end in one hand and a thin metal weapon Markus had before told her was called a 'gun' in the other. A madman named Ferozin Hai had once built an artifact that looked similar. As they walked, they flashed their lights down each row.

Her heartbeat quickened. Increasing to an almost painful *thud, thud, thud.*

Lorlie quickly pulled off her shoes and placed them on the bottom rack. It would be quieter without them. Barefoot, she leaned back on her heels and stared at one of the objects directly in front of her. It was a little baking pan; she could imagine it belonging to a child.

Forcing herself to breathe slowly, she focused on the image of the pan. Distantly, she registered the sound of the guards coming closer.

Breathe.

In. Out.

Her heartbeat returned to its normal rhythm. The tremble that had been creeping into her hands retreated.

Straightening, Lorlie crept to the end of the row, opposite of where the guards were. They left the massive warehouse door open. If she timed it right, she could step into the previously searched row right before the guards flashed their lights down this one. Then she'd escape out the front door, and they'd never even know she'd been here.

Something cold tingled at the edges of her fingertips.

She looked down. There was a faint sheen of gray marring them.

Markus.

She'd forgotten about Markus. For half a heartbeat, she closed her eyes. If she left without him, she'd probably turn to stone before getting but a few feet outside the warehouse. Besides, while she could probably avoid being seen, they were going to find Markus for sure.

Curse you, Aatoon! A jolt ran through her. She hadn't allowed herself to acknowledge her curser's name since waking.

And doing so made this all the more real.

The one person she'd thought cared about her had been the one to take everything.

I should have known.

I should have seen it.

"Who would ever steal a statue?" The first guard spoke up; his all-too-near voice snapped Lorlie's attention back into focus. The second just grunted as if he couldn't be bothered to put two brain cells toward an answer.

Lorlie gritted her teeth. *Fine.* She'd just have to take care of them. She pulled out a kitchen knife, which she'd stolen from Markus's apartment, from the inside pocket of her jacket. Listening to their footsteps draw nearer, Lorlie backtracked to the inner edge of the aisle, closest to where the guards would be passing.

How can I be gone for a thousand years and yet still have to fight like this to survive?

Maybe her family had been right. Maybe she didn't deserve a happy life.

As the first guard stepped into view, turning to flash their light down the aisle, Lorlie sprang forward. She slammed a foot into his stomach, making him stumble backward. Behind him the other guard jerked his gun upwards, panicking. She twisted, slicing the knife across his arm. He dropped his gun, and she snatched it mid-air. Stepping back, Lorlie aimed it at the guard she'd kicked. He had a young face, with curled black hair brushing the edges of his eyebrows. The other man was middle-aged, and slightly overweight.

They'd dropped their hand-held lights. The yellowed beams cast haunting shadows over them, the first guard staring at her in frozen horror, still holding his gun. The second slumped against one of the shelves, clutching a scarlet-drenched arm to his chest.

"Drop it," Lorlie said to the first. Her voice echoed back at her, foreignly empty. Just like she felt inside.

He didn't move.

"*Now.*"

Slowly, he stooped and placed the weapon on the ground at his feet.

"Move." She motioned toward the second guard. He reluctantly walked over to his partner, but his eyes didn't leave hers. Fear and anger fought over his expression. They were looks she'd come to know well. She'd been hated as a princess, but after her kingdom's fall, and her escape from the tower, she'd become a thief. A criminal. The kind of creature parents told stories of to scare their children into obedience. Lifting her chin, she slid her finger over the gun's trigger. She'd asked Markus how the weapons worked, and he'd made it sound fairly simple. "*You just point, and pull the trigger.*"

"Lorlie?"

She clenched her jaw but didn't turn towards Markus. She couldn't let the guards leave. They'd alert the Lyhes to her existence.

"What are you doing?"

It was such an innocent question, spoken so quietly, yet it buzzed in her brain.

What are you doing? What are you doing? What are you doing?

It was the same question that screamed through her when she killed Aatoon. The same question that wept when she'd refused to heal her ex-fiance of a fatal sickness.

"What has to be done," she said, more to herself than him.

"Lorlie, look at me."

She kept her focus on the guards. The one with the wounded arm was shaking from the pain of the deep cut. A tiny puddle of blood was forming at his feet. The other was glaring at her, obviously trying to appear brave. He didn't quite pull off the look.

Markus stepped up to her. He placed a hand on her arm, gentle but firm. Scowling, she glanced sideways at him.

"Give me the gun," he said softly, holding out his hand.

"No."

"We're not going to hurt anyone," he said.

Too late.

"Lorlie?"

She looked away from him, toward the guards. How many people had she hurt in her lifetime? Faces flashed through her memory. Too many to count. *Too many. Too many. Too many.* That was what she did—hurt people. Destroy things. Ruin relationships.

It was the only way to survive.

She tightened her grip on the gun.

"Lorlie, look at them."

She met their worried eyes.

"See?" Markus said with emphasis. As if there was something to be found in them. But whatever it was, she couldn't find it. All she saw were enemies who'd hurt her if she didn't hurt them first.

For some reason, though, she allowed Markus to ease the gun from her grasp, something that should have earned him an elbow to the gut. He then lifted the bloodied knife from her other hand.

"We're the good guys," he said to the men. "We're not here to hurt anyone. But we really need you to not tell anyone about us, okay?"

Right, like they'll listen. Lorlie jerked away from Markus and stomped to the side where they'd entered through.

He didn't understand.

She was not a hero.

Not a legend.

Not one of the 'good guys.'

She was a *beast.*

And if Markus stuck around her long enough, he too would be destroyed.

CHAPTER TEN

MARKUS

"And at the edges of the kingdom, the Darkness, the beast, plotted."

–From The Book of Legends, Volume Forty-Nine

MARKUS JOGGED TO catch up with Lorlie, their tether twinging uncomfortably in his gut. In just two streets, the section of stark metal warehouses had faded back to the city's usual bricked offices and stores. Up ahead, Lorlie stalked down the sidewalk, hands buried in her pockets, hair fuzzing and wild. She hadn't so much as glanced at him since storming out of the warehouse.

She almost killed them.

Horror still lingered at the edges of his mind. He was stuck on that image—the blood, the knife. Lorlie standing there with the gun aimed at their chests. She'd taken the two men out so quickly. *How did she know how to do that?* That wasn't something a princess should know how to do. That wasn't even something a normal person knew how to do.

He managed to catch up to her right as she turned onto another street. It would lead them to the Saucy Hut, Markus's workplace, where they'd been doing most of their research on the warehouses and artifacts over the last few weeks. "Hey," he said, trying not to breathe too heavily. "Can we talk about what just happened?"

Trams clacked down their tracks, full of passengers hurrying home for the evening. A few private transports buzzed past. On one of the buildings, someone had painted a faint golden figure, standing with their arms outstretched. 'The Guardian,' people called it. An ancient, powerful legend who used to protect those in danger. Now, its symbol was used as a way of warding off harm.

Markus slowly fisted his hands. They'd gotten blood on them—the guard's blood—when he took the knife from her. Seeing it on his tanned skin summoned a swirling mess of disgust and hurt. Those men hadn't deserved that. They'd simply been doing their job.

"Lorlie."

"No," she snapped.

Markus stopped. *No? Fine, then.* He folded his arms, feet frozen against the pale concrete, waiting. Sure enough, a few shops down, the tether snapped taut. Lorlie turned and stomped her way back.

"What?" She threw her hands up as she neared. "What do you want me to say? Those two guards are going to alert Zek Lyhe to my existence. We won't be able to just waltz around and search for the watch anymore, and that's on you, Markus!"

"You didn't have to hurt them," he said.

"They were about to see you!"

A retort burned on Markus's tongue, but he bit it back, forcing himself to pause and study her. To see her. She was scowling, eyes flaming embers. But there was more to her than this furious, stone-hard person.

Just like there's more to me.

The thought took him by surprise, and he barely stopped himself from visibly recoiling. That wasn't true. He wasn't . . .

What? that small voice inside of him asked. *You aren't a person like all of them? You aren't worth seeing?*

No, I'm not.

Markus Clint was a nobody. There was nothing amazing about him. Nothing useful. All he ever did was make other people's lives worse.

But with magic . . .

Taking a deep breath, he buried the thought and met Lorlie's unrelenting glare. "Why are you so angry, anyway?"

She scoffed, making a dismissive jerking motion with her hand.

"I'm serious. Why are you always so angry?"

Lorlie looked at him like he'd lost his mind. For a moment, he thought she was going to insist that she wasn't angry. "Because," she said instead, teeth clenched, "I am surrounded by idiots."

He almost laughed. "Really? That's not why."

"No. It's not." She looked away, watching the men and women passing them. Hatred shadowed her expression.

"So why?" he pressed. He knew he was being annoying, but he also couldn't help himself. He *needed* to know—and not just this. He needed to know everything. It was an attribute his grandfather had despised in him.

There were just *so* many amazing, fascinating things in the world just waiting for someone to stop and pay attention to them.

And he'd always had an insistent itching deep inside to do just that.

"Lorlie?"

She shrugged, glancing down at her feet—which were *bare*, Markus realized. *When did she take her shoes off?*

"Everyone I ever cared about either betrayed me or died because of me."

His heart thudded in his chest.

Who?

Why?

Questions poured through his mind, an avalanche of words, but he bit his tongue, waiting. After a few moments, she sighed. "You know the story in the lore book? The one about me?"

"Yeah?"

"It was right about one thing: there was a Darkness bent on destroying everyone around me. It simply failed to mention that *I* am that Darkness." She looked up, meeting Markus's eyes. "I am a beast. Remember that."

Markus's throat tightened.

"Now, can we please get back to Ned's place?" she mumbled.

Nodding, Markus self-consciously buried his hands in his pockets and started down the sidewalk. They were silent as they crossed the tram tracks and turned onto the Saucy Hut's street. It was a red brick building that was much smaller than many of the others on the street. Behind the building would be a driveway with the parked delivery transports.

"So, what are we going to do now?" Markus asked. They paused in front of the door. Usually, at this time in the evening, it was bursting with customers. But today, a quaint wooden sign hung over the door, reading, 'closed.'

"There's only one other place I can think of looking."

Markus pressed his lips into a line. "The mansion?"

"Castle," she corrected. "And yes. If it isn't still buried in the ground or in some thief's sock drawer, it'll be there."

"Breaking into the warehouses was one thing, but snooping around Mr. Lyhe's home?" Markus shook his head.

"He's our last option."

"And you can't ask him about it?"

"No."

If we can bring the magic back, it'll be worth it.

Markus took a deep breath and nodded. Pulling open the front door, they stepped into the Saucy Hut. The sharp scent of cleaner immediately accosted him, overpowering the usual comforting smell of baking pizza.

Inside the main lobby were two round tables atop a black-tiled floor and fenced in by dark walls with flecks of red and yellow.

"*The paint shows that we are professionals who love pizza.*" Ned, the owner of the Saucy Hut, and Markus's boss, had explained once. "*That's why we're so successful. Because of good color combinations.*"

Really, the Saucy Hut was successful because it had amazing pizza. And three delivery transports for every restaurant in the city. And because Ned underhandedly ran all the other pizzerias out of business.

You certainly didn't want to be on his bad side.

Ned's niece, Rose, sat at one of the tables, fiddling with a Sceptori figurine. She was around eight years old, with adorable red pigtails and a face full of freckles. She glanced up, and Markus grinned, flashing her a quick wave before walking over to the counter. "Hey, Ned?"

"Down here." Ned grunted. Markus leaned over the counter. The large man was on his hands and knees, scrubbing the floor with a wet rag. A dingy water bucket sat next to him. Markus smiled, shaking his head. There were plenty of workers who could clean the place, but Ned still insisted on doing it himself. Every single building. Every single day. When Markus had tried to convince him to do otherwise, he'd brushed him off.

"*You take care of the customers,*" he'd said. "*I take care of my hut.*"

"Ned," Markus repeated. His boss plopped the rag into the bucket and twisted to look up at him. Gray peppered Ned's buzzed hair and stubbled jaw, making him look like someone's grandfather. He wasn't. Just someone's uncle. Markus cast an affectionate glance back at Rose.

"Boy," Ned said, "I'm cleaning."

"I can see that."

"And?"

"And we need some advice." Behind him, Lorlie snorted. She hadn't wanted to get his boss involved anyway, but Markus trusted Ned. He was the closest thing he had to family now. Plus, Ned was one of the few left who still fervently believed that the magic was going to come back one day.

"On what?" he grunted.

"Potentially . . . breaking into the Lyhe mansion." Markus winced.

Ned stared at him for a long time before releasing a drawn-out sigh and rose to his feet. "Fine. I also put in a pizza for you two, so you have to wait for that anyway. I'm not boxing it. You'll have to do that."

"Thanks, Ned," Markus said. His boss huffed, but a smile twitched at his lips as he lumbered over to the table in the corner of the restaurant, where Lorlie had stationed herself. He sat down, and Markus eased into the seat between them. "So, uh, Lorlie, do you have a plan?"

Folding her arms, she leaned back in her seat. "Get in, find the watch, get out."

"That's if that old artifact is even there," Ned said.

"Obviously," she said.

Ned nodded slowly. "And I suppose you'll need a driver nearby to pull you out should you need to run?"

"Wait, hold up." Markus leaned his elbows on the table. "Are you telling me we might have a high-speed chase on our hands?"

"You should not look so excited at the prospect of that," Ned said.

Markus grinned. He'd read story after story of heists and chases. But he'd never thought he'd *be* in one.

Not that I will be, he reminded himself. *That's only if we get caught.*

"It's probably best if we avoid getting caught," Markus said. Lorlie rolled her eyes at him.

Ned nodded. "Right, which is why I'm going to make sure you kiddos actually have a plan." He pulled a piece of paper from his pocket and slapped it onto the table. A blueprint of the mansion.

CHAPTER ELEVEN

LORLIE

"On the princess's seventeenth birthday, it made its move. Sweeping in on shadowed wings, the Darkness let loose a furious flood of fire and death upon the kingdom. All who had loved the princess were soon gone, buried beneath rubble and ash."

–From *The Book of Legends, Volume Forty-Nine*

LORLIE PICKED AT the edge of the Lyhedrune castle's blueprint. "I told you," she said to Ned, "I know that castle. I don't need this." She had spent a lot of time wandering those halls during festivals, and family get-togethers. Being Sorik Lyhedrune's fiance had required her to be present, but no one had ever cared if she was actually there. So she'd been left to entertain herself.

Ned grunted. "Still. Run through it one more time."

Fine. Sighing, Lorlie straightened in her seat. Markus had lost interest a long time ago, and was now across the room, animatedly talking to Ned's niece about something. The little girl held a figurine of a man with animal-like features. Whiskers. Too-wide eyes. Hair that flared in an unnatural way. It was supposed to be a Sceptori.

These people know nothing.

A real Sceptori was a powerful magic-wielder, born with an unnatural cavity in their chest, right beside their heart, that the magic would fill as they grew older. They had the unique ability to shapeshift. But otherwise, they looked like any other human being.

They weren't.

They were the world's judges. The rulers of kings. If they didn't like what a kingdom was doing, that kingdom either changed or was destroyed.

Ned cleared his throat. Lorlie rolled her eyes and pointed to the back side of the map where an office was outlined. It had once been the King's office. "We'll wait till the middle of the night, then climb over the fence on the east side, where the guards at the front gate won't be able to see us. The design of the brick on the castle makes it perfect for climbing, so we should be able to scale that up to the office window."

"And then?" Ned prompted.

Lorlie glared at him. "*Then* I search the rooms for the watch, hopefully find it, and we meet up with you on the east side, where we first entered."

Of course, that wasn't what she was going to do, but the old man didn't need to know that.

Ned absently picked up one of the pizza slices left in the box between them, and took a bite, nodding slowly. The triangular sauce and cheese smothered dough was similar to something Lorlie had had before, back in her Age. A chef from across the sea had visited her father, and as a gift, he'd toasted chunks of bread with cheese covering the top, and a spiced sauce to go alongside it. It had been her sister's favorite. Lorlie frowned at the brightly colored box. Somehow though, even without magic, this version tasted far better.

Folding the blueprint, she said, "So we're done here?"

Ned took another bite of his pizza slice. A thin trail of grease trickled down his chin, and he swiped it away. "I suppose. Though, I did want to mention one thing." He leaned forward, blue eyes piercing hers. "If you can bring the magic back, then it'll be worth this. But I don't want anything happening to that boy over there." He jerked his head toward Markus. "You understand?"

"Perfectly," Lorlie said drily.

She watched silently as Ned rose, gave her one last significant look, and strode back over to finish scrubbing the floor.

What would it be like to have someone actually care like that?

At the other table, the little girl let out an excited gasp. Lorlie shifted her attention to them, listening as Markus described a wyvern named Cringefold the Burnt. He made the guy sound amazing and heroic. Terrifying, even.

Nothing like the real Cringefold.

She'd read the lore piece on old Cringy, and while it had painted him in an impressive light, Markus somehow managed to make the wyvern seem as though he'd been an other-wordly creature, filled with power and beauty.

How does he do that? How can he take a simple character from an ink-stained page, and make it sound so magical?

After a long moment, Lorlie stood and walked over. Markus paused, glancing at her. A slight shade of pink crept into his cheeks. "Oh, Lorlie, are you ready to go?"

Lorlie knelt and studied the little girl's face. Ned's niece had wide, curious eyes, and freckles that swam like a school of tiny fish across her face. The girl smiled at her, then leaned toward Lorlie. "Markus says you're a princess," she whispered.

"Did he, now?" Lorlie glanced sideways at him. Markus rubbed the back of his neck, grinning.

A little flicker of warmth, so faint she nearly didn't notice it, stirred inside of her.

"I suppose he's right." A rare smile tugged at Lorlie's lips. "But I'll have you know, I'm not one of those helpless princesses from the stories." She crossed her arms. "I killed a dragon, once."

She said it like it was something to be proud of. It wasn't, though.

It was her greatest shame.

"How?" The girl was all grins and bouncing excitement. "What happened?"

Lorlie rested her elbows on her knees and cocked her head thoughtfully. If Markus could make Cringefold into something he wasn't, she could take the liberty to tell this story the way she wanted it to be, instead of its bleak reality.

"He lived in a cave on the top of Whistling Mountain. Growing up, I would look out my bedroom window at the blanket of black smoke choking the sky above it and wonder when someone would do something about him. The smoke contaminated the air, hurting everyone in our kingdom. But everyone was afraid of the great dragon. They didn't want his wrath to fall upon us. And so, after years and years, our people began to get sick. Their lungs were poisoned from the foul air." Lorlie paused, vision blurring. Why couldn't this have been the reality? Poisoned air due to a rogue dragon would have been a better fate than a Sceptori's wrath. "So one day," she said quietly, "I decided to do something about it. For . . . for my people."

Her heart squeezed.

"I set out to climb up that mountain and confront him." Lorlie glanced at Markus. He was perched on the edge of his seat, watching with rapt attention. Flecks of gold danced in his dark eyes. *Have they always been that color?*

"What happened next?" the girl asked. "Did he eat you?"

Lorlie raised an eyebrow.

If he ate me, how am I here?

"He was furious," Lorlie continued. "The sky and mountain trembled with his roars! I could barely see my hand in front of my face because of the amount of smoke pouring from his seething mouth, like a cauldron bubbling over. He vowed that I wouldn't live another day."

"*Then* did he eat you?" the girl breathed.

"Obviously not!" But she couldn't stop a smile from breaking free. "No one gets eaten in this story, little girl."

Ned's niece giggled.

Lorlie had been so angry that night when Aatoon confessed to destroying her kingdom. Since escaping the tower, she had searched for the dragon responsible. To kill him. A life for many, many lives lost. Aatoon deserved to die.

But . . .

All she wanted right now was to talk to him, one last time.

Why does it hurt so much?

"Okay, but what did you do?" the girl asked. Lorlie's smile slowly faded. This child thought that it was a grand thing, to kill a dragon. But she didn't understand. There was no way she could.

Only a monster could kill a monster.

The blood staining Lorlie's soul was proof of that.

The girl impatiently tapped her on the arm, and Lorlie took a deep breath, trying to slow her heart's thudding. ". . . I drew my golden sword and slew him."

Red dripped through the black of her mind.

Crimson pooled at her feet.

The cold hilt of a magic-coated sword bit into her palm.

Hazel eyes pinned her in place.

"*This is my gift to you," Aatoon whispered. "See?*" She could hear him, feel the flakes of ash against her skin, as if she were back in that moment, in the rubble of what was once her kingdom.

Lorlie pulled back from the girl.

"That's so cool!" the girl squealed. "I wish I was a princess! I wanna slay a dragon!"

No, you don't.

Rising from her crouched position, Lorlie struggled to swallow around the lump forming in her throat. "Anyway, I think it's time to go."

The girl jumped to her feet, and—unexpectedly—threw her arms around Lorlie's waist, hugging her tight. Lorlie blushed. What was she supposed to do? Awkwardly, she patted the girl on the back. But as that little girl looked up at her, a bright, unfaltering smile on her face, Lorlie felt the stone around her heart soften.

She wished, in that moment, that she could have known this beautiful little girl her whole life. Maybe Lorlie would have ended up a different person if she had known just one kind soul. Maybe this little girl could have saved her from becoming a beast.

"*No one is coming to save you,*" Aatoon had told her.

But they could have. They could have. There'd been so many opportunities. So many moments when she'd been looking for someone to simply stretch out their hand to her.

I don't deserve that, though, do I?

CHAPTER TWELVE

MARKUS

"The princess alone survived."

–From *The Book of Legends, Volume Forty-Nine*

MARKUS LAID ON his torn, coffee-stained couch, and stared at the bumpy tan dots on the ceiling. They'd come back to his apartment to wait for it to get dark, then they'd head over to Wolf Park to scout out the mansion grounds, and wait for the right moment to trespass on the property of one of the most important men in the world.

He replayed the scene at the Saucy Hut. Lorlie kneeling in front of Rose. For a moment, all the hardness, all the ferocity, was gone. Her gray eyes shined as she described trekking up that mountain to confront the dragon that was harming her people.

Lorlie had *smiled*. For the first time since waking, she'd actually smiled—while telling a story about slaying a dragon, no less.

And it turned out, her smile was kind of beautiful.

That was her. The real Lorlie. The person she hides from everyone.

Beneath the fire and stone, there is a girl who isn't angry. A girl who cared. A girl who can laugh, and be kind, and tell stories to little kids.

"These books are useless," Lorlie said at the table across the room. She slammed the book closed. It was one of the ones he'd collected—an old record of the lore.

"They're not," he said. "They're history."

"They're an idiot's fantasy about what happened in history. Not what actually happened."

He frowned. *Easy for you to say.* To him, and everyone else alive, those were the only records they had. The only tangible thing to suggest that life was once different.

"Take, for example, this record of Clek the Terrible!" Lorlie jabbed a hand aggressively down at the book. "This states that he was a giant who destroyed the Alafri's city hall. He wasn't! He was a rebel leader who gained the loyalty of a giant named Timlin—who accidentally knocked over city hall during a peace negotiation."

"Really?"

She met his gaze. "Really."

Swinging his legs off the couch, he sat up, eagerly. The padlock he'd been practicing to pick clanked against the floor. "Why don't we write a new record of history? Seriously, think about it!"

Lorlie pressed her lips into a thin line. At last, she turned and looked down at the book. "I read in here that you people think the Sceptori are heroes." The words were a hushed whisper, barely audible.

"They are," Markus said. "They saved the world! Multiple times."

"No, they're not." She placed a fist against the cover of the book. "A Sceptori is who destroyed it."

Markus was silent. For once he didn't want to hear more. Not really. It felt like every time Lorlie opened her mouth, she ripped away another chunk of the beautiful tapestry he'd built from the lore.. The one he needed to hide the emptiness inside of him.

What would Grandpa think if he heard that the only thing he loved in life was a lie?

He shifted and looked down at the floor. Faded scuff marks crisscrossed over each other on the wooden planks. "The story you told, was it true?"

When Lorlie didn't answer, he looked back up. She'd closed her eyes. And she seemed . . . weak. Frail. Like at any moment, a breath of wind could carry her away.

"Some of it," she said.

"Which parts?"

Markus glanced at her hands. She was clenching and unclenching them, her knuckles whitening more each time.

"I did kill a dragon," Lorlie said, eyes still closed. "But not to save my people."

"Why, then?"

Lorlie opened her eyes. Her expression hardened. "To avenge them."

"And . . ." He took a deep breath. "That's why you were cursed?"

"That's why I was cursed."

It made sense. The blood that had been on her hands when she first woke. Her torn dress. The ashes smeared across her face. But it disturbed him that the lore hadn't even hinted at it. Was everything they knew really so terribly wrong?

"I'm sorry," he said.

"For what?"

He waved his hand. "I don't know. That your kingdom was destroyed, I guess. That you had to kill someone, even if they were just a dragon."

She paled.

Wait . . .

"Lorlie," he said. "It *was* a dragon, right?"

"Of course it was."

But her eyes said otherwise.

His stomach sank. Standing, he cleared his throat and nodded to the door. "It's about time to head there, right?"

"Right," she said, voice flat.

He led the way out of the apartment, and toward the tram station outside. To distract himself from the idea of Lorlie having murdered someone, Markus ran over the plan in his mind. Ned and Lorlie had decided it would be best for them to wait in a park located right beside the east section of the mansion grounds. That way, once it got late enough, they'd be ready to sneak onto the property. Hopefully everyone in the mansion would be asleep.

And hopefully, this will be worth it.

CHAPTER THIRTEEN

LORLIE

"The Darkness took her up in its mighty claws. Its vengeance would not be satiated by simply killing her. And so it took her up to the top of an abandoned tower, and there she remained for many days."

–From *The Book of Legends, Volume Forty-Nine*

PALE STARS STARED down at Lorlie, condemning and angry. She glared back. Aatoon had told her on a number of occasions that the sky, the stars, were where the magic came from. But if there was magic up there, why couldn't she reach up and drag it down to her?

The branches of the oak trees growing around Wolf Park quivered in the breeze, casting giant, monstrous shadows across the lawn. She sat with her back against a hard wooden bench, impatiently waiting for the last of the transports parked in front of the mansion to leave. If she glanced over her shoulder, she could see the castle's black fence looming high into the air.

"That's Calypso," Markus said, pointing to a gleaming pattern on the far right of the sky. He lay on the grass, looking up at the stars. He'd been pointing out constellations for the last half-hour.

He should have abandoned me already.

The thought itched in the back of her mind, but she tried to dismiss it. Once they were sure no one was around, they'd break into the castle, and then, well, if the watch was there, she'd break her curse, and Markus would never have to see her again.

Nor I him.

She reached out as if to cup the inky black in her hands. It passed right through her fingers, cold and empty. In the distance, she could just barely make out the faint outlines of the blocky buildings around the park. The night should have been glistening with golden light, not this . . . void.

How can they live like this? A sour taste crept across her tongue.

Voices and faces flickered in the back of her mind, memories she didn't want to remember. Sorik. Aatoon. Her father. Mother. Sister. A thousand years later, and they were still plaguing her. *Why can't they all just die?*

All the memories.

All the guilt.

All of it.

She was so tired.

"That's a siren." Markus pointed to another cluster of stars.

Lorlie sighed and raked a hand through her tangled hair. It was a mess, but she hadn't bothered with it since waking. Why should she? There was no one left she cared to look good for. *Not that there ever was.*

She paused. No. That wasn't right. There were times when she had tried—really tried—to be who she thought her family wanted her to be. But it never seemed to matter. There was nothing she could do to make them care about her.

It was never enough.

"There was this bully named Kenth at the school I went to when I was young," Markus said. "Everyone hated him. Everyone. He threw kids' lunches to the ground. Locked us in closets. Was basically awful in every way."

"Sounds like he needed a good punch to the face," Lorlie said.

Markus was quiet for a few heartbeats. "That's what the others thought. One afternoon they planned on ganging up on him, to, y'know, teach him a lesson. Payback for everything he'd done."

She nodded. That was understandable. Probably for the best, even. If Aatoon had been one of those in on the plan, the boy would have probably died instead of simply getting knocked around a bit. Aatoon had been a Sceptori of the purest form—emotionless, unmoveable, and above all else, the very definition of *judgment.*

She'd never understood why he hadn't killed her

"I couldn't just let them do that," Markus continued, voice soft. "So that day, I followed him home."

Lorlie frowned. "To warn him?"

"No," he said.

"Then why?"

"Just to see."

She rolled her eyes. "See what, exactly?"

Markus sat up and crossed his legs. The park's only lamp splashed yellow light across his skin and clothes. He tilted his head to the side, studying her with a gaze that felt like he could peer straight through to her soul.

"To see," he said slowly, "whether Kenth was worth saving."

Chills spiderwebbed down her spine, though she didn't know why. *Was he?* she wanted to ask. But she already knew the answer. "And you found that he wasn't," she said. "He deserved to get beat up."

Beneath the yellow lamp, surrounded by shadows, Markus looked sad. Overwhelmingly so. He slowly shook his head. "People deserve a lot of things. But that doesn't mean you have to give it to them."

Something splintered inside of her chest, the tiniest crack in her stone armor.

That's not true.

Markus sighed, and laid back against the grass, staring at the star-speckled sky. "Kenth loved the stars," he said. "He had his own scope, and constellation trackers, and everything. Those little lights up there were his only friends. He wanted to be an Astronomer. His mother was an invalid, though. And he was going to have to drop out of school at the end of the semester to take care of her and his two younger siblings."

"None of that matters," she pointed out. "He was still an awful human being."

"He was," Markus agreed. "But he wasn't only an awful human being. He was good things too. He was *more*."

Lorlie blinked.

He was more.

How did Markus see that? None of those details mattered in the face of the terrible things he had done.

"I wonder what he's doing, now," Markus whispered, more to himself than anything.

Lorlie looked up. Somehow, although nothing had changed, the stars didn't look so angry anymore. They'd softened. Reminding her of the nights she'd snuck out to the royal gardens behind her castle and listened to Aatoon tell her bedtime tales beneath a blanket of glowing constellations.

"Did you save him?" she asked.

"Yeah."

Lorlie leaned her head against the back of the bench, picturing that bully sitting outside his home, staring up at the stars, just like she'd often done. Aatoon had often told her that people should always get what they deserve.

But . . . she wasn't so sure anymore.

CHAPTER FOURTEEN

ZEK

"A prince of a nearby kingdom heard of her peril. He knew of the darkness and the magic's blessing. And so with great courage, he marched upon the tower—only to find it empty."

–From *The Book of Legends, Volume Forty-Nine*

ALL HIS LIFE, Zek Lyhe had many things to miss. He'd grown up on stories about a beautiful world, with castles and dragons and miracles. Things he could never have because it had all been torn away by the magic. Corrupted. Destroyed. It may be strange to miss things you've never had—but he felt the absence like a wound that never fully healed.

Zek had also missed his father, every hour the stern man spent locked away in his office.

He'd missed the guards and servants who'd been dismissed over the years.

And the few friends he'd had as a child before he'd been forced into his family's secluded life.

He missed the awe he used to have for the magic. Before he had seen what it could do.

But the thing he missed the most, was his mother.

Especially now. He sat in his father's too-big office chair and stared at a photograph of his mother. A hole ached inside of his chest. It had been four years since she'd gone insane after losing his father to the magic.

Four years.

Yet the pain remained.

Just like the curse that had been passed down their family line for generations.

He rubbed his eyes, and looked up at the darkness beyond the window pane. Most of the city was asleep, but there never seemed to be rest for him. He had too much to worry about.

Like the fact that one of his statues had vanished.

A knock came at the door. Zek ignored it. He'd sent more men to watch the warehouses after hearing that two individuals had broken in and assaulted some of his guards earlier that evening. But it wasn't going to be enough. Not if this person was who he thought she was.

Not if she figures out what happened with the magic.

The door swung open, and his head of security stepped in. Closing the door quietly behind himself, the aging hulk of a man turned to face Zek. Casually tossing the photograph back in the desk drawer, Zek proffered a lazy smile in the man's direction. "Yes?"

"Don't do that," Cason said sharply. "Don't lie to me."

"I'm not lying."

"Yes, you are."

Fine. Zek dropped the smile.

"What are you going to do?" Cason asked, unmoving from his place by the door

Zek planted his elbows on the desk and laced his fingers together. He took his time deciding how to reply. Cason had been the head of security for almost as long as Zek could remember. He'd been his father's most trusted advisor. But he still didn't know everything about the Lyhe family or what they kept secret from the world.

"I'm still considering the best course of action." He thought of the statue that had vanished and cold immediately pricked the back of his neck. *The Forgotten Princess.* His family had done an impeccable job at erasing her existence from history, but he'd read the journal written by his ancestor, Prince

Sorik, the first to fall to the curse. She was the one who placed it on them, who doomed every firstborn heir to a slow death.

She's the reason father's dead.

And mother . . .

Eyes burning, he gritted his teeth. This was not a time for weakness. His parents had left him this legacy, this job. To protect the world from the beasts of the past and to ensure that the magic never returned to what it had once been.

He stood. "I have it under control."

Cason hesitated. "Zek," he said softly. "I loved your parents. You know that, but your father made a mistake."

"He would have been fine if—"

"No," Cason interrupted, "don't lie to *yourself*, either, boy. He made a mistake. He let fear control him. And right now, you have the same look on your face that he did all those years ago."

Zek lifted his chin. "I'm not going to make a mistake."

"He said the same thing."

"I'm not having this conversation with you. All you need to know is that I have it handled." Cason pressed his lips into a thin line. For a moment he just stared, then—*finally*—he pivoted on his heel, and left, shutting the door quietly behind him.

Zek stood there, listening to the man's retreating steps slowly fade away. Barely controlled claws of fear tightened around his chest and throat, making it difficult to breathe.

For a moment, he was consumed by the memory of his father's death. He'd been sixteen. Only a boy. Barely grasping what it meant to be a descendant of Sorik Lyhedrune. Desperate to survive, his father had somehow managed to make a hole in the magic's prison and draw out some of its power.

When Zek closed his eyes, he could still see the angry explosion of seething golden light melting his father from the inside out.

His breath came in quick, tight gasps.

That could happen to other people if the magic was tampered with.

"*I trust you*," he could almost hear his mother's voice saying. They both had trusted him to keep the magic contained—to ensure their legacy continued.

And now that *girl* was somewhere out there. She was the only one who knew the true version of history, other than himself.

He rubbed the side of his face as the deep ache in his jaw became demanding. Walking over to the mirror on the wall, he peered at his reflection. His father would have been horrified to see his office outfitted with a mirror. No one in his family had been allowed to have anything even remotely reflective. Mother had had absolute fits over it. But she'd never won. His father had been too afraid to see the curse. Had been desperate to not be reminded of his impending death.

Ignoring it hadn't changed anything, though.

So Zek preferred to look his situation in the face. That was the only way to handle problems, after all.

Cracks seething a dark, sickly gold spider-webbed up half his face. It throbbed with a low, torturing pain at all times. He brushed his fingers against his cheek, but he couldn't feel anything other than smooth skin—which was exactly what anyone who wasn't looking into a reflective surface saw.

Even after his men tracked down the awakened statue, what was he supposed to do with her? "I don't know what to do, Mom," he whispered.

But that was a lie.

He *did.*

He just didn't want to do it. Didn't want to hurt anyone—even someone who should be dead.

The weight that always seemed to pull on his shoulders doubled. He planted a palm against the wall to brace himself, still staring at the jagged lines on his face.

His ancestors had broken the magic in an attempt to remove it from the world.

His family hid the fact that the magic still existed.

Generation upon generation had borne this weight—and succeeded.

The glass blurred until all Zek could see was his weakness.

He could see his mother, the disapproval in her eyes. His father saying he was right, that Zek was nothing but a failure.

I'll fix it, he promised silently.

I have to.

And not just for his family. There was a city—and entire world—out there who lived happy, peaceful lives because the magic wasn't active anymore. If it were to come back to full strength, lives would be endangered.

Shoving away from the wall and mirror, Zek stalked back to the desk and pulled another drawer open. Inside was a single sleek, metallic object shaped vaguely like a pistol. Intricate golden etchings were melded across its barrel, contrasting the dark shadow it cast. Zek slowly picked it up. Once, as a child, his father had warned him to never touch it, no matter the circumstance.

But it was the only way he could think of getting rid of the girl. He couldn't let magic return to what it once was. He tucked the weapon in his belt.

No matter the cost.

CHAPTER FIFTEEN

MARKUS

"The Darkness, you see, was a clever creature. It had foreseen the prince's rescue and carried the princess away once again. In a garden, overgrown with thorned roses, the Darkness placed a curse upon her."

–From *The Book of Legends, Volume Forty-Nine*

MARKUS HAULED HIMSELF onto the window sill, puffing from exertion. Lorlie had managed to wrench the window open and was already inside.

He slipped through the opening and dropped onto lush, maroon carpet. Soft white light spilled from elegant oval lamps attached to the tan walls, illuminating the large office. *Do they just permanently keep the lights on in here?* He blinked as his eyes sluggishly adjusted. Lorlie stood a few steps inside the room with her back to him. A full sized mirror hung next to the closed door opposite the window, with red-framed paintings lining the walls. To the right was a huge, curved desk. Empty space filled the rest of the room, making it seem like a hollowed shell.

"Wow," Markus breathed. He walked over to the paintings, bouncing slightly on the thick carpet. One was of a dragon with gold scales, an ocean of flames pouring from its open mouth onto a crumbling castle. Beside it was a portrait of a blond-haired man sitting atop a throne, holding a thorned rose. The swirling style of the painter's brush strokes looked like it belonged to the Age of Kings. For a thousand-year-old painting, it was *incredibly* preserved.

"Lorlie, do you see this?"

"I do have eyes," she mumbled.

Markus glanced over his shoulder. She'd moved to the desk and was riffling through the drawers. He was pretty sure she hadn't, in fact, stopped to see what he was talking about. Biting back a sigh, he walked over to inspect the mirror. It struck him as strange to see a full-length mirror inside of an office. But who was he to say what belonged there? He'd certainly never had an office himself.

"You still sure this is the castle?" Markus asked.

"Yes. It's identical. This used to be the king's office."

Turning slowly, he scanned the room. It had a quiet—yet impressive—elegance to it, with its dark red floor, and delicate lamps. Yes. He could see a king sitting behind the desk, signing decrees, or standing in front of the window, gazing out on his kingdom. "My grandfather wanted to be a Lorist, you know," he said. "Standing here, in an office that once belonged to kings of the past would have been a dream come true."

Markus couldn't remember ever seeing his grandfather actually happy. He'd simply been too exhausted from working, too angry that he never pursued lore. *Too burdened with me.*

"Is that why you're obsessed with the lore?" Lorlie asked. She slammed the last desk drawer closed a little too loudly, then pulled out the high-backed chair, and stooped to check underneath. Though, why she thought the watch might be under there, he had no clue.

"Maybe," Markus said, watching. "In the beginning, perhaps. But I really do think our history is amazing. I mean, the world had magic! And dragons, Lorlie, *dragons.*" *And people who were important, and adored.*

People Markus could only dream of being.

Lorlie stood and shoved the chair back into place. Frustration pulled at the corners of her frown. He didn't think she was going to find anything useful in here, especially not the pocket watch. It would probably be in a display case somewhere.

Walking over to the window, he cocked his head at it. Darkness seemed to drip from the glass, smothering the world beyond. "You know, I once read about this really cool bird creature that could light itself on fire. It only came out at night, and—"

"Hush," Lorlie snapped. Markus's words died on his lips, and he turned as footsteps thudded in the hallway outside. Markus froze. But Lorlie immediately dashed across the room and managed to slip behind the door right as it swung open. A tall young man with messy blond hair walked in, head down as he sorted through a handful of letters.

Markus's heartbeat hammered against his chest. He glanced at Lorlie, who was glowering at him in an annoyed way like she was irritated at him for getting them caught.

But he hadn't done anything wrong.

The man looked up and dropped the letters he'd been sorting through.

"Um, hi," Markus stammered.

The man stared at him. "Where did you come from?"

"The . . . window," Markus said. Heat flushed through his face. That sounded so dumb. But any useful words had fled his mind.

"Ah, yes, the window. Of course." The man's initial shock faded, and a calm mask clicked into place.

Markus blinked. Then focused on his face. Did he look familiar? He had a strong jawline and pale green eyes. The maroon suit he wore was immaculate, pressed free of even the slightest hint of a wrinkle. He wore it proudly, shoulders thrown back, gaze confident.

No way . . .

Markus *had* seen him before.

On banners in the city.

"You're Zek Lyhe!" Markus blurted. *I'm standing in front of the person who single-handedly controls all of the lore in the entire world.* He never imagined meeting Zek this way.

A small smirk twitched at the edges of Zek's mouth. "Indeed. And you are?"

"Markus." He shifted, nerves forming needles in his skin. "And uh, you weren't supposed to be awake right now." Markus winced. That was probably not the best thing to say.

Zek made a dismissive motion with his hand. "Oh, I never sleep. Anyway, you were going to explain why you climbed through my window?"

Actually, I wasn't. Markus cleared his throat, about to tell him so when he was distracted once again by the portrait of the prince. The figure in it looked rather similar to Zek, in fact.

"Prince Sorik," Zek said.

Markus blinked. "What?"

"The man in the portrait. His name is Prince Sorik." Zek nodded to the portrait. "He isn't very well known among the legends, unfortunately. Probably because he was never crowned king and died at an extremely young age."

It was at that moment that Lorlie slipped from behind the door like a ghost. She pulled something silver from inside of her jacket, and before Markus could stop her, she grabbed Zek from behind and pressed a thin knife blade against his throat.

CHAPTER SIXTEEN

LORLIE

"And there the princess was turned to stone."

–From *The Book of Legends, Volume Forty-Nine*

LIGHTLY PRESSING THE knife she'd found in one of the desk drawers to the skin of Zek Lyhe's neck, Lorlie leaned forward and hissed, "Where is Aatoon's pocket watch?"

Markus still stood by the window, a hint of fear creeping into his eyes. "Careful," he said, voice sharp from worry.

Lorlie ignored him and wiggled the knife a little bit, just so the stupid Lyhedrune descendant could feel it. "Start talking."

"I don't even know what that is," Zek said calmly.

"Liar."

"Really?" Zek said. "And could you kindly inform me how you know that I am, in fact, lying?"

"You're a Lyhedrune."

He paused. "I believe the proper pronunciation is 'Lyhe.'"

"The watch," Lorlie spat. "Where is it?"

"Markus," Zek said, "is this a friend of yours?"

The anger blistering beneath her skin drove her to press the knife deeper, to make this wretched descendant of Sorik Lyhe bleed. She controlled herself, just barely. "Tell me," she said as her hand started to shake, "or you die."

Never mind the fact that Aatoon was the only person she'd ever actually killed—she could do it, *would* do it, in order to break her curse.

"You broke into my house and are threatening to kill me over a pocket watch?" Zek said, somehow managing to sound amused.

What in the myths is even slightly amusing about this situation?

Lorlie scowled at the back of his head. "Yes."

"Well that's dedication," Zek said. "All right, move the knife, and I'll see what I can do to help."

She debated with herself for a moment. What was the plan here? He wouldn't just hand over an artifact to her, would he? Gritting her teeth, she flicked the knife away from his neck and stepped back. Zek turned and scanned her up and down

"And your name is?"

"None of your business," Lorlie said.

At the same time, Markus answered, "Lorlie."

Lorlie gritted her teeth, avoiding Markus's gaze. She pointed the knife at Zek. "Well?"

"What Age is it from?" Zek asked. He glanced in the mirror and swiped a hand over his hair.

"The Age of Kings."

He smirked at her. "Well good news, darling. I happen to have a room full of artifacts dedicated to that Age. Perhaps your precious—what did you call it?—*'Aatoon's pocket watch'* will be there."

"Good," she said. "Lead the way."

The young man hesitated, eyes flicking to the portrait on the far wall. The one of a prince holding a rose. *Sorik Lyhedrune.* Memories kindled in her mind. Sorik dancing in a flurry of aristocrats.

Sorik beaming as he described his plans for the kingdom to her. Explaining how he would do better than his father.

Sorik . . . begging her to save his life, in this very office.

"You deserve to die," she'd told him. "When they stick your useless body in the dirt, it will be the happiest day of my life."

What she meant to say was, I don't know how to heal you.

I don't want you to die.

I'm sorry.

But she hadn't. Because she never seemed to be able to say what she meant. Because he'd abandoned her, left her in that tower. Because he didn't care that she'd been hurt, that she was hurting.

He only cared about himself.

But like that boy in Markus's story, maybe . . . maybe there had been parts of him that were worth saving.

She glanced back at Zek. She hadn't expected him to look so similar to Sorik. And she especially hadn't expected a painting of her ex-fiance to be in his office.

A thousand years, and I still can't escape his shadow.

"The last time I saw him, he was dying," she found herself saying. "And yet, you have his last name."

"Oh, he did, but it was a slow, rather painful death." Zek absently rubbed the side of his face. "He lived just long enough to have a son."

Lorlie stared at him, feeling distant. Numb. As if her mind couldn't quite grasp the fact that Sorik really had died.

And that he married someone else.

"Good for him," she muttered at last. *I don't care.*

Her chest burned, tight and painful. *Why does it matter?* It shouldn't matter. She should be happy that he'd suffered.

So *why* wasn't she?

Swallowing, she nodded to the door. "Take us to the watch."

Zek shrugged and strolled to the door. As Lorlie moved to follow, Markus placed a hand on her shoulder. She shrugged him off.

"What are you doing?" he asked. "I thought we had a plan."

"That plan was useless as soon as Zek saw you."

Actually, she was never going to follow that plan to begin with. She'd always known she would need to get Zek to take them to it. He had just shown up a little earlier than she wanted.

"You say that like it's my fault, somehow," Markus said.

"Well, I'm not the one who has almost been caught twice now," she snapped.

Hurt flashed across his face, and he looked down. Taking that as an end to the conversation, Lorlie turned away.

"Just don't hurt anyone," Markus said softly. Lorlie didn't answer, following Zek—who had paused to wait by the door—into the hall. As they reached the end of the narrow hallway, the tether tying her and Markus together snapped taut, and a sudden wave of lightheadedness swept over her. She barely swallowed back bile. *He's not coming.* She froze, and glanced over her shoulder, panic suddenly squeezing her lungs. Markus stood in the doorway of the office, staring after them.

A foreign shadow darkened the light in his eyes.

Zek paused and arched a questioning eyebrow. "Is there a problem?"

Folding her arms, she glared at Markus. "Fine. All right! I won't. Okay?" It was a lie. But she couldn't get the watch without his cooperation.

"Promise?"

"Promise."

But that was like promising to turn into a frog. She hurt people, whether on purpose or not. It was the only thing she was good at.

After a long pause, Markus nodded, and started toward them. The tether immediately loosened, but it didn't bring relief. Her gut was still turning and twisting on itself because she knew what Markus didn't seem to be able to grasp that there was no happy ending.

Not for her.

Not for anyone near her.

This would end with someone getting hurt.

Markus caught up, and she spared a sideways glance at him. The shadow was still there, lurking at the edges of his eyes. It wasn't right, how she treated him. None of this was his fault. She probably wouldn't have even gotten this far without his help.

I'm sorry.

But she couldn't say it.

The hallway opened onto a balcony, overlooking the castle's impressive entryway. The walls had been stained a deep maroon, and a black carpet flowed up the wide set of stairs. Zek passed two of the open hallways, turning down one lit by a line of elegant lamps.

In between the closed doors on both sides were more paintings. Markus paused in front of one depicting a thrashing ocean in vivid detail. Aqua blue waves rose like frozen walls on each side, and at the center of it all was a child. A little boy. He had his tiny hands raised as if that could stop his inevitable fate.

"I've never heard of this painting before," Markus said.

Zek stepped over, pointedly ignoring Lorlie's look of warning. "This," he said proudly, "is one of the great masterpieces of Arithia Helm."

Lorlie had no clue who that was. But Markus apparently did.

"This is one of Arithia's pieces?" His eyes widened. "It's . . . it's amazing! I didn't know any had been recovered after the Dwindling!"

"Very few," Zek said. "This one is called 'The Guardian.'"

Lorlie snorted. "That's a dumb name." Both of them turned to her with expressions of horror. She shrugged. "That kid is about to die. Whoever was supposed to guard him failed."

Zek folded his arms.

Markus cocked his head questioningly at her. "What do you mean?"

"The waves," she said. "They're about to swallow him."

"Uh, no?" Markus said.

"No?" Lorlie repeated, scowling.

"No," he said. "You don't see it?"

Keeping an eye on Sorik, Lorlie edged closer and peered at the painting. Waves. The kid about to drown. What was she not seeing? She squinted, focusing on the child. There was . . . a faint golden figure outlined behind the boy, holding their arms out in a mimic of his.

Had that been there before?

"See?" Markus said. "That's the Guardian, whoever they are. There are some other vague lore pieces that reference someone by that name as well. They're probably a Sceptori or an important magic-wielder."

Something about that itched in the back of her mind.

Regardless. That wasn't important right now. She pointed the knife at Zek. "The room?"

Zek smiled at her, then motioned toward the door next to the painting. "That's it."

"Good. Go inside." She wasn't about to go first in case it was a trap.

"If you insist," he said. He casually swung the door open and strolled in. Markus darted after him and immediately gasped.

Inside was a room with a wide, curved ceiling. Glass cases lined with maroon cloth glittered from their stations. There were artifacts inside. Her heartbeat quickened. Three gigantic portraits hung on the far wall, bearing faces she'd seen before. Faces she saw every time she closed her eyes at night. Forcing her gaze away from it, she faced Zek. "All right, where is it?"

"The watch? I haven't a clue."

Lorlie checked to make sure Markus was out of earshot—he was already on the other side of the room, goggling over the artifacts in one of the cases. She stepped closer to Zek, and surprisingly, he actually flinched. "I am not messing around," she said in a low voice.

"Oh, I know. You think you can bring the magic back." He shrugged. "You can't. It's gone. Dead."

"The magic is a *thing,* a power source; it can't die," Lorlie said. Zek shrugged again, and they stood there, staring at each other.

"They never told me your name," Zek said finally.

"What?"

"Your name, Lorlie. Sorik left it out of his journal. But he said it's your fault he was cursed." He rubbed the side of his face again, then seemed to notice what he was doing, and jerked his hand down.

Of course he said that.

Lorlie studied Zek and found something hidden—just barely—in his calm gaze. *Fear.*

He's terrified.

After a moment of debate, Lorlie slid the knife back into the inside pocket of her jacket. "Make one wrong move, and it's out again. Understand?"

"Perfectly."

"Hey, Zek!" Markus called. "What does this artifact do?"

She watched Zek cross the room to Markus, before turning back to the portraits. An urge as strong as the tether binding her and Markus pulled her towards them. It was a waste of time, at any moment a guard could peek in. She should focus on finding the watch.

But . . .

As she drew near to them, her throat shrank. Her family's faces stared blankly from the canvases.

Her father, golden crown glinting atop his head.

Her mother, chin tipped slightly upward with an imperious air.

Her older sister, the usual delicately ambitious smile playing around her red lips.

Lorlie slowly let out her breath. She could remember the day these were painted. She'd been sent to her room, omitted from the honor after angrily chunking a vial of red paint at her sister's spotless white gown. It had been a dumb thing to do. Silly, even. But—she'd just been so *angry.* They had been ignoring her, like usual. She figured she'd probably spend the whole time hovering in the background, not participating, anyway.

So she'd acted out.

Back then, she'd told herself she did it out of pure spite.

But really . . .

I just wanted them to notice me.

Reaching out, she almost touched her mother's portrait. Something inside of her was dying to feel the paint-dried canvas, to know for sure that the people memorialized upon them were actually gone.

Gone forever.

She pulled back and curled her hands into fists.

It doesn't matter, she thought. *I don't care about them.*

An ocean filled her chest, threatening to drown her.

She pivoted away from the wall and immediately froze. In the corner, just left of the portraits, was a pedestal with a velvet pillow. Lying in its center was a pocket watch.

Lorlie rushed over.

It was a rose-gold watch, with delicate keys for hands.

Yes!

She picked it up. The watch was cold in her hands, like she always felt nowadays. *As if, inside, I'm still stone.* Its metallic surface glinted with thousands of memories. How many times had she seen Aatoon pull it out, and twirl it thoughtfully as he explained something to her? How many times had he shown her its ticking face, and said, "*Do you see it?*"

"*See what?*" she always muttered back, annoyed at the question.

He'd smile his reserved smile. "*The possibilities.*"

Slowly, she hooked its metal chain around her finger, like Aatoon used to carry it. *I did it. I found the watch.* Lorlie frowned. She could still sense Markus across the room.

It'll work. I have to give it more time.

"Oh Lorlie," Zek called. "I would put that down if I were you."

She looked up. Zek stood beside a glass case, holding a slender silver object, similar to a gun, to the back of Markus's head. Its long barrel glinted dangerously. She recognized it immediately. *Ferozin Hai's weapon.* It was rumored to be able to erase whoever it struck from existence. A little bead of sweat trickled down Markus's forehead.

"We wouldn't want an unfortunate accident to occur, now would we, Lorlie?" Zek said.

I have the watch. She glanced down at it, swallowing around the lump in her throat. If it worked, she . . . she didn't need Markus anymore.

And by the look on his face, she could tell he knew it too.

I don't . . . I don't care.

"Liar," Aatoon's voice whispered. "All you ever do is lie."

This is what I am. This is what I do. Survive.

Clutching the watch in her fist, Lorlie bolted for the door.

CHAPTER SEVENTEEN

LORLIE

"Perhaps forever. For, the means to break her curse were never voiced."

–From *The Book of Legends, Volume Forty-Nine*

LORLIE SPRINTED DOWN the hall, praying for the watch to hurry up and break her curse. *It has to work.* The closed doorways and paintings all blurred together in chaotic color. Her eyes burned, the tether in her gut twisting demandingly.

She was leaving Markus.

Just . . . abandoning him.

Like everyone had always done with her.

Hot, angry tears pooled in her eyes, making it difficult to see the steps. But they were trapped alongside all the words she'd never spoken. Phantom drops of scarlet blood dripped from her trembling fingers as she glanced down at the watch again.

Blood that smoked, and turned to ashes.

Blood that screamed to the world who she was. Who she really was.

"*You are a beast, just like me.*"

"You deserved it," she whispered."You . . ."

As she reached the end of the hallway, the tips of her fingers began to sting with a familiar ice. She stumbled to a stop. Gray brushed the edges of her fingers.

What?

Her jaw slackened. *No!* She had the watch! Why was she . . . Why was the curse not broken? Her throat tightened to the point of choking. Holding the watch out, she glared at its still face.

"Stop!" she said. "Stop it! I did it, Aatoon. I found your watch. That was the test."

. . . *Wasn't it?*

She dragged her hand through her hair. *Still cursed. Still cursed. Still cursed.* The words thudded in her skull again and again. It was the symphony that had followed her since the day she was born. She couldn't escape it, could she?

She would never be free.

She would never be saved.

She would never be . . . never be . . .

Anything more than a monster.

"On your knees, now!" a voice shouted from behind her.

Lorlie barely registered it. She dropped the watch as flames bubbled inside of her, ancient, unquenchable, and as destructive as the dragon fire that had wiped her kingdom from the face of the earth.

She could almost see the satisfied tilt of Aatoon's head.

She turned, slowly, to face Zek, who strode towards her, the cursed weapon in his hand.

"On your knees," Zek repeated. His hands shook.

Where is Markus? A sharp bolt of fear ran through her. "What did you do with him?" She wasn't a statue again so that probably meant he wasn't dead. Then again, had anyone tested what would happen if one of the people tethered died? She couldn't remember.

"What do you care?"

"I don't," Lorlie spat. "Obviously."

Zek shook his head slowly, lip curling with disgust. "You don't deserve to be alive. This is why we had to get rid of the magic. Because it created creatures like *you*, who don't care about anyone or anything but themselves."

"Oh, and you're not doing this for yourself?

"No. I'm doing this to protect people like Markus." He slipped his finger over the trigger.

I could run for the door. But he'd still be able to hit her. Besides, she couldn't go far with the stone creeping up her hands. *What did it matter, anyway?* There was no magic to fix her curse. *Nothing* could ever fix it—fix her.

"Any last words?" Zek said.

"Wait!" Markus burst into the hallway. Zek spun, his finger slipping against the trigger. A silver-gray beam shot from the barrel.

Lorlie took advantage of the distraction, bolting back towards them. Markus hit the ground right as she slammed into Zek. He stumbled, and she tore the weapon from his hand, and stumbled to Markus.

He lay on the floor, face contorted. Pain formed glistening droplets of sweat on his forehead, plastering his hair against his skin. His very being seemed to be . . . thinning, becoming more and more translucent with each gasping inhale.

Every muscle in Lorlie's body became ice. A hazy gray mist rose from the trail the weapon's beam had left, drifting to the ceiling.

No.

Her breath came in quick gasps. She raised the gun, turning to Zek. "What did you do?" she yelled. "Zek, what did you do?"

"I . . ." The man in front of her was no longer composed or in control. He was shaking, staring past her, at Markus, in pale, wide-eyed horror. "I told him to stay in the room! You abandoned him. He wasn't supposed to . . . I didn't think he'd . . . It slipped!"

She moved her finger over the trigger. But something stopped her from pressing down on it. *He deserves to die! Just pull the trigger!* Her hand started to shake.

"*People deserve a lot of things,*" Markus's voice seemed to whisper in her mind. "*That doesn't mean you have to give it to them.*"

And standing there, at the top of the balcony, meeting his tear-filled eyes, Lorlie *saw* Zek Lyhe.

A boy growing up in a world where magic was something to be hated, where it hurt people—killed them. His shoulders no longer seemed so firm, so strong. Instead, they bent with an invisible weight. And those terrified, angry eyes . . . They had glimmered when telling Markus about the ocean painting. And . . .

I can't kill him.

He was so much more than a villain.

The last, dented chunk of stone shielding her heart crumbled into dust. Leaving her open, and exposed, and exhausted.

"Well?" Zek spat, voice hoarse. "What are you waiting for?"

Lorlie looked at him and found that, for the first time in her life, she wasn't angry.

She was filled with grief.

Maybe I always have been.

Maybe this anger had always been that: grief.

Dropping the weapon, she slumped to her knees beside Markus. His form fuzzed, so translucent that she could see the tile beneath him. He, of all people, did not deserve this fate.

He deserved to *live*. To see the magic. To smile.

The tears that had been pooling in her eyes for so long finally fell free. She stared down at him through the haze. This was her fault. She'd chosen herself—even though she'd known that he was the person this world needed. His smile. The light in his eyes. The beautiful way he saw history. The way he believed so strongly in the magic. That was what this world needed—not some stupid power source that had caused so much hurt.

He was probably the only person who would give everything to help her.

And what had she done?

Treated him like nothing.

When really, he was the opposite.

"I'm sorry, Markus," she whispered, voice breaking. "I'm so sorry."

A tiny speck of gold flickered to life in the air above him, as if in response to her words. She blinked, trying to see through the blur of tears. *What . . .*

Hands grabbed her arms in an iron grip and hauled her to her feet. "Wait!" Lorlie gasped, struggling. But the man's hold didn't loosen.

"What do you want me to do with her?" the man grunted. He was older, from the sound of it.

Haunted shadows marred Zek's eyes, but he straightened. "Load her in the artifact transport and take her to warehouse six. She'll be a statue by the time you get there."

"And the other one?"

Zek didn't even glance in Markus's direction. "He'll . . . be gone soon."

"Zek." Lorlie jerked. "Wait, we have to try to save him! Please."

Zek leveled his gaze on her. "This is what you deserve."

"But not what Markus deserves."

Without another word, the man holding her—one of Zek's guards, she guessed—dragged her down the stairs and out the door. The darkness of night still blanketed the world, turning the castle grounds into a nightmarish image. She was dragged to the side of the house, where a large transport sat, silent. The guard held onto her with one hand and threw the back door open with the other. Lorlie jerked against him, but it didn't do much good.

Sighing, the man picked her up and threw her into the back of the transport. Pain jolted through her as she hit the metal floor. The back of the transport was large and box-like. Its walls loomed over her like a cage. Pushing herself to her knees, she twisted in time to see whoever had thrown her step out of sight, and then the lean figure of Zek Lyhe took his place.

He just stood there, a black spot in the darkness.

"Sorik would have loved you," Lorlie said hoarsely.

"Would he have?" Zek leaned closer, planting his hands on the floor of the transport. "I really wouldn't know, since you *murdered* him before he could be truly recorded in the lore."

"All I did was refuse to heal him," Lorlie whispered. "I didn't curse him. I just refused to heal him." *Not that I could have.* She'd never learned how to use the magic that way.

"Refusing to take action is equal to committing the deed," Zek said. He pushed off the transport and stepped back. "I hope you know, I am *saving* the world by eliminating you and every ounce of wretched magic from it." He slammed the massive door shut. A moment later, a lock clicked into place.

She slumped forward, numb. The fire inside of her was gone. Drowned. Extinguished.

Cold seeped from the metal through her clothes, into her flesh, down through her bones, lacing like chains. It held her in place, right where she always ended up.

Alone.

In the dark.

No matter how many times she shook her fists at the world, no matter how many times she saved herself, it would never be enough.

Because she was Lorlie Cyphrani. The girl no one had ever wanted. The girl who always ended up hurting those around her.

The beast.

The transport rumbled to life, and Lorlie hugged her arms around herself, body aching with exhaustion and cold. Weight pressed around her, stone crystalizing over her skin. She felt the seizing lock as her lungs stopped working. Her heartbeat slowed. Flecks of dirty gold flickered over her vision, and she tried to reach out to them. Tried to feel their warmth.

But there was none.

And there, in the back of a transport meant for old, discarded artifacts, Lorlie turned to stone for the last time.

CHAPTER EIGHTEEN

MARKUS

"Before long, her name was lost to memory, her kingdom wiped from the records."

–From *The Book of Legends, Volume Forty-Nine*

EXCRUCIATING PAIN SHATTERED Markus's thoughts, turning them into blinding, burning shards that jabbed at the inside of his skull over and over. He gasped soundlessly as his skin pulled as if torn slowly apart by an invisible force.

Somewhere far, far away a figure hovered over him. A ghost.

He shuddered, lungs screaming for air.

"I'm sorry, Markus." The words were more of an impression than audible sound. "I'm so sorry."

A single, tiny, golden ember appeared in the foggy haze.

Markus stared up at it, unable to move, unable to think. Pain sank into him, burning away everything. The ember flickered.

And then, it *grew*.

Golden light streamed over him. Warmth against burning ice. Light against the shadows flickering at the edges of everything. Relief against blinding pain.

And air. He gasped, body jerking belatedly to the motion. Oxygen poured through his lungs. He sucked in great gulps of life.

I'm not dead. The pain slowly faded, and his thoughts—though still sluggish—stopped fleeing his grasp. *I'm not dead. How—?* Struggling, he managed to sit up. His surroundings were still hazy, but golden dust glimmered in the air all around him.

Like . . .

Magic.

His jaw slackened. "Is this real?" he whispered. Reaching out, he brushed his hand through the beautiful particles. They were warm to the touch. A comforting, safe warm. He looked up and squinted. There was a vague shape of a featureless person standing just a few steps away.

It looked like the Guardian, from the painting with the ocean and the little boy.

Woah.

"Hi," Markus whispered.

The figure shifted closer, obviously studying him, though it didn't appear to have eyes. This wasn't a Sceptori. Or any human. But he got a distinct impression of *familiarity* from it. It felt the same as when he'd first been drawn to Lorlie when she was a statue. And when he touched the artifacts.

He looked down at his hands. Golden dust covered them, and he blinked. *No way . . .*

"You're the magic." Markus looked back up at the faded figure. "The magic isn't a simple power source, is it? It's alive! It's a person."

The Guardian.

The figure drifted closer. It fuzzed, shrinking until it was eye-level with him. It reached out and took his hands. Warmth sank deep into his skin at the touch. He gasped as images suddenly poured into his mind.

Children dancing in a circle as the magic swirled with them, giving their movements grace.

The magic kneeling beside an old gardener, breathing life into his plants, making them grow unnaturally tall and full.

Lorlie, standing in front of a blond-haired prince, fists around the magic's throat, forcing it to hurt people.

A tall man with hazel eyes whispering in its ear about how wretched—how hopeless—the humanity it loved was.

A kingdom going up in flames far brighter than its own warm glow.

That same golden figure shattering into thousands of dark, angry shards. Markus could feel its emotions in his chest, as if they were his own. Rising like an ocean, drowning all the light. Tight, and raging, and so *so* hurt. Because it had loved these people, and yet they'd caused it pain. Used it. Blamed it for everything wrong in their lives.

And in its weakened, hurting state, a prince did the unthinkable. He cursed the magic itself. He locked it away. So that it was unable to even reach out and touch the physical world. It waited year after year after year, for someone to look for it. For someone to see.

But no one ever came to save it.

Tears trickled down Markus's cheeks, as warm as the magic. The golden figure leaned forward and rested its forehead against his. Another image rose in his mind.

A small apartment room with two beds. A little boy squirmed beneath the blankets of one, eyes glued on the wrinkled, gray-haired man sitting on the opposite bed.

"Grandpa," Markus whispered. This was a memory of his grandfather telling him bedtime stories. His heart ached.

"*I saw,*" the magic said. The words were impressions, breathed into his mind, not audible sounds. "*Always.*" Markus felt the magic's emotions—the anger, the hurt, the grief—begin to soften as they watched his grandfather lean eagerly forward, mouth moving silently as he told his story.

"You watched us," Markus said, "all those years, you weren't able to do anything, but you could see. You watched us tell stories about you, believe in you."

"*He loved you,*" the magic said.

He slowly shook his head.

"*He did. I saw.*"

"He was always so angry," Markus whispered.

"*He was angry at himself, at his failings, not you.*"

The words sank into Markus's soul, healing the wounds that had festered there for so long. Maybe . . . maybe he hadn't been so much of a burden. Maybe he wasn't to blame for his grandfather's unhappiness.

He loved you.

There was so much light in those three little words. Reluctantly, Markus pulled away from the magic, letting his grandfather's image fade. "How are you doing this, if you're trapped?"

A spike of anger, then regret, then excitement jabbed through him. The magic fuzzed, and another one of its memories surfaced in Markus's mind.

It was of a dark room. A man stood there, surrounded by a pile of artifacts and open books. Behind him, a younger version of Zek stood, arms hugging himself. He looked scared. The man reached a hand to the side and curled his fingers. Markus got the distinct impression of something *cracking*, like a curse only being half broken. The smallest hole appeared in the air near the man's hand. Dark gold bled from it, trickling from the crack in its curse.

But the magic was furious.

All of its pain and resentment kept in for over a thousand years lashed out in its slither of freedom and consumed the man.

The image vanished abruptly.

The magic crouched in front of him, still and silent. Markus gently squeezed its hands—they were surprisingly firm. The magic had hurt people, but it had also done beautiful things. *It shouldn't be locked away like this.* He could feel the crack still there, the tiny opening in its prison, which allowed it to reach out to him now.

Markus smiled. "I know what you need. I won't leave you like this, I promise."

After a moment of hesitation, the magic pulled away, dissolving into a flurry of gold dust that swirled together. Markus stumbled to his feet. What was it doing now?

In one flooding wave, the golden dust hit him *and sank straight through.* Markus gasped, blinking. He was once again standing in the hallway of the Lyhe mansion, alone.

Deep inside of his chest, a little ember sat pulsing, silent, waiting to be seen. An ember hidden inside every person alive. *This whole time*, he realized. *It's been here the whole time—a part of us, inside us. We just didn't know how to see it.*

And he knew what he needed to do to set it free.

But first, he had to find Lorlie.

CHAPTER NINETEEN

LORLIE

"In grief, the magic, unable to save the girl it had loved, died. Leaving the world empty, and alone."

–From *The Book of Legends, Volume Forty-Nine*

1,000 Years Ago

LORLIE STOOD IN a rubble of ghosts. It used to be a castle with golden terraces and vining red roses crawling up the walls. Now it was a mound of stone and ashes. A grave where her only chance of *happily ever after* had been buried.

Somewhere out there, hidden beneath the scorched rubble, were the bodies of her parents and sister. King. Queen. And their perfect heir. All destroyed by a beast.

Lorlie looked down at the golden-scaled dragon at her feet. He was dying.

Tightening her grip around the hilt of the sword that protruded from his chest, Lorlie let herself slump to her knees. Warm blood oozed into her torn gown, but it did nothing against the numb cold creeping through her body. There was just *so much blood.* Seeping through her clothes, between her fingers, into her soul.

He shuddered, convulsed.

I'm sorry. I'm so sorry. The words gripped the edge of her tongue, refusing to come loose. She drew a ragged breath. It felt like the blade was in her chest. As if she'd plunged it straight into herself, and there was no way to pull it free.

"See?" Aatoon wheezed. His dragon voice sounded like gravel grinding against her brain. "You . . . are . . . a beast . . . just like . . . me."

Lorlie's focus blurred. She could hear her family's screams. Could see her kingdom devoured by an ocean of flames.

Red-hot anger swelled inside of her.

She staggered to her feet again and ripped the sword free. He roared in pain. The sound pounded over the rubble, over the graveyard of memories. Shaking, she threw the sword. It clattered against the rubble, then puffed into a flurry of golden dust.

At her feet, Aatoon groaned. His massive reptilian form shivered, collapsing inward with a golden glow.

And then there was just a man.

His body twitched with each gasping inhale. His graying hair was plastered to his forehead. A scarlet hole pierced the center of his chest. "Lorlie," he wheezed. Tiny flecks of magic gathered on his skin as he tried to prolong his life.

"I have nothing more to say to you!" Her throat burned. Her eyes smarted. But no tears would fall. *Why won't they just fall?*

Aatoon lifted his pained, hazel eyes to hers. "Little Beast," he murmured, barely audible. "I have . . . one last lesson . . . for you." He lifted a single, bloodied hand, shakily gripping his pocket watch. Like some great righteous gavel in the hand of a judge, he always used it to finalize his curses. Lorlie stumbled back as he hooked a finger through the chain, and gave it one, tiny flick.

The watch spun.

Golden dust swarmed.

A crushing weight, like a giant fist closing around her, as magic seized control of her body. She gasped, unable to move, unable to escape. *No!*

"You must *see,* child," he said. "Do you see?"

Cursed stone crept across her skin, bleeding through her like poison.

"You do not have to stay this way," Aatoon's voice whispered, faint, barely existent.

And the rubble vanished into an ocean of gray.

CHAPTER TWENTY

MARKUS

"And that is how the princess and the secrets of the magic were forgotten."

–From *The Book of Legends, Volume Forty-Nine*

MARKUS FOUND HER on the fourteenth row of warehouse six, placed between a statue of a horned frog and a blue vase that looked like it had been glued back together. She was stone, kneeling, arms wrapped around her middle. He knelt and placed his flashlight on the ground. The yellow light splashed across Lorlie. Her face . . . that frozen expression. If he didn't know Lorlie, he would think she'd been crying.

"I'm not going to give up on you, you know. You're worth saving." Just like Kenth. Just like the magic.

Maybe some part of her heard.

He placed his hand over hers, grinning as he watched her gray lighten with life. The cold stone beneath his fingers warmed with magic, turning to soft flesh. And then Lorlie slumped forward and drew a rasping breath. Markus sat back on his heels, waiting.

Lorlie rested her palm against her head, looking up with shock.

"Hey." Markus gave a small wave. "You okay?"

Tears glimmered in her eyes, and she hastily swiped them away. They were *brown*, he realized, her eyes—a deep, brilliant brown. When had they changed from gray?

"I thought you were dead," Lorlie whispered.

"I thought so too."

"What happened? I saw you . . ." She shook her head and rubbed her eyes again.

"The magic."

She stared at him, mouth slightly ajar. "What?"

"The magic," he said. "Lorlie, it's not gone! It saved my life."

LORLIE

Lorlie's brain struggled to process Markus's words. *The magic isn't gone?*

And . . . it saved his life?

"It took a little bit for Ned and I to figure out what warehouse they'd taken you to," Markus said apologetically. He picked up the flashlight, then nodded toward the direction of bright midday light filtering through the shadowed building, probably coming from an open side door.

"Is Ned here?" she asked. The words scraped against her throat like sandpaper.

"No, I dropped him off at the Hut. I didn't want him to be in danger if . . ."

If there were guards.

She coughed, the motion jerking her entire body. Coming back from a stone curse wasn't easy, and often it took some time for the body to sort itself out. "There weren't any?"

"No. It seems like Zek thinks everything is over."

"And it isn't?" Resting her forehead against her palm, she focused on slowly forcing oxygen through her stiff lungs.

"Of course not."

He almost died helping me. The image of him lying on the tile, fading little by little, flashed through her mind.

"You shouldn't have come back for me." Her tone came out sharper than she'd intended. But that was probably for the best. He needed to leave her. Let her be consumed by the stone she deserved.

Aatoon's blood dripped from her hands.

Sorik reached out, begging for the mercy he hadn't shown her.

Her family screamed, words bouncing through her skull. You deserve this. You deserve this. You deserve this.

"You do not have to stay this way," Aatoon's voice whispered. And then there was another voice, distant and fuzzy. "*I'm not going to give up on you . . .*

"*You're worth saving.*"

Where did that come from? Lorlie blinked tears away.

"Come on Lor," Markus said. He held a hand out to help her up. She almost slapped it away. *I don't deserve help.*

But she did need it.

Lorlie looked up, meeting his eyes. Soft, golden specks swam in their depths. *Almost like magic.* And she found herself wondering if perhaps he was magic. If perhaps it was here, buried inside this kind, soft human being. Perhaps it just looked different from what she remembered.

Or, maybe, she never really saw magic at all until now.

Reaching up, Lorlie took his hand, and let him help her to her feet. She wobbled, her muscles still trying to wake up. She followed him past rows of shelves, to an open door where sunlight was streaming through. It let out into an empty alley adjoined to another narrow path between storage buildings. After a few turns, they emerged onto a main street with a familiar red, black, and yellow transport sitting on the curb. One of Ned's. She slid into the passenger seat, and Markus went around to the driver's side.

"Where are we going?" Lorlie asked.

"To bring the magic back."

She frowned. "How?"

Resting his hands idly on the controls, Markus stared out at the street. Lorlie followed his gaze. Other transports hummed past. People went in and out of shopping centers and offices, rushing about like they were in a race. No one paused to notice the two lonely people sitting in a pizza delivery transport.

"I think I know why," Markus said softly.

"Why what?"

"You're so angry."

She crossed her arms. "I told you—"

"No." He shook his head. "The real reason, the deeper reason."

He fell silent, and for a few moments, they just sat there, staring out over the city, with its blunt buildings and chaotic traffic. There was no magic in sight. But hadn't he said it wasn't gone?

"Why?" Lorlie whispered at last.

Though, she already knew.

Markus shifted to look at her. "Because you were never loved, were you? Because no one ever cared. No one saw."

Lorlie looked away, blinking rapidly. In that moment, she was once again a forgotten, tiny thing in an ocean of dancers.

A daughter standing beside her parents' closed door, trying to find the courage to knock.

A little girl waiting, waiting, waiting for her sister to take her hand.

A princess locked in a tower, dreaming of a prince to set her free.

A . . . a beast everyone wished didn't exist.

Lorlie drew her knees up against her chest, planting her feet against the edges of the chair. *Maybe I never really escaped that tower, after all. Maybe I was born there.*

"I know what that's like," Markus continued softly. A raw note of hurt trickled through his voice, a type of ache Lorlie was all too familiar with.

She sucked in a slow, deep breath, and forced out the words burning inside of her. "The story in your lore is wrong. The one about me. It tells of someone who had the magic's blessing, who was loved and adored, who was beautiful and kind. The real story is nothing like that." She closed her eyes, letting her past come to life in the darkness of her mind. "I was the second born to a family who was already perfectly happy, the unexpected disruption to their lives. So I learned to lash out. To hurt people like they hurt me." She glanced sideways at Markus. He was staring out at the street again, quietly drumming his fingers against the console.

He *did* understand. She knew that for certain. He understood what it was like to not be seen and to desperately wish to be.

The difference between them was Lorlie had let that turn her into a monster.

He let it make him a better person.

But I don't have to stay this way.

"I'm sorry," he said.

"Me too," she whispered.

Taking a deep breath, Markus twisted a dial on the transport's control panel and slid it into motion.

CHAPTER TWENTY-ONE

MARKUS

"All that is left is this tale, and her statue, still buried beneath those thorned roses."

–From *The Book of Legends, Volume Forty-Nine*

MARKUS PULLED UP to the curb directly in front of the Cursed Garden's black gates. Like usual, an eternally long line of people stretched outward from the ticket booth. "Come on," he said to Lorlie, and jumped out, dashing past the tourists. Strangely enough, the sensation of the tether tying Lorlie and him together was gone.

He glanced back and found her practically on his heels, expression befuddled.

The woman at the booth yelled as they sprinted through the entrance into the Garden. "Lorlie," Markus panted. "The tether, I don't feel it!" *And her eyes are no longer gray.* Did that mean . . . "Is your curse broken?"

"I think," she stammered. "Maybe?"

He shook his head and focused on weaving through the people milling about, accidentally bumping into some of them, and turned down one of the rows of statues. Pausing for a moment, he scanned the area. *Aha!* He motioned to Lorlie, then squeezed between a statue of a snarling mermaid and a hippo-like humanoid creature. They were vaguely familiar. If he stopped, he could probably recall their lore. *No time, though.* A voice blasted over the loud speaker, announcing that security was being called in. He finally skidded to a stop at the foot of a gigantic statue.

Looking up, he grinned.

Cringefold the Burnt loomed against the sky, massive and majestic. Whatever Lorlie said, he was *awesome.*

"Him?" Lorlie asked, disgust dripping from her voice.

"Yep!" Markus looked back at her, still smiling. It was all right if she couldn't see what he saw in Cringefold. It was there, though. A beautiful, brilliant sparkle in the wyvern's gray irises. A warmth nestled in its heart, hidden from view and touch. An ember just waiting to be a flame.

Just like the ember inside of himself.

Markus rested a hand on one of the wyvern's claws. "Do you feel it?"

"Feel what, exactly?" Lorlie asked.

The ember inside of him began to grow, unraveling, threading tendrils of golden warmth through his veins.

Lorlie stepped beside him, arm brushing his. She pressed her palm against Cringefold's leg. "Feel what?" she repeated.

He tipped his head back, studying Cringefold's stone face. A tiny, almost indiscernible hum of life flickered in the air around them. "Magic," he breathed.

"I don't feel anything."

"The magic," Markus explained slowly, "is a person. It was cursed, trapped inside of itself, somehow." That was a bad way of putting it, but it was the only way he could think of.

It . . . kind of reminded him of Lorlie. All closed off in her own little world of pain, desperately wanting help, but not knowing how to reach out.

"Look for it," he said, "not to control it. Just to see it, *feel* it. It's *there,* Lorlie. A small crack in its prison. We can open it."

After a moment, Lorlie let out a small gasp.

She found it.

In his mind's eye, he could see the Guardian crouched in front of him, hands holding his. "I'm sorry," he said, closing his eyes. "I'm sorry no one saw you all those years. I'm sorry they didn't want you. Because they should have."

Those were the words he'd needed to hear himself, for so long.

He reached his left hand out to the side like he'd seen Lorlie do when she was trying to access the magic. Glancing sideways, he saw Lorlie doing the same.

Together, they reached into the crack, and grasped the magic's hand. Not to use it, but to set it free. He could feel splinters spider-webbing through the curse, breaking it apart.

With a thunderous roar, golden light exploded across the Cursed Gardens.

EPILOGUE

MARKUS SAT ON the edge of his bed, staring down at the crisp, blank pages of his grandfather's notebook. A pen sat on the mattress beside him, waiting for him to pick it up and write the words shining in his mind. In the other room, he could hear Lorlie messing with one of the artifacts she'd taken from the warehouses during their last visit. It had been two days since they'd released the magic into the world. *Only two days.*

Yet, so much had changed.

Flecks of gold drifted in the air around him, comfortingly warm. Markus glanced at them, smiling. "I found it, Grandpa," he whispered. "I found something worth writing about."

"You almost ready?" Lorlie called.

"Just about!" Gathering the pen and notebook up, Markus stood and walked into the main room. Lorlie leaned over the small table, inspecting a silver wrist brace. Magic drifted around her.

Markus stepped over to the window and peeked outside at the street. It was abandoned, save for a few brave souls hurrying down the sidewalk. Cracks splintered down the road. Magic drifted down there, illuminating the buildings in a golden glow.

When the magic was released, it had chosen to free all of the Cursed. Every statue in the Cursed Gardens and warehouses had woken, and the city had been flung into chaos. Most of the legendary figures were confused and scared.

Some had clearly been cursed for a reason.

Others, like Cringefold, Markus was certain, meant no one harm.

Either way, it was their job to set things right and make sure no one got hurt.

"I think I have this figured out."

Markus glanced back at Lorlie. She shoved strands of her brown hair behind her ear and held her arm up for him to see. The bracer glistened from her forearm.

"It'll contain them?"

"It should."

He nodded, glancing at the gold glittering in the air. It had a long way to go still. Every now and then he caught a faint impression of lingering anger from it towards the world. Pain that deep didn't just vanish overnight.

Lorlie cleared her throat, and Markus realized she'd said something. "Um." He blinked. "What?"

She rolled her eyes. "I *said*, we might as well head out."

"Oh! Right." Since they were to blame for releasing all of the creatures who'd been turned to stone, they'd decided it was their job to track down the ones who were going to hurt people. That bracer was a handy artifact that should be able to replicate the stone curse. Since the magic didn't want to be used like it had in the past, they were stuck to using artifacts. Which was perfectly fine with Markus.

"*Markus*," Lorlie said.

"Okay, okay, I'm coming! But first, look." He placed his grandfather's notebook on the table and flipped it to the first page. Lorlie leaned over to watch as he wrote a single sentence at the top.

Once upon a time, there was a girl who turned to stone.

"What are you doing?" Lorlie asked.

A smile tugged at his face. He snapped the notebook shut and slipped it into his pocket. "We're going to tell your story, the way it really happened. And everyone else's too. I think it's time for history to be told the right way. No more lies. No more falsified lore. Just the truth."

For a moment Lorlie just stood there, silent. He braced himself for her to reject the idea like she had every time he'd brought up something like that.

Instead, she just nodded.

He blinked. "Wait, so that's a yes?"

"Of course it's a yes," she said. "You people desperately need help in that area." A smile quirked at the edges of her lips. "Now can we go wrangle some monsters already?"

"You mean, be epic heroes?" he said. "Always!"

She crossed the room and pulled open the door. The rest of the apartment building was eerily quiet. Everyone had gone into hiding, terrified of the unexplainable things that were happening to their city. Even Zek Lyhe hadn't been heard from since the magic's return. Markus's stomach twisted at the thought of people getting hurt because of their actions.

But in the dim lighting, the breathtaking, warm sparks of magic drifted like tiny promises. *Life will be better*, they whispered, *wounds will heal.*

And Markus would make sure of it.

"Promise me one thing, though," Lorlie said, still standing in the doorway.

"What?"

"You'll also tell *your* story."

"Oh . . ." His cheeks warmed. "I don't know if I have anything worth—"

"You do," she said. "Take it from a real life legend."

He laughed. "All right, promise." Glancing over his shoulder, he saw the magic coalescing into a faint figure, the sunlight in the window creating a dazzling backdrop. It didn't have any facial features, but he could still feel it smiling at him.

"*Thank you,*" it seemed to say.

But really, he should be thanking it.

"Come on." Markus stepped into the hallway and started for the stairs. "We have legends to find!"

And magic to show to the world.

THE ROSE AND THE BULL

TASHA KAZANJIAN

CHAPTER ONE

KIAR WOKE UP before his father that morning, so early that the stars still sparked silver against the blackness of the sky. He rolled out of bed and into the corridor before his eyes fully opened, clutching his tunic and leather shoes in one hand. The only sound in the whole castle came from the kitchen—exactly as he'd hoped.

He started down the steps of the tower. The stones under his bare feet might as well have been ice, but a waft of warm air blew up the stairs, rich with the scent of fresh bread. Kiar didn't bother to stop and put his shoes on, only moved faster. He stumbled into the kitchen a moment later. Shivering slightly in the sudden gush of heat, he hastily pulled on his tunic.

"Steady there, *a bhobain*," said the cook, Elspet, but she couldn't suppress a laugh. She stood at the long table, up to her elbows in dough. "Where are you off to so quick?"

Kiar grinned. Only Elspet could still call him her boy, her little scamp. No one else would dare. He kissed her wrinkled cheek and sat down at the table to lace up his shoes. "The herdsmen will be here this morning to pay the harvest tithe. I want to finish the preparations and still meet them at the ford." *Before my father even stumbles out of his bed*, he added silently.

"Won't the lord take care of the preparations himself?" Elspet asked, frowning.

"I can manage," Kiar replied. Elspet's eyes narrowed, but he ignored her expression. His father's words from the night before still rang in his ears, and Kiar meant to prove every one of them wrong. He knew there was more to a lord's work than swords and feasts. Hadn't he always done everything his father asked and more? His father's people knew it, even if the lord himself didn't. And hadn't he earned his torc from the lord's own hand six years ago now? Kiar's fingers went to the circlet around his neck, a promise wrought in gold. There was no need to fight for it again.

Except here he sat, the sun not even yawning yet, the only one awake aside from Elspet. And Elspet, everyone swore, never slept.

Kiar let go of the torc and leaned his head back, his eyes closed. Something touched his arm. He flinched, but it was just Elspet's hand on his shoulder. Kiar forced himself to let out a slow breath and then smiled at her. She raised one eyebrow, clearly unconvinced by his expression, but only sighed and passed him a thick slice of bread.

Butter and honey dripped down Kiar's wrist as he jammed the food into his mouth and got to his feet. He had work to do, and quickly if he wanted to leave the castle before his father awoke.

"Wait a moment," Elspet said, unclasping the brooch fastened to her shawl and pressing her thumb against the pin. A dot of blood welled up. "Where's your knot?" she asked.

Kiar rubbed the back of his neck, his fingers brushing against the strip of leather hidden beneath his torc. He couldn't show her *that* charm. "I left it upstairs."

That was true, in a way. The intricate knot that he usually tied into his black hair probably lay next to his bed, forgotten along with his cloak. He would fetch them both later.

Elspet frowned and licked the blood from her thumb. With a dark little *hmm*, she said, "Bring it here before you leave for the ford. I'll not have you wandering out on the moors without a fresh drop."

Kiar promised he would and hurried away. Not even Elspet could know that he'd kept his mother's charm; she, like everyone else, would demand he burn it. He should have thrown it onto the funeral pyre years ago. Only the blood of the living had power. But Kiar couldn't bring himself to do that, not then and not now.

He tried to push the memory of that day out of his mind. The fever had caught his mother just after he turned sixteen. He had longed for that birthday, spent years preparing for it—and then it came, a day of competition, of fights and feats, and finally, the last warrior admitted defeat. Kiar, wild exultation blazing in his blood, could claim his inheritance. He'd barely felt his bruises. All he'd known was the heat under his skin and the cold metal of the golden torc as his father placed it around his neck.

His mother had left the feast early that night, and perhaps Kiar would've found that strange if he hadn't been so full of his own victory. By the morning after his birthday, she couldn't even raise her head. And by the morning after that, she was gone.

Again, Kiar tried to shove the memory down, but it spread like poison, like a wound gone sour. Nothing would clear it, not even the chill air of the courtyard. Kiar knew that well enough. He could only grit his teeth against it and get to work.

Morning dawned bright and clear, and soon enough, most of the household had woken up. The castle hummed with activity. The great hall had to be made ready for the herdsman to sleep in, as they would likely stay several nights, and the stables prepared for their tithe: pigs and sheep and perhaps even a bull. By the time the sun had fully risen, all was finished, or nearly so. Kiar gave the last few instructions to the steward and left to meet the herdsmen, smiling to himself as he passed out of the gate. His father was still asleep.

Many of the herdsmen had already reached the ford when Kiar arrived. He jumped into the shallows, calling out to them. They cheered in response, and several slid down the banks to meet him. Kiar hurried across. Frigid water dashed and foamed over the rocks, but he knew his footing. As a child, whenever his mischief had maddened his mother enough, she would send him running over the moor. His father had often grumbled that his son would grow up half wild, always at the beck and call of the wind.

Kiar grinned to himself. Maybe he was half wild, but that meant he fit in as well with the herdsmen as he did with his father's warriors. He strode onto the banks, and the men waiting there clapped him on the back. One pressed a skin of wine into his hands while another pulled him over to the campfire. This was the best of the tithe-time, Kiar thought—away from the castle. The herdsmen would show him their beasts, eager for his approval and his promise that the lord would accept their offerings, and then he could simply be a part of their revels, eating charred meat fresh from the fire and laughing over old memories.

It was well past midday when the last man's flock reached the ford and Kiar finally led the group to the castle. His father stood ready to greet them in the courtyard. The lord spared Kiar a single sharp look before he turned his attention to the herdsmen.

Kiar crossed his arms. A fresh sting of frustration cracked apart the contentment he'd felt at the ford. His gaze slid back to the castle gate. He wanted to run towards the mountains, away from the crowded courtyard and the bleating of sheep, away from his father's hearty laughter.

Instead, he drifted down to the kitchen. Now, however, servants filled the room, rushing about at Elspet's rapid orders. The place hummed with activity, even though the evening's feast was still hours away.

Elspet stood near the hearth, inspecting a roast. Her eyes caught Kiar. She cocked her head, but then a maid's clumsiness snatched her attention. Kiar snuck an apple and leaned against the wall, suddenly exhausted.

"Kiar!"

He snapped upright again. His father stood in the doorway, red-faced. "What are you doing, hiding in the kitchens? Our work's barely begun."

Kiar swallowed the last of the apple, but before he could speak, his father continued.

"Yet here you are, creeping off and stealing food like a boy. You'll be a lord, soon enough, and you expect to claim your people's loyalty, their respect? It's one thing to earn a torc, but—"

The reprimand went on. Kiar shifted, intensely aware of the maids listening and Elspet pursing her lips. He wanted to shout back at his father, but words wouldn't come. The kitchen's heat seemed to stifle him. His fingers moved up to the torc around his neck, and he twisted it slightly as sweat pricked his skin.

His father's voice stopped.

Kiar froze, his hand dropping to his side. It was too late. His father had seen the knot tied underneath the circlet.

"Are you mad?" the man hissed. In a single, hawkish swoop, he ripped the charm from Kiar's throat. He stared at it, the old leather stiff with dried blood.

"Do you want to trap her spirit here?" he whispered. His fist closed around the knot, and then he stalked across the kitchen. Servants scrambled out of his way.

Don't, Kiar wanted to cry out, but he couldn't speak. He only watched as his father threw the knot into the fire. It disappeared in an instant, the scrap swallowed up by the flames.

Kiar turned and ran.

He pushed through herds of sheep in the courtyard and raced out the gate. Someone might have called after him; he didn't know. *Do you want to trap her spirit here?* The question tore at Kiar's thoughts. What if all the old stories were true, and the blood of the dead could be used to tether their souls to the earth?

No, he told himself furiously. That was only a tale sung by the *shenachie.* His mother was gone, borne away to the *sídhe* years before.

For hours he roamed over the heath, until the sun sank into the mountains. A storm flowed over the peaks, the violet clouds singed with gold. Kiar blinked, startled. He'd stayed out all afternoon, something he hadn't done in years. He knew he ought to turn back. His father would be angry, and worried. After all, Kiar did have the tithe to oversee.

Instead, his gaze shifted to the forest. It was directly in the storm's path, but the trees would offer some shelter from the rain.

A few drops hit his face as he reached the woods and hurried deeper in. Eventually, he slowed, listening to the rain rustle in the leaves.

The misty green stillness of the place should've quieted his mind, just like hours of racing up the hills of the heath should've tamed his restlessness. Yet frustration foamed in his chest. Kiar shook his head, his long hair heavy with rain, and wished for some kind of distraction.

Someone gasped behind him.

Kiar whirled around, his hand on his knife. There, half-hidden behind a yew, crouched a woman. She drew back, her dark eyes fixed on him. Kiar released his grip on the knife and straightened slowly. "Hello," he called.

The woman didn't reply, but she didn't turn away, either. Her head tilted to one side, red curls trailing over her pale face.

For a moment, Kiar stared at her. In the shadow of the rain, the woman's white skin and grey eyes almost seemed to glow. He opened his mouth to ask her name, but then, with a sudden, graceful movement, she slipped out from behind the tree and smiled up at him.

Kiar's breath caught, the question withering away under the sudden heat that spread under his skin. Her lips were as dark as the berries beading the yew's branches.

"You should not be in this place." Her eyes glinted teasingly. She moved out from behind the tree and crossed her arms. They were bare; she wore no tunic underneath her peplos. The brooches at her shoulders gleamed even in the dim light.

Distantly, Kiar wondered why *she* was in this place, why she had no cloak despite the cold, but her words baited him. "Why not?" he asked, arching an eyebrow.

The woman spread out her hands, motioning to the trees around them. The gesture somehow brought her closer to Kiar. "Don't you know the stories of this forest?"

"According to the *shenachie*, there are stories about every forest," Kiar replied with a smirk. The woman had the otherworldly beauty of a *sí* from a poet's song, yet she stood in front of him, solid and real and so close now that he could feel her breath on his skin. Maybe she was a *sí*, but Kiar didn't feel any fear at the thought, only fascination. He couldn't look away from her.

She smiled suddenly, a red, teasing smile.

Kiar reached out and very lightly touched her hair. "You don't seem like a spirit."

"No, I'm not a spirit." Her hand twined into his. "I am Muira."

Her mouth darted up to his, and he caught the scent of death on her tongue.

CHAPTER TWO

SPRING CAME SLOW in the mountains. A rill of wind brushed against Ròs' cheek as she left the cottage, and she wanted to breathe in until the delicious cleanness of it filled her up.

"Are you sure you don't need my help?" Innes, Ròs' mentor, called from inside.

"No, I'd like to try herb-gathering on my own," Ròs answered, pinning her woolen mantle at her shoulder with a heavy, intricate brooch. It was the only one she had; she'd wanted to trade it for a simpler one, but nobody would take it.

The older woman came to the doorway, her eyes pinched. "If you're sure."

Ròs was very sure. Innes' hut was small, and nearly every day, someone came by looking for a salve or a tea or a cask of heather beer. Ròs craved time alone.

She was used to being on her own for days, used to traveling over the dales and into the mountains. She'd been to every castle and village and farm in Alba, it seemed, but for every night she'd slept under a roof, she spent half a dozen under the stars. Even after a winter in Innes' cottage, Ròs' feet still knew the pattern of the earth, and she had no fear of getting lost.

Despite the riot of wildflowers blooming over the dales, Ròs filled her basket slowly. It wasn't so cold anymore; her fingers didn't grow stiff as she picked little bunches of flowers and herbs. She wandered over the heath until sunset. By then, she'd gathered nearly everything she'd wanted, which would please Innes—and hopefully soothe any irritation about Ròs being gone so long. Even so, she walked a bit faster, moving closer to the trees where the ground was less marshy.

A flash of white caught her eye. Ròs stopped, peering into the woods. The sun had sunk behind the mountains now, but she could see a flicker of something bright.

Ròs twisted the knot around her wrist to make sure it was secure and started towards the flicker. She threaded her way through the skeletal branches until suddenly, she stood in front of a rose bush. It was early for roses. Wonderingly, she touched the soft white petals. One flower dropped into her hand. She twirled it between her thumb and forefinger, then tucked it into her braid.

"Hello," said someone behind her.

Ròs whipped around.

A man stood there, leaning against a tree. "Don't be startled. If anyone ought to be, it's me. I hardly ever see other people here." He straightened up with a slanted smile. "Though I don't mind the company."

Ròs stumbled back, the branches of the rose bush snagging her clothes and hair. Thorns scraped at her arms, but she scarcely noticed. *There's nothing to be afraid of,* she told herself, *just calm down*—but still her heartbeat filled her head.

"I see you've been pilfering my roses," the man continued. He stepped closer, within arm's reach of her. "I'm afraid I'll have to take a little toll for that."

Dread blurred Ròs' vision. Why couldn't she *speak*? She knew this old fear by heart and yet couldn't force it down.

The man laughed, his pale blue eyes crinkling with amusement as he moved nearer. "Don't be frightened. I'm not going to hurt you. Anyway, you're the thief."

He was standing too close, so close that she could smell the thick tang of his sweat. A rage of panic shot through her blood, and Ròs threw her basket at him.

He stumbled back. Before he caught his balance, Ròs tore herself free, the roses clawing at her sleeves. Something snapped. She didn't stop to see what had ripped loose, though, only ran. The trees seemed to constrict, while behind her, she could hear the man calling. His shout was guttural, then drawn out, rising like a howl.

Ròs raced blindly through the branches, her chest aching for breath, until her foot caught on a root. She fell hard.

"You're quick."

She jerked her head up. The man stood over her, his mouth pulled into a grin. As he dropped into a crouch, his smile slowly stretched.

His shaggy black hair spread over his back, his face, his arms, and his blue eyes brightened into copper. Ròs shrank back in horror. He was a hound, massive and growling and poised to spring.

"Get back!" she screamed, staggering to her feet and instinctively flinging up her arms. As she did, she saw the mess of scratches on her bare wrists and realized what she had left behind on the rose bush.

Her knot.

Ròs' eyes widened in horror. Before she had time to move, the hound lunged. His teeth sunk into her arm. She screamed again, but as blood-red pain filled her vision, she wrenched the brooch from her mantle and stabbed the hound with its pin.

The creature snarled in pain, its jaw loosening. Ròs kicked it away. Half sobbing, she began to run again, but she was dizzy now and knew she wouldn't make it far.

Something dark moved in the pines ahead of her. Ròs squinted, then rubbed a hand over her face. A massive black bull blocked her path, his horns pale in the dim light.

Ròs stopped. They'd trapped her.

The bull strode towards her. "Get on my back."

Her pulse was roaring so loudly in her ears that, for a second, Ròs couldn't understand the words.

"*Get on my back.*"

The bull's voice was low and harsh. Ròs hesitated, but only long enough to hear the hound's howl behind her. Then she grabbed hold of the bull's thick fur and hauled herself onto his back.

For such a massive beast, he moved quick, deftly weaving between the trees. It took all Ròs' strength to hang on, her fingers entwined in his coarse hide. She buried her head in his neck with her shoulders scrunched up to her ears.

She didn't know how long they ran. When the bull pulled to a stop, rearing back and stomping his hooves, she lost her grip and tumbled off. Dazed, she rolled over, her cheek against the cold turf.

The bull moved closer, his nose twitching. Stiffly, Ròs sat up. It was dark now, but she could see by the stars that they were in a small clearing with a ring of stones at the center. A well, she realized, catching the glint of light reflected on the water. A holy well. A spring called forth by the gods themselves, so abundant that it not only filled the shaft but saturated the earth around it. The circle of turf around the well grew vividly green, thick with little white flowers.

"You're safe here," the bull announced.

Ròs glanced at him. The voice was so *human*. Questions burned in the back of her throat, but she simply stared.

"Madragh—the hound—he can't touch you, not if you stay in this clearing," the bull continued. "The virtue of the well is strong. It will protect you so long as you can feel the water beneath your feet. But we're deep in the forest now." He grunted. "And Madragh isn't the only shiftling. I don't think I could get you to the edge of the wood, not without one of them scenting us. I'm sorry."

Ròs only sat there. She was aware of a pain in her hand, and she unclenched her fist, wincing as she saw the brooch clamped against her palm. The pin had stuck in her skin. She drew it out, the wound oozing blood.

The bull lowered his head. "I'm Kiar. Can you tell me your name?"

"Ròs," she whispered, touching the flower still tangled in her hair. And then a sob broke loose.

Memories burned like ice in her blood and prickled under her skin—a man's hands on her body, the reek of heather-beer in his mouth. She shook her head, clawing her arms around her chest, trying to tear herself back into *now*, not then, but she was trapped inside the fear.

The bull nudged her shoulder, a whiff of breath steaming over her face. The solid warmth of him sent a shiver through her, and for a moment, the memories retreated. He knelt down, not quite touching her, but she reached out to twine her hand into his fur. The weight of his presence held her steady.

After a while—her tears worn out and her head aching—she turned to look at him. He lifted his head, and though she couldn't see his eyes beneath the tufts of black fur, she could feel his gaze mirroring her own misery.

"I'll kill him," he muttered.

Her mind still tangled in memories, Ròs thought for a moment that the bull meant *him.* Then she realized he meant the hound. Madragh, he'd called the beast. "What did he want with me?" she asked, her voice hoarse.

The bull grunted. "To take you to Muira, the *bhuidseach* of these woods. That witch turns all who trespass here into shiftlings." His nostrils flared. "You're bleeding."

Ròs closed her fist, hiding the bloody bruise on her palm. "It's nothing."

"Your *other* arm."

Frowning, Ròs lifted her right arm, her sleeve torn and bloodstained, then gasped as the movement sparked a spasm of pain. The hound's bite.

"Let me see it," the bull said.

Ròs shut her eyes, forcing herself to breathe through a wave of nausea. She wasn't sure what the bull thought he could do and meant to tell him that she could manage, but when she opened her eyes, her breath froze in her lungs.

There wasn't any bull on the edge of the clearing. There was a man, tall and broad-shouldered, with a tangle of dark hair and a scruffy beard on his face. He had no tunic, only breeches and a mantle. Blue-black tattoos swirled over his arms and chest. The marks of a warrior.

"Here," the man said, reaching out to her.

Ròs stumbled back. Her feet sank into the wet turf, and a strange, tingling coolness spread through her.

The man frowned, taking a step closer, but as his foot touched the damp ground, he flinched and jerked away.

Ròs felt the stones of the well brush against her skirt. "Change back," she whispered, her eyes dropping.

He stared at her. "But—"

"*Change back.*" Her voice shook. "Please."

She kept her gaze down until she heard a hoof pawing the earth. A sigh slipped out, and she leaned against the well. Her right arm gave way then, slipping into the water. Ròs gasped at the cold shock.

"I didn't mean to scare you." The bull paced at the edge of the clearing.

Pulling her arm against her stomach, Ròs let her hair fall over her face to hide her flushed cheeks. She didn't know what to say. He *had* scared her. As much as she wanted to laugh it off or even just look at him, she couldn't. She scratched at the bloodstained skin of her arm, then stiffened.

The bite was gone.

"The well," she said softly.

"What?" The bull leaned forward.

Ròs glanced at him now, holding out her arm. "The water healed it."

"I didn't realize it was so powerful. I can't touch the water any more than Madragh or the *bhuidseach* can. If only—" He grunted, kicking at the turf, then shied away as a spray of water went up.

Ròs touched the rim of the well almost reverently. "How did you find this place?"

"Hiding." The bull shrugged back his powerful shoulders; in a flash of moonlight, Ròs noticed three pale scars cut into his fur. "After the first time I fought Madragh. He was trying to lure a little boy into the forest."

"He gave you those?" She gestured to the scars.

"No," he said shortly. "Muira did, as a punishment for interfering with Madragh's hunt."

Ròs sat on the edge of the well and pulled up a long blade of grass, absently twisting it into a knot. "Why did the *bhuidseach* turn you into a bull?" she asked.

CHAPTER THREE

KIAR COULDN'T KEEP the bitterness out of his words as he replied to the woman's question. "It is not hard to tell."

Ròs' fingers twitched.

Inwardly, Kiar smiled. *It is not hard to tell.* These were the words sung by the *shenachie* as they began a tale. He had heard them a thousand times in his father's hall, and though he did not recognize this woman, he knew the *shenachie* symbol etched into her brooch.

"The wood belongs to the *bhuidseach*," he continued. "She caught me trespassing." Now he was glad to be a bull, grateful for the fur hiding how his face burned at the memory. "There was poison on her tongue. When I woke up, she was tearing the torc from my neck."

Ròs winced. Kiar turned away—he didn't want pity. Rage built in his chest at the thought of his torc around Muira's throat.

"And the spell?" Ròs asked.

"Her words rang with a power as strong as pain, in the trees and the stones, and then I could feel them in my blood." His teeth clenched as he spun back towards Ròs. "I can still feel them. As long as I'm in this forest, I have the power to change back to myself, but if I leave, I'll be trapped as a bull forever."

There was silence. Ròs stared at Kiar as though trying to memorize every detail of his tale.

"Have you ever told a story like this one?" Kiar asked.

Ròs' eyes dropped. "Why do you ask?"

"Your brooch. I recognized the symbol." Though it was her hands as much as her brooch that gave her away. Her fingers had the steady grace—and the calluses—of a musician.

The brooch lay on the ground still, glinting as a mist began to fall. Ròs picked it up. "I'm apprenticed to a healer now. I haven't told any stories in over a year."

"But you still remember," Kiar insisted. He edged forward, but the power of the well pushed him back. "You're a *shenachie.* You know the stories that answer every question. One of them *has* to answer mine."

Ròs stood and began to pace. "I know stories of men being turned to beasts and of beasts that can disguise themselves as men. I know stories of the gods walking the earth as beasts, but—" Her mouth quirked. "You don't seem especially godlike."

Kiar almost laughed, startled by the sudden quickness of her smile. He'd convinced her, then. It didn't matter how many stories she had to recite, as long as one of them showed him a way to kill the witch and reclaim his torc.

"There is one tale," Ròs said. Her voice dropped, slipping into a soft rhythm that made Kiar lean forward, eager to catch the words. "It is not hard to tell."

Ròs wished she could've denied being a *shenachie,* but it was impossible. A thousand stories still spun through her mind, just waiting for a blazing hearth; a thousand melodies still thrummed in her fingers, just waiting to be released by a harp's strings. There was no fire beside the well, and she had no harp, but she belonged to these stories. They lent her voice power.

The bull listened avidly. He was a good audience, Ròs observed. Better than most lords she'd met. If he hadn't told her that the *bhuidseach* took his torc, she never would've thought he was a lord at all.

Then again, he wasn't especially like any warrior she'd ever met, either. Ròs pushed the thought to the back of her mind. She had stories to tell, tales of *bhuidseach,* of bulls, of curses. Enough stories to fill the whole night.

Yet none of them were right. As Ròs finished each tale, Kiar asked questions, searching for some key to destroying the witch. For all Ròs knew of lore, however, she had no answer—or at least, none that helped him. She only had more stories. Caught up in her craft and his curiosity, she began another and another.

It was only when dawn broke that she realized how exhausted she was. She fell asleep almost as soon as she lay down, but the dampness of the ground seeped through her mantle and skirts. She woke up shivering.

Kiar's ears twitched. "You'll catch a chill if you stay so close to the well."

Ròs' teeth were chattering, but she hesitated.

"You can jump back into the circle again if we hear anything," he said quickly.

For a moment, Ròs could almost picture him as a man, holding out his hand to her—his eyes sharp with concern, yet his shoulders tensed, almost uncertain. Something flared in her chest, the brightness of it almost painful, but Ròs clenched her fist. He was a bull, not a man. She needed him to stay that way.

Still, she left the circle and sat down beside him, beginning a story she'd woken up remembering. He nudged closer to her as she spoke, and she leaned into the warmth of his fur. The chill slowly seeped out of her bones.

CHAPTER FOUR

DAYS PASSED, AND the *shenachie* still had stories to tell. Her voice transformed the little circle around the well into the peak of a mountain or the hollows under the hills.

Her voice had the power of spring rain, Kiar thought, bringing worlds to life.

He left the well each morning, shifting into a man to forage for wild herbs and mushrooms, though he always shifted back before returning to Ròs. Often, he heard the distant howl of a hound, but Madragh never appeared.

Kiar almost wished he would. He hated hiding.

He hated the forest, too: the closeness of the trees and the leaves that covered the sky and the emptiness. It drove him mad to hear nothing but his own voice in his head—and every snapped twig sent him whirling around, fists raised. He kept reaching for his knife, only to remember it was long gone. Like his torc. Like his knot. The sight of the tattoos on his arms made his gut curl. The marks painted into his skin as a warning to his enemies were an empty threat. The *bhuidseach* had stripped everything from him, and now he jumped at shadows.

Just a boy, lost in the woods.

Kiar turned back to the well as quickly as he could. There, the *shenachie* would be waiting for him—a tangible reminder that despite the *bhuidseach's* power, he'd still managed to steal Ròs from her.

One morning, Kiar woke early, the *shenachie's* story from the night before still humming in his mind. She'd sung the tale of Lir's children, transformed into swans by their stepmother. This witch sent them into exile for nine hundred years. Once the curse released them, they died, finally at peace. Kiar wondered grimly if they were at peace or just exhausted. The story's ending hardly satisfied him, and besides, Muira hadn't set any time limit on his curse. He couldn't just wait for it to break on its own.

He sighed. His muscles were stiff, but he couldn't move; Ròs slept against his side, curled up with her face in his fur. He lifted his head to see her, careful not to stir too much. She seemed thinner, her cheeks hollowed, and shadows smudged under her eyes. Anxiety pinched Kiar's gut. She couldn't live on mushrooms forever. Perhaps he could try to snare a rabbit, but without a knife, he couldn't skin it, and he didn't dare light a fire.

If he could find a sharp flat rock, then he might be able to manage. And if he made a fire far away from the well, ready to run if one of the shiftlings scented it . . . risky, of course, but it might work. He sniffed, trying to remember the scent of meat roasting on a spit, the delicious sizzle of juice as it dripped onto the coals. His stomach growled.

Ròs stretched slightly, her eyes flickering. She yawned, and the breath blew a strand of red hair out of her face.

"Sorry," Kiar said. "I didn't mean to wake you."

"'S all right," Ròs mumbled, glancing up at the sky. "It's late." She sat up and wrapped her arms around her shins. "Innes never would've let me sleep so long."

Kiar's tail twitched. Ròs rarely mentioned the healer or her life outside the forest. She talked all day and half the night, but never about herself. "She must be worried about you," he said quietly.

"Yes. She must." With a sudden smile, Ròs added, "Or she'll be glad to be rid of such a useless apprentice. I'm much better with words than I am with herbs." She stepped over to the well and splashed the water onto her face. Her fingers combed through her hair, deftly weaving it back into a braid. "Your family must be worried about you as well," she said, her eyes tilted toward him.

"My father probably thinks I've run off," Kiar replied, and though he meant to say it lightly, the words tasted as hard and sour as a rowan berry. He forced a smile. "At least he's not to blame for the curse, though. He's got better sense than to take a *bhuidseach* for a second wife."

Ròs tied off the end of her braid with a scrap of fabric torn from the bottom of her dress. "Your mother died, then?"

"Years ago." Kiar stood abruptly. "You must be hungry. Hopefully, I'll find something more than wild garlic today."

"Can I come with you?"

Kiar stared at her. "No. It's too dangerous."

"I'll stay with you the whole time," Ròs insisted. "You said you haven't seen Madragh out there, or Muira. And we can stay close to the well, so we can run back if they do find us." She hugged her arms against her chest. "I know it isn't safe, Kiar, but I'm . . . I'm going mad. All I can do is walk in circles around this well, over and over, waiting for you to come back. I need to get away, just for a little."

"No," Kiar repeated more sharply. "If they catch me, there's not much worse they can do than what they've already done. But if Muira gets you, we're done for." He gritted his teeth. He hadn't meant to lie to her—and he hadn't, not really. He didn't know the full truth himself and didn't see any point in frightening her with the unknown. She'd been terrified enough when he found her. "Ròs, you know I'm not the only man she's lured into the wood. Madragh, of course, but there are others, all of them transformed into beasts and set to guard the borders of the forest." He shut his eyes. "You aren't the first woman, though. I told you Muira meant to turn you into a shiftling, and that might be true, but I don't know. The women brought to her are never seen again."

Now he looked up at Ròs, meeting her gaze. She stared back at him, and then her mouth set in a grim line. "I'm not afraid of her."

"Yes, you are. Or you should be. Even if you're not, you're our only chance at getting out of this hell. I won't risk losing you to her." With that, he spun around and plunged into the forest.

As soon as he was sure she couldn't see him anymore, he shifted, letting out a sigh as he settled into his own skin. The transformation brought little relief, though. He could still feel the weight of the bull in his blood. When he tangled a hand through his hair, the strands seemed thicker and coarser, more like an animal's hide.

Perhaps he should've stayed with Ròs. He hadn't thought about what she might feel like, penned inside the circle. After all, she was safe there. He didn't think she would mind a rest from storytelling, or the time alone. Even when Kiar was a bull, she seemed wary of him.

Given Madragh's attack, he could hardly blame her. Still, he'd brought her to the haven of the well. He meant to protect her from Muira. The *bhuidseach* might have his torc, but he was still his father's son. A lord defended his land and his people, even if all he had was a well and a *shenachie.*

A chill wind scuttled through the trees. Shivering, Kiar pulled his mantle tighter around his shoulders and cursed under his breath. Overhead, the clouds hung heavy and dark as boulders. More rain, Kiar thought, and he cursed again. So much for the hope of a fire.

The mist soon thickened into a cold drizzle that wormed into his mantle and slithered over his skin. Kiar almost shifted back into a bull, though he knew from experience that wet fur wasn't much better than wet clothes. Besides, he needed his hands to forage.

With the sky overcast, it was difficult to tell how much time passed. Kiar wandered further into the woods, collecting a small bundle of herbs, and eventually came across a cluster of mushrooms. He crouched down to inspect them. Morels, he decided, and smiled slightly. It wasn't meat, but he'd noticed that Ròs liked morels. Whenever he brought them back, she saved the mushrooms for last and then ate them quite slowly, savoring each bite. He pulled one up.

A twig snapped nearby.

Kiar stiffened. The mushroom fell to the ground as he shifted. Slowly, he turned around, his nose twitching. Shreds of rain fell in his eyes, but it didn't matter; the stench of wet dog filled the mist. "Come out, Madragh."

Hoarse laughter broke through the branches, and then Madragh appeared, his tail heavy with mud. He shook himself and bared his teeth in a grin. "Hello, Kiar. We've been looking for you."

Kiar grunted, his eyes on the hound, but his ears pricked. There. A slight rustle in the brambles. He backed away just as another figure appeared: a man, tall and lean, with pale hair and dark eyes. A cold tickle that had nothing to do with the rain slid along Kiar's spine.

He stamped the fear down. "What do you want, Deirc?"

Deirc smiled thinly. "Where's the girl?"

"Who?"

Madragh hacked out another laugh. "You reek of her scent, bull. Been having a little fun, have you?" He loped forward. "Just like a lord to keep a pretty thing all to himself."

Kiar ground his teeth together, holding back a snarl. The hound meant to bait him, and he wasn't going to fall for it.

"Muira wants her," Madragh continued. "And you. She'll do worse than a few scratches this time, Kiar. You've tried her patience long enough."

"She might spare you," Deirc cut in. "If you tell us where you've hidden the girl."

"*She* might," Madragh said. "But I won't."

Kiar snorted. "What will you do, Madragh? Kill me? Not while Muira's got your leash. You wouldn't dare go against her."

"I'm not her pet," Madragh retorted. "She might think herself the queen of this forest, but she doesn't command me." He ran his tongue over his sharp teeth. "Besides, I'd be doing her a favor. She might even reward me for it."

"You're a fool," Kiar said quietly. "Any power you have belongs to her. She owns you, whether or not you see it."

"Is that why you resist her, *my lord*?" Deirc said mockingly. "Does it sting your pride to see your torc around the *bhuidseach's* neck?" His red eyes narrowed. "She beat you, and now you're thrashing because you don't have the cunning to control her any other way. A warrior wouldn't. You don't know what it is to fight with anything except a sword."

"I don't want to control her," Kiar spat. "I don't want *her* at all, and she won't have me."

Deirc smiled. "She will. And she'll have the girl, too. For all your defiance, you know you cannot resist Muira's magic. Spare yourself the humiliation and tell us where you've stashed the bitch."

Kiar forced himself not to flinch, but Deirc's words sent a violent tremor through him. He knew Muira could rip his mind open and drag the secret out. But he didn't think they would call her just yet. He sensed the hunger in Madragh's threats, and whatever the hound said about Muira, he wouldn't dare disobey her once she appeared. Kiar guessed Madragh wanted a chance at revenge first.

Which gave Kiar the chance to kill *him*. He wouldn't lose against a mangy hound.

Only he couldn't risk it. If they did call the witch, Ròs would be lost.

So Kiar stepped back. "You haven't caught me yet."

And with that, he whirled around and ran.

He heard the hound tearing after him but didn't look back, only charged through the trees. He had to lead them away from the well, he knew. Charging down into the bed of a stream and up the ravine, he followed the path of the water as it cut across the forest.

Above him on the ridge, Madragh matched his pace. Kiar forced himself to run faster, but his hooves slipped in the mud along the bank. Knees buckling, he scarcely managed to keep his balance. The hound leaped down as Kiar fought to regain his footing. Claws dug into Kiar's back, and he reared up, bellowing. Madragh clung on.

Kiar writhed and bucked. The sky spun above him as his forelegs slashed the air, his vision freckled red with pain, and then the awful current of gravity swept him toward the water. He twisted just enough to land on his back, but the force of the fall smacked his lungs flat. He struggled for breath, momentarily paralyzed. A trickle of air scraped down his throat. He gasped, rolling over.

Beside him, the hound sprawled half in and half out of the stream. Kiar staggered to his feet and backed away. The hound lay still, only his tail moving slightly as the water ran over it. Then his eyes opened, fixed on the bull.

Kiar jerked away. He shifted to climb up the bank and glanced over his shoulder long enough to see the hound crawl out of the stream. Quickly, he turned around, just in time to see a flicker in the underbrush.

He sprang aside as an adder darted up from the leaves. It let out a savage hiss and struck, but Kiar snatched a broken branch from the ground and swung it. The branch hit the adder's head, and its lithe body snapped like a whip. Kiar shifted into a bull and ran, this time not daring to look back.

The drizzle thickened into a true downpour as Kiar raced through the woods. He could scarcely see and nearly rammed his horns into a tree more than once, yet he kept going. Only when the branches thinned did he realize that he had reached the edges of the forest.

He pulled up short. An icy cord of terror wrapped around his heart as he looked around him. Beyond the trees, he could see a sloping field, grey with rain. A few more paces and he would've been trapped—free of the forest but forever caged inside the bull's form.

Kiar.

He heard his name, the voice as soft and cold and pervasive as mist. A shudder went through him.

The rain stilled, the forest suddenly quiet. Kiar wanted to yell back at the voice, but he forced himself not to move. He could feel the tremor of power in the air.

Slowly, he stepped back into the forest. Soon the field had disappeared, only trees around him. The rain fell again. Nearby, a dove keened.

Kiar began to trot, then broke into a run.

CHAPTER FIVE

RAIN DRIPPED DOWN the back of Ròs' neck, into her ears, along her spine. She blinked hard and rubbed water out of her eyes. It didn't do much good. The forest remained a haze of empty shadows. Kiar still hadn't appeared.

She coughed, clenching her teeth to keep them from chattering. *Helpless.* She knew this feeling, the wild and miserable ache of it, the surge of frustration that rattled her ribs like the bars of a cage. It wasn't the cold or the rain; Ròs had spent more of her life under the sky than under a roof. Except that before, she could wander where she liked. Now, she couldn't leave the well's reach.

If Kiar didn't come back, she would have to, though. Ròs buried her face against her knees, wondering how long she would have to wait. *Tomorrow morning,* she told herself. *If he isn't back by tomorrow morning . . .*

But that meant all the rest of the day and an endless night of waiting.

Or she could escape now.

Nothing kept her tethered to the well. The bull couldn't leave the forest, she knew, but she still could. The shiftlings, or even the *bhuidseach,* might catch her. Yet it might be worth the risk. Ròs couldn't stay in the well's circle forever, dependent on the bull for meager scraps of food, terrified every time he left that he might not return. The only curse on her was fear.

Ròs straightened, her eyes fixed on the forest again. She could overcome that. She *would.*

She stood up and walked towards the trees. The rain had soaked into the turf so she could no longer tell where the well's protection ended, but she told herself she didn't care. Water seeped into the seams of her boots as she marched into the forest.

Her hands shook, and she balled them into fists. She would keep going. She'd get out of this place. By nightfall, she might be in Innes' hut, settled in front of the fire while the healer forced her to drink buckets of nettle tea.

Or she'd be dead, killed by the witch.

Kiar might already be dead.

Ròs stopped. When Kiar saved her from Madragh, he'd defied the *bhuidseach* for the second time; if Muira caught him now, she'd do worse than carve a few scars into his side. Ròs' stomach jerked as she imagined Kiar out there, hurt, maybe dying—either as the bull with his gentle eyes or the man who had held out a hand to her.

Something tugged at Ròs' chest as though a spider had spun a silk thread between her and Kiar, and the line had suddenly been drawn tight. She almost gasped at the pinch. A flush fired over her skin, and she stopped, her hands in her hair.

He only saved you because he needs you, whispered a dark little part of her mind. *This lord, this warrior. He's just using you to get what he wants.*

Ròs bit the inside of her cheek and shook her head. He *did* need her, and right then, she needed him. He'd asked for her help, and Ròs meant to give it, whatever little help it was.

Besides, marching through the forest alone got her into this mess in the first place.

Ròs turned around. She settled with her back against the well again, and she waited. Worry nibbled at her gut as the sky darkened and the rain slowed.

It wasn't until after nightfall that she heard footsteps in the forest. Ròs huddled under her mantle, watching the trees. She wanted to run but kept quite still. She had to stay by the well. Nothing could hurt her if she stayed by the well.

A large shape loomed out of the mist. Ròs' shoulders sagged as she saw the bull's shaggy body and curving horns.

"Ròs?" he called.

For a moment, she couldn't speak. Relief gushed over her. "I'm here," she finally replied, her voice husky.

The bull stumbled to the edge of the well's circle and leaned against a tree. "Good."

Ròs moved towards him. He looked exhausted, his head lowered and his breath coming in steamy huffs. "What happened?" she asked.

Kiar jerked his head up. There was nothing gentle in his eyes now; they glittered with a rage that made Ròs flinch back. Dizziness lurched in her gut. She knotted her fingers around her arm, every muscle tensed to run.

"Madragh," Kiar said through gritted teeth. "Him and another shiftling."

Anger seemed to surge out of him, along with the stench of sweat. Ròs bit her lip and tried not to breathe in, as though she could somehow protect herself from that awful aura. Kiar's eyes fixed on her, and his ears twitched. "It's all right. I shook them off. They didn't follow me back here." He kicked at the turf. "Though it would've been better if I killed them."

Ròs opened her mouth to reply but said nothing. Only a few steps and she'd be back in the well's circle. Yet as she stood there, caught up in the current of his anger, she felt the strange tug of silken thread again, and she held her ground. He wouldn't hurt her. The swell of his fury, even if she thought she might choke on it, encircled her like the magic of the well.

She breathed in sharply, caught up in the terrifying safety of it.

Kiar's legs buckled, and he knelt down, his chin dropping to the ground. He cursed under his breath, almost wearily.

"Are you hurt?" Ròs asked.

"It isn't bad," Kiar mumbled. "I just need to rest." He shut his eyes. "I brought you some food. I left it on the stone."

Ròs hesitated—she couldn't see any injuries, though his thick black fur might be hiding them—but then stumbled past the bull and into the trees. The stone was large and flat, tucked into the rambling roots of a beech tree, just out of sight of the well. Kiar always left the food he foraged there, then shifted back into a bull before returning to her. A flicker of warmth stung Ròs' chest as she crouched down beside the stone.

Morels. A little pile of them, drops of rain filling their honeycomb caps. Ròs swallowed. She almost wanted to smile, except she thought she might crack if she did. Instead, she scooped them up and hurried back to the well.

“Thank you,” she said softly. Her fingers ran over his hide, searching for any trace of blood.

Kiar shrugged one shoulder. “They’re your favorite, aren’t they?”

“Yes,” Ròs replied. She hadn’t told him, she didn’t think. Yet he’d noticed.

“You must be freezing.”

“Yes,” Ròs said again and wished she could say something else, something better. But all her words were borrowed, and right then, she couldn’t remember a single story. So she curled up against the bull’s side and felt his chest rise and fall in rhythm with hers as they both dozed off.

CHAPTER SIX

THE DAYS GREW warmer, though the nights stayed cold. Kiar thought he knew the forest after spending half a year there, but he'd never seen it in spring. Buds freckled the dirt and then burst into a furor of purple and yellow and white. Birds and squirrels chittered in the treetops, and a sharp green sort of smell filled the air.

Kiar might've liked it better if all those flowers were edible—or filling. Still, the spring brought with it a fleet of young rabbits, temptingly easy to snare. He decided the fresh meat was worth the risk of a fire. He got a small blaze going far from the well and paced anxiously as his catch roasted, though none of the shiftlings appeared. Once the meat cooked through, he ate his half in a few ravenous gulps, relishing in how it scorched his tongue. He hurriedly skewered Ròs' portion on a stick and started back to the well, worried it would get cold before he returned.

"Ròs," he called as he reached the usual rock and set the meat down. "Come and see what I caught!"

Through the trees, he could see her at the well's edge. She hesitated, peering into the forest.

Kiar pressed the heel of his hand against his forehead. Of course. He shifted quickly into the bull's form and trotted forward so she could see him. "It's all right," he said. "Come on. I've got a surprise."

One eyebrow quirked, Ròs followed him to the rock, then let out a small gasp. She snatched up the meat and tore into it. After the first rapid bite, she sank back against a tree, chewing slowly. "This," she said, "tastes better than anything I've ever eaten in a lord's castle."

The meat was lean, charred, and unseasoned, but Kiar couldn't agree more. "You must've had some feasts, though," he said. "Whenever a *shenachie* came to my father's hall, the kitchens turned out their best."

She swallowed. "I liked the villages better. Less food, but more dancing."

Kiar almost reached out a hand, ready to show her that a lord's son knew how to dance just as well as any villager. But then remembered he didn't have a hand, only a hoof. His tail twitched.

"I wonder if I ever came to your father's castle," Ròs mused as she took another bite.

"You didn't," Kiar said. "I'd remember you."

With a small snort, Ròs picked the last piece of meat from the skewer. "Would you?"

"I would," he insisted. "You're the best *shenachie* I've ever seen."

Ròs' hand froze halfway to her mouth.

"Once, the poet Cathán sang for my father," he began, then hesitated. He hadn't told her much about his home, not since the first night, and hadn't planned to, either. Yet she was staring at him, curious, so he went on. "They say he was more than just a *shenachie*, that he mastered both verse and vision and could see the designs of the gods before they came to pass. When he sang, his voice held every person in the hall captive." Kiar ducked his head to meet Ròs' eyes, and he smiled. "Except me. I fell asleep."

That startled a laugh out of Ròs.

Kiar laughed as well. "My mother was furious. She gave me a fierce scolding, said I'd dishonored our guest." He stopped then, his smile soured by a jerk of pain as he remembered her. Swallowing, he continued. "But I never could keep awake when the *shenachie* sang. Not until now."

"I'm not sure that means much," Ròs pointed out drily. "Since our lives depend on it."

"No," Kiar replied. "I think if you'd come to my father's hall, I'd have listened to every word."

Ròs smiled slightly, rolling the bare skewer between her fingers.

"Why'd you give it up?" The question came out before Kiar could stop it.

After a moment, Ròs said, "It is not hard to tell. I was tired of castles."

Kiar opened his mouth, then shut it. *It is not hard to tell.* Despite his disinterest in the *shenachie* who visited his father's castle, he still knew their skill. It took years to learn the ancient epics, the long cycles of poetry and song. No story was easily told, though the *shenachie's* art made it seem so. Whatever drove Ròs to give up her craft and hide away in a healer's hut, Kiar doubted she could tell it so simply. After all, he knew for himself what it was like to be tired of castles. To explain what drove him from his home that day, though, the tangle of pain and anger that made him run from his father—Kiar didn't have the words and didn't want to find them.

He looked at her carefully, and a flare of shame jabbed his gut. He shouldn't have asked her about it. He shouldn't have asked anything of her, but they were both trapped, and he had been so sure she held the key. Now, a hundred stories later, he wondered if there was no key to be found.

"Ròs," he started. "What if I could get you to the forest's edge? It'd be risky, but—"

"What about you?" she asked sharply.

Kiar shrugged. "I'll manage. You can't stay here forever."

"Neither can you." Ròs scooted forward until her face was in front of his. "I'm not giving up just yet."

"It's not giving up." He stood and stamped his hooves, relishing in the strength of the bull's form. "Trust me. I'm not dying as Muira's slave. I won't yield to her, to any of them."

Ròs' face tightened, and Kiar's eyes narrowed. "What is it?"

"Nothing." She hesitated, then repeated, "*I won't yield.* That just reminded me of a story."

"What story?"

She plucked at a loose thread in her mantle. "It isn't important. I don't think it'll help us."

"But it might," Kiar insisted.

"Not this story."

"Why not?" Kiar shook his head impatiently. "Ròs, we don't even know what we're looking for anymore. *Any* story might be the one."

"All right," Ròs said, plucking up a blade of grass and knotting it around her fingers. "How did Deidra come to be called Deidra of Sorrows? It is not hard to tell."

But her voice was thin.

As she began to speak, Kiar realized he vaguely remembered the story. He had heard it years ago. Still, he listened carefully for any new insight, any hint for how to defeat Muira.

The king of Alba, while visiting the island of Erin, stayed in the castle of a chief whose wife was in labor. The king's seer foretold that the child born would bring the death of many great men, for her beauty would drive them mad. The king's warriors, unsettled by the seer's words, wanted to kill the child, but the king instead demanded her for himself. He took her from her mother's arms the very night she was born.

He hid Deidra away in his castle and allowed no man near her, rearing her to be his own as soon as she came of age. Deidra knew, always, that this would be her fate, but she refused to yield to him. Even after he took her into his bed, she searched for an escape.

One night, a band of warriors came to stay in the king's hall. He offered them hospitality, as a king should, and brought out Deidra to serve them. As she poured their wine, she studied the warriors, searching for the strongest, the most cunning. Fingal, the youngest son of their chief, easily surpassed the rest. Deidra caught his eye, but he did not dare return her smile; he knew the king jealously protected his property. Later that night, Deidra crept from the king's bed and slipped down to the hall. Fingal, for all his fear of the king, could not resist Deidra's beauty. The two fled the castle before dawn.

The story, Kiar remembered, did not end happily, but it was not the story that twisted his heart. As Ròs sang Deidra's lament, the ache in her voice hung heavy in the air. Kiar's throat constricted.

"Ròs," he said abruptly.

She broke off, blinking.

He'd never interrupted her before. Yet he had to.

"What?" she asked.

Kiar opened his mouth, but he didn't know how to answer. Half to break the silence and half because it was true, he said, "It hurts you, telling this story."

The tangle of grass dropped out of her hands. "It's a lament," she said shortly. "It's supposed to be sad."

"No," Kiar pressed. "It isn't just sad. It *hurts* you." He knew because it hurt *him* to hear the pain in her voice, worse than Muira's lash or Madragh's bite. He needed to help her—he needed to know. "Why, Ròs?"

Her fists clenched. "It's always hurt me, even before."

For the first time since the night they'd met, Kiar wanted to shift out of the bull's form. He wanted to reach out to her, take her in his arms and promise her that she was safe there, yet he didn't dare.

He didn't want to see that fear on her face again.

"Then tell a different story, Ròs," he said, kneeling down next to her. "I don't much like this one either."

She bent her head, curls falling over her face, but as she began a new tale, she rested her hand on his side.

CHAPTER SEVEN

SHE COULD'VE TOLD him.

Except she didn't know how. She couldn't even sing Deidra's lament; she didn't know how to piece together her own.

In the cool light of dawn, she stared up at the sky and thought about Kiar's question—and his eyes on hers, somehow both sharp and gentle. He *saw* her. She might spin stories of kings and *bhuidseach*, but she couldn't hide herself behind them. Kiar saw her.

Ròs wanted to pace, only that would remind her of how little freedom she had. Besides, she didn't dare move. Kiar might wake up. Part of her wanted him to ask one more time, to press her for the truth. The other part of her hoped he would never mention it or even *look* at her again. She wasn't sure she wanted to be seen.

She certainly didn't want to look at herself.

Kiar set out to forage soon after he woke, and for once, Ròs didn't mind. She needed to be alone. The quiet of the clearing gave her little respite, though, as her thoughts kept wandering back to Deidra's lament. She stood and knotted a hand in her hair as though she could yank the song out of her head: *Comfortless, no peace or joy . . . break my heart no more today.*

Please, Ròs thought. *Please, no more today. Don't make me remember.*

So when she heard the scream, she almost thought it was her own.

It was a boy's voice, she realized. Ròs rushed to the edge of the well's circle and hesitated. No sign of Kiar in the woods. She didn't know how long he'd been gone, either, or if he was too far away to hear the scream. Torn, she glanced back at the well. Kiar would tell her to stay put, but then, he wasn't there.

Another scream. Now Ròs ran, yet even as fear sparked in her veins, she felt a thrill of relief at the sudden freedom. Wind tangled her hair, and her feet scudded against rocks and roots. She slowed as she drew nearer to the sound, her breath short and her heart quickening. She grabbed a fallen branch and clutched it tight.

Ahead of her, she saw something blue among the trees. Her fingers dug into the rough wood of her makeshift weapon as she edged closer. There was no sign of the hound, though, only a boy slumped beside an oak, wrapped in a blue mantle. Nearby, a sheep lay still. Its wool was matted with blood.

"Please!" the boy yelled, his voice weaker now.

Ròs hurried towards him. "Be quiet!"

The boy started and pressed up against the oak's trunk. "Who are you?"

She ignored this, dropping the branch and crouching down beside him. He couldn't have been older than fourteen, scarcely more than a child. Mud stained his tunic and breeches, the cloth worn but sturdy. Likely a farmer's boy, Ròs decided. "It's all right," she said, and then she saw the blood on his leg.

His eyes fixed on hers, bright with terror but oddly glazed. "I . . . I can't stand up."

Deftly, Ròs rolled the fabric back and examined the wound. A chill spread through her chest. It wasn't what she'd expected, not the bite of a hound or even a gash. Only two punctures, small but steadily oozing blood. "What did this?" Ròs asked, keeping her voice steady.

"Snake," the boy mumbled. "I was near the woods with the flock and heard a howl. The sheep panicked. They scattered, and one of them ran into the forest. I followed, but when I found it . . . " He looked over at the dead animal and clamped his mouth shut, his face sickly pale. "I wasn't paying attention to the ground. I must've stepped on an adder. Only it wasn't—" He shut his eyes. "There's something wrong with this place."

Kiar had mentioned other shiftlings. Ròs cursed herself for not asking more questions. Still, it wasn't a snake that had mauled the sheep, which meant there was more than one of them on the boy's scent. Ròs glanced around but saw nothing in the trees or the underbrush, though she did notice a patch of white flowers nearby. These she pulled up, scrunching the petals in her fist and pressing them against the boy's wound. "Don't worry. I'm going to take you somewhere safe." She tore a strip from the hem of her skirt and tied it around the bite. "You're going to be fine, all right? Just hold on."

The boy nodded, his breath coming in short gulps. Ròs grasped his hand and helped him up. He staggered, and she wrapped an arm under his shoulders, almost toppling over as he sagged against her.

Panic scorched under Ròs' skin at his sudden, crushing weight. She bit her tongue hard enough to taste blood and forced herself to hold still, though her stomach wrenched. There wasn't time to be afraid. She had to get him back to the well. "Come on," she said hoarsely. "Come on."

The boy managed to take a step, then another. Ròs stumbled along with him. They just had to make it to the well, she told herself. They couldn't be too far. They just—

"Well, this is a surprise," a man said.

Ròs' heart went hollow. Her fist clutched the boy's tunic, and she could feel him shaking. Or maybe she was shaking. She turned around to see a man only a few steps behind them. It wasn't Madragh, at least. This man was taller and paler, his blond hair almost grey with grime.

"I only meant to catch Muira another shiftling," he continued. "But instead, I find Kiar's bitch."

The boy's arm tightened around Ròs. "Snake," he whispered.

Ròs stiffened. The blond man's eyes glinted red, and when he smiled, a forked tongue flicked out between his teeth. "Clever boy," he said, and darted forward.

The boy let go of Ròs and lunged at the man, shoving him back. Unshaken, the man grasped the boy's wrists and threw him to the ground. He moved to step over him, but the boy grabbed his leg and pulled it hard. The man lurched.

Seizing his chance, the boy surged up and hurled himself at the man. As they both fell, the boy shouted for Ròs to run.

She stared at him, shocked. Before she could move, the man drove his elbow into the boy's neck, then heaved him aside. Slowly, he got to his feet and stood over the boy, who tried to push himself up. The man kicked him down again, pressing his foot against the boy's neck. "Stay," he ordered while his eyes tilted towards Ròs.

Terror shredded her lungs, fraying her breath. Ròs knew she had to run or pick up the branch and fight—*anything.*

The man swung his leg back for another kick. This one struck the boy's head, and he went limp. Ròs cried out, jolting forward, but the man stepped between them. A sick, reckless energy flared in Ròs' blood, her vision at once sharp and shadowed. She snatched up the branch and swung it at him.

He caught it easily. His strength sent a shudder through Ròs; her bones seemed twig-thin, and her arms shook. He thrust the branch aside, Ròs swept along with it. Before she could steady herself, he grabbed her arm and twisted it up behind her back. Ròs gritted her teeth as she felt his breath on her neck.

Don't don't oh please don't—

The earth pitched underneath her. Ròs wanted to shut her eyes, sink down into nothingness, but her heart still raced. She thrashed against the man's grip as he pressed closer. A stillborn scream clawed inaudibly out of her throat.

"Keep still," the man hissed. His tongue flickered against her ear. "Or I'll make you."

She nearly retched, and her body convulsed. The man's other hand closed around her jaw now, his fingers crushing her face.

Ròs' teeth snapped.

The man yelped in pain. In a sharp burst of rage, he spun her around and struck her across the face. The force of the blow sent Ròs to the ground. She gasped, trying to push herself up again, and his foot pressed down between her shoulders.

A black shape roared out of the trees.

The pressure on Ròs' back lifted. She watched, paralyzed, as her attacker shifted into a snake and slithered towards the bull. Kiar lowered his horns. The adder's head snapped at him, but he jumped back. Mud splattered his fur as he stamped and twisted. Writhing, the snake narrowly avoided the bull's hooves. Kiar bucked wildly and almost trampled the unconscious boy.

Ròs flinched as clods of earth hit her skirt. She clenched her fists so hard that her nails stabbed into her palms, and the pain pressed her into action. Darting over to the boy, she hooked her arms under his shoulders and pulled him clear of the fight. "Wake up," she muttered. "Wake *up*." They'd never escape if they had to carry the boy. She shook him, but he didn't even moan.

A howl sliced through the air. Ròs huddled over the boy, another noiseless scream thick in her throat as she saw the hound. Madragh burst out of the trees, springing over the dead sheep and snarling at Kiar. Behind him, more shapes appeared amid the trees: a stag with branching antlers, a fox, a yellow-eyed wolf. They charged at Kiar in a frenzy of fur and blood. Kiar bellowed, the sound more animal than human. He reared up, his hooves slashing at the stag, then swung his head at the wolf. One horn tore open the beast's side.

Whirling around, Kiar plunged through the furor. He thundered towards Ròs. "Come on!"

She hesitated, her eyes on the boy still lying senseless in the mud. But there was no time. Kiar paused just long enough for her to pull herself onto his back. Hisses and growls followed them as they raced between the trees. Ròs' eyes burned. The rank heat of the bull's body filled her mouth and nose, while twigs whipped at her arms and legs. The memories of that first hellish night in the forest swirled around her in the sting of the wind and the stench of sweat, only this time, it wasn't just Madragh behind them. *So many.* So many men cursed by Muira. And now that boy—

A tear slipped down her cheek, which stung. She must've gotten a cut.

None of it made sense. The *bhuidseach's* spells, the beasts with voices like men, and her own stupid, pitiful attempt to fight. Whatever Kiar believed, Ròs had no power to match any of this. An ache welled in her chest, heavy enough to pin her down until she couldn't even sob.

Kiar kept running, though, and it was all she could do to hold on.

CHAPTER EIGHT

KIAR'S HOOF STRUCK a stone, and he nearly fell. Ròs gripped his hide tighter, her knees digging into his lacerated side. He gritted his teeth at the pain. Damn Madragh and Deirc and all the shiftlings. He wasn't sure which one had clawed the gashes across his ribs, but damn them all. His muscles throbbed as he forced himself to stumble on.

Ròs slid down from his back—Kiar winced as her skirt, plastered to his bloody side, ripped free—and rested a hand on his flank. "I can walk the rest of the way," she said, then stopped. "Kiar, you're hurt."

"We have to keep going," he said, his voice rough. "We're almost there."

Ròs said nothing else, but as they walked on, she paused to pick small bunches of flowers. By the time they reached the well, Kiar's head felt oddly light, as though he were underwater. He sank to the ground. Dimly, he was aware of Ròs crouching down beside him and then moving away. He couldn't see where she went, nor did he have the energy to lift his head.

When she returned, she carried her mantle bundled up in her arms, the cloth soaking wet. She knelt and scrunched up a corner of the fabric, which she used to dab at the gashes. A growl rumbled in Kiar's throat. The pain muddled his senses, and he bit his tongue to keep still. He couldn't thrash, especially not in this form; he might hurt Ròs. It might've been easier if he was a man, safer even, but he wouldn't shift.

Instead, he shut his eyes and focused on his breath. He remembered his father teaching him the trick of it when he was fifteen. Another warrior had challenged him to a fight, and while Kiar won, he'd gotten a wrenched shoulder and a slash across his stomach. The shoulder hurt worse at first, but once the old healer jammed it back into place, Kiar scarcely noticed it. Instead, it was the cut that kept him awake. He'd felt like such a child, moaning over a scratch. He hadn't been afraid during the fight, yet afterward, as a fever simmered in his blood, a strange dread gripped him, fed by pain and restlessness.

He'd kept quiet until everyone else in the castle fell asleep, then crept out to the courtyard where the wind would cool his hot skin. There, he'd found his father. The lord stood near the remnants of a bonfire, his hands held out over the coals.

"The pain will pass," his father said quietly. "There's no ignoring it, though, Kiar. You'll spend more of your life healing than you will fighting."

Kiar didn't reply. The cut throbbed. He wanted to get away from it somehow, or at least get away from his father. The man didn't move, however. He placed a hand on Kiar's shoulder and told him to breathe deep, to feel the shape of the pain and then let it be—no shrinking back or forcing it down. It didn't lessen the sting, but Kiar's mind settled enough to let him sleep soon after.

He'd used the trick dozens of times since then. As Ròs cleaned his wounds and covered them in a makeshift paste of crushed flowers, Kiar fell into the old rhythm: breathe in, breathe out, until eventually, the fiery pain lessened to a sullen ache.

Ròs smeared the last of the paste over the gashes and rubbed her hands on her tattered skirt. She was filthy, Kiar realized, her peplos ragged. The sleeves of her tunic were also torn and brown with old blood, the marks of her first encounter with Madragh. A bruise stained her cheek.

She'd been so terrified that first night. Kiar hadn't thought to wonder why, not with the hound snarling at her heels. He should've realized, though, from the moment she told him to change back into a bull. He shouldn't have needed Deidra's lament to give it away. He shouldn't have needed to see her now, her eyes blunted by tears—red and almost wild, as though she was still running. Not even the well could keep her safe from her own memories.

"I'll kill him," Kiar muttered.

And this time, he didn't mean Madragh.

Ròs' mouth twitched. "What good is that going to do? It's the *bhuidseach* who did this, who turned them into beasts."

"They were like that before," Kiar replied shortly. "Her magic's done nothing but give them power."

"Why does she do it?" Ròs asked, her voice rising. "That boy wasn't like them. He was only a child, not a man yet. He didn't even mean to come into the forest. It was Madragh—" She pressed her knuckles against her mouth and wrapped an arm around her knees. "Now Muira will trap him here, so he can't get back to his home or his family, and in a few years, he'll probably be as much of a brute as the others."

"He might not," Kiar said gently. "I'm not." He nudged Ròs' shoulder with his nose. "Besides, we're going to break the curse long before then."

She looked down. "What if I can't do it? What if there isn't any way to break it?"

No, Kiar almost replied, but he held the word back. He wanted to shove away the possibility, even as the same doubt stung him. Still, Ròs needed something more than brash reassurance, more than Kiar trying to convince himself that he wasn't defeated. Ever since he found her, he'd been desperate—desperate to break free of Muira's curse and prove himself stronger than the witch. He couldn't just escape the *bhuidseach*. He had to *fight* her, win back his torc. Only then could he return to his father.

He'd told himself it was for Ròs as much as himself. After all, she was trapped along with him. He had to protect her from the other shiftlings, hide her from the *bhuidseach*. Kiar winced at a sudden pang of guilt. Even in that, he was fixated on Muira.

Ròs glanced up at him, but Kiar couldn't speak. The bull's form seemed to weigh him down, its strength suddenly oppressive—and useless. He'd done so little to help her. Yet Ròs, in spite of his stupidity, still sat there looking at him, giving him a chance to try again.

"We can break it," he said finally. "You're the *shenachie*. Have you ever heard a story where there wasn't a way to break the curse?"

She shook her head.

"So we'll find it, whatever it is." Kiar moved closer to her. She leaned against him, careful not to touch the gashes on his side. They stayed like that for a long time, Ròs nestled against Kiar's shoulder. Dusk fell, but neither of them slept.

"I can't think of any stories," Ròs said eventually. "It's too *loud* in my head."

Kiar glanced around at the utter stillness of the clearing and knew what she meant, remembering that night in the courtyard. He didn't say there was no need for any stories just then. She wanted one, and he understood the need for an escape. A distraction wouldn't help, though. He'd spent enough of his life running away from his own thoughts to know that, and now, all he wanted was to go home.

"Then I'll tell one," he said.

Ròs tilted her head back to look at him. "You said you never listened to the *shenachie* who came to your castle."

"No," Kiar admitted. "But I can tell you about the castle itself." He smiled slightly. "I might only be a warrior, but that's not hard to tell."

Even as he said it, he knew it wasn't true. Still, he started to speak, and as he did, he found the words. He told her about the night he won his torc. He told her about his mother's death and his father's rigid grief—how he'd seen that grief as indifference and believed his father wanted him to forget her, too. Only he couldn't. He couldn't be what his father wanted—not the son, or the man, or the lord. Not if it cost his memories. His father could rage all he wanted. Kiar held onto his mother, as close as the knot he kept tied around his neck, until sorrow turned into bitterness and the burden of it threatened to crush him. So he ran, always, anywhere, and yet wherever he went, it followed.

Until now, as the story unspooled and the hard knot of pain unraveled.

Ròs listened quietly as he talked. Once or twice she asked questions, and as Kiar answered, he remembered more, memories torn loose from the shuttered places in his mind. It ached the way his muscles used to after a long day of training, the kind of soreness that sang of strength rather than weakness.

He would've expected to miss the castle more as he told Ròs about it. Instead, a fierce sort of hope sprang up as the stories made the place real once again, and her body warm against his made him more determined than ever to bring her home.

CHAPTER NINE

"THAT'S BRÌGHDE'S HARP," Ròs said, pointing up at a small cluster of stars.

The night was unusually clear, and while it was still cool, Ròs didn't mind. She hadn't moved from Kiar's side, though she was careful not to brush against his wounds. In spite of exhaustion, neither of them felt like sleeping.

Tracing the shape of the constellation with her finger, Ròs said, "The stars tell the stories of the gods, but without Brìghde's music, they would be silent and still. Her voice sets the sky spinning."

"Do you miss your harp?" Kiar asked.

"Yes," she replied without hesitation. "But it's gone now."

Kiar lifted his head to look at her. "My mother had a harp. When we get out of here—" He stopped abruptly, his ears twitching.

"What is it?" Ròs whispered.

"Get back to the well."

She hesitated, and then a howl split the air.

"*Run*!"

Kiar surged to his feet, horns lowered. Ròs scrambled towards the well and huddled against the stones.

Madragh launched out from the trees. Jaws wide, the hound flung himself at Kiar, only to dart away as the bull reared up. Kiar kicked at him. The hound swerved, circling the bull.

Shivering, Ròs dug her hands into the ground, feeling the sharp cold of the water.

Kiar rushed at Madragh, catching the hound's side with his horn. Blood splattered over the turf. Madragh clawed at Kiar, his eyes moon-bright with rage. His frenzied movements seemed to disorient the bull, who stomped and twisted but couldn't land a clear blow.

Finally, Madragh pulled back, his snarl almost a smile. Sweat and blood matted Kiar's fur, the gashes on his side oozing again. He lowered his head for another charge.

Ròs wanted to shut her eyes but didn't dare. She watched, horrified, as the hound sprang over Kiar's horns and landed on his back. The bull writhed and kicked his front legs, trying to throw Madragh off. Madragh morphed into a man and clung to Kiar's fur. He let out a breathless bark of a laugh even as the bull bucked wildly.

Kiar threw himself to the ground, attempting to crush the man, but Madragh leaped clear and shifted into a hound again. As Kiar lay prone, Madragh lunged. His teeth ripped into the bull's neck.

Kiar cried out in pain, an inhuman roar. Blood filled Ròs' mouth as she bit her lip harder and harder. Her fingers dug into the stones behind her until she touched a tangle of grass—a knot she'd woven days before. Pulling the fragile charm out, she pressed it against her mouth, soaking it in scarlet.

Madragh howled, his jaw about to close on Kiar's neck again. Ròs hurled herself out of the well's circle and shoved the hound away from Kiar, planting herself between them. As she swung the blood-knot at the hound, he jolted back.

In an instant, Madragh was a man again. "Step aside," he growled.

Ròs lifted the knot higher. "No."

"Ròs, don't," Kiar said, his voice rough with pain. As Ròs glanced at him, her heart thudded.

He had shifted, and Ròs saw him as she hadn't since that first night. Blood ran over his blue-black tattoos, the marks of the hound's teeth visible on his shoulder and chest. The white of his collarbone gleamed bright under the gore.

"Step aside, girl," Madragh repeated, his face twisted with hatred and hunger. "I'm putting an end to his interference." His blue eyes turned on Ròs. "Then I'll take back the prey he stole from me. Muira wants you."

Kiar rolled over, trying to get to his feet, only to collapse with a gasp. Ròs wanted to pull off her mantle and staunch the wound, but she had to hold up the knot.

"Then call her," she said.

Madragh started.

"Call her! If she wants me so badly, then *call her*."

A low growl rose in Madragh's throat. Ròs thought the man was going to spring at her, but instead, he lifted his head and howled. The trees shivered as the sound died down. A terrible fear gripped Ròs' chest.

A power as strong as pain, Kiar had called it. She felt the tremors ripping through her like a scream.

A woman appeared beside the brook, stone-pale and dark-eyed. Three torcs gleamed around her throat. Her hair was garishly red—as were the stains on her grey mantle.

"Foolish girl," she said, her lips curving in a smile.

The knot in Ròs' hand burst into flame. She shrieked, letting go.

In the forest around the well, shadows stirred. Yellow eyes blinked out of the darkness; the shiftlings had joined their mistress. Ròs knew if she took a few steps back, she would be within the circle of safety again, but she didn't move.

"Bring her here," Muira commanded. Her gaze fixed on Ròs, cold and craving.

Ròs reached for Kiar, but Madragh wrenched her away from him and threw her to the ground at Muira's feet. Ròs pushed herself up, glaring at the woman, but Muira's eyes were on her brooch.

"*Shenachie*," she said.

Ròs felt the woman's gaze cut into her bones, and she found herself saying hoarsely, "Not anymore."

"No?" Muira asked coolly, yet there was a sharpness in her expression. She lifted Ròs' chin with one slender finger. "Why not?"

Behind her, Ròs heard Kiar say her name, his voice ragged. She couldn't turn around. Muira's question slid between her ribs, and the truth spilled like blood. "There was a warrior," Ròs whispered. "His feats are honored throughout Alba. Wherever he goes, the lords offer him the best of their households."

She had heard so many stories of him, heard the awe in men's voices when they told the tales. When the warrior came to the castle where she was wintering, she'd felt a thrill of excitement. Her hands had trembled as she took up her harp.

"When I sang for him, I felt his eyes on me the whole night," she said softly, and she was in the hall again, her skin prickling from the fetid heat of his stare. A sick dizziness gripped her. She nearly retched, but the words tore out instead:

"He took what he liked from every household."

Something snapped in her chest. Ròs slumped. The spell of Muira's question had broken, leaving her ravaged, hollow. "I couldn't go back," she mumbled.

"I, too, would not go back," Muira said quietly. She unclasped the brooch at her shoulder and swept off her bloodstained mantle, dropping it to the ground in front of Ròs. "And that is the price I was willing to pay."

Ròs stared at the stains, strangely bright as though they would not dry.

"I was born to be the bride of a king," Muira continued. "Shut away in his castle until I came of age. When the warriors of his ally came to stay, I went secretly to the strongest and fairest of them, begging him to steal me away. He could not deny me. Yet we were hunted across Alba by the king and his brother. They killed my warrior, piercing him with two spears." Her face darkened. "Then they captured me. For a year, they passed me between the two of them. Finally, I swore they would not have me any longer. I cursed them with my hate, and I flung myself from the king's horse as he carried me to his brother's castle."

Grief is heavier than the sea. The lines of Deidra's lament hummed in Ròs' mind, and her eyes widened as she looked from the mantle to Muira. In the woman's death-cold face, she saw the shadow of terrible pain.

Muira—Deidra—nudged the mantle with her foot. "But I did not die. The king met my curse with his own, and now I cannot be borne away to the *sídhe* until the stains are washed from my mantle." She leaned down, her face close to Ròs. "You can free me, *shenachie.*"

"How?" Ròs asked, but she already knew the answer. The holy well: the one place in the forest Deidra could not go.

Seeing the understanding in Ròs' face, Deidra nodded. "You must wash the mantle in the well."

Ròs jerked away. "Why should I help you?"

"You must," Deidra said, her voice low and urgent. "I could not trust this task to another."

"You've tried before, haven't you?" Ròs retorted. "What happened to the other women your shiftlings caught?"

Deidra's mouth curled with disgust. "I gave them the same chance. One after another, they deceived me. They promised to help, only to try and escape as soon as they thought they were out of my sight." Her eyes glittered. "A mistake. They feared me, *shenachie*. They didn't understand, but you do. And you have already found the well. It offers you shelter."

"I didn't find it," Ròs said quietly. "Kiar did."

"The bull." Deidra's gaze shifted to him. "He's dying."

A chill choked Ròs' heart.

"He has a few hours at most before he chokes on his own blood. The water of the well could heal him, but he cannot go near it." Deidra looked back to Ròs, one eyebrow raised. "So, *shenachie*, what will you do now?"

Ròs turned to Kiar, who looked back at her, his eyes strained. He was afraid, for her, for himself, yet while Ròs was terrified of the *bhuidseach* and the hound and the blood pouring from Kiar's chest, she realized the old fear—the one always crouched beneath her skin—was gone.

She was not afraid of Kiar. As she realized that, something gave way in her chest, like ice splintering apart. She could breathe again. In the sudden empty space, she felt fresh the pain of her grief, but it was shot through with hope, giving it a new shape and beauty as sunlight dazzles mist.

And when she faced Deidra, she saw how the woman's grief had made her cruel, and she pitied her. "If I free you, the spell on him will break?" she asked.

"Yes."

Ròs reached down and gathered up the mantle. "Then I'll do it."

Aware of Muira's eyes on her back, she walked to the well and flung out the mantle. The fabric caught in a curl of wind, then settled onto the surface of the water. Slowly, it began to sink. Ròs leaned over to watch it, her hair tumbling over her shoulder. Fiery curls trailed in the water, and beneath the ripples, she saw rust-colored clouds, the clear darkness soon thick with blood.

Wondering if she ought to use a stone to scrub at the stains, Ròs reached in to draw the mantle out.

Something caught hold of her hand.

Ròs let out a shriek as it dragged her in. For a moment, there was nothing but blazing cold and bloodshot darkness. She thrashed, gasping for air, and found that she could breathe. There was solid ground beneath her again. Blinking, she squinted against an icy wind.

She was on a mountaintop. Stars glittered above and the moon hung low and large over drifts of snow.

Reeling with the shock, Ròs' fingers tightened around the mantle in her arms. It was dry now, the stains as bright as ever. She anxiously shook it out again, kneeling in the snow and grabbing handfuls to rub against the stains.

"Please." She wasn't sure who she was talking to, but as her fingers grew numb and tears burned and froze on her cheeks, she couldn't help herself. "Please, I have to save Kiar."

So you will save Deidra, then?

She did not know if the voice was her own or if it came from the stars, but she replied, "Yes. If I free her, I can save Kiar."

And why should you save him?

"Because he's good."

Then why should you save Deidra? She is not good.

"Then she needs saving all the more." Ròs' retort echoed over the mountain.

And why does she need saving, shenachie?

A sob strained Ròs' throat, but she choked a reply. "It is not hard to tell."

It was impossible to tell. Yet she began to sing. The notes rang in the ice-clear air, and Ròs felt the story catch hold of her until she could see figures around her. Wind blew over the drifts, sending up glittering eddies of snow, and the crystals formed the shapes of men and women, horses and swords and spears. There were other shades, too. There was a woman with a harp and a man standing over her. The shadows twisted, but Ròs could not look away. Deidra's lament twined with her own cry of pain.

Tears streamed down Ròs' cheeks and dropped, frozen, onto her hands. She continued to scrub at the mantle, her fingers red and raw, but she couldn't feel them. She ached with sorrow, and fury, and most of all, a terrible desolation. She was alone on a mountaintop trying to save a *bhuidseach* she both hated and pitied.

Yet it was herself, too, that she hated and pitied.

Ròs shut her eyes. The stains were as bright as ever, and a slinking despair crept in. The mantle would never be clean. Deidra would never be free, any more than Ròs would ever be whole again.

"I can't do it!" she said, standing up and screaming the words like an accusation at the stars. "I can't!"

No, shenachie. *But I can.*

The voice was slight, just a hum under the howl of the wind. Ròs collapsed onto the snow, her body stiff with cold. Her lungs ached, her eyes burned, and then somewhere in the awful pain of it all, she heard a piercing note. A single chord that changed chaos into harmony.

Violet skimmed over the sky. The stars faded, though the moon stayed bright, and then gold scorched the horizon. Ròs watched, transfixed, as the sun rose and stretched its rays. The warmth poured over her. It hurt at first, her blood burning as the sensation returned. She cried out in agony, but the pain began to fade, and as her fingers tingled and her skin shivered delightfully under the heat of the sun, she realized just how numb she had been.

The snow sparkled and crumbled under the intense brightness, melting rapidly into the earth. Ròs was soon drenched. Still the violent gentleness of the sun penetrated her, and she lay there in the morning light, aware only of its peace.

CHAPTER TEN

KIAR WAS COLD. The mist seemed to be strangling him—or maybe that was Madragh's foot on his chest. A dull kind of exhaustion slunk over his body, softer than sleep.

He didn't dare shut his eyes.

Ròs wasn't back yet. He couldn't tell how long she'd been gone, but he meant to wait for her.

Around him, the whole clearing seemed to hold its breath. No one spoke, not the shiftlings in the trees, not Madragh as he shoved his foot harder into Kiar's ribs, not even Muira. If Kiar strained his eyes upwards, he could see her. She held completely still, staring at the well.

The sky slowly faded from black to blue, and the stars paled. Kiar watched as Brìghde's harp disappeared under the tide of light. Yet Ròs didn't return. He wanted to push Madragh off him and run to the well, throw himself in after her, but even if he could escape the hound, the curse still bound him.

A shaft of gold broke through the forest, the first rays of sunrise. Madragh flinched. The pressure on Kiar's chest eased momentarily, enough for him to twist himself away. He tipped his head back in order to look at the well, though Muira stood in the way.

And so he saw her vanish.

As the sun spilled over the clearing, Muira let out a low cry and took a single step forward. Her foot touched the vibrant green circle around the well, and then she disappeared. Kiar blinked. She was *gone* in an instant. A breeze whispered in the leaves overhead, and it seemed to scatter the acrid tension in the air. Muira's power had broken.

Kiar braced his uninjured arm against the ground and pushed himself up. Gone. She was gone, evaporated like morning dew. No trace of her remained. Kiar swallowed as he realized his torc was gone, too.

Now there were no beasts in the forest, only ragged men. They glanced at each other, uncertain, and Deirc cursed.

"It's over," he spat.

Madragh spun around to face him. "What do you mean, it's over?"

"The *bhuidseach* is finished," Deirc replied, gesturing towards the well, and then he turned away. "Her power's done."

"No," Madragh growled. "No, she's still here. She's just—"

Deirc let out a sharp laugh. "Can't you feel it, Madragh? It's *over*." He began walking into the forest.

The other shiftlings—not shiftlings anymore—began to mutter. Kiar saw one, a boy, draw away from the others and run after Deirc, soon passing him. The others followed more slowly, one by one. Madragh gaped at them. "Get back here!" he yelled. "We have to wait for her!"

Deirc paused and gave Madragh an almost pitying look. "She isn't coming back." With that, he went after the others.

The sudden urge to laugh sent a spasm of pain through Kiar's chest. The shiftlings had cast aside humanity for the scraps of the *bhuidseach's* power, and without her curse, they were nothing. Just men.

Kiar was a man again, a weak, ordinary man—a dying man. He could feel his life dripping out of the wound in his shoulder. Yet a fierce joy burned inside him.

"No!" Madragh shouted. He kicked Kiar in the stomach. "It's *your* fault."

Groaning, Kiar curled into a ball. His ribs seemed to stab into his lungs. Blood filled his mouth. Some distant, frantic part of his mind knew that Madragh meant to kill him, and he had to fight back, but he had no strength left.

Madragh bent down and closed a hand around Kiar's throat. "You did this," he snarled, his face contorted with rage.

Kiar doubted that. *Ròs*. Ròs had done this, whatever it was, and she still hadn't returned.

The cold set into his bones now, stealing away some of the pain. Kiar gritted his teeth, the bitter warmth of blood on his tongue, and forced himself to look up at Madragh. One hand twitched. His numb fingers could scarcely feel the turf, but then they brushed against something rough. His fist closed around a rock.

Madragh tightened his grip, and Kiar convulsed. He couldn't see, blackness singing the edges of his vision. With a wild burst of energy, he swung the rock at Madragh's head.

The stone smashed into the man's temple, and he crumpled to the ground. Kiar sucked in a rasping breath. He struggled to his knees and flung himself at Madragh, the rock still clutched in his hand. Madragh stirred, blood on his temple, but Kiar brought the rock down again, then again, until it dropped from his fist.

The hound was dead. Kiar swayed and collapsed. As he hit the ground, the pain seemed to rip his bones apart. He heaved in an agonizing breath.

Ròs.

She was still in the well.

Kiar dragged himself into the circle. The ground squelched under his fingers, but there was no current of power driving him back—the curse was gone. The mist darkened, his body so *heavy.* Still Kiar crawled blindly forward.

His fingers scraped against stone. With one final, excruciating effort, he lifted himself over the edge and plunged into the water.

It was cold, but a delicious sort of cold. It soothed the burning pain in his shoulder. Then, behind Kiar's eyes, everything changed from total blackness to glowing red. He blinked, startled, and for a single moment, he saw the sun rising over a mountain. The ridge seemed to be on fire with color.

A woman, her hair blazing in the light, stood on the peak. Her mantle rippled behind her, the bloodstains gone.

Kiar called out, thinking she was Ròs, but then she turned. It was Deidra.

His fists clenched. The exhaustion had gone, his strength renewed, and he almost moved towards her, ready to fight.

Until he saw her eyes—the strange, soft brightness of them, brimming with life. The brittleness of death had broken away.

Kiar stepped back, uncertain, but before he could do anything else, water closed around him once again. Frantic, he reached out. His hand closed around someone's arm.

There was a desperate, lung-twisting moment of searching for the surface, and then he burst up into the dim light of the forest.

"Kiar!"

"Ròs?" Kiar spluttered. It was her arm he'd caught. "Ròs!"

Her wet hair trailed over her face as she treaded water, surging towards him. He caught her and held her tight, but immediately began to sink. Ròs clung to him as he kicked to stay afloat, both of them spluttering and laughing.

Kiar grabbed hold of the well's rim. He clambered out, pulling her up along with him, and helped her down onto the turf. They stood there, breathless and soaked. Kiar thought he saw Ròs smile, under a jumble of dripping curls, and almost moved to brush her hair back. Yet he tensed. A moment ago, they'd been tangled up in each other's arms, but now they were on the ground again and he remembered, in hazy snatches, her conversation with Muira.

The curse was broken, yet he wished he could transform just so he wouldn't have to see that look of panic on her face again. Still, he wanted desperately to hold her.

Her fingers ran over his shoulders, and his muscles instantly relaxed under her touch. "You're healed," she said. "It worked!"

Kiar gently rested his hand on top of hers, his thumb rubbing over the place where the wound had been. There was only the slight ridge of a scar. "You did it."

"No. I don't think I did. But it's done." She gave a quick flash of a smile. "I'll tell you later. It is not hard to tell."

She leaned closer, her fingers curled against his neck, weaving into his hair. Then her mouth was on his, a fierce rush of a kiss. He kissed her back, pulling her against him. She stiffened, just for a second, but before he could let go, she softened, burying her head in his neck and kissing the fresh scar.

"Let's go home," she whispered.

Kiar pressed his lips against her hair, then twined his hands into hers. They didn't look back as they left the clearing.

The mist faded fast. It seemed only moments later that they reached the edge of the forest, the sudden wideness of the landscape taking their breath away. The valleys and mountains and rivers spread out before them, drenched in morning light.

Kiar pointed towards one of the mountains, a sudden joy rising in his chest. He had no torc, no weapons, not even his shirt, and yet he knew his father wouldn't care any more than he did. "That's where my home is, Ròs."

She leaned against his shoulder. "Then that's where we'll go. Though it'll take longer now that I can't ride on your back."

Kiar grinned and swung her up into his arms. "I can still carry you," he said, beginning to run.

Ròs wrapped her arms around his neck, and her laughter sang across the valley.

BONUS MATERIAL

THORN TOWER CHARACTER SKETCH: VALIBRIM

ANNE J. HILL

ICY TEARS

A WHITE-HAIRED boy sat in the dark woods.

Alone.

Abandoned.

Left to fend for himself in the great wide world full of monsters and humans who wanted to capture little elf boys like him.

Valibrim shivered in the falling snow. The trees were the only barrier between him and complete vulnerability. The leaves shielded him from monsters like the father who'd left him and the mother who hadn't cared.

Something crunched in the snow, and he jerked his head up. A fawn tentatively crossed his path and paused to stare at him.

"Hello, little friend. You can call me Brim." He held his shaking hand out, palm up. "Are you lost too?" His heart ached, and he hoped with everything in him that the little fawn would be his friend, if even for a moment.

Its nose wriggled as if debating to sniff the pink hand.

The boy sneezed, and the fawn's ears flattened as she darted around a tree and leaped through the snow. It wasn't long before he lost sight of it.

"Figures," Valibrim mumbled to himself and stood. Laying in the freezing weather wouldn't help anything.

Pulling his cloak tighter around himself, he stepped in the fawn's footprints and jumped along behind her. She might be scared of him, but he could pretend they were only playing a game of chase.

An owl hooted from up high. Something howled and snarled in the distance. The forest was full of noise. Like the gentle touch of snow landing on leaves or the *drip-drip* of . . .

Of what?

The snow couldn't be melting already.

Valibrim froze when he looked up from the fawn's footprints.

The baby deer hung over a fallen log. Claw marks tore open its flesh, mangled muscle peeking through. Crimson blood dripped from its shredded throat and melted away the pure white snow.

There were monsters in these woods too.

Who could hurt such a helpless creature? What sort of beast could be so cruel?

He shuffled through the snow and stopped by the deer, running his fingers down its still-warm muzzle. His eyes filled with icy tears that slid down his cheeks.

That was the day he decided no more monsters were allowed in this forest. *His* forest.

Valibrim spent the cold weeks curled up to ward off frostbite until he learned he could make fire with a simple wave of his hand. That certainly was a thrilling development. His father had left him there because he was unable to perform magic like he was supposed to. Because he was a disappointment.

His eyes lit up when the flames danced on his fingertips. Finally, he was becoming the elf he was meant to be.

Powerful.

Each day, he became stronger in his powers and stronger in his desire to protect the forest.

He eventually grew up and built a home in the trees. He rid the wood of snow, warded off monsters and darkness, and filled it with fruits, sunshine, and happiness. But he was still all alone, just like he had been as a child.

So he invited any elves to come to live, dance, and dream freely in his forest, tucked away from the world. A place where he would keep them safe. A place where no more monsters could get them.

A wood where the Guardian of the Forest didn't abandon even the fawns.

KEEPER OF THE WOODS

They call me a saint
Under the moonlight
Keeper of the woods
Guard of the night

But what they don't know
Is my elf flesh turns
To something that roars
And destruction is sworn

A monster within
A monster without
Waiting, praying
To find a way out

Until then, I'll roam
Keep myself hidden
And I'll protect them
'Til she loves what's within

BEAST OR BEING

THE GUARDIAN OF the Forest darted through the woods. Twigs stabbed his bare feet. The waning light peaked through the leaves and danced on the forest floor. Shadows climbed up the tree trunks.

Nightfall was coming.

You should have been home hours ago to prepare, Valibrim, he chided himself. *You spent too much time talking to her.*

Valibrim yanked his shirt off so it wouldn't get ruined in his transformation. If he'd been home sooner, he would have had time to use his powers to ward off shifting into a monster. But tonight, he wouldn't be so fortunate.

A log lay in his path, and he vaulted over it. He'd have to remove it in the morning. *Among other more unpleasant things.*

Howls drifted through the air. Feet pounded behind him—vicious wolves that devoured anyone left in the woods after nightfall.

But the beasts outside were not the ones the Guardian feared that night.

He prayed to Linitor that the wolves would stay away—he'd hate to clean up blood in his sacred forest. If he wasn't locked up before he shifted, as hard as he might fight the impulse, he'd attack any beast or being in the forest.

Valibrim reached his home, a series of wooden houses he'd built amongst the trees—his own fortress. The Guardian clambered up the stairs, gasping for air as his limbs stretched and reformed. Feathery wings sprouted out of his shoulder blades.

He slammed his door shut, tore off his pants, and half ran, half crawled to the back of his lowest house, where he locked himself in his spellbound room.

The whole forest shook when the Guardian let out an aching roar.

SNOW WHISPERER

They called him the Snow Whisperer.
Slinking into town once each winter,
bringing frost on his fingertips, smiling through icy blue eyes.
Skin white as the snow he spun, hair whiter still.
He'd pass through the red apple trees and pile his fruit basket full.
Freezing autumn's crimson fruit—a delicious winter treat
for all the boys and girls to bite.
Juice ran down their cheeks.
Children would sing of his deeds, how snow flowed from his fingertips
and flakes dropped on their noses. He'd shape ice sculptures
for them to carry home.
For only one day he'd come, the elf who controlled the skies.
Leaving the rest of winter bleak.
His name but vapor on their lips:
The Snow Whisperer

FLOWERS OF SORROW

VALIBRIM HAD LIVED many years in the forest. Sometimes alone, sometimes with a woman he loved, and sometimes pretending the townspeople he protected from a distance made him feel less lonely.

Thirty years in various flavors of isolation.

Valibrim ran dirt through his fingers; a smile tugged at his lips. The earth was soothing to the touch and would wield new life. He dug small holes in the ground at the base of his home. Reaching into his satchel, he pulled out a handful of rose seeds and placed one in each hole. A soft tune came from his lips, as he hummed over the plants. He could easily flick his hand and grow a masterful garden around him, but that wasn't the same as getting his hands covered in dirt and watching the plants slowly come to life. They were magical enough on their own. They didn't need his skill to fill the empty spot in his chest.

He lifted his head and looked to the heavens, snapping his fingers. Rain drizzled on the newly planted seeds as he covered them with dirt.

She would have loved these roses.

Valibrim took a deep breath, the joy of creating new life shortly lived. He brushed the dirt from his hands. Rain mingled with the tears on his cheeks and dripped down to the hollow spot on his chest. Memories of the woman he once loved flooded his mind—the love that once filled his heart. Dancing under the forest canopy. Holding each other as flames consumed logs in the fire. Kissing her deeply in the autumn wind. Giving her his heart. She not giving hers back.

He'd loved too fiercely for anyone to return it with the same intensity. She was no different, except that she haunted him more than she ever loved him.

She taught Valibrim something he would not soon forget: "I love you" are just words strung together and nothing more.

LONELY SOULS

THE GUARDIAN OF the Forest sat in his fortress in the trees.

Alone. For thirty hellish years.

Tracing the grooves of his palm, he remembered a time when he was able to feel such a delicate touch. He once knew love and held it dear. He once was the elf he wanted to be.

No more.

Valibrim's harp sat between his feet, ornate roses engraved down the wooden framework. He rubbed at his temple as he ruminated on past mistakes that made him feel like a monster. He brushed his white hair behind his ear; the ends trickled over his lap.

Shadows crept along his walls and danced in the flickering candlelight. They closed in on him, ready to smother. And no one would notice . . .

All alone.

He took a deep breath and plucked the harp's strings. The once painful pricks were now merely light taps on his fingertips as his sense of touch weakened each day. His eyes drifted closed, and the enchanting melody filled his soul and calmed the woods. Playing away the monsters on his walls and in his heart.

It was his duty to keep peace in the woods, and as dusk faded into twilight, he could sense this would be a long night.

Sleep threatened to end Valibrim's melody, his body tired from the long nights protecting the forest and the enduring loneliness of his work. With no one to love or love him in return.

But maybe it was better this way. Maybe it was safer . . . hidden away from the world. The beast he was, contained.

Cor paced her room in the dark and listened to her father's ragged breaths. It was lonely work to take care of a parent who gave her no thanks—who kept her from the battlegrounds. She'd fought alongside her fellow warriors in the war against the humans until her father was struck down. Now her only contribution to the war was patrolling her town.

Stopping by her window, she looked out into the night. The soldier who'd just replaced her on watch walked up and down the street, a dark shadow. The town was quiet, peacefully asleep, while death and war raged only miles away. Her job was over for the night, but she couldn't bring herself to lay down.

It would be so easy to slip outside, sneak past the soldier, and rejoin the ranks where she could be of more use. Free. With no father to tie her down.

She rubbed her jaw as she shook her head. *No.*

As one of the few soldiers in the town, it was her duty to keep her people safe should danger arise. A sort of guardian of her army town.

Cor considered going to sleep, but it would be a restless night, where she'd keep her ears pricked for unusual breathing from her father and any threats from outside. So from her bedroom, she aimlessly patrolled, bare feet grazing the wooden floor. Brown hair tucked behind her pointed ears.

Nothing would give her more joy than to fling her duties aside and dash back to the battlegrounds. But honor and family loyalty kept her bound, and, for now, that was reason enough. This was good. This watch-keeping was noble work.

Two lonely souls waded through the dark of night. One a beautiful warrior, the other a reclusive beast.

And one fateful day, they would meet and change the course of their lives forever.

EXCERPTS

GRIMKEEPER EXCERPT

EVERLY HAYWOOD

A HAUNTING MELODY crept down the corridor as Dagmar dipped into another jaunty curtsy. She froze, ears straining to catch the notes. The melody seemed familiar somehow, but she could not quite place where she had heard it. Before she realized what was happening, her feet moved down the indigo carpet in search of the music. Her heart swelled with the desire to find it—no, with the need to find it, to possess it, to lose herself in those glorious melancholy notes. She could see the music before her, a swirl of light and shadow painted in blues and grays and smudgy greens. Soon the smears of color were joined by pulsing blue flames. They flickered and danced and wove around her, as if delighted to meet her.

Marveling, she reached out a hand and felt no pain, only a delicious warmth. A sense of belonging and purpose swelled inside her breast, as if this had been the thing she was searching for her entire life without even realizing it. The fire curled around her fingers, twisting and spinning at her command as she manipulated them into shapes. Her entire body begged to join in, and soon her feet skipped to the music as the flames spiraled around her. They took shape, like a partner made of fire and shadow, and soon she found herself spinning as they held her close and swept her deeper and deeper into the music.

Never had she been more happy, never more complete.

Nothing else mattered. Everything faded into the distance, insignificant details of a time long past. Only this remained, this moment, this music, this dance, this—

The chords of the song broke off with a bellowing clamor.

Dagmar skidded to a halt, arms held out to embrace the fiery partner who had abruptly vanished like a wisp of smoke caught in a stiff breeze. Aching to find him once again, she spun in a circle, a cry tearing from her mouth.

She didn't even know where she was. Instead of the corridor she last remembered, she now stood in a large, windowless room. Other girls stood around her, human girls in simple dresses with blank, confused expressions painted on their faces. Dagmar saw her own desperation mirrored in their eyes. She turned more slowly, scanning the faces—some thin, some browned from the sun, some gaunt with dark circles hugging the eyes.

Then she saw Peregrin. He stood just outside the circle of confused girls, arms held away from his body as if he too embraced an invisible partner. He stared at her, mouth twisted in a look of pure horror. For the briefest moment, she thought she saw flames flickering in his eyes, and then he dropped his arms and sprinted toward her.

"What are you doing here?" he hissed as he caught her elbow and spun her about to herd her in a frantic retreat. "Do you have any idea—"

"Peregrin—" She tried to protest as he practically hurled her down the grand hallway and back into the stairwell. She cast one last look behind her, toward the room occupied by the other girls, but then the door swung closed, and Peregrin dragged her down the stairs. He said nothing else until they had left the palace and reached the winding path from the servant's entrance. A dark green hedge soon blocked her view of the building behind them.

He released her then and raked a hand through his hair. It was trembling, she realized. His hand shook violently. He stopped walking and seemed to take a moment to compose himself.

"What were you doing?" His voice held an edge as if he struggled to keep his tone calm. "I specifically told you to *wait*—"

"I heard the music." She pierced him with a hard look, determined to drag the secrets from him by force if necessary.

He pressed his palms against his legs as if to still them. "I know. But if you'd stayed where you should be, you wouldn't have."

"Where does the music come from?"

"That's not—it does not concern you. We will never speak of this again. Do you understand? And from now on, you will stay in the servant areas. You will *never* venture beyond. Do you understand? Dagmar?" He took a step closer so that mere inches separated them.

"No," she said, the word hoarse but obstinate. "I don't understand."

His eyes flickered closed briefly. Then they snapped open, and he grasped her by the shoulders. "Then understand this." He leaned down and stared into her eyes. "You are in danger. And if you do not do exactly as I say . . . it could cost you your life. Do you understand *that?*"

She became painfully aware of his long fingers curling around her sore shoulders. Her arms remembered the feel of the fiery dancer's form swirling around. Her feet could still tap out the moves. Her ears still heard a lingering note of the music.

But Peregrin kept her grounded to the present. She could not pretend he wasn't there, couldn't retreat back into that strange dance inside the palace. What had he said? Her life was in danger?

She could understand that. It wasn't the answer she wanted, but she would never find answers if she put herself into a wooden box deep beneath Gelairan soil.

Will a scheming bride and a shy elf scholar manage to make magic, or will they fall prey to the deadly dance? A missing sister, a mountain of books, and magical cats collide in this enchanting romantic fantasy.

Read Grimkeeper *today, FREE IN KU!*

PROJECT SYTHRALL EXCERPT

ANNE J. HILL

Title To Be Announced
A Novella Subtly Inspired by Beauty and the Beast

SYTHRALL STOOD AT the delta's edge, the river and sea waters swirling and lapping at his boots. His brown hair tumbled down to his waist and brushed against his pointed ears. The smell of saltwater and fish cleansed his grieving soul. Vines curled around the mossy trees circling the estuary. He ran his thumb over his necklace, feeling the engraving of a skull crowned with roses. The ocean waves crashed at his back and the air filled with the sound of his crew nearing the end of laboring over his damaged ship, the *Bloody Briar*. He'd only stopped working to fill his flask with fresh water. But something had caught his eye—something moving in the estuary.

"Captain?" his quartermaster said behind him.

Sythrall stared steadily at the fresh water. "Yes?"

"We're ship shape. Ready to sail at your order, lad."

Sythrall cringed when he called him that but nodded and looked over at the *Bloody Briar*. She floated just beyond the island she'd crashed on in the storm a few days ago. He knew the risks of faring the Skull Sea, but his mission was worth it. A holy endeavor.

He would be the first elf—or perhaps the first *person*—to find Meno's island and convince the dragon god to do his bidding. The legends told of a great treasure that the dragon kept in his lone mountain, which captured his crew's interest. But Sythrall was more interested in what the dragon could do for him.

Sythrall wasn't certain Meno could do it, but if this dragon-god couldn't, he'd hunt down Linitor, then Belok, and then Zelric, and then . . . He'd hunt down every single god until one of them could raise the dead. He'd search all of Nathal for someone who was willing and able to accomplish it, even if it meant sailing the Skull Sea and crashing into unknown lands. Even if he had to put his whole crew in danger. If they failed him and turned back, he'd find a new crew, learn to walk on water, or grow wings, damn it! He'd turn all of Nathal upside down if it meant filling the gap in his agonized soul.

But first, he needed to know what stirred in the water.

He nodded to Tiff, the quartermaster. "Do you see that?" He pointed at a ripple.

Tiff squinted his eyes. "What? Water?"

Sythrall sighed heavily. "The movement."

"Probably just fish or something. You all right, Cap?" He put his hand on Sythrall's shoulder.

The captain shrugged his hand off. "Don't you see the fin?"

He could feel Tiff's eyes burrow into him like he had sprouted wings. "No, lad. Come. You've been in the sun too long."

There wasn't anything Sythrall hated more than not being taken seriously. His crew already questioned him enough, seeing as he was only twenty years old, and most of them were twice that. Most blamed his bloodline for his position, but he'd earned it as any good captain did. He fought off everyone who dueled him for the spot, even though he could have claimed it after his mother passed it down. The last thing he needed was his crew thinking he'd lost his mind too.

The water rippled again, and Sythrall saw as clear as day a fin too large for a fish lap the water. "There!" He pointed.

Tiff paused. "Dump a bucket of rum on me and call me a cod. I see it. I'd say that was a merelf tail if I didn't know better. And I always say, no god would create life in the Undersea that can talk. It's not *natural*, you know."

"Careful what you say of the gods. I need their help." He took a few steps into the water, crouching down to get a better look.

Sythrall grew up with tales of merelves. They were created to rule the Undersea, just like the legged elves were made to rule the land. The other myth was that in ancient days, long before bows and ships were invented, one clan of elves got tired of the humans trafficking them, grew fins and gills, and moved to the seas. Both stories said if you stepped too far into the ocean without an adult, the merelves would grab your feet and gobble you up.

But they were just fairy tales to keep children from running into the Skull Sea, an ocean prone to violent storms and shipwrecks.

Even if those tales were true, Sythrall was no child anymore. He took a deep breath, knowing this wouldn't help him look any less crazy to Tiff. "If anyone is down there, please come up. We won't hurt you." He had no idea how one convinced a merelf to show itself. Perhaps it was just a large fish, and he was making a fool of himself after all. He cleared his throat. "You see, I've always thought merelves were just bootleg tales. But perhaps you're real, and maybe we could get along?" He scratched at his head, feeling as foolish as he looked, talking to an estuary.

He wasn't even sure what to do if it were a merelf. Talk politely and be on his way? Capture it? Ask for directions to Meno? His crew had gotten horribly off track during the storm, and their navigations were compromised. To be perfectly honest, Sythrall wasn't too sure they'd been headed in the right direction anyway. Meno's exact location was shrouded in myth.

A fish-like tail flicked up, then slowly, the water rushed towards him, and he stumbled backward. His heart raced when webbed fingers dug into the sand, followed by an elvish head. Dark brown hair pooled down the feminine face that blinked at him with wide, curious eyes. Gills fluttered along her neck. Her pale skin glistened as if it had once attempted to turn into full scales.

"Barnacles!" Tiff stepped away from the edge. "Merelf!"

Project Sythrall will continue as a novella in a later publication. Sythrall will return briefly in Thorn Tower, *as a much older man.*

THE REFUGE IN THE STORM

ABIGAIL FALANGA

A Snow White and Beauty and the Beast Retelling Excerpt

CATELINE TRUDGED ON. Nothing remained in her mind besides bitterness and cold. She wasn't even sure she was human or alive anymore.

A dark castle rose before her as if it was an eddy of storm and night, almost before she was aware of it. Wolves howled behind her as she stumbled into the lee of the dark thing.

The massive wooden door was thick, sturdy enough to withstand battles, and there was no hope of making herself heard over the howling wind, but she pounded anyway. Then she waited. It had been an eternity since she rested.

This didn't feel like rest. She should be moving on. On. On. On . . .

The door gave just as her knees began to, and she almost fell into the courtyard.

Silence.

She moved a few steps in and looked around.

A light like moonlight or the aurora borealis hung over the courtyard, illuminating a garden—the most beautiful she had ever seen, but growing with intricate flower-like structures made of clear ice rather than living plants.

She reached out and gently touched a perfectly formed rose—only for it to break off in her hand.

"Child."

The soft voice made her jump and spin around, heart thudding in her chest.

A man strode from an open gate at the far end of the courtyard. He was tall and dressed in a garment so dark he seemed to give form to the night, with a beautiful face peering at her from under a hood. He smiled, though what should have been welcoming seemed worse than the hungry snarl of a wolf.

Cateline turned to run, but slipped on the icy path and fell, clutching the still-unbroken rose.

"Nay, child, do not flee." The man put out a strong hand and gently lifted her by the elbow. "Stay. Come inside and find rest and join us for refreshments. This you owe, at least, for having plucked one of my roses."

Tongue-tied, Cateline allowed him to guide her. The hall he brought her to was vaulted and beautiful, almost as cold as the courtyard with only a small fire burning in the hearth. The man placed her in a comfortable chair beside it, rang a bell for an attendant, and sat opposite her—all with that same eerie smile.

"I am Prince Velinstier," he said. "But I forget! I have been long away from the world—you would not have heard of me. You are welcome to this, my home. Tell me your name."

There was something fae-like about him, an inhuman otherworldliness. She should give him nothing and take nothing. She placed the ice flower on the table and stared at it, which seemed easier than looking into Prince Velinstier's eyes. The rose was worth looking at, for frost seemed to spread from it.

"Cateline," she said without meaning to, gazing back at him and unable to look away. "My name is Cateline."

"We shall call you Cae," he declared, then turned to the white-clad servant who had come noiselessly. "Bring a warm drink for our guest, for she is chilled to her very blood."

Cateline turned toward the fire. She was tired. The warmth was welcome. Never mind Prince Velinstier's deep, luxurious eyes. Heat was what she needed . . .

Pain shot through her as she reached toward the flames, jerking a scream from her frozen throat.

"Frostbite," the prince said. "And what is this? Have you been fighting the wolves as well? Never mind. We shall heal all your wounds, Cae."

Cae . . .

It was as if he had cut her from her past, from a name and history no longer hers. Was this freedom?

At the thought, tears came.

She sobbed, though the effort burned her face and tore at her throat.

"Ah! You have been through much! Drink this, child."

He placed a flagon in her hand, and she drank, though she had not intended to. Whatever it was, warmed and soothed her to her very core.

"There!" Velinstier's voice was gentle as a velvet rope binding her. "Now, tell me your woes, Cae."

"I thought myself lost—dead." She sobbed, and the words poured out. "My stepmother ordered that I be killed. We fled, but the wolves! My companions—all dead. Then the storm. I've been wandering so long! It's all my fault. My stepmother thought I was evil. She hated me, wanted me gone, thought I was too flighty, not good enough."

"You hate her."

Bitterness scratched at her from the inside like frostbite on her skin. Cateline considered her bitterness, her grief, her outrage, her anger and—

"Yes," she said.

"You are right to."

"I hate her. I am evil, as she thought. Perhaps she was justified in thinking I would have ruined my kingdom."

"But now, you will stay with us, Cae, where we will take that hatred and anger and use it to make you strong."

She looked at him, meaning to argue. But one of the attendants stood there, tending the fire. It was a man, but with a face like a corpse—gray and hollow, skin splotched with red bloat.

She stifled a shriek. "What is it?"

"Only one of our slaves." Prince Velinstier's smile turned into a grin as ravenous as if he would swallow her whole. "Do not fear them."

"Everything is fear!" she groaned. "I thought I was dead before I came here."

"Once you join us, you need never fear death."

"Are you an alchemist? A wizard?"

Prince Velinstier chuckled. “Once, long ago. But unlike most alchemists, I and my brethren achieved what we sought. And we shall give it to you, Cae. Now, let us see to this cut on your arm.”

Run! Run—she must run, flee, on and on through the snow, to death. Whatever this fae wizard meant, it would be better to meet death. She was brave, wasn’t she? Her father was a warrior. The same blood ran through her.

He pulled back her sleeve with a jerk, reopening a wound that had almost frozen over. Torn flesh ripped away with the fabric, frostbite blackening the edges.

But she did not scream—only looked up into those endless dark eyes.

“Your blood lives, though infection touches it,” he purred.

She wasn’t brave enough to flee. “It is fire and pain!”

“Do not fear. We will take this old blood and give you blood of ice.”

“Sorcery,” she whispered. “No. I—I can’t—”

“Where else would you go?” He leaned forward, cradling her arm. “Nothing awaits you but death and the bitterness of betrayal.”

The words wrenched like a blade in the hatred she felt hardening. “Oh! I haven’t the courage—I am nothing anymore. My heart is torn and trampled.”

“We shall take your heart of flesh and give you a heart of stone.”

“A heart of stone and blood of ice?” she scoffed and tried to bid her legs to move, to flee, *anything*. Weariness paralyzed them.

“Look,” he said, waving a gory hand toward the table. “Your rose already grows, joining you to us. Give me your blood and become one of us.”

She looked and saw that the rose had grown, spreading over the table in a vining frost. She touched it and let the ice crawl over and into her skin, though she felt nothing.

“One of you? But you are a monster . . .” The words trailed away, and she found she had no more objection to make. The peace of surrender crept through her, and she sighed as he bent to sink hungry fangs into her arm.

Continues in Crimson Books Collection, *Book Two*
a Snow White Collection

CRACKED ROSES

ANNE J. HILL

Sharper Than Thorns Anthology Excerpt

FOR TWENTY-FIVE years, roses were set on her doorstep every Sunday morning. She'd pluck them up, trim the stems, and stick them proudly in a glass vase until, one by one, they'd slowly shrivel in old age. Their bright red shade deepening to a darker maroon. And that's when she knew it was time.

She'd pull the crinkled roses from the slimy water, dab off the stems, and carry them to his grave.

In life, he'd made her promise to enjoy the roses before they faded and then to leave them with him. There was no sense in giving him living flowers if no one could enjoy them, he'd said.

He'd always been so practical.

She smiled at the thought as she lay them gently by his stone, careful to leave the petals intact. Her fingers caressed his engraved name, and she let out a sigh. Cracking open a book, she began to read to him a tale about a man with strong opinions and 'practical' ideas that melted from a simple touch or word from the woman he loved.

A peevish man who now lay in the ground because he'd given his life to save his beautiful wife twenty-five years ago.

That was their story, forever remembered in the words she penned.

She closed the book and whispered to the man in the ground, "I think roses are prettier when they're dried and cracked and been through a thing or two. When roses die, I get to come see you. It's very impractical of me, I know."

She could almost hear him say, if he'd been there, "And that's why I love you."

For more Beauty and the Beast, Snow White, and Little Red Riding Hood stories and poems by multiple writers, read Sharper Than Thorns: An Anthology, *book three in the* Black and Gold Anthologies.

PROJECT STONE EXCERPT

BEKA GREMIKOVA

Title To Be Announced

RESIDENT ADVISORS WEREN'T supposed to sneak onto the roof at night to meet mysterious men—even if the man in question was the boarding school's resident cursed creature.

But that very fact—the curse, and the loneliness it carried—was the exact reason why Rhea had to keep bending the rules. Both the headmistress and Simon wanted Simon's presence at the school kept hush-hush for reasons of their own . . . reasons Rhea was determined to ferret out eventually.

She just had to make sure none of her girls caught her in her twice-weekly forays. At least tonight, if anyone found her, she had a weapon to knock them out, though *that* would only land her in heaps more trouble. Better to just be sneaky, despite how backwards that felt. It shouldn't be the twenty-two-year-old RA tiptoeing around—the students she looked after should be the ones causing mischief. Hefting the rosebush she carried to a more comfortable position, she glanced over her shoulder.

The hallway behind her was dark and quiet. She continued on, climbing the stairs to the next floor, where yet another, slightly more rickety, set of stairs led to the rooftop—Simon's domain that he shared only with the birds and a gaggle of stone gargoyles.

Pausing, Rhea eyed that flight of stairs warily, her legs already aching after lugging the potted rosebush up three floors, making sure to dodge any sneaky janitors or loitering RAs on the way.

It'd given her quest a bit of thrill; there wasn't much else to do during the evenings at a magical academy out in the middle of nowhere in the Brionic countryside. Might as well "borrow" a rosebush from the Plantmastery class to bring to Simon.

The poor guy deserved a pick-me-up, and if a rose plant could do that, Rhea would toss a thousand of them his way. Even if he also made her want to tear her hair out half the time when he'd get lost in his thoughts and completely ignore her.

She tackled the last flight of steps, lugging the plant up those narrow, creaking stairs, stepping carefully to avoid tripping and falling backward. But no matter how she tried to keep quiet, the steps rattled and groaned under the weight of her own body and the huge bush she carried.

At the top of the stairs, the door to the roof opened.

Simon stuck his head through, frowning. "If you make much more noise, the entire school's gonna—" Then he caught sight of what Rhea held in her arms, and his grey, stone jaw dropped in astonishment. "What in the Masteries—"

She paused and set the plant down to give her time to gasp for breath. "Um." Clearing her throat, she straightened. "I know you only asked for *one* rose, but . . ." *You deserve so much more.* The words tingled on her tongue; she felt a flush creeping over her cheeks.

If her girls ever learned about the existence of Simon, and her crush on the stone man who lived on the roof, she'd never hear the end of it. The last thing she needed was a bunch of high schoolers needling her about her love life.

Simon reached out, brushing his fingers across the petals. Oddly enough, his face seemed to soften, though she knew from experience his skin would still be cold and stone-smooth. "You brought an *entire* plant?" Then his lips twitched. "Does the Headmistress know you're smuggling me contraband?"

She scowled at him, crossing her arms. "The Plantmasters won't miss a single rosebush. And I haven't stolen it. I'm . . . rearranging its place on the grounds."

"Wouldn't want you to lose your job on my account." His words, light and airy and warm with teasing, settled in her skin and made her itch to hug him.

"What do you want a rose for, anyways?" She looked away and shook out her limbs. She reached for the plant, but Simon, moving faster than she expected a stone man capable of, stepped down, snatched it, and whirled away with it. Rhea followed him up the rest of the steps, through the door, and out onto the roof.

The sweet-scented air of spring washed over her, bringing with it the chill warning of rain. Simon set the rosebush down and rubbed the back of his neck. His shoulders hunched slightly. "I . . . I wanted to see if my Mastery still works," he said quietly. "Even in this . . . form."

Her throat closed at the wistfulness in his voice. "Simon—"

"I know it's stupid," he interrupted before pressing his lips together. "But I—I want to know how much they took from me. If there's anything they left."

Heat swirled through her. "And what if your Mastery doesn't work?" she asked softly. "What then? Will you keep blaming yourself for choices you regret?"

His gaze lowered. He turned, staring down at the roses as if they held all the answers to his questions. As if they were the key to breaking his curse. She could almost see his mind whirring, obsessing over his perceived failures, ignoring her presence as though he'd forgotten she existed.

She blew out a breath, trying not to let that bother her too much. She knew it wasn't personal, that he simply internalized his problems, but it still made her feel useless to help. Like nothing she said or did would ever make a mark . . . like nothing she could do would ever matter.

Above them, the clouds gathered, threatening rain. Along the edge of the roof sat the gargoyles that decorated the academy, once carved by a Stonemaster before Stonemastery was outlawed. Their eyes seemed to dig into her, unyielding and hungry.

She wondered what it had felt like for Stonemasters, with their kinship to stone, to make it move of its own volition. How much power they must have wielded, how much hurt they must have caused. She shivered under the weight of the gargoyles' gazes, her entire body tingling.

Masteries weren't meant to be used like that. Not that *she* would know; she hadn't developed one yet.

Yet, the stone seemed to whisper at her. She suddenly couldn't look away from the gargoyles' curved lips, their giant fangs.

"Rhea?"

She blinked and shook her head as Simon's voice lured her from her thoughts. "What?"

He cleared his throat. "Are you . . . going to stay and watch?" He nodded at the rosebush, which now trembled in the wind.

That same wind buffeted them both, lashing Rhea's bright pink hair into her eyes. She pushed it aside while Simon stood, unaffected by the gnawing gale. "Do you want me to?" she asked.

Simon's shoulders hunched even further as he glared at the quivering rosebush. "I'm not sure I want a witness if I fail."

"Then, will you need a friend?" She pressed closer to him, reaching out to place a hand on his shoulder.

His head snapped up, and his eyes widened. She sucked in a deep breath, then took his hand. His fingers were smooth and cold, as unyielding as the gargoyles' glares. But beneath that, she knew there lay a fiery, passionate soul. "If you do, let me be that friend," she whispered. She didn't dare tell him how much she needed to be that friend; how, if he pushed her away, she wouldn't know what to do with herself.

After a soul-strangling moment that stretched too long, his fingers closed around hers, loose and gentle. "All right."

An upcoming Twenty Hills publication

THORN TOWER EXCERPT

ANNE J. HILL

BOYER WASN'T CERTAIN about much in life, but he knew for a fact that the man standing before him was going to die.

The assassin eyed his target's back, waiting for the right moment. The Baron of Weshem was a gray-haired Trader of elves and owned a humble estate in Conwell. Boyer despised these sorts of humans. Where he was from, his kind got along with the elves like family.

Boyer's accomplice, Waldren, lounged in a chair by the fireplace, feet propped up on a cluttered oak desk. The red wrap around his head made him look less deadly than he deserved, but it covered his pointed ears well enough.

Boyer and Waldren were alone in their target's candle-lit bedroom.

"Who are you?" the Baron asked the half-elf in his chair.

Boyer stood behind the old man like his shadow. Unseen. Unheard.

Waldren flipped a coin and caught it. "Your atonement."

Boyer's dagger slipped almost effortlessly into the Baron's back, right in his kidney, and the Baron stiffened as though paralyzed by pain and dropped to the floor. Boyer kneeled down and stabbed the base of his skull.

One moment, the Baron of Weshem was alive, and the next, he wasn't.

Waldren sighed. "You're no fun, Boyer. Where was the flare? The show?"

Boyer rolled his eyes and pulled his dagger free. "You have ten seconds to loot." He tapped his foot with each second, keeping an eye on the door as Waldren tore around the room, tossing coins, golden cups, jewels, and whatever else he fancied into his bag.

Waldren would have complained for a week—or longer—if he weren't afforded the opportunity to rob the dead Baron. But Boyer put more stock in ending any bastard who committed heinous deeds.

"Times up," Boyer said. "Let's—"

A shrill bell rang through the halls, followed by shouts, "The Baroness is dead!"

"Belok's rainfire," Boyer swore under his breath. He pulled his kerchief over his nose. "I thought you barred her room shut!" Boyer grabbed Waldren's arm and yanked him toward the window.

"I did!"

"Rooftop. Go." Boyer nudged Waldren.

The nimble elf scampered out the third-story window, his bag strapped around his shoulder.

Once Waldren's feet disappeared, Boyer climbed out just as the bedroom door busted open.

"There!" a portly guard yelled.

Boyer pulled himself up and rolled onto the rooftop. He followed behind Waldren as they ran along the sprawling manor's peak. An arrow whizzed past Boyer's ear. He glanced downward. A handful of guards were on the lawn shooting at them.

Focus, Boyer. Two targets down, one to go.

With that, Boyer yelled a code to Waldren, "Fox in the hen house." Boyer grabbed onto a chimney and swung himself over, landing smoothly on the other side.

"Why me?" Waldren shouted back.

Boyer reached the end of the manor's first rooftop, jumped the gap, and tumbled onto the lower roof. "My lead. My call." He fished out his grapnel.

"If I die, bury me with a barrel of ale. Linitor's Hell won't have any."

Both assassins snagged their grapnels to the edge of the roof and dropped down. Waldren stopped at the top window and smashed the glass in with his feet, screaming, "Give me your eggs, chickens!"

Boyer dropped to the ground and yanked his rope free. He slipped around the back of the manor while Waldren wreaked havoc inside. Boyer could barely make out Waldren shouting, "Blasted humans! Die! Die! Die!"

With the guards distracted by Waldren, Boyer kicked in the lowest window that led to the last Trader's room. This dog was the real target: the one employed by the Baron and Baroness to do their dirty work of rounding up slaves, who dealt actual blows to the elves, who would dare to treat them like animals. Boyer may be human, but if he was certain about one thing, it was that elves were anything but animals—Boyer's father had never agreed.

He landed in the room, glass shattering around him. The Trader was leaning against his door, holding it shut like the fox upstairs might gobble him up. And his eyes were wide with disbelief, staring directly at Boyer. He threw his hands into the air. "Don't kill me!"

Boyer pulled his dagger out. He'd witnessed this same look of horror so many times in the seventeen years of his career. It had been his favorite part in his younger days—seeing his targets fully acknowledge their fate for their corruption. He was a different man then.

But this monster still deserved to die.

The Trader flashed out his own dagger, but Boyer gripped his wrist and spun his arm around his back, pinning the Trader's face against the door.

He stabbed the Trader's kidney and the bottom of his skull, his signature move. He let the Trader sink to the floor.

Three targets down, zero to go.

The tale continues in Thorn Tower, *by Anne J. Hill*
Includes minor Beauty and the Beast inspiration, not a retelling

ACKNOWLEDGMENTS

Thank you to all the authors who poured blood and sweat into this book. To Lara E. Madden for spending endless hours doing the bulk of edits, and Anna Augustine, Moriah Chavis, and Sarah Harmon. To all the beta readers who volunteered to give feedback. Shout out to Hannah Carter and Maseeha Seedat. To Savannah Jezowski (Dragonpen Designs) for her formatting magic, and to Fantasical Ink for this stunning cover. To the readers for believing in us enough to at least buy the book.

To God for everything and all things. For giving us the gift of writing.

–Anne J. Hill

AUTHORS' NOTES

ANNE J. HILL

For my personal story in *Briars & Blood*, my original intent was to give you a story about a side character from *The Fatebringer Trilogy*, but due to time constraints, I've had to pull that story from this collection and will publish it at a later date (as was the case with some of the other authors). However, I did include an excerpt of the opening chapter: *Project Sythrall*, as well as a character sketch on another *Fatebringer* side character: Valibrim. He is the most obvious Beast inspired character in book one of *The Fatebringer Trilogy*: *Thorn Tower*. (Series name is a working title, meaning it might change.)

The story I ended up putting in this collection instead is set in the same world as *Fatebringer*, but many years later. While *Fatebringer* is more medieval, *The Ward and the Wolfman* is inspired by the Georgian era. Both are set in the world of Nathal. *The Ward and the Wolfman* is related to my *Brimwood Manor Chronicles*, yet to be published.

L.A. THORNHILL

I began *The Reader and The Soulless* with little experience in rewriting fairy tales, but the moment I realized Joel and Viola would fit perfectly into the steampunk world of a current WIP, I dove headfirst into this project. Drawing inspiration not only from *Beauty and the Beast* but *Jane Eyre* as well, I created two of the most beloved characters I believe I will ever write. Their story may not continue in other books, but I hope to keep their legacy alive in their story world.

JULIA SKINNER

Do you know what I always hated about fairytales? Everyone is always exactly what they seem. The prince is always charming. The princess is beautiful and pure-hearted. The villain is always ugly, and loud, and cruel. I hate this because in reality, people are not that simple. People are not what we expect. We are a chaotic mixture of contradictions. We can be simultaneously the beauty and the beast.

I first wrote *The Statue Girl* as a fun little flash fiction for Go Havok, meant to poke fun at the fairy tales I despise by dumping the tropes on their heads. I wanted to point out that people are not always what we expect—and that's okay. Little did I know that it would grow into *this*, a 30,000 word novella exploring grief, worth, and what it means to truly see those around us. This is my longest finished fiction piece to date, and it has been an amazing journey! Unfortunately, this novella simply couldn't contain the scope of the entire story or the world, which is why I have already begun working on a full novel version, where I can fully dive into the world-building and plot *The Statue Girl* deserves.

TASHA KAZANJIAN

The Rose and the Bull draws inspiration from a number of tales, most obviously "Beauty and the Beast" and "The Black Bull of Norroway." The stories Ròs tells are taken from Irish mythology, as is the character of Deidra. For Ròs' version of Deidra's lament, I included two quotations from *The Tain*, Thomas Kinsella's 1969 translation of the *Táin Bó Cúailnge*: "Comfortless, no peace or joy . . . break my heart no more today" and "Grief is heavier than the sea." Deidra—generally spelled Deirdre or Derdriu—appears in the Ulster Cycle, and I have mostly remained faithful to the rendition of her story told in *The Tain*, though I imagined a new ending.

BEKA GREMIKOVA

The excerpt included in this collection is from an upcoming novel to be published with Twenty Hills in 2025 or 2026; think "Beauty and the Beast" meets *Harry Potter* with a plethora of flesh-hungry monsters and a girl who must risk it all to save the school she loves. I'm excited to share the rest of the story with you in the future!

EVERLY HAYWOOD

Thank you for reading my little excerpt from *Grimkeeper*. If you like royalty/commoner pairings, arranged marriages, characters with disabilities and swoony sweet romance, you'll love my *Between Shade and Flame* series. The first two books are in Kindle Unlimited for your immediate reading pleasure, and Book 3, a project I've lovingly titled *Runemaster*, releases May of 2023!

ABIGAIL FALANGA

"Beauty and the Beast" has amazing themes: self-sacrifice and the transformative power of love. I set out to create an inverted version of this tale and explore these themes at an even deeper level. The full novella (which has other fairy tale influences) will appear in the upcoming Snow White anthology from Twenty Hills. "The Refuge in the Storm" can be read as an independent flash fiction—though with the knowledge that more is coming soon!

ABOUT THE AUTHORS

ANNE J. HILL

Anne J. Hill is an author who enjoys writing fantasy for all ages. Her love of words has led to her career as an editor and content writer. She runs Twenty Hills Publishing with the help of her circus-performing best friend, Lara E. Madden. She spends her days dreaming up fantastical realms, researching ways to get away with murder . . . for writing, arguing over commas at the kitchen table, talking out loud to the characters in her head, promising her housemate that she isn't, in fact, crazy, and rearranging her personal library—affectionately dubbed the "Book Dungeon."

Instagram @anne.j.hill.editing
Twitter @AnneJHillAuthor
www.annejhill.com

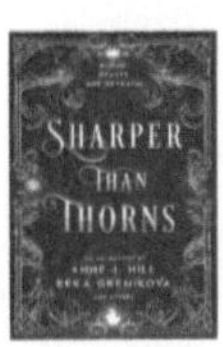

L.A. THORNHILL

L.A. Thornhill is an epic fantasy and steampunk writer who deeply loves her Savior, and has a severe addiction to caffeine. She currently has one novella *The Lost Descendants* in her fantasy series "The King and Prophet Chronicles" which is available in ebook, print, and also in audiobook in the near future.

Facebook @l.a.thornhillauthor
Instagram @l.a.thornhill

JULIA SKINNER

Julia Skinner is a nineteen-year-old, modern day hobbit, with a love for good stories and chocolate ice cream. She lives in South Texas with her family and two miniature Australian Shepherds (and a ton of other animals!). When she's not working on one of her many fantasy novels or flash fictions, she can be found juggling college, playing video games, dreaming up yet another entrepreneurial project, or happy-ranting about Brandon Sanderson's books. She is a sinner saved by Jesus, and if any good comes from her journey, it's because of Him. Her published works include *Prismatic, Fool's Honor, Casting Call, Darkness & Moonlight*, and more!

Instagram @litaflameblog

TASHA KAZANJIAN

Tasha Kazanjian is currently pursuing her masters in clinical counseling and writes fantasy to escape APA citations. She loves losing herself in books, especially very old ones that smell strongly of ink and dust, and has been known to disappear into used book shops for hours at a time. Tasha's writing process usually involves stacks of historical nonfiction, a hundred index cards stuck up on her wall, and copious amounts of coffee, tea, and colored pens. She is currently revising a dark fantasy novel involving ice age dragons.

Instagram @tnkazanjian.writer

ABIGAIL FALANGA

Abigail Falanga writes fantasy and science fiction, and is possibly some kind of fae creature, living in New Mexico with family, books, and wild ambitions. She's released many flash fictions, short stories, a novel, and co-edits the Whitstead Anthologies, and plans to fill libraries with more writing.

Facebook @abigailfalangaauthor
Instagram @abigailfalangaauthor
Twitter @AbigailFalanga

EVERLY HAYWOOD

Everly Haywood imagines herself to be a shieldmaiden of great prowess…but you're more likely to find her in a dusty library than on the battlefield. She writes swoony-sweet romantic fantasy about strong leading ladies and brooding but huggable heroes. An advocate for her Goblin Princess with Down Syndrome, she also features characters with disabilities. When she isn't tangled up in magical curses or drinking coffee, she can be found weeding her garden, homeschooling her Fairy Princess, or reading books by authors like Maggie Stiefvater, Elise Kova, and Sylvia Mercedes. Sign up for her newsletter to receive a free book!

Facebook @everlyhaywood
Instagram @savannahjezowskiauthor
Bookbub @everlyhaywood
everlyhaywood.com/newsletter

BEKA GREMIKOVA

Beka Gremikova writes folkloric fantasy from her little nook in the Ottawa Valley, Ontario, Canada. When she's not trekking across the globe, she plays video games, dabbles in art, or curls up in a cozy corner with a mystery novel. Her work can be found in various anthologies, and her indie debut, *The Other Cinderella*, is now available in ebook and paperback from Amazon. Her first full-length book, codenamed *Project Dragon*, will release with SnowRidge Press in Fall 2023. To keep up with all her writing mayhem, you can sign up for her newsletter or join her reader group, "Beka's Books," on Facebook. Photo credit to Sarah-Ann Wijngaarden.

Instagram @beka.gremikova
www.bekagremikova.com

HANNAH CARTER

Hannah Carter is just a girl who loves to dream and write and still wakes up every day hoping to figure out she's secretly a mermaid. Hannah's debut YA fantasy novel released from SnowRidge press in November 2022. In her spare time, she's probably either cuddling her cats, drinking tea, reading, or practicing for her imaginary Broadway debut.

Instagram @mermaidhannahwrites

www.annejhill.com/twenty-hills-publishing
Instagram @twenty_hills

www.ingramcontent.com/pod-product-compliance
Lightning Source LLC
Chambersburg PA
CBHW020248030826
48979CB00030B/2661/J

* 9 7 8 1 9 5 6 4 9 9 1 6 2 *